THE PRIVATE CHEF

SAMANTHA VÉRANT

Storm
PUBLISHING

Ebook ISBN: 978-1-80508-645-1
Paperback ISBN: 978-1-80508-646-8

Cover design: Blacksheep
Cover images: Depositphotos, Shutterstock

Published by Storm Publishing.
For further information, visit:
www.stormpublishing.co

ALSO BY SAMANTHA VÉRANT

The Lucky Widow
The Writers' Retreat
The Perfect Catch

This one is for my mother, Anne, and our time in Malibu.

AMUSE BOUCHE

(A taste of the meal to come.)

Fire that's closest kept burns most of all.

—William Shakespeare

FADE IN:

INT. A LUXURIOUS MODERN KITCHEN—SUNSET

A hand whisks cream to high peaks.

A WOMAN (V.O.)

Cooking, like acting, has its own set of
methods and rules.

EXT. A MALIBU BLUFF—SUNSET

The sun sets over a frothy ocean. Waves crash onto rocks. Seagulls soar and squawk.

A WOMAN (V.O.)

When cooking, one gets to the heart and soul of a meal using ingredients, tools, and techniques. When acting, one takes the ingredients of what makes a person who they are—the sour, the sweet, the bitter—to capture the essence of the character, creating an authentic feast.

INTERCUT—BLUFF/KITCHEN

A hand slices beets, red juices run off a white marble cutting board, drip onto the floor.

A WOMAN (V.O.)

It's all about the method…

SOUND of sirens wailing in the distance.

A WOMAN (V.O.)

Revenge comes with its own set of rules and methods, too.

A WOMAN (V.O.)

A bit sweet, a bit salty…

A wooden spoon rises to lips, tastes… A hand
adds a dash of brown sugar. Some salt.

                    A WOMAN (V.O.)

   …sometimes—after simmering and coming to
   the boil—revenge can lead to unforeseen
   events and circumstances…

On the stove, a red sauce boils…

                    A WOMAN (V.O.)

   Then again, it depends on the recipe and
   the exact methods and techniques used to
   settle the score…

A human form is splayed out on a sandy cove.
Waves crash. Blood mixes with ocean water.

FADE to black

ACT ONE

L'ENTRÉE

(The first small course to whet your appetite.)

If you prick us do we not bleed?
If you tickle us do we not laugh?
If you poison us do we not die?
And if you wrong us shall we not revenge?

—William Shakespeare, *The Merchant of Venice*

FADE IN:

INT. LAX AIRPORT—DAY

A pretty twenty-something, JULIA, races off a
plane and into the terminal with a carry-on
and a cat cage. She takes off her hoodie while
standing in line at security, wrapping it
around her waist. A SECURITY GUARD ushers her
forward. Visibly nervous, she whispers to
the cat.

JULIA

Are you ready?

FADE OUT

ONE

JULIA

The thing about Los Angeles is that you can slip into darkness, oblivion. Unless you are somebody important—or if you know somebody important who can get you into a film or a coveted party so you can rub shoulders with the A-listers—nobody pays any attention to the so-called masses. The hoi polloi. A fake wave. A fake kiss. A fake smile. And even faker laughs and promises. Don't call me, I'll call you—unless you have stellar connections. People drive into their garages, close the door. People come, they go.

Veni, vidi, vici.

I came. I saw. I conquered. That's the dream, right? Well, it's the dream if you know somebody. And I don't know anybody. Not anymore.

After a twelve-hour flight from Charles de Gaulle to LAX, I've finally landed on US soil—home sweet dreaded home. Drops of perspiration roll down my back. My nerves are in a tangle because I haven't been back to California in eight years. Part of me is excited, but the other part is nervous to face my former life, all the memories. I shudder. I don't want to think about the past, not when I should be focusing on the present and the future.

Right about now, I could really use a shower.

After waiting over an hour to get through airport security, I'm finally standing in front of the conveyor belt waiting for my bags—two suitcases filled with almost everything I own, specifically cooking tools. A chef never goes anywhere without their knives. And I love mine—a set of stainless steel Claude Dozormes with sleek black handles, a graduation present from my family when I'd finished my culinary studies at Le Cordon Bleu two years ago. I think they might have been a bribe to come work and cook with them. And I did for a while. But now I'm moving on, spreading my culinary wings and carving out my own path.

I really hope airport security didn't confiscate my knives.

I pull out my phone to text Jasmine, the woman who'd hired me to be the private chef for Hollywood's Golden Couple— Erica, the actress, and David Drake, owner of Drake Entertainment.

All I really know about this couple is that they're insanely rich, hence my killer salary of $170k a year with added perks, like living rent-free in their guesthouse with a view of the ocean, a car, and, get this, a clothing allowance. Although I haven't spoken to either one of them, I do know what they look like. She's drop-dead gorgeous, often compared to Charlize Theron —with a figure most women would kill for, blond hair, and a perfect complexion offset by steely blue eyes. As for David, he's a slick-looking fifty-year-old, compared to Ben Affleck. Definitely not an eyesore.

Honestly, I don't care about their looks or their celebrity status. I'm only focused on living out my dreams: opening a chain of French bakeries in SoCal, exact locations to be determined.

JF:

I'm here. Waiting for my bags.

Three dots. I let out a sigh of relief.

JA:

Not working for the Drakes anymore. Driver is
waiting. You have his number.

I stare at the screen, dumbfounded. Jasmine had told me
that she was going to meet me at the airport, give me some last-
minute advice on the ride over. She's quit and she's just telling
me now? In addition to worrying about my knives, my heart
races. After rummaging through my purse like a hamster
hopped on Red Bull, I find the printout with all of the pertinent
details on it, specifically the driver's cell number.

JF:

Through security. Waiting for suitcases.

A:

Text on way out. Meet you out front. Ground
level. Have sign. Look for the rolls.

I scratch my forehead with confusion. Rolls? Maybe he'd
meant baguettes. Like a welcome basket? I don't know. I'm
practically sleepwalking.

A few minutes later, the conveyor belt groans to life. Immediately, I spot one of my bags—the big orange one with the black
ribbon belt—the one with my tools of the trade. I jump toward
it. Beurreboule meows inside the kitty carry-on as I move her
out of the way with my feet. I'm yanking the bag by its frayed
handle, bumping into the cart behind me and it jolts backward.

A man wearing skinny jeans and aviator shades helps me
lug the sack off the belt before I topple over. "Thank you," I say,
giving him the once-over. He's cool, or trying to look cool. And,

well, he's kind of cute with his sandy blond hair tucked under a purple Laker's cap.

"Merci," I say out of habit. "Uh, thanks."

The guy smiles and lifts my bag onto the trolley. As he gives me a double take, I see my reflection in his tinted lenses. I look like a vagabond. "You look familiar," he says, tilting his head to the side with a shy smile. "You must be an actress."

He's actually pulling that line on me? Flirting with somebody who has plane skank all over them? I'm also wearing a tank top and I'm wondering if I'd remembered to shave my armpits. It got hot on the plane and even hotter in line for the airport security checkpoints. I'd pulled my hoodie off and now I look like a hoochie mama.

I grimace. "No, I'm not an actress."

But, perhaps, I could be one.

I've made a few changes to my appearance. I've dyed my hair from strawberry blond (as we say in France—Venetian blond) to a darker blond with golden highlights (châtaine). My green eyes are now a slate blue, thanks to colored contact lenses. And I don't have braces anymore. Plus, my figure filled out. Basically, at twenty-three, I'm not a gangly fifteen-year-old anymore, a bit curvier than the stereotypical pencil-thin French woman.

One of my dad's favorite songs, the Rolling Stones' "Sympathy for the Devil", plays on repeat inside my brain. Smoke and mirrors. I'm in LA, baby. And nobody, not even my new employer, will know who I really am.

"I know I've seen you somewhere," says the guy, and my eyes go wide with panic.

By the way his eyebrows pinch, I have to say something to throw him off. "Please tell me you're not a stalker." My gaze flickers to the corner of the room. "There are police. Just over there..."

He holds up his hands in mock surrender. "I'm not a stalker.

We were on the same flight. You were watching a movie and I thought you had a nice laugh." He tilts his head to the side. "What were you watching?"

A terrible movie my soon-to-be employer made, so bad I'd teared up, wondering what I was getting myself into. "*Love at First Latte*."

He cringes dramatically, his neck tightening. "Ooh boy, saw that bomb. Erica Drake. Her first movie before she made it big time. Man, so bad."

"So bad," I agree.

I go silent as my other suitcase rounds the belt, then let out a grunt as I try to grab it. The guy takes it easily, hoisting it onto my other bag. "Thanks," I say again.

Beurreboule lets out a tiny meow and the guy clears his throat. "Is that a cat in there?"

"Ssh!" I hold my index finger to my lips. "Don't tell her that. She thinks she's human."

He clutches his stomach and snorts like a donkey. "You're funny. Comedian?"

My eyes go wide. I have no idea where this conversation is going. Nobody has ever told me that I'm funny. And if they did, I'm pretty sure they were just trying to bolster my confidence. I do know a lot of foodie jokes, though, like "why did the chef become a musician?" The punchline: "because she could get a good beet." Just as pathetic as the ones I'd seen in Erica's disaster of a movie. "I'm not a comedian."

"What brings you to La La Land?" he insists.

"Why are you asking so many questions?"

"Sorry. I'm originally from Chicago." His eyes meet mine and he laughs softly. "And I can't shake the urge to talk to strangers, especially one that almost fell on her cat."

Damn it. He's nice. But I'm not here for a meet-cute with a stranger, no matter how cute he is. "Thank you for grabbing my suitcase before I did. As you may have noticed, I'm kind of a klutz," I say with a self-deprecating laugh.

He grins and shuffles his feet. "You didn't answer my question. What brings you to LA?"

I tilt my head to the side, trying to gauge what he wants. Everybody in LA wants something. Maybe he's just nice. "I'm a chef," I say, waiting for a spark of recognition. There is none, so I clear my throat and continue, "I've heard the food scene in LA is booming and I thought I'd try my luck here."

"Oh," he says, shifting his weight. "Cool. What restaurant?"

"No restaurant. Not anymore. I'm actually a private chef now."

He lifts his sunglasses to the top of his head, his blue eyes lighting up. "For who?"

The woman we were just talking about.

I'm staring into his eyes. I love the color—like an azure ocean and all dreamy. I shake my head and then cough. "Sorry. Can't tell you. Signed an NDA and everything. They like their privacy."

He nods in thought. "Where'd you get your training?"

"Le Cordon Bleu," I say proudly. "And my family owns Fouquet."

This is another thing about LA—all the name-dropping. It's a talent and I might as well fit in instead of sticking out. I know all about twirling tongues, especially when it comes to food prep and creating delicious meals. At least my meals aren't fake.

"The Michelin two-star?" he asks, and I raise a brow. "And you w-worked there?"

The more I take in his appearance, the more I see he's trying to fit in, too. I kind of like his geeky awkwardness—the stuttering.

"Sous-chef. And now I am here." I narrow my eyes into a mock glare. "Is this an impromptu interview—?"

"Maybe." He holds up a finger and then pulls a business

card out from his wallet. "I own a couple of high-end boutique hotels. I was in Paris, scoping out talent for our properties. Should you ever want to throw your toque into the ring—"

Good one. Chef humor. I'll give him credit when it's due.

"Merci." I pause, looking at his card. "Mr. Boyd."

"It's Paul." He grins and, well, I like his crooked, goofy smile. "And your name?"

"Julia. Julia Fouquet." I tuck his card into my purse and then place Beurreboule's carry case on the trolley, balancing her as best I can. "Should anything change, I'll keep your company in mind, but my driver is out front and I have to go."

I turn to leave.

"Wait," he says. "I've eaten at Fouquet—most memorable meal I've ever had. I'm serious. Should you need other options, give me a call."

I look over my shoulder. "For a date? Or a job?"

"Not a date." He shrugs and his cheeks flush pink. "Don't get me wrong. You are gorgeous. But I play for another team."

Boy, did I have him pegged wrong.

Never burn a bridge.

"I have your card, Paul," I say with a sly grin. "And thanks for helping me with my bags. My cat thanks you, too."

The driver waits curbside with a sign—JULIA F—and I head toward him. He gives me a slight nod and opens the rear door of a black Rolls-Royce Phantom, vanity plate DRAKE. Oh. He hadn't been referring to baked goods. My purse is slung over my shoulder, and I grab Beurreboule's case before he snags it. "Precious cargo," I say and, as if cued, my fuzzy lump of a butterball meows.

He shakes his head and guffaws. "Does Mrs. Drake know you've brought a cat?"

"Of course," I say.

He sneers. "I'll take care of your bags."

"What's your name?"

He doesn't answer so I crawl into the back seat, floored by the luxury—the smooth, leather seats. Flying first class, now this. I feel like I'm on another planet. Beam me up, Scotty. A couple of minutes later, the driver hops in. "There's bottled water, Julia."

I don't respond because I'm not sure if he's talking to me. The driver holds up a bottle of chilled Pellegrino. "Julia, do you want water or not?"

His harsh tone has snapped me to attention. Damn it. I've got to get my head out of the clouds.

"Thanks. I'm good," I say, leaning forward. "I'm the new chef—"

"Please put your seat belt on," he barks. "It's the law."

I do as he's instructed, buckling myself in. I press on, trying to glean any information. "How do you like working for the Drakes?"

He snaps, "Did you sign a nondisclosure agreement?"

I nod.

"So did I." He shakes his head slowly as he glowers at me in the rearview mirror. I can only make out the color of his eyes—such a dark brown they're almost black. Unnerving. Before I can utter one more word, he rolls up the privacy window.

Got it. "Kind of rude," I whisper to Beurreboule and unzip the front of her case so I can stroke under her chin. Her purrs resonate from my fingers to my chest. "At least you're a people person." I pull out a spare tank and a clean blouse from my bag. "And I can change my top."

Beurreboule meows as if to say good idea. I spray myself with a sample perfume I'd snagged in duty free. *J'adore Dior.*

I'm feeling a bit breathless on the drive to Malibu—everything is so familiar, yet oddly different. Bumper-to-bumper traffic on the 401 to the 10. Check. Smog. Check. Beautiful weather. Check.

My heart rate picks up as the car glides onto Pacific Coast Highway, or, rather, PCH, the beaches on our left. I roll down the window and inhale deeply—the salty brine of the ocean I've missed infiltrating my nostrils, although I could live without the exhaust from the cars.

When the iconic Santa Monica Pier comes into view, I can't help but grin. The colorful Ferris wheel stands tall against the clear blue sky, its vibrant hues beckoning us closer. I can hear the laughter of children and the faint music from the amusement park rides drifting through the salty ocean breeze. In my head, I hear my own childhood giggles while remembering my mom swooping me in her arms, spinning me around, before passing me on to my father.

The rhythmic crash of waves against the shore fills the air, a soothing backdrop to our coastal drive. Surfers of all ages and skill levels dot the horizon, their silhouettes gliding gracefully across the shimmering waves, their colorful boards cutting through the turquoise waters. The sight fills me with a sense of longing, a desire to join them in their aquatic dance.

I catch glimpses of families picnicking on the beach, their colorful umbrellas dotting the sandy landscape like confetti. Joggers, cyclists, and rollerbladers bob to the beat of their own music as they glide down the path.

Every so often, we pass scenic overlooks offering panoramic views of the coastline. I crane my neck to take in the rugged cliffs, the azure expanse of the ocean, and the pristine beaches. The beauty of it all is overwhelming. Coming home is overwhelming.

Finally, we pass Malibu Pier. Its weathered wooden planks stretch out into the ocean, a symbol of the town's rich history and charm. Seagulls swoop and dive, adding to the electric atmosphere. A tried-and-true water baby, I can't wait to buy a new board or two. I lean back into my seat and sigh. So many waves are crashing down upon me, so many emotions, so many memories.

My dad was a rocker and loved to play the guitar—The Clash, the Rolling Stones, Tom Petty—and I'd inherited his tastes in music. I find myself humming the Mamas and the Papas's "California Dreamin'."

I take a deep breath. This drive is not just a journey from LAX to Malibu—it's an adventure for my spirit, an awakening for my soul.

Welcome back to California, Julia Fouquet—a place where dreams can be made and sometimes crushed at the same time. I laugh to myself. The only things I'll be crushing are those waves outside my window and, well, garlic.

TWO

ERICA

The clock on the wall ticks relentlessly, each passing second amplifying my irritation. It's almost ten in the morning and the new chef I've hired is annoyingly late. Granted, I understand plane delays and traffic, but I've been pacing in our foyer for what feels like an eternity. I have our day planned and it's time to get on with it.

Finally, the intercom crackles to life. "Mrs. Drake, your driver is here with a Julia Fouquet," announces the guard.

"About damn time," I mutter.

I shake out my hands, preparing myself for her arrival, connecting to the character I'm about to play—my emotions, my thoughts, and my motivation.

And action. I stomp up to the intercom and press the button to answer.

"Send them in. And put Julia's name on my list. She's my new employee," I assert, a flicker of annoyance evident in my tone.

"Will do, Mrs. Drake. Have a nice day."

I usually respond with, "you, too, Kyle," but today I don't. I can't because I'm pouring myself a glass of wine. Julia's probably sitting in the back seat, wondering if she'll be working for a super bitch. According to David, it's one of my powers.

As I open the front door, our sleek car—one of David's "look at how successful I am" extravagances—glides into the driveway. The Phantom pulls up to the front walkway and Julia slowly steps out from the back seat, her eyes darting around our magnificent compound and then toward the bluff leading toward the ocean. Pictures—even the ones featured in *Architectural Digest*—don't do our estate justice.

She mouths, "Wow! This place is incredible."

I want to respond, "It is. Welcome to Wonderland, Julia," but refrain, letting her take everything in.

Nestled into a verdant landscape, our twelve thousand square foot home sits on three acres, complete with breathtaking ocean views and an enviable private sandy beach with cabanas and lounge seating, accessible by a gated path only available to us. Add in the guesthouse, the infinity edge pool, the state-of-the-art gym, and, well, Julia will never want to leave, especially after she sees our restaurant-worthy kitchen.

Then again, she might want to leave when she meets me. She'll need a backbone made of iron steel rather than cast-iron pans to prepare what I need. And I'm counting on that. If she doesn't show any signs of strength, she's useless to me, no matter how well she cooks.

When she lets out an amazed gasp, I do, too, because she's prettier in person than the screenshots Jasmine had sent me, cuter than the taped video I'd seen. She's hiding her saucy little figure underneath a grape-patterned, button-down top, but she's curvy.

Although I hate what she's wearing, David will adore her. He likes them young—sweet and innocent. Just like I'd been when he'd fallen in love with me. I find myself staring at her, thinking.

"Mrs. Drake, it's so nice to finally meet you in person." Julia clears her throat when I don't respond. "I can't believe the view you have."

"Yes, it's the reason we chose this property." I snap my gaze onto the driver. "Please take Ms. Fouquet's luggage to the guesthouse. Then you can leave. I'll call you if I need you."

"Yes, Mrs. Drake," he retorts gruffly, sending a glower in my direction.

Enrique will get over it. I've known him for years. He's used to me. But Julia isn't. I focus my attention back on her. "Just wait until you see the view from your living quarters. Shall we head inside?"

Julia nods yes and blinks, her long eyelashes brushing against the top of her cheeks. I wonder what kind of lash formula she uses or if she was simply born with good genes. She's still standing in the driveway, wringing her hands nervously, looking slightly gobsmacked.

"I'll be right there," she says, holding up a finger.

"Don't take too long. I've been waiting for your arrival, and I have plans."

I don't tell her that my plans include her.

She shoots me a slight smile and then pulls something out from the back seat of the Phantom. As she walks toward me, she's carrying what looks like a soft animal crate, confirmed when the inside of said crate meows.

Don't get me wrong. I love animals, grew up with a bunch of strays. But I didn't know she'd be bringing one here and I'm not prepared for this surprise. I guess sometimes you need to improvise. I cringe. "Is there a cat in there?"

She goes silent for a moment.

"Yes, Mrs. Drake, I told Jasmine I was bringing her. She said it was OK."

Her accent? It's like she's trying to sound more French, almost like that skunk cartoon character Pepé Le Pew or that Canadian mouse Savoir-Faire. It's absolutely ridiculous. Julia's mouth twists with confusion when I respond with a slight laugh. She shifts her weight from side to side.

"Julia, call me Erica," I finally say, jutting out my chin. "It better be an indoor cat. I don't want any coyote incidents. And it's to stay in your living quarters."

She looks down and mumbles "*it?*" I understand I'm probably insulting her fur baby, but I don't want to be too nice. Julia gets positive points for politeness. Negative points for the cat. Let's see how she prepares her meals. Let's see how *everything* goes.

"Coyote incidents? Here?" She eyes the property, waves her hand toward the ocean. "We're not in the canyon."

I raise a brow. "Coyotes have legs. They walk. They run. They're wily. They snatch small dogs and cats from yards all the time."

I'm not lying to her or trying to instill fear. It's true. Sometimes I hear the cunning dog-like animals howling at night. And I've seen the stories on the news, how these predators are skilled in the art of stealth. Like ninjas, they venture into yards cloaked in darkness, seeking unsuspecting prey. The little dog let out for a late-night pee. The little cat who escaped through the sliding door. And, on rare terrifying occasions, even small infants have been snatched from their cribs.

Her mouth rounds into a small o and she shudders, shaking her head, eyes wide. "She's definitely an indoor cat. A Paris cat. Lived in my apartment—"

"If *it* destroys any of the Italian linen-upholstered furniture with its talons, you'll be replacing it with your very high salary. The one I'm paying you."

She cringes and then lets out a tired sigh. "Where eez Jasmine? I thought she was meeting me at the airport."

I hide another grin. After meeting me, I would have asked for Jasmine too, possibly to renegotiate a higher salary. But Jasmine is not here. She's long gone.

I shake my thoughts off with a shrug. "She disappeared. Didn't even tell us that she was quitting. Just left. But good thing for you, I found your file and you'll have free run of the guesthouse." I wave my free hand toward the crate. "But I didn't know about the cat."

Julia's eyes, such a strange color—slate blue with hints of lavender—go wide. "I'm sorry," she says. "But she's here with me and she's part of the deal. I adopted her when she was a kitten—"

Little tiger—already playing the take-away. She's got spunk. I like her. I see where this conversation is headed, and, honestly, I don't care that she brought her cat.

"The cat is fine," I say, cutting her off. I let out a puff of annoyance. "I should have handled the interview. It's so hard to find good help these days. I hope you're everything Jasmine has said you were." I turn on my heel. "Come, follow me. Leave the cat outside on the front stoop."

Julia doesn't budge. She clutches the carry case closer to her chest. "What about zee coyotes?"

First day and she's already causing problems when she's supposed to be a solution. Enrique is stomping up the path that leads to the back of the house, probably angry I'd had him take care of Julia's bags, but I don't care. "Driver! Come take Julia's cat. Bring it to the guesthouse."

He shoots me another glare before answering, "Yes, Mrs. Drake."

"And close the door when you're finished. Don't want a coyote to get in."

I turn to face Julia. Her face visibly blanches. "Come inside. And we'll talk more about your position here at Hummingbird House."

"I'm happy to be here. Very excited," she says nervously. "And it's not exactly a house."

"You are very right. It's a lifestyle. But don't get too

overzealous with your excitement. You do realize this position starts with a one-month trial period," I say, turning my back on her to lead her into the house.

I do not hear her footsteps. She doesn't follow me. Just stands in the doorway, her mouth agape. She crosses her arms over her chest. "I thought my contract was for a year."

I lift up my shoulders. "It shouldn't be a problem if we like the way you cook."

Her eyes narrow with a challenge. "You'll love the meals I cook for you. I worked at a Michelin—"

"I know," I say and then I point, my eyes narrowing into the tiniest glares. "The upstairs levels are strictly off-limits. It's our private space for family only, but you'll have free run of the downstairs and the rest of the compound. Although I do have some rules."

"I understand."

She looks like she wants to bolt right out of here. With my demeanor, I wouldn't blame her if she did. But right now, I'm testing her every reaction to me. She'll either pass with flying colors or she won't. What can I say? Every relationship is based on trust and honesty. And I'm going to need both from her.

THREE
JULIA

I have no idea what I've gotten myself into. But it definitely wasn't this. No warm welcome. No happy you're here. Just Erica's steely eyes blazing into mine as she sips a glass of rosé. Plus, her blond hair is matted down on her head, her eye makeup is smudged, and she's wearing some weird bathrobe with a hummingbird print. It's not even noon yet. I've only been here ten minutes and I'm already thinking about Paul's offer and the card tucked away in my purse. Based on my first impression of Erica, I definitely need a backup plan.

I realize that I shouldn't be judging her, but I can't help it. In the real world, life doesn't come with a built-in TikTok filter. It's easy to get caught up in the glossy perfection of celebrities on magazine covers, forgetting that in person, they're just as human as the rest of us. Most glamorous stars don't have flawless skin or perfectly sculpted features without the magic of airbrushing—a reminder that true beauty lies in our imperfections, our quirks, and the stories etched into the lines on our faces—not in the artificial glossy pages of a magazine spread.

Erica's personality definitely needs a filter, but her home doesn't need one.

She walks me through a massive foyer, our feet clicking on stained concrete flooring, her back to me as I take in the details, both Mediterranean and Moroccan in style, notably all the graceful, curved arches leading to other rooms, rounded at the top and coming to a pointed end. The tin-covered, ivory-colored painted ceilings are vaulted with exposed wooden beams, creating a sense of warmth, and Moroccan tiles in colorful intricate patterns add pops of color here and there. There are quite a few wrought-iron details—the handrail leading to the upstairs, the light fixtures, and other design elements.

My gaze focuses on all the beautiful Moroccan chandeliers and lanterns, casting beautiful lights and patterns on the white walls. I think I spy with my little eye a cozy nook decorated in rich fabrics with Moroccan lights resembling glass and iron stars. I kind of want to hum The Clash's "Rock the Casbah", but refrain.

Erica leads me into a large living room with an expansive view of the ocean. It's similar in style to the rooms I'd peeked into, save for the many hummingbird paintings adorning the walls. "So, Julia, have a seat."

She ushers me to sit on a pale blue linen couch. I'm hoping I don't leave a stain. Even though the AC is blasting, I'm sweating bullets. From a chilled ice bucket, she refills her glass of wine. An American-sized glass—not a French pour. My gaze shoots to the floor-to-ceiling windows and the ocean outside. I want to swim... away from here.

"Julia, I lost you there for a minute. Tell me more about your culinary background. What makes you the right fit to be our private chef?"

One thing I know is cooking.

Poised and confident, I respond, "After finishing my studies at Le Cordon Bleu, I honed my skills at Fouquet, specializing in creating bespoke menus tailored to individual preferences. My culinary philosophy revolves around blending flavors to evoke unique experiences for our guests. I've even created my own additions to the recipes—"

"And your family owns Fouquet?"

Name-dropping has its uses. "Yes. I learned everything I know in the kitchen from them. The moment I was old enough to pick up a knife, I learned every slice, every chop from them—brunoise, chiffonade, julienne—"

"I've eaten there. At Fouquet," she says. "I loved that soup with the Parmesan crisp."

"That's my recipe," I reply, nodding with pride. "The ginger added to the potimarron velouté and the Parmesan crisp—"

"Your family also owned the restaurant l'Ondine in Santa Monica. Correct?"

"That's right. It served seafood, mostly—l'Ondine means water sprite in English... We moved back to Paris when I was six."

Her mouth twists to the side. "I thought you were eight?"

I gulp. I've just messed up my story again. I've got to get with the program. "Six? Eight? I was so young I really don't remember. Eight. Six. Eighty-six—that's what we would say when we'd run out of something at the restaurant..."

"I see," she says with a bored yawn. "Can you recall a challenging situation you've faced in the kitchen and how you've managed it? I'm only asking because my family can be a tad difficult." She pauses. "Tyler, my son, is easy. He mostly likes chicken nuggets, only organic in the shape of dinosaurs, and only with their heads and tails on, or hamburgers, but Madison is a handful."

Jasmine didn't mention anybody by that name.

"David's adoptive daughter from his first wife," Erica continues. "She's dead—not Madison, but Valerie is six feet under. David made a movie about it. Have you seen it?"

"I don't see many movies. I'm always in the kitchen. And

when I'm not, I'm vegging out in bed, usually with a cookbook or binge-watching *Chef's Table—*"

"Have you seen any of *my* movies?"

"I just saw one on the plane." I pause, trying to keep from cringing. "*Love at First Latte.*"

"That's my first one, when I was starting out." She scoffs. "The critics hated it. I still remember some of the reviews."

So do I. I'd googled a couple on the way over and I remember phrases like *lackluster script* and *lack of chemistry* and *should never have seen the light of day.*

Erica leans forward, a glint in her crazy blue eyes. "What did you think? Tell me the truth. Wasn't I hilarious? I mean, I think the critics were a bit harsh."

I don't know what to say, so I spout off one of the horrific lines from the film's bizarre coffee-making competition. "Their reviews were more tangled than a latte art masterpiece gone wrong."

She meets my eyes with so much intensity I have to sit back into the couch. "You really liked the film?"

"You were great. The dancing scene took the cake."

I'm not lying, and I have to hold back a laugh. A dance-off in a coffee shop?

"What about my accent?"

The way she says this with force I'm wondering if she's already picked up on my over-the-top French accent. Admittedly, I've been laying it on pretty thick. Perhaps I should tone it down a notch or two.

"I thought you were Irish."

"Right," she guffaws. "I'm sure you did." Her eyes darken to a steelier blue. "You're an excellent liar, Julia. I know the film is absolute shit. I just wanted to see if you'd be honest with me. But you weren't." She shakes her head from side to side and then shoots me a death glare. "I'm disappointed in you."

She wants the truth. She'll get the truth. Maybe it's my get out of jail free card. I just hope she doesn't ask me to reimburse her for the first-class ticket. I'll take the risk. "Honesty? You want honesty?"

"I do."

"I thought it was horrible. Not funny at all. Just like the critics said."

Erica hunches over in unrestrained laughter. "Finally! God dang! Finally!" She raises her glass, taking a healthy sip of wine. "To you! Somebody who isn't kissing my ass. I like you, Julia."

Once again, I've been rendered speechless and I honestly don't know how to respond. Maybe I should tell her that I didn't mean to be so rude, even though she'd appreciated it.

"Mrs. Drake, I..."

"Please call me Erica, darling," she slurs, drawing out darling like dahhhhh-ling. Oddly, doing my research I'd read she'd grown up in Fresno. I saw a replay of the tearjerker of an interview with famed reporter Tabitha Sinclair, the latest Barbara Walters or Diane Sawyer, on YouTube. I can practically quote Tabitha's opening, hear the story in my head.

Erica Drake's childhood was filled with hardships that seemed insurmountable. Growing up in a cramped trailer park, she often went to bed hungry, her dreams fueled by the faint glimmer of Hollywood glamor she saw on an old TV set. Despite the worn-out carpets and peeling paint of her surroundings, Erica found solace in the stories she created in her head, weaving tales of far-off lands and daring adventures to escape her reality. With a heart full of hope and determination, she saved every penny from odd jobs and school performances, dreaming of the day she would walk the red carpet herself. This tenacity, born from adversity, would be the very essence of the star she would one day become.

"Julia, you've gone quiet," Erica says, snapping me back to the present.

"Sorry. Just thinking." I adjust my weight, leaning forward, trying to get the conversation back on track. "You mentioned Madison?"

She rolls her eyes, feigning annoyance. "Yes. She's always on a new diet. This week it's keto or paleo or raw. The next week it's something else." She throws her hands in the air, wine spilling on the floor. "Kids these days. I don't know anymore." She leans forward. "Honestly, I think she changes her tastes every week to get under my skin."

My gaze darts to the window. "Where is she?"

"Darling, it's spring break. Madison went to Europe with friends. Tyler is at a basketball retreat. And David is filming in Vegas." She pours another glass of wine. "Which leaves us two women alone to get to know each other better. I can't wait to see what you prepare for me tonight."

I gulp. "I thought I'd have a few days to settle in."

"I'm paying you an exorbitant salary." She places her hands on her hips. "Why on earth would you think that?"

Because it's in my contract. "I talked to Jasmine about this. I have to buy a new surfboard, maybe a paddle board—"

Erica's sneer silences me. "I'm paying you to cook, not play in the water like a little mermaid."

"But I do get two days off." No, screw this. Screw everything. Dreams are made by sticking to your guns, not letting other people—especially a crazy bitch—control them. "Mrs. Drake, I'm sorry but I'm backing out of our deal. Where are my things? I'll call an Uber."

To go where? I don't know. Just far, far away from here. Panic rises in my chest. A lump forms in my throat. I only have two solid connections in LA. Both are strangers.

Erica swallows and meets my eyes. "Look, Julia. I'm a bit stressed out, not my normal self with the nomination..."

"Nomination?"

She nods her head vigorously, her messy blond hair brushing her shoulders. "Best actress. The Oscars. A movie called *Swerve*. I have a copy. Blu-ray. We'll watch it in our home theater later." Erica stands up, wobbles. "I'll take you on a tour of the property. As mentioned, the upstairs is off-limits." She circles a finger toward the second level and shrugs. "We'll start with the kitchen—and then your space." She meets my eyes and puffs out her bottom lip into a pathetic pout. "Please."

I suck in my cheeks, deliberating for a moment. I do need some time to figure out my next move. I must be a glutton for punishment. "A one-month trial period? Right?"

"Right." She links her arm into mine. "You're going to love it here."

Am I? Because I already hate everything about this situation and I'm planning on leaving once I figure out where to go. At least I have my knives, a form of protection.

"Is something wrong?" she asks.

"Sorry," I say. "I'm a little tired."

"Feeling the jet lag, yes?"

And suddenly she's concerned? "I am."

"I'll show you around and then you can get some rest. How does that sound?"

I nod. "Perfect."

On the tour, Erica explains the house rules. I can use the pool, but only on my breaks and when David isn't around. I can have guests over, but they need to have background checks and nobody should spend the night. I can help myself to wine, but not the Miraval, her rosé. It's from Brad Pitt's vineyard in France. They're *great* friends. David only likes red, but mostly drinks Scotch.

The moment I step into the kitchen of this magnificent Malibu home, a wave of pristine elegance washes over me. The marble countertops gleam under the soft glow of the pendant lights, untouched by the chaos of culinary creations. And, believe me, having worked in a Michelin two-star, it gets chaotic, one of the reasons I'd even considered working as a private chef. That, and the salary Erica is paying me.

On the far wall, a grandiose stove commands attention. A masterpiece of stainless steel and sleek design from La Cornue's château collection, this professional-grade appliance promises out of this world wonders with the turn of a knob and costs around $200k.

I can't help but wonder if this kitchen has ever witnessed the sizzle of onions in a hot pan or the sweet aroma of freshly baked pastries. Everything is in its place, from the rows of gleaming copper pots hanging above the island to the perfectly aligned spices in ornate glass jars.

As I gaze out of the window above the sink, I'm met with a breathtaking view of the Pacific Ocean stretching endlessly to the horizon. The sun casts a golden hue over the water, its rays dancing on the gentle waves below. Far in the distance, a pod of dolphins frolic, their sleek forms breaking the surface in graceful arcs.

But what truly captures my attention are the humming-birds. They flit and dart among the vibrant flowers that line the edge of the bluff, their iridescent feathers shimmering in the sunlight. Each tiny creature is a masterpiece of nature's design, a fleeting burst of color.

I watch in awe as they hover near the window, their delicate wings beating so fast they seem to blur. One brave soul ventures closer, pausing to inspect the glass with a curious tilt of its head. For a moment, our eyes meet, and my mind is blown.

FOUR

ERICA

Life sometimes follows a script, especially when you're the one writing it. Sometimes, though, you need to improvise. I'm back to thinking about my motivation for hiring her. As Julia surveys the kitchen with her jaw dropped, I meander over to the intercom. "Ladies. Kitchen. Now," I say with force, my voice echoing throughout the house.

I know Silvia and Karla are cleaning the master bedroom, the sound of the vacuum rumbling. I'm not lazy. I'm taking in Julia's every reaction—to me, this kitchen—and I just don't feel like moving. Plus, I don't like raising my voice too much because, should I win the Oscar as I'm hoping I will, I have to save it for my awards speech.

I watch Julia, running her hand across the countertops, the stove, the Thermomix I'd ordered for her, and I run my lines in my head. "I'd like to thank the members of the Academy, the cast and the crew—" I pause, smiling to myself.

A couple of minutes later my cleaning ladies meander into the kitchen with a bounce in their steps and large smiles. I know why. They've been kissing up to me all week. They're looking forward to next Sunday. I give them most of the swag I receive at the varying events—the jewelry, the clothing, the tchotchkes, the chocolates. Very expensive things. Designers and brands hope that I'll wear or talk about whatever they've bestowed on me. Sometimes I do. Most of the time I don't because I enjoy spreading the wealth.

I'm also looking forward to walking the red carpet, to the flashes of photographers and the screams of my adoring fans. Because after next Sunday, if I win, I'll be retiring from acting on a high note. If I don't win the Oscar I'll need a new script—a better one, and Julia could definitely supply some inspiration. I'm trying to figure out which character I want to play, which character Julia's going to play.

Silvia clears her throat and Julia turns, cocking her head to the side.

"Julia, this is Silvia and Karla... our house staff. They're sisters from Mexico." I nod at the ladies in acknowledgment and then I introduce Julia. "This is our new chef from France."

Silvia regards Julia. "Julia, we're not from Mexico, but Guatemala. And Karla is not my sister, she is my daughter."

Teasing them that they are sisters from Mexico is an inside joke between us. Silvia is flattered with the reference, making her younger. Karla is not. At any rate, I sponsored both of them when they got their citizenship and, well, they are like extended members of the family and they love being spoiled.

I shrug. "Same thing in my mind. Spanish is Spanish. It only rains in Spain. What was that expression?" I tap my chin. "And the rain in Spain falls mainly on the plain."

Silvia blurts out a laugh. "Then what happens in Guatemala?"

"She wouldn't know. She's never been there," says Karla.

Julia blinks, probably feeling a mixture of surprise and sympathy for Sylvia and Karla. How could I be so clueless, or worse, indifferent? By her expression, I can tell she admires them. She doesn't admire me.

"Nice to meet you, Julia," says Silvia. "Welcome to Hummingbird House. What do you think of your workspace?"

I grab another bottle of rosé from the refrigerator and, set to uncork it, I look at the clock on the microwave. It's only half past eleven and I'm now on my third glass.

Julia spits out a soft laugh.

"What's so funny, Julia?" I demand, and she turns to face me, her teeth digging into her bottom lip. "Let me in on the joke. As I've told you, I'm really under a lot of stress. I could use a laugh."

Her eyes dart to the side, to the stove, to my hands. It's obvious she's trying to come up with something to say aside from "you are a raging alcoholic and an absolute asshole." So, she surprises me when she says, "Your kitchen is so beautiful. But it doesn't seem like it's ever been used."

Clever girl. I'm liking her even more, coming up with that on the fly while my eyes shoot daggers at her. And to be honest, it is quite funny because I've only used the stove or the microwave to heat up premade meals. When I was young, save for frying an egg, I never learned how to cook... hard to do when there wasn't food in the house. But Julia doesn't need to know that.

"We order in a lot. Or go out. You know how it is." Her nose scrunches again and I straighten my posture. A chef, no, she doesn't know how it is. "Choose a day for them to clean your home. They work Monday to Friday from 10 a.m. until whenever they leave. They like taking long breaks by the pool."

Karla grins. "It's a really nice pool."

I turn my gaze toward the window. The pool is one of the estate's crown jewels—an infinity edge masterpiece looking out over the ocean. Right about now, I'm sure Julia is itching to jump into both. "I can clean my own place," she says.

"But you cannot. I like things done a certain way."

"She does," says Silvia with a roll of her eyes.

I wink at the ladies. I have a feeling she'll agree to working on a barter system. "Julia will cook your lunches... no need to bring them here anymore. Agreed?"

Silvia and Karla smile.

"Agreed," says Julia after a moment of baffled hesitation.

"We always eat ours by the pool or on the beach. You're welcome to join us," says Karla. "Do you ever make desserts?"

"I do," replies Julia. "My specialty is pastries..."

"And my specialty is avoiding them," I say with force. "It's the way I stay so trim. No carbs for any of us until after the awards. I have a dress to fit into."

Silvia and Karla groan. Julia eyes the bottle of rosé and she thinks I don't notice the disgusted judgment flickering in her eyes. But I notice everything. It's what I do, comes with my job. I study people, their every reaction, including the way they speak—the pauses, the tone, the volume. Their accents. I can always tell when somebody isn't being honest.

"It's a very stressful time. And I'm mostly on a liquid diet now." I raise my shoulders apathetically. "You'd understand the pressure I'm under if you knew what I was going through."

She lowers her gaze. "Believe me, I understand pressure."

"I'm sure you do," I say, my tone more snappish than I'd intended. "Which day do you want them to clean?"

"Do I have a choice?"

"No."

"I guess Wednesdays."

I look to Silvia. "Wednesday good for you?"

"Of course, Erica," she says.

I walk over to the drawer with a combination lock on it. I flip up the carved silver plate, revealing the keypad. "The code is 14344, which ironically means I love you very much, or so

I've heard. Although I love both of them, do not share the code with Tyler or Madison."

I open the drawer and Julia lets out a gasp when she sees stacks and stacks of hundred-dollar bills. Julia nods dumbly and blinks. I get it. Seeing this much cash is disconcerting. There's over $100k in it. Under the cash is a scale. And I know the weight of every bill and when the drawer needs to be replenished. "This is the petty cash drawer," I say.

"That's a lot of money. Aren't you worried about being robbed?"

"Not with our security system. And not unless you're the thief. With that said, I want all receipts put in this envelope—for food, when you shop." I eye Silvia and Karla. "They know the drill for cleaning supplies and any extras. Every single receipt."

"What extras?" asks Silvia.

"All those little things you sneak in—the razors, the makeup. I don't care. But I do notice them."

"You're the one who told us to buy those things," says Karla. "So we look presentable."

Julia cringes. By now, she probably thinks I'm some kind of monster. "I just like things done a certain way. It's the way I grew up."

"I thought you grew up in a trailer park," says Julia, dumbfounded. She clasps a hand over her mouth. "Sorry. It wasn't my intention to be rude. I, uh, I saw clips of your interview, the one with Tabitha Sinclair."

She's done her research on me. I won't hold it against her because I've also done my research on her.

"Exactly," I say, going silent for a moment. "And it's the reason I like everything just so. I never want to live like that again—unkempt and in filth. I like everything to be perfect. As for the cash, I like keeping a lot of it around because I didn't have any growing up."

After I'd married David and was nominated for *Valerie* six years ago, the tabloids usually concocted their stories with headlines like this: FORMER TRAILER PARK TRASH ERICA DRAKES STRIKES IT BIG. It didn't help when the press also learned that I'd had an ongoing affair with David while he was married to Valerie and that Tyler was David's biological child born out of wedlock. Enter the new headlines: ERICA DRAKE: SLEEPING HER WAY TO THE TOP and the speculative article ERICA DRAKE KILLED FOR HER CAREER.

David never defended me, just told me to laugh it off and to get used to being targeted by the press. And that time, the torture, has come to an end. There are no crosshairs on this woman's back. I've paid my dues. Now that I have the potential to achieve my childhood dream of winning best actress for *Swerve*, it's time to count my blessings and move on. I walk over to the pantry, open the door.

"Everything you need should be in here." I indicate a hook in the back. "Save the planet. We bring our own shopping bags when we shop."

"Are those Chanel?" she asks, pointing to the burlap bags with a logo.

"No, they're knock-offs," I say with a shrug. "I saw them in a shop in Santee Alley and I just had to have them. Might as well be stylish when you run errands. Anyway, have a look around; if you need anything else, you know where the petty cash is."

Julia shifts her weight from one foot to another. "I should probably settle in, maybe take a shower—"

"A very good idea," I say, eyeing her up and down. "But before you make an escape for dreamland, follow me to your suite."

Her eyes are saying what her lips aren't: I want to get away from you. Honestly, I would, too. We all have something we want to escape from. As a young girl, living with an alcoholic mother and her revolving door of abusive boyfriends, I used to dream about escaping my past and I did just that. Now, I need to escape my present and I've been planning my freedom for years. Whether she likes it or not, Julia is an integral part of my story.

FIVE

JULIA

Erica leads me past the pool and towards a slate path in the perfectly manicured garden, the heady scent of sage wafting up to my nostrils. She's stumbling in front of me, her glass of rosé in hand, the drink splashing on the ground. I've already come up with a nickname for her: Lushika. Glorious kitchen or not, I *am* definitely thinking about running, getting the hell out of here, and she knows it.

"In addition to coyotes, sometimes we find snakes in the brush." Erica glances over her shoulder with a look of warning. "Be extremely wary of rattlers. The gardeners found a few last week and had to call the fire department for removal."

My heart skips a beat at the mention of rattlesnakes. I can't shake the image of slithering creatures hidden in the bushes, ready to strike. And then Erica adds, almost casually, "We've had a couple of tarantula sightings, too."

Tarantulas? The thought sends a shiver down my spine. I'm trying to keep my composure, but my fear is palpable, my gaze latching onto my feet, darting left to right. Even if I wanted to run, I don't think my legs would cooperate. Plus, I need to get my things and, more importantly, my cat.

Coyotes, and snakes, and tarantulas, oh my. Add in Erica and, although the grounds are jaw-droppingly beautiful, this could be hell on earth. What in the world did I sign up for? My wildest dream has turned into the wildest of nightmares.

Watching my every step, I notice belladonna plants bordering an herb garden and my mind instantly leaps to an even darker place. Also known as deadly nightshade or devil's cherries, belladonna, although striking in appearance with its waxy, oval-shaped leaves and bell-shaped flowers ranging in deep purple hues, is highly toxic after the flowers fade and the plant produces shiny black berries that look like cherries. If ingested, these berries are lethal. Along with knowing which mushrooms are poisonous, I also learned which berries are hazardous from hiking in the mountains one fall and looking for cèpes—a large French mushroom like a portobello, or large cremini. If you're not sure, pharmacists in France will tell you yay or nay regarding your haul.

I stop in my tracks and yelp, "Erica, those are poisonous."

She freezes mid-step, her shoulders tense. "Did you see a snake?"

"No," I say, thinking, *oh, God.* "Those plants. The belladonnas, the ones with the purple flowers—they're extremely poisonous."

"I didn't have the gardeners plant them. David did."

"I don't understand. Pourquoi? And why are they planted near an herb garden? I smell the aromas of—"

"He thinks that they're pretty, that they go with the rustic landscaping of the grounds. And that's not an herb garden." She waves a hand into the distance. "We do have one, though—fresh basil, thyme, other plants. It's over there, on the other side of the swimming pool."

My eyes shoot back to the purple flowers of the belladonnas. "But those... they're extremely toxic. You might want to think about having them removed."

"As if we're going to eat them?" she scoffs, and continues down the path.

A bright green hummingbird with a red chest and pointy little beak hovers in front of me for a moment and then flies on like a tiny rocket into the distance. My heart lurches. "What about the hummingbirds?"

"Silly girl, hummingbirds are only attracted to flowering plants with nectar—and the reason I have plants like grevillea, lavender, and salvia in addition to the feeders in the hummingbird garden." She pauses. "Oh, that reminds me, I have to tell the gardeners to refresh the feeders." She turns and grins, a dazed, glassy look in her eyes. "It's a magical place, the garden. I often sit for hours on one of the stone benches, just watching them. You could say I'm slightly obsessed with those tiny creatures, their iridescent wings, the way they can fly backwards and forwards..."

"Yes," I reply, wondering where this conversation is headed. "I love them, too."

"See? We have something in common."

I don't think so.

In the distance, the sound of loud hammering snaps me to attention. A crew of workers are installing something on the bluff. "What are they doing?"

"Oh, just another of David's latest phases. Apparently, thanks to Madison and Tyler, he's taken up rock climbing, and he's having them install rock-climbing grips or clamps. I don't know what they're called exactly. But there is a little cove at the bottom, our personal paradise. Although there are no private beaches in California, this one is hard to get to, and David thinks rappelling down to it would be fun. To each his own, I suppose. And David can do whatever the hell he wants with his money. And I'll do as I wish with mine—the reason I hired you."

Her grin fades into a frown. I'm at a loss for words so I blurt out, "Where is he? Your husband?"

Erica's eyes lose their glimmer. "I already told you, he's in Vegas. The movie is called *The Sunset Stripper*." She mumbles, "David told me I was too old for the part."

My heart goes out to her for a beat. And then I think, *bring out the tiny violins*. She has everything. Before my mind debates the subject of privilege, Erica continues down the path and I follow her. She stops in front of a mini replica of the main house, complete with a little terrace decorated with two elegant chairs and a small wooden table.

"This will be your new home," she says with an eager smile. "Welcome."

Stepping inside, I'm immediately struck by the breath-taking beauty of the Pacific Ocean stretching out before me from a large floor-to-ceiling picture window. The waves crash against the rugged bluffs, the sound soothing my tangled nerves.

Even with Erica's looming presence, the space itself exudes tranquility, with clean lines accentuating the natural light flooding the space. The two-bedroom layout is thoughtfully designed, with minimalist decor in soothing blues and whites. Open and inviting. Calm.

I can't help but admire the small kitchen, complete with a backsplash of shimmering mother-of-pearl tiles and modern appliances. The idea of cooking here, overlooking the ocean, has me licking my lips, imagining the aroma of my dishes mingling with the salty ocean air. Mussels in savory white wine sauce with garlic, finely chopped parsley, garlic and two more of my special ingredients—fennel and ginger. I'm craving them right now. The dining room table, positioned in front of the window, seems like the perfect spot for meals. It's almost romantic, although the idea of sharing it with someone is a distant thought.

As I unzip my cat free from her crate, Erica's eyes widen in disbelief. She points. "That's a cat? More like a guinea pig..."

"Non, she's not a rodent," I say with a huff. "Meet Beurreboule."

Erica cringes. I suppress a tight smile, finding mild amusement in Erica's reaction as my little orange-and-white love bug scurries under the bed.

"Burble?" Erica's top lip lifts with confusion. "Weird name. And weird cat. It's so—so tiny."

"Her name is a combination of beurre, meaning butter, and boule, ball. Tu comprends? Butterball."

Shoot. I've used the informal "tu" when I should have used "vous."

She shakes her head, her jaw dropping ever so slightly. "Well, what do you think of your new home?"

"It's absolutely stunning," I reply, genuinely appreciating the elegance of my new living space. The open living room is almost twice the size of my apartment in Paris, which I'd been able to rent out. "I think Beurreboule and me will really like it here," I say, my eyes once again locking on the ocean view.

Erica nods perfunctorily as if to say, *how could I not?* "Do you have a uniform?"

"I brought my chef's coats."

"Can I see them?"

I thought she was going to let me settle in, yet here she is, breathing down my neck. Good thing I'd had my coats cleaned and pressed before I left. I unzip one of my suitcases, pulling out a crisp white coat and hold it up. Erica scowls. "Can you put it on?" she demands, and so I do.

She surveys me and then her nose pinches into a sneer. "Ugh, that simply won't work. At all. I hate it. It's so shapeless and formless. Basic."

Of course it is.

"I'll be cooking in it, not wearing it on the red carpet."

"No, you won't be wearing it all," she says with force.

"We're going shopping. And you'll also need a couple of dresses."

"Dresses?"

"We're having a party after the awards. Here. Next Sunday. Fifty or so people." She rolls her eyes. "Our closest friends. I really hope I'll be celebrating a win, because my friends can be quite nasty. If I lose, they'll rub it in my face—not with words but facial expressions. Or they'll talk about me behind my back."

This woman needs a huge reality check. And new friends.

"I was hired to cook for your family and the occasional dinner party. I can't cook for that many people," I say, keeping my tone level.

"I didn't say you had to," she scoffs. "Silvia and Karla can help the caterer, too. I've already hired Mel B..."

I blink. "The Spice Girl?"

"Are you daft?" She shakes out her hair. "No, the caterer. She and her crew will do all the cooking, but the recipes will be yours. I'd like to see a proposal for them. I hope you can come up with something this weekend. Those little appetizers. It won't be a sit-down meal, not for so many people. It's that French theme..."

"An apèro dînatoire," I sigh.

"Ooh, I do love how everything sounds better in French."

I rub my eyes.

"I'll leave you to settle in. And I'll be back in an hour or so. I just need to clean myself up a bit. We'll go to the Country Mart, have lunch at Tra da Noi, and then I'll take you shopping. I have just the perfect store in mind for you. It's actually French." She pauses. "Like you." She blows me a kiss and then eyes me up and down. "Maybe you should clean yourself up, too. The paparazzi is always out in force especially during the awards season." She shrugs. "And, well, you'll be with me."

After the she-devil leaves, I flop down onto the bed, which is so comfortable I don't know how I'll get out of it. I prop myself up on my elbows, staring blankly at the ocean. Beurreboule hops up next to me and climbs onto my stomach, purring and kneading my belly. I pet her sweet little head, deliberating. If I ignore Erica's eccentric demands and overbearing personality, I have one month to come up with a new plan or I could pack up my things and leave right now. The chorus to the Clash's epic song "Should I Stay or Should I Go?" infiltrates my brain.

Silvia knocks on the door. I wave her in and she smiles. "I brought you fresh towels. I'll just set them here on the table."

"Thank you."

Since I have Silvia alone, I have the opportunity to pump her for information. Like me, she's hired help. No time like the present. I swallow and then get on with it. "How do you like working for the Drakes?"

She grins. "We love it."

"You do?" A foreign concept, I can't imagine loving working for Erica. I can be honest with Silvia, but need to be tactful. "Erica is a bit..." I shrug, like it's not a big deal. And now I'm thinking about my dad again and one of our favorite songs— "Hard to Handle" by the Black Crowes. I think Chris Robinson lives or used to live in Malibu. "She seems a lot to handle—"

"Not really. She's very kind." Silvia puffs out her bottom lip. "Erica is just very stressed out with the awards. You should have been here the last time she was nominated. She didn't win and it crushed her. Couldn't leave her bed for a month..." She pauses. "Just ignore her behavior like my daughter and me do. She'll have her ups and her downs, but then she snaps back."

Snaps. Interesting choice of word. Because I don't know if I can deal with a roller coaster of emotions right now. Each crashing wave reminds me of when my dad taught me to surf. I was five years old and we were at Zuma Beach. The way we'd laugh when I'd tumble off the board. The way my mom would dance in the sand, pretending she was Esmerelda, and cheer me on.

"Madison, Karla and I have first pick with the swag she'll receive. The last time it was valued at over one hundred and thirty-five thousand. Erica keeps most of the cosmetic treatments—the lipo, the Botox, the hair stuff. But we'll keep you in mind, too."

I don't know if I should be insulted. I realize I probably look pretty gross, that my hair is greasy and ratty, but I have the excuse of a long travel day. "What's wrong with me?"

"Nothing. You're absolutely gorgeous." Silvia laughs. "We get the rest of the goods—the candles, the chocolates, and sometimes trips. It's a bonus of dealing with her meltdowns." She places a finger on her lips. "You're not hearing this from me, but, believe me, there will be many. Just ignore them. She's all bark and no bite."

I go silent. Maybe she is truly stressed out. Maybe drinking and acting like a bitch is a defense mechanism. Beurreboule meows and snakes around Silvia's ankles. "You have the cutest furball. I love her!" She picks my cat up and cuddles her under her chin. "She's so tiny. Is that how you snuck her in?"

"Erica knows she's here."

She clucks her tongue. "Keep her inside. Nature can be dangerous..."

"Yeah, yeah, I know. Coyotes and snakes." I shudder. While we're on the subject and she's preoccupied, I have one more question. "What about Mr. Drake? What's he like?"

Silvia shrugs. "He's not around all that much."

"Is he nice?"

"To us, yes."

Her words give me pause.

"To Erica?"

"I've already said too much." Silvia forces a tight smile. She places Beurreboule on the bed. "I'll leave you to shower and settle in. I hear you're going to lunch and shopping. Erica is going to spoil you rotten."

"Has she taken you and Karla shopping, too?"

"Have you ever seen cleaning ladies wear designer clothes to work?" Silvia grins. "Look, Julia, the one thing you truly need to know about Erica is that she came from nothing. Now that she has everything, she likes spreading the wealth." She pops her lips. "You've only been here for a couple of hours. You'll soon realize what she's really like."

Silvia leaves with a wave, closing the doors behind her. I sit staring at the ocean, wondering if my first impression of Erica is completely wrong. Then again, it was almost like she was purposefully being nasty.

One month. It's not like I'll be living in a prison. Not with this view.

SIX

ERICA

Perhaps I'm being too demanding with Julia on her first day. I really don't want her to leave. It's time for scene two, take one. She's going to think I'm completely bonkers. But that's the point. I need to gauge her every reaction to me.

Before I hop in the shower, I pull out my phone to check messages on Snapchat and smile.

MOONBEAM:

How's it going?

SUNBEAM:

Plan's on. Might be overdoing it.

MOONBEAM:

Don't push too hard. We have our future to think of.

SUNBEAM:

I can't stop thinking about it.

I watch as our messages vanish. Poof. They're gone.

The future. I need something tangible to hang on to. I set my phone down. To be safe, Moonbeam and I have never met in public and we don't use our real names when communicating. We're not having a sexual affair, so David could never accuse me of any wrongdoing, but it is emotional. Moonbeam and I have a lot in common, namely we both hate David with every fiber of our being. My monster of a husband probably wasn't expecting that I'd be nominated for best actress again and he won't want to lose face. I know he's been making plans to get rid of me. And I've been making my own plans, too. Until the pieces are in play, I'm doing what I always do—playing my role of the nagging wife.

After trying to call David, I walk into the bathroom to take a quick shower, wash my face, put on some makeup, and do my hair. I laugh at my reflection. Julia must have been terrified of me.

I'm in the process of getting dressed when my cellphone rings. I look at caller ID. David. "Erica," he grunts. "You've called me ten times. And texted me at least twenty. Aside from accusing me of having strippers on my lap, what do you want?"

It's not an accusation. I know David takes his casting calls too far. I'd hoped and prayed he'd go down like the others during the height of the #MeToo movement, but not one actress came forward to accuse him of anything. He'd made it out of that storm unscathed. Which means that he's probably paid them all off. Lord knows, he has the money.

He was only twenty-five years old when he took over the helm at Drake Entertainment, the company his father started, and made his first film—producing, directing, and writing a low-budget horror film, *Evil Ignited*. He'd invested $3 million into it and, an instant cult classic, it grossed over $180 million at the box office. From there, he became the executive producer of other films, made bundles of money, and became a household name. Throughout the years, he's written, produced, and directed other films like *Caught in the Ripcurl*, *Women on the*

Edge, Valerie, Swerve, and now *The Sunset Stripper.* Who knows what's next?

"Erica, for fuck's sake," he huffs. "Say something. I'm busy."

Well, hello to you, too. It's hard being even remotely pleasant to him. I have to fake it until I make it away from him and ride the tide to a place I shall call happiness and bliss. Out of the dragon's lair. Like I've been doing with Julia, I need to keep him off-balance. "I just want to know how filming is going, darling."

I call everybody darling. It's not a pet name or term of endearment. I'd rather have said *how's filming going, you cheating sociopath.* But I know David's limits.

He lets out a labored sigh. "Kind of a nightmare. Luna Starlight is—"

I cut him off. Luna was once my friend, but her *real* name is Eleanor, or rather, Nellie. "If you'd put me in that role..."

"Damn it, Erica. We've gone over this. You're too old for the part."

"Old? I'm only thirty-eight. I have a few good years left—"

He snorts. "Not in Hollywood, you don't."

Every time he says this, I see red—and not the red carpet. Hollywood is so messed up, always looking for the next hottest, youngest thing. Unless you're Meryl Streep or Julia Roberts, you don't stand a chance at my age.

"Nellie is *only* two years younger than me. Makeup could have aged me down or up—whatever was needed."

Last night, David was on the news. Well, not the actual news, but TMZ, flashing photos of him canoodling with Luna Starlight (a.k.a. Nellie Jones) and inferring that they're having a wild affair. Even though she tells me she isn't, I know Nellie is sleeping with David. When she was up for the role, she'd told me that she'd always wanted my life. She can have it.

Before we both hit it big, we lived together, sharing a one-bedroom apartment in Hollywood Hills. Both of us small-town girls, escaping our former lives. Both of us wanting to make it big. Both of us big dreamers.

My, how things have changed.

"You can't dance," he says. "She's a tried-and-true burlesque performer..."

"I could have learned."

David chokes out a laugh. "You can't teach an old dog new tricks. Plus, you're extremely difficult to work with. And, no, you can't have a part in my next movie—unless it's about a useless actress who has the world at her feet but drowns in a pool of wine."

Oh, no, he didn't just go there again. He's the one that started the rumor in the first place—probably to make sure I wouldn't be able to work again without him. It started as a joke on one of the late-night talk shows and escalated on from there. And, although it wasn't true, his plan had worked. Even with all of the accolades, nobody will go near me. I can't get auditions. My agent has tried. David has blackballed me from working unless it's with him. My blood is boiling. I've got to calm down and bring this home.

"Well, Nellie—forgive me, Luna—hasn't been nominated for an Academy Award. Twice."

"Thanks to me," he says with a cackle. "And maybe she will. The film is looking spectacular so far. Luna is just timid with a couple of scenes. Doesn't want to handle a live snake. But she'll get there."

"She's dealing with you."

I want to high-five myself for that quip.

"Jesus, Erica, I don't want to go through this with you again."

I take a steadying breath. "Fine."

He coughs. "Did you just agree with me?"

"I did," I reply, but only to keep him on edge. I have fun tipping the scales, mostly so they end up in my favor.

"You've already had a glass or two—"

I am not slurring my words. But he likes to think I'm constantly drunk, mostly because that's what I want him to think. Sometimes, to deal with him, I do get quite buzzed, but I keep my wits about me, most of the time.

"I was celebrating the arrival of our new chef, Julia. Julia Fouquet. She's from Paris."

"She's quite beautiful," he growls with a pleased moan. "Hmmm, a French chef. Reminds me of somebody I used to know..."

My throat catches. "Wait a second. How do you know what she looks like?"

"I pulled up surveillance. Somebody has to keep an eye on you when I'm not around."

I look around—left, right, my eyes wide. "Are there cameras in our room?"

He lets out a laugh. "I was talking about the front of the house. I saw you standing in your bathrobe, glass of rosé in hand and I saw her step out of the car." He pauses. "But you do look nice in blue. It's my favorite color—matches your eyes."

A heavy silence hangs in the air until David clears it with his gruff voice.

"I'll be home tomorrow night. Get the guest room ready. Luna will be coming with me for a costume adjustment. Then we're flying back to Vegas for the final scene. So as long as we have this chef, I'd like boeuf bourguignon. I've been craving meat."

The line clicks to a close. I straighten my posture. I'm playing the biggest role of my life. And whether Julia likes it or not, she'll be acting right alongside me—best supporting actress.

SEVEN

JULIA

It's been over an hour and Lushika hasn't come back to capture me for the afternoon of torture she's planned. After showering, I've just been chilling out, staring at the waves lapping in the ocean and listening to Beurreboule's purrs. Save for Erica, the surroundings, the kitchen, everything is beyond perfect. But I know there is no such thing as perfection and dread pinches at my stomach.

While I wait, I thumb through the file Erica's left behind with the house rules. Erica's handwriting is illegible—chicken-scratch scrawls. From what I can read, Tyler has a food allergy to nuts of any kind. Madison's dietary preferences: she's on a paleo diet, which puts the kibosh on pastry making. No grains? No dairy? I wonder if Lushika has a spiralizer so I can whip up some zucchini noodles. No carbs!

I'm trying to remain positive but, based on first impressions, I'll be working for a walking nightmare.

Antsy, I reach for my suitcase and pull out the one photo of my parents I'd brought with me, my favorite. In it, I'm about six or seven years old and our faces all have wide smiles. We're on the beach, me holding a bright blue boogie board, the Ferris wheel on Santa Monica Pier in the background. My mom's eyes are so bright and cheerful. She has a big floppy straw hat on her head. My dad has his head thrown back in laughter. He was always so jovial, joking around. Really bad dad jokes. Like, "Why don't scientists trust atoms? Because they make up everything!"

I stare at the photo. I remember that day so well. After the beach, we'd walked over to the pier, passing by a man in a gold-painted suit and hat, his skin gold too, who stood like a statue until somebody gave him money. Then, he'd slowly started moving, and then quicker, finally break-dancing. I'd stood in awe. We all wandered to grab ice cream cones—Mom and me taking strawberry, Dad more than happy with his chocolate mint.

It was the perfect day.

My mother was estranged from her French family for moving to the United States and marrying an American, so I'd never met them, don't even know if they're dead or alive. My dad's parents were old, living in a retirement community. Dad always joked that he was their greatest mistake. I'd visited them a few times, and kept in touch with them via FaceTime, and letters, until they died a couple of years ago.

I pull out my phone, trying to call everybody to tell them that I've arrived OK. My parents are on a permanent vacation and it's impossible to get hold of them, but it's after 9 p.m. in Paris—a good time to call my aunt, Marie, not quite busy with the dinner rush at Fouquet's. She picks up quickly, but the camera is facing outward, toward the kitchen. I can hear her speaking rapid-fire French, but I can't see her. "Finally! We were wondering if you'd arrived OK!"

"Oh, I'm here. I've arrived. Safe and sound..." I pause. "Auntie Marie, switch the view. I can't see you. I can only see the butts of the line chefs."

"Sorry," she says with a laugh. "You know me and technology. Une minute."

As Marie fumbles with the phone, my eyes survey my living quarters. Riku, the stuffed panda bear, looks right at home on the overstuffed chair. Me? I'm feeling very much out of place.

Staring at the bear, my thoughts spin to Liam. He was two years older than me. I was a sophomore in high school when we met; he was a senior with sandy brown hair, a dimpled smile, and an infectious laugh. He was smart and studious. He liked to watch me surf. Terrible at it himself, never able to stand up on a board. My first love, I've kept all the letters and notes he wrote for me stuffed inside the giant panda bear he won at a stand at Santa Monica Pier. For some reason, I had to bring it with me.

"Punaisse," puffs Marie. "Une minute un plus."

"Take your time," I say.

Marie is ten years older than my mom. Growing up, they called each other big sister and little sister—Auntie M to me. The common thread between them was food. My mom was a pastry chef, Marie's specialty was seafood. My dad and Bernard ran the businesses—not that Marie or my mom couldn't do that side of things. They could. They were both trailblazers. But they both wanted to focus their energy on doing what they loved. And it wasn't money or budgets—it was creating out-of-this-world recipes that kept their customers coming back for more.

I lick my lips, thinking about the meals and desserts I'd been introduced to at a very, very young age. I revel in the memories of being smacked by their aprons while trying to put my own flair into a dish—namely cocoa powder. I'd snuck in what I now call a spice into one of Marie's daube de boeuf when she wasn't looking. And let's just say that addition stuck. I think I was five years old. All the flavors, all the teachings, melded together.

And that's the reason I became a chef.

Finally, Marie's face comes into view. Suddenly, I miss her

crinkled eyes, her smile. Uncle Bernard squeezes into the frame with his bushy white mustache taking up half the screen. We smile at one another for a moment until Marie pointedly says, "You don't look happy."

I shrug. I'm not about to tell them of my first impressions of Lushika. I mean, it's quite possible Erica was just having a bad morning. "I'm happy. I am. Just a little tired. Long flight."

Bernard nods. "Oui, and you're too far away."

"Look at my place. Look at this view." I turn the camera and sweep through my living space, landing on Beurreboule, and then la pièce de résistance—the view. "Isn't it amazing?"

I flip the camera view back to me, nodding furiously.

Silence.

"It's nice. Superb. But there is more to life than a beautiful view. Are you sure you want to stay in California?" asks Marie. She can barely meet my eyes. A tear slides down her cheek. "You can change your mind. You'll always have your place here, especially in my kitchen."

They don't know how much I've been longing to come back to California. And I'm not going to tell them, because it would hurt their feelings, make them think that I don't appreciate my French roots. Although I've thought about hopping on the first flight back to Paris, I don't want to be a quitter. I can't give up when I haven't even started. I lower my head, shaking it. "I miss the ocean, surfing the waves. I miss the sun—"

"We have sun in the City of Light," says Bernard.

"You surf in Biarritz every summer," Marie pipes in, nodding her head vigorously. "We have an ocean. We also have the sea..."

"It's not the same thing. And I hear the rain," I say with a sigh. "Alors, you've both done so much for me. And you know how much I love you. But it's time for me to carve out my own life."

"By being a private chef to some celebrity?" Marie guffaws. "It's beneath you. You're wasting your time and your talent."

"I'm fulfilling a dream. I want to do what you and Mom did. Open my own restaurant here." I swallow. We've had this conversation before. She can't argue with me on this. She knows about the killer salary Erica is paying me.

"What's she like? This actress? She's all over the news—something about an Academy Award for a movie called *Swerve*." She shakes her head. "She's quite beautiful."

For somebody so off-kilter, I think. And she really needs to gain some weight. She's five foot seven and looks like she weighs one hundred and ten pounds—when wet.

Bernard lets out a frustrated gasp. "It's not out in France or on Netflix yet. We'd go see it, but have to wait a couple of weeks. It only came out last November." He shrugs. "I guess there was a problem with the voiceovers or the translation."

"I haven't seen the movie."

"But you've met her."

"I have." And what a meeting it was. If I tell them she'd been drinking wine at half past ten in the morning, they'd probably hop on the first flight over here to drag me back home.

"Is she nice, charming? On television interviews she seems like she's very down to earth."

If Earth was located on another planet.

"She's, um, interesting," I say, not wanting to worry them. "It's going to be an adventure—"

A knock comes at the door. "Julia! It's Erica! Are you ready for our big day?"

I clench my teeth.

"Une minute," I shout, thankful she doesn't barge right in. "Auntie M, Oncle B, I'm going to have to call you back. She's here. She's taking me to lunch. And then shopping for clothes."

Bernard raises a bushy eyebrow. "You didn't bring clothes?"

"Of course, I brought clothes. We're shopping for a new

uniform. She wasn't too keen on the chef's coat—too formal for home entertaining."

"Oh," Marie replies, clucking her tongue, her brown eyes wide. "I guess that's nice."

I hear the sarcasm in her tone. I know she won't push the subject, even though she looks mildly insulted. She'd designed the chef's coats at Fouquet. "I better get going. I'll call you next week."

She and Bernard blow me kisses. "Nous t'aime, ma puce."

"Je vous aime, aussi. Bisous."

I click the line to a close, scramble out of my chair, and after tucking the photo of my parents into Riku the panda's back, I open the door with dread. To my surprise, the Erica standing in front of me is a completely different person.

EIGHT

ERICA

Julia's mouth drops open when she takes in my appearance. Instead of wild-looking hair, I'm now perfectly coiffed, my makeup minimal instead of smudged and running down my face. Before coming over, I'd changed out of my bathrobe into something a little more appropriate—a green cashmere sweater, skinny jeans, and brown suede boots that hit below the knee with a two-inch square heel.

I smile. "Do you have everything you need? Are you settling in OK?"

"I am," she replies, twitching ever so slightly.

"By the way, you can have everything Jasmine left behind—"

Julia grimaces. "Where did she go?"

"I have no idea. I told you she just up and disappeared." I shrug. "Water pressure good?"

She grins and nods her head. "Fantastic. I had the best shower. Totally woke me up."

"Wonderful," I reply with a satisfied grin. Totally? She sounds so American.

I look over her shoulder, noting she hasn't placed any personal effects—save for the tiny orange-and-white cat on the bed and a raggedy stuffed panda on the reading chair. I hand her the basket of goods I've been hiding behind my back. Julia, obviously, had been too taken in with my costume change to notice it.

Her eyes go wide. "What's all this?"

"A little welcome gift." I lift my sunglasses to the top of my head, meeting her stunned gaze. "I meant to give it to you when you first arrived." I shrug and then let out a soft laugh. "But I forgot. I can be a bit scatter-brained." I titter, but pause when she doesn't laugh. "Have a look."

Julia sets the basket down on the dining table and I watch every facial expression as she pulls out one extravagant gift after another—the Dior perfume, the expensive candles, the soaps, the shampoos, the Chanel sunglasses. Finally, she opens the blue velvet jewelry box. In it rests a necklace—platinum with diamond-studded fork, knife, and spoon pendants hanging off the chain. Her mouth almost hits the floor.

"Erica, this is all too much," she says, her voice quivering.

I wave a dismissive hand. "I didn't pay for any of it. Brands send me things all the time."

So I'm lying a little bit. Just a tad. I did buy the necklace for her.

She's silent. In shock. I would be, too. I threw in the Dior perfume after I'd caught a whiff of her upon her arrival. I must have twenty bottles of the stuff.

She shakes her head from side to side. "Yes, Silvia told me."

I'm a bit taken aback. "You talked to Silvia?"

"She was dropping off fresh towels and, well, we chatted a little bit."

Well, now I'm more than curious. I hope my staff doesn't talk about me behind my back like my so-called friends do.

Julia's cat snakes its way around my ankles. I pick her up. She's so tiny and, dare I say, adorable? "What did Silvia say?"

"Nothing much. Just that she loved working here. And she told me about the perks."

I'm wondering what else Silvia has shared. I make a mental note to speak with her later. The cat jumps out of my arms and scurries under the bed.

Julia puts everything back into the basket, eyeing the goods with longing. "This is all amazing, but I can't accept this."

"But you can." I cluck my tongue and reach into my purse, grabbing the Tiffany key chain. "Shall we take your car?"

"M-my car?"

"Well, it's a loaner while you're working here. You can keep the key chain, though." I pause. "I thought you'd like the SUV, especially on your days off. Shall we go check it out? Because I told the driver to go home and nobody, I mean nobody, walks in LA."

She nods, nervously, and then bites down on her bottom lip. "I haven't driven a car in over a year."

"But you drove in Paris?"

"I did."

"Well, if you can handle Paris, you can handle driving in Malibu. Driving, it's just like riding a bike. The SUV is automatic, not manual." I snap my fingers. "Easy, peasy. Bring your new sunglasses. You'll need them when you're with me. And I apologize in advance." I wave toward the basket. "That's one of the benefits. The paparazzi? Well, let's just say working for me does come with its disadvantages."

Julia slips her tennis shoes on. I look down and don't hold back my sneer. "I guess I have to buy you new shoes, too."

"What's wrong with my shoes?" she mumbles.

"Everything," I say, leading her to the garage. "Come on, now. Let's go. I don't know about you, but it's after one and I'm starving. I'm thinking of having my one cheat day today."

"Cheat day?"

"I've been dying for carbs," I say with a laugh, and she blinks rapidly.

Oh, Julia, my darling, I'm full of surprises. Just you wait.

We meander up the path taking us to the garage and her jaw drops even more when she sees all the cars in it—Madison's BMW, David's Maserati (red, of course), the enormous Escalade, the Phantom, David's Lexus, and the brand-new silver Mercedes G Class SUV painted in brushed silver, which I point to. "That was Tyler's car. It's yours to use now."

I throw her the keys, but she doesn't catch them and they land by her feet.

"Won't Tyler need his car to get to school?"

"No," I say. "I didn't tell you. Tyler is being homeschooled for the rest of the year. And, well, he's grounded from driving." By the way her mouth twists to the side, I can tell she wants to ask why, yet she doesn't. Probably because she knows it's none of her business. I point toward all the gear on the back wall. "Also, feel free to grab anything you want. We have inflatable paddle boards, which you can inflate with the generator pump thing on the beach, and boards in every size and color. Save your money. Use ours."

"Really?" she says, her eyes wide.

"Really. Tyler is a surfer. Took lessons from Ollie Shore. David made a movie about him, too. I was in it. Played the little surfer girl. I couldn't surf, but they used a body double. Anyway, you have the key for the gates to the beach on your key chain." I hop in the passenger side and then lean over, opening her door. "What are you waiting for? Our carbs are waiting. And then we're going shopping. Such a fun afternoon."

Julia nods, gets in, and puts the key in the ignition. She lets out a shaky wheeze and looks over at me. "The first couple of minutes might be a little rough."

"That's OK," I say with a wink.

. . .

We have a lighthearted conversation at Tra da Noi, where we order a bottle of wine, both of us starting with salads, followed by the delectable gnocchi with shrimp, the paparazzi out in full force. They don't get too close to me, and Julia seems to be handling the attention well, only slumping slightly or grimacing with every flash or whisper behind our backs. As I hand over my credit card to pay for lunch, I lean forward, focusing in on her.

"What's your dream?" I ask. "I know it's not to work for me. I mean the big dream."

She clears her throat. "I don't know what you mean."

"I think you do." I lower my sunglasses to the bridge of my nose. "I see a lot of myself in you—the drive, the ambition. If we ignore my first film, the one you saw on the plane, I can tell you that I've worked very hard to get where I am."

"I saw your interview with Tabitha Sinclair," she replies, her voice almost a whisper.

"See? We have a lot in common. Now you know the real me. I want to get to know the real you." I tilt my head to the side. "So, tell me. What's your big dream?"

Her jaw clenches slightly. "To open up my own restaurant. Here." She looks around. "Well, not here at Country Mart, but in Los Angeles somewhere."

"Like your parents," I say with a thoughtful nod.

She lets out a sigh. "Oui. Like my parents."

"That's a solid dream." I lean forward. "My dream was to get away as fast and far as I could from my family." I stand up, brush my hands off on my pants, my past life hitting me in the stomach like a sledgehammer. "It's time to share the wealth. Now it's time for shopping."

Thankfully, I don't have to shoplift anymore. Not with this wonderful life I lead, the money I've made in my films, and, well, David's credit card. He can write off everything as a business expense. It's a win-win.

"Tomorrow, I have a luncheon so you can have most of the day off. Use one of the boards in the garage, if you'd like. But tomorrow night, David's coming home with a guest. He's requested boeuf bourguignon."

She mumbles out what sounds like a slightly irritated agreement.

At l'Agence, a very bourgeoise store, I insist on shirts and pants that are a tad too tight. "You have a lovely figure. You should show it off." I snap my fingers and the salesgirl comes running. "Julia needs a couple of dresses. And some shoes, too—heels and sneakers."

The salesgirl scrambles out of the dressing room and into the showroom.

Julia turns to face me, her eyebrows furrowed with confusion. "What is up with this 'Pretty Woman' day? Is there something you're not telling me?"

I've already told her everything she needs to know. Well, all she needs to know for now.

"Funny, it just hit. Your name is Julia. Like Julia Roberts," I say with a laugh. "Vivian. I wish that role had come at a different time. Not exactly the right part for a five- or six-year-old." I lift my shoulders and then I let out a dramatic yawn. "Julia, I think we're finished here. Don't worry about dinner tonight. I'm stuffed from lunch. And so very tired. You settle in more, swim in the pool."

"B-but," she replies, looking at the price tag on one of the dresses. "Again, this is too much."

I guffaw. "Not when you have everything. And the clothing allowance was in your contract because I like things to be a certain way."

"I don't get it. I'm only here to cook," she replies.

"I know. But you're working for me." I meet her shocked gaze. "Hate to say it, but LA is all about appearances."

That and sometimes people do things to get what they want —sometimes no matter the consequences, repercussions, or risks.

NINE

JULIA

Today has to be the most messed-up day of my life. I think I'm working for Sybil, that woman in the film with, gosh, I don't know how many personalities. The weirdest thing is—Erica didn't act drunk at all, and she'd had not one, or two, but three or four glasses of wine before noon. And two more at lunch, when she ordered a red, Montepulciano. I'd only had one glass because I was driving. We didn't even finish the bottle.

I don't get her personality shifts—nasty as a hungry junk-yard dog this morning and sweet as a summer breeze this afternoon. Maybe she holds her liquor well or sobers up quickly. Maybe she gets hangry and really needs to eat more carbs.

And what's up with all the gifts? If this is her way of apologizing to me for her behavior this morning she'd gone completely overboard. I'm hanging up four bags of clothes and placing shoes in my closet. My eyes sweep each price tag. The dresses, there are four of them, all silk and completely inappropriate for cooking in, considering oil splatters, cost around one thousand dollars each. Add in the tops, pants, and blouses—all very stylish, although a bit snug. I love them, and she must have dropped $20k like it was nothing, not to mention the shoes or the completely outrageous gift basket.

We'd talked about dreams, connected. A random $20k investment could light mine on fire. But, no, oh no, that would be silly. My mind is spinning. What is she buttering me up for? She must have an agenda.

When we came back from our shopping adventure, before Erica entered the main house and I'd headed to my quarters, she'd said, "I had fun today. Oh, and by the way, don't forget, David's coming home tomorrow night. He's requested boeuf bourguignon. As mentioned, he likes the meat from Gelson's—the one in Calabasas. You just take Las Flores Canyon and cut over via Piuma."

"I thought I got the weekends off," I'd replied, cringing.

"You do if everything is prepared in advance," she said with a nod. "And this is a special request. Plus, you'll have most of the day off tomorrow." She winked and then turned on her heel, looking over her shoulder. "I have the best idea! David won't be here on Sunday evening. You and I will have a dinner and movie date, get to know each other better! A girls' night! I'm craving mussels. You can get them at Malibu Seafood."

I sigh. So my day off isn't my day off. And I'm back to thinking about dual personalities.

Another thing that's really pulling at my gut is she keeps mentioning, no, insisting, that I go to Gelson's in Calabasas when there are plenty of fine grocery stores in Malibu—Whole Foods, Ralph's, Trancas Market, and Vintage Grocers. And I know the closest Gelson's is in West Lake Village. Why Calabasas?

I eye Riku the panda, thinking about getting in touch with Liam if I can find his contact info. Surely, he must be on one of the social media channels, the ones I'd deleted when I'd moved to France.

I owe Liam a huge explanation and I'm not quite ready to

give it. When we left LA, he came with us to the airport, where we'd shared a teary goodbye, me promising to keep in touch. What would I say? Sorry, I just bolted and never contacted you again? I shake the thoughts of him off.

One step at a time.

The guesthouse has its own Bluetooth sound system, so I link my phone to it, putting on the song I'm in the mood for, one of my dad's favorites: "Hotel California" by the Eagles.

Basically, the lyrics, which my dad had explained to me when I was twelve, sum up the exact way I'm feeling.

A weary traveler (me) stumbles into a hotel (Hummingbird House). On the outside everything is seemingly glamorous with champagne and pretty people (Erica). But despite the allure, all the gloss, something isn't sitting right with the traveler, a sense of unease.

And then the traveler becomes trapped in this hedonistic and material place.

I shudder, reminding myself I can leave anytime I want to. The song on this playlist switches to Boston's "More Than a Feeling" and I continue unpacking my suitcases with a sigh. I will stick to the deal I'd made with Erica of giving this job one month, but if her personality switches at the flip of a switch, I definitely can't handle a year and I'm packing up my knives.

As I finish unpacking my belongings, I can't shake the feeling that I'm being watched. That somebody is outside. I walk over to the window. There is nobody. Just the bushes scraping the front porch. Beurreboule meows and then snakes around my ankles. I nearly jump out of my skin.

"You little stalker," I whisper, hitting myself on the head with my palm. "Hungry?"

After feeding the cat and giving her fresh water, I throw on a pair of shorts, a long-sleeved T-shirt, and my new Erica-approved five hundred-dollar gym shoes, deciding to head down to the beach to watch the sunset. Before leaving, I remember that earlier, Erica had pointed out the key I need to use to open the gate. I grab my keys, my phone, my earbuds, and set off down the path, keeping my eyes focused on the ground.

A five-minute and slightly snake-fear-inducing walk later, I'm finally on the beach. The Drakes' little stretch of sand looks like it belongs to a private hotel. There are two open wrought-iron cabanas with gray-and-white striped canopies, around ten sun loungers, a large table and chairs for seaside dining, and a smaller coffee table and chairs for doing laissez-faire.

I'd thought the outdoor terrace and pool were killer, but nothing had prepared me for this. It's like having a slice of my own personal paradise. And I'm here experiencing it all alone.

My gaze searches for the air pump until I find it. Tomorrow, I can't wait to go paddle-boarding. Right now, I just want to relax, dig my toes in the sand, watch the waves and the sunset, breathe the ocean air in. I click the playlist on my phone, listening to the Eurythmics "Sweet Dreams."

I'm going for mine.

Sitting in the sand, I try to shake the nagging suspicions out of my head by focusing on my surroundings. My eyes scan the horizon. In the distance, I can see the island of Catalina, now bathed in an orangish hue. To my left, the Malibu Pier and the twinkling lights of Santa Monica.

The sun dips toward the horizon, casting hues of a glorious orange and fiery pinks across the sky, the waters reflecting the change from day to dusk. The waves rhythmically kiss the shore, filling my ears with their soothing melody. A lullaby. In the distance, a playful pod of dolphins leap, their silhouettes highlighted against the backdrop of the setting sun. I lean back, just watching, listening, a warm breeze tousling my hair. Then, I close my eyes, letting the tranquility of this moment wash over me, the salty brine of the ocean filling my nostrils. I stay in a trance for a good ten minutes and then I stand up, brushing the sand off my legs. It's getting darker out, a couple of bats swooping in the sky.

Important to our ecosystem, I'm not afraid of bats and they are magical to watch as they glide in the air, but I am afraid of snakes. It's time to head back. After dusting off my feet, I put my shoes back on and make my way up the path, thankful for the motion sensor lights illuminating the way. Just as I'm approaching my living quarters, a humming bird whizzes over my head, whirring its wings. To my surprise, the bird flies back and hovers in front of my face for a moment or two before darting off.

I whisper, "Good night, Mom or Dad. I love you."

Before turning in, I unroll my knife bag—the blades polished and sharp. I can see my reflection in the largest one and a creepy feeling overtakes me again. A shiver shimmies its way down my spine and I step toward the window. There's nothing, nobody outside, just the sound of the waves crashing on the shore, the rustling of branches.

I flop down on the bed. This day has definitely caught up to me. I lower the blackout blinds with the remote. And then I fall asleep—but it's not deep or soothing, not with nightmares of snakes and coyotes and crazy actresses.

TEN

ERICA

Our driver has picked me up to drive me to some vineyard in Malibu. Before Julia hops into the SUV to do whatever it is she wants to do, I call out to her and she ambles over, swallowing back a sigh. I'd given Julia the day off to unwind before she really has to start working tonight. It's not like I'm a complete ogre. I do understand jet lag. And driving me around isn't in her job description.

"Julia, this is Antoine, our driver," I say. "Antoine, meet Julia, our new live-in chef."

He grins. "Nice to meet you."

She scratches her cheek and tilts her head to the side. "Nice to meet you, too. But haven't we met before? I thought you picked me up yesterday?"

Antoine blinks. "Nope. I had the day off."

I cut in. "I called in a favor, hired somebody to drive the Phantom. I'd forgotten about Julia's arrival. And, as you know, I don't drive."

"That could have been dangerous, Mrs. Drake—"

"Oh, everything worked out," I titter. "Julia got here safe and sound. And the car is fine."

Antoine's brows pinch together. "Why didn't you have Jasmine pick her up?"

"Because she up and disappeared," I say, turning my back on him to face Julia. "Julia, have fun today. Don't forget David is coming home tonight. Take Las Flores to Gelson's for the meat."

I jump into the back of the Phantom, leaving Julia standing, her face strained with utter confusion.

Although the mountain and vineyard views are sublime, the people surrounding me, shall we say, are less than desirable. I can't stand these luncheons. And I can't stand anybody I'm sitting with at the table I'd been assigned to. Among the other industry movers and shakers, I'm stuffed in between Miriam Steinberg, wife of Bob, and Cindy Wexler, wife of Harry, both of their husbands friends of David.

"Erica, I love your dress," says Miriam. "Tory Burch?"

I honestly don't remember the designer. All I do know is that it's blue, it's comfortable, and I've paired it with a blue cashmere cardigan in case it gets cold. Smile, nod, and agree. "Yes, exactly."

"You're always so fashionable," says Cindy. "Oh, to be young again."

"I'm old by Hollywood's standards," I mumble.

Nobody responds. Because nobody really listens unless they are talking about themselves or gossiping. After a photographer takes our photos and everybody angles in for a shot with me, elbowing one another for the best position, I know why they've invited me here. If I win the Oscar every single person at this luncheon, and there must be at least seventy women in attendance, regardless of whether I speak with them or not will say something along the lines of, "Oh, Erica Drake, we're the closest of friends. I just saw her. We had lunch together."

Vapid sycophants.

I sit in silence, staring at the vineyard. My fake smile hurts and I can't wait to get out of here. This is sheer and utter torture. A high-pitched whine brings me to attention.

"Why on earth would these people think that women of our stature would like to sit at picnic tables? However beautifully decorated, it's like we're at some kind of hoedown."

And so the bitching and complaining begins.

"Maybe they'll bring in some cowboys," I say, and all the women smile like hungry hyenas and nod their heads.

"Now that would shake things up," says Miriam. "These things are so dreadfully boring."

It's difficult to mask my grin or burst out into laughter. Does she talk to herself? One day, she'd told me that she'd wanted to spice things up with her husband and then laughed, saying she was swapping out different tea flavors for breakfast. Yes, *that* will certainly get him interested in her again.

Cindy Wexler leans closer to me and whispers in my ear. "You won't believe it. My chef quit. She said I was too high maintenance with my requests."

What am I supposed to say? You *are* high maintenance and I can barely handle eating lunch with you. Instead, I pull out my acting skills, placing my hand over my mouth as I gasp, my eyes wide. "No! I can't believe it. It's unfathomable."

Her jaw clenches. "You don't have to be such a drama queen all the time."

Shifting my gaze off hers, I wave one of the servers over and point to my wineglass, which he immediately refills. I mouth *thank you* as he saunters over to another table. If there's a time for alcohol, it's now. The chatter, the laughter, coming at me from every direction, is worse than the relentless and deafening buzz of cicadas on a hot summer's day, notable on my honeymoon with David in the south of France. Thinking of David, perhaps I should drink more. One of these women will surely gossip to their husbands and it will get back to him.

"It's so hard finding good help these days, isn't it?" I say, raising my glass to my lips. I swallow back a rather large sip, all eyes on me, and then say, "I've been thinking about hiring a new personal assistant—"

"Whatever happened to the last one?" somebody asks.

"I don't know," I say with a shrug. "She just up and disappeared the other day. Didn't even leave a note."

"Because who would put up with you?" says Cindy, and the other women laugh.

Touché, Cindy. And true. I shoot her a tight smile.

"Maybe David is working on a new film, another one based on a true story," says Miriam. "Maybe the assistant was trying to get away from a crazy wife. And maybe the crazy wife killed her."

Or maybe the husband did. Somebody—usually a woman—dies in almost every one of his films—either that or the poor soul is sent to prison. David's films are dark and based on true stories. Whatever. I know this was another dig made toward me. Bring it on.

I take a swig of wine and then lift my chin up. "Funny. Do I look like a crazy wife to you? I've been nominated for another Academy Award and there's nothing crazy about that." I meet Miriam's gaze, holding it steadfast. "Anyway, before we hire a new assistant, I'm going to let our new chef settle into the swing of things."

"You hired a chef?" asks Cindy, jaw dropped.

"I did." I can't wait for this coup. "She's from Paris."

The women let out gasps and talk over one another.

A pretty server coughs, interrupting the conversation before it escalates, placing salads in front of us. When she's finished serving, she just stares at me. Or maybe she's glaring at me.

"Did you want an autograph? Not here," spits Miriam and

the women snicker, chins raised. She leans forward to the group of cackling hyenas. "The audacity of some people."

"The things we put up with. I mean, we are at a charity event," says Cindy with a condescending snort.

The girl's lips twist and she lifts her thin shoulders into an apologetic shrug. "Sorry, Mrs. Drake. I'm just a really big fan—"

Miriam grins and waves a hand in my direction. "Of course you are, my dear. You're in the presence of Academy Award winner Erica Drake. If she wins—" She cackles. "Maybe the second time is the charm."

"We'll find out soon enough," I retort.

I can't decide who is worse. Miriam or Cindy. Probably Miriam. Should I mention her plastic surgeon really messed up one of her eyes? It's actually quite comical. So high, it's almost as if one of them is constantly looking in the other direction. But I'm not laughing now. Her words "second charm" send shivers down my spine because she got the expression wrong. I'm David's second wife and his first wife, Valerie, died, leaving Madison, his adopted daughter, in his care. I know a lot about her situation because my first nomination for best actress was playing Valerie in David's eponymous film. And now I'm wondering who will be his third wife. I know he's had it with me. I'd been fun in the beginning—a challenge. Now I'm just challenging.

"I think you'll win the Oscar, Mrs. Drake," replies the server with a sweet smile, breaking me out of my thoughts. "*Swerve* is incredible, a really powerful film and..."

Her accent. So beautiful. "Are you French?"

"Oui, I am."

This explains her look—gamine, I think they call it. Young, pretty, innocent—almost childish or boyish. Impish. Like that actress Audrey Tautou or Audrey Hepburn. Those pouty lips and hazel doe eyes.

"Can you cook?" asks Cindy.

"Non, I only serve and chop things here. I'm actually an actress." She blinks in thought when somebody huffs out a cough. "But I do know a French chef. Her name is Julia."

"Julia Fouquet?" I ask.

"Yes, that's her name. Do you know her?"

"I do," I say with a smile. "She works for me."

"Oh, mon Dieu! What a coincidence! I'm Chloe LeFevre and she's a good friend of my sister's. We are supposed to get in touch when she arrives. Has she?"

Oh, she's arrived. "Just yesterday."

"I have a new phone and I have a new number..."

I reach into my purse, handing over my card. "Text me your information and I'll make sure Julia gets it."

Chloe stands in shock, staring at the card. It is quite pretty, ivory with gold embossed lettering. But that's not why she's stumped. It's me. I've given her my personal number. "I-I-Merci, Mrs. Drake. That's really kind..."

Miriam silences Chloe with a glare. "Can you stop babbling on about how wonderful Erica is? I'd like to know why we're here. What cause are we supporting? I mean, because Erica is a lost cause."

God, I hate her. I chirp out another fake laugh.

"It's a fundraiser to clean up the beaches and the ocean," says Chloe.

My thoughts turn to Julia. Hopefully, she's taking advantage of her free time because, regardless of what her contract says, she won't have much of it. Not with what I have planned for her. Today, we're eating mussels as the main course. I pull out my phone to text her.

ED:

Changed mind. Would like flambéed shrimp Sunday night. Not mussels. Sure u have a good French recipe.

Miriam scoffs as Chloe tells us all about plastic and how it poses grave threats to marine life through ingestion, entanglement, and the disruption of ecosystems, also how the pollution impacts human health, as toxins from plastic can be ingested through seafood consumption.

I tap my chin, now wondering if I need to avoid seafood. I shrug the thought off. Surely, flambéing or boiling would destroy any threats. And I don't want to scare Julia away by changing my mind every two seconds.

"Good cause," says Cindy. "And good thing we all brought our checkbooks."

Chloe just blinks, awkwardly, and then refills our wineglasses. "Merci, Mrs. Drake," she says.

All eyes latch on Chloe as she saunters over to another table.

"Is your French chef as pretty as that girl is?" asks Miriam, tsking.

I nod, knowing she's digging for information so she can cut me down somehow. I don't care. "Prettier. She looks like a rockstar version of Brigitte Bardot. Back in the day, of course." I pause. "She's twenty-three years old."

The women exchange amused glances.

"I don't know," says Miriam, whispering loudly enough for all of us to hear. Her breath—awful, tinged with acid—fans across my face. And they think I'm the drinker. She pauses dramatically. "On second thought," she continues, "I wouldn't want a pretty French temptation like that around my husband—"

"She'll only be tempting us with her meals. She attended Le Cordon Bleu and worked at Fouquet."

"Fouquet. In Paris? Two stars?" Cindy wheezes, spitting her wine on the table.

"The very one."

That meal at Fouquet was one of the best of my life, when

I'd received my first nomination as best actress for *Valerie*. So much acclaim. That meal was also the last time I'd celebrated anything because my relationship with David took a hard nose-dive. I lift my shoulders, shrugging my thoughts off.

"Et voilà."

"I'm going to steal her away from you," says Cindy. "I believe that I told you that I wanted a French chef a couple of months ago."

She's the one who gave me the idea.

I grin. She's always trying to one-up me. Sure, her husband is successful, and she has a bigger house right on Carbon Beach —one she'd outbid us on. But she's not taking my French chef away from me. Over my dead and lifeless body. I rub my hands together underneath the table. "Good luck with that," I reply, looking at my watch, and stand up. "And, on that, it's almost four and I've got to get back home."

"Hope you're not driving," says Miriam.

I send her a death glare and force out another fake laugh "Why would I? I have a chauffeur." As I walk away, I look over my shoulder. "See you next Sunday at our party to celebrate my win. Dress code required." I eye their outfits, sneer. "Just so you know, I'll be wearing Dior." I lift my chin. "An original."

Before any of them respond, I pick up my pace, my heart beating wildly. I have to win the Oscar. It's part of my plan—the endgame. After that, I'm going to disappear and Julia's going to help me.

ELEVEN

JULIA

My head throbs. I've gone to Malibu Seafood for Erica's shrimp. Her menu change was mildly irritating, but I hadn't picked up anything yet. Tomorrow night, I'll be flambéing them in Pastis—the French way. I'd been a bit floored at the price of Pastis at the liquor store. Over fifty dollars a bottle for what is twenty in France? Crazy. But I don't care. Before I'd left, I'd grabbed a stack of "petty cash" from Erica's drawer. She seems to love her alcohol. And she will adore my shrimp.

Now, it's time to go to damn Gelson's in Calabasas. I'm at the stop light on Las Flores and my hands are shaking and I can barely breathe. A deathtrap, I know this road is laden with hairpin turns. Instead of turning left, I make a U-turn. Screw going to Gelson's. I'm going to Whole Foods.

Some day off. I just want to get into the water. When I return to Hummingbird House I eye the ocean with longing, my gaze locked onto the waves as I prep on autopilot. Finally, the boeuf bourguignon is simmering and will be ready in three hours. Just as I'm putting the lid on the Le Creuset cocotte, Erica sashays into the kitchen. "Julia, I need your help."

Internally, I sigh, and then I turn around, forcing a smile. "Sure, Erica. You need my help with what?"

"Just a little advice," she says. "I haven't seen David in two weeks. And I simply don't know what to wear." She turns on her heel. "Follow me."

Behind her back, I send invisible bullets of anger into her, thinking about how easy it would be to push her down the stairs. What a terrible accident. A tragedy. I never used to think this way—not until I'd met her. No, I've never, ever been this bitter.

We enter the master bedroom and it's like a nuclear war zone, clothes strewn everywhere—on the couch, on the bed, on the floor. She must be having one of her meltdowns.

I pick up a blue silk dress, hold it up. "What about this?"

I swear her face pales for an instant and then she smiles. "It's perfect. Blue is David's favorite color. OK, Julia, you can go now," she says, waving a hand dismissively.

After leaving Erica, I decide to take a dip in the pool to clear my head. Swimming relaxes me. I'm allowed to unwind—when nobody is around, that is, and the dish is simmering. Sometimes I like to practice apnea and would do so at one of the many pools in Paris. Holding my breath until my lungs feel like they may burst. Swimming under water. So, that's what I do, thinking about Beyoncé's "Runnin' (Lose It All)" video, which features a couple, two French apneists.

I'm ready to face everything.

Except for the sight I see when I emerge.

Breathless, my eyes lock onto a large shadow, looming over the pool. My gaze focuses. I choke, taking in his appearance. He's insanely good-looking in person, doesn't look his age, and has an athletic build. Must work out a lot. He's wearing jeans, black loafers, and an expensive black designer T-shirt—the same brand Erica had bought me: Vince. "You must be Mr. Drake?" I ask once I find my voice.

"And you must be our new chef, Julia." He grins, his teeth so white they're nearly blinding. "Call me David."

He's caught me off guard in the tiniest of red surf bikinis, the boy shorts riding up my ass. I can't help but shuffle my feet, nervously. "I'm sorry. I didn't think anybody was around. I'm allowed to use the pool when nobody is here."

"Where's Erica?"

Probably passed out in her room. "I don't know."

"Welcome to Hummingbird House," he says. "Erica tells me that you're French."

Merde. I have to sound more French. I mean, it's not like I'm a criminal, a murderer, or a deranged psychopath. I'm just Julia Fouquet, a chef.

"Oui, I am." I curve my lips into what I think is a grin. I probably look deranged. "Enchantée."

He holds his hands in prayer position, looks up to the sky. "Please tell me you know how to make buttery croissants and baguettes."

A shiver runs down my spine—despite the warmth of the pool, the air. "I do. Bien sûr—so flaky, they melt on your tongue. Like butter."

"Thank the heavens!" He licks his lips. "I used to go to a bakery in Calabasas—would drive a half hour out of the way just for the croissants. Best in the world. Better than Paris."

I bite down on my bottom lip. He takes off his sunglasses, tucking them into the top of his T-shirt, his hazel eyes meeting mine. "Sad story, really. The owners died. Terrible car accident. I made a movie about it. A murder–suicide. Have you ever seen *Swerve*?" He lifts up his chin. "I'm up for two Academy Awards—best director and best original screenplay."

He doesn't mention Erica's nomination for best actress, just stares at me.

My jaw wants to unhinge. I'm shaking. I'm trying to step

out of the pool, but my legs won't move. "How are you settling in?" he asks.

I can't answer because my teeth are chattering. I'm not cold, the air is warm and the pool is heated to seventy-eight degrees. I'm in the process of flipping out, my entire body trembling.

"Cold?" he asks, and I nod, stepping out of the pool. He hands me a towel and I wrap it tightly around my body. He takes a step forward. I take two back.

"Are you sure you're a chef? You're too pretty. In fact, gorgeous. I've got a role in an upcoming movie that I think would be perfect for someone as captivating as you." He eyes me up and down. "You've got a Brigitte Bardot look about you—but sexier, darker."

I have to get away from him.

"I'm not an actress. I'm a c-chef," I stutter. "And I'm here to work for you and your wife."

David, undeterred by my rebuff, smirks and responds, "Come on, Julia. I'm just appreciating beauty. No harm in that—"

A blond woman wearing the highest heels I've ever seen, at least six inches, saunters up behind him, linking her arm into his. "I thought you appreciated me."

"Oh, Luna, you know I do."

She smiles at me, flashing her pearly whites. "I'm Luna Starlight, the lead actress in David's latest film," she says, eyeing me up and down. "Are you sure you're just a chef?"

I wrap the towel tightly around my body. "I'm a chef. And dinner will be served in one hour."

"Thanks, Julia," says David, running his tongue over his lips. "Can't wait."

Luna whispers something inaudible in his ear and he grins.

Shaking ever so slightly, I race back to the guesthouse, fearful of snakes. Not the ones possibly lurking in the garden—but the slippery ones standing by the swimming pool in designer slacks and a tight red dress. I'm about to hop into the shower when I notice a bouquet of lavender sitting on the small dining room table. My mother's favorite flower. Beurreboule meows as my throat catches. I pick her up, snuggling her under my chin, thinking and pacing. In every nerve, every fiber of my being, I know darker dynamics are at play.

TWELVE

ERICA

The moon is full and orange tonight, reflecting in the pool. A blood moon. A ball of fire. Luna and David sit on the terrace, drinking and laughing. I watch them for a moment, see how she gingerly touches his arm, his thigh. Shaking my head, I grab a wineglass and my bottle of Miraval from the refrigerator to join them. I stumble onto the deck. "Nellie, it's so nice to see you after all these years. Making a guest appearance, are you?"

Sensing my sarcasm, her mouth curves into a tight smile. She sticks out her chin like a disgruntled child. "It's Luna now, Erica."

"Right. Luna," I scoff and take a seat, pour myself a large glass of wine. "My, how things have changed."

"They have," she says and then she mumbles, "We used to be friends."

"Friend? You're the best of them all," I growl. "What's that expression..."

"Just stop it with your quips, Erica," snaps David.

Julia walks by to head into the house and David's gaze glides with her every step, his lips ticking into a repulsive grin. "I'm looking forward to dinner tonight."

"She's not on the menu, David," I snigger.

Before Julia disappears into the house, she freezes, her spine rigid. Then, she turns, her jaw set. "Will you be eating in the dining room tonight?"

"No, the kitchen," I say, my tone snappish. "The dining room is for special occasions and family meals."

Luna rolls her eyes, her fake lashes fluttering like butterfly wings.

"Julia, did you want to join us?" asks David.

"Why would she do that?" I take a swig of my drink. My breath forms clouds of condensation on the glass. "She's here to work."

Julia blinks and excuses herself.

"Jesus, Erica, sometimes you're as nasty as a snake," says Luna, tsking.

I take another swig of wine. Grin with my teeth bared. "Then you should be petrified of me."

Nellie, Luna, whatever you want to call her, is scared of the slithery creatures. I know this because when we were room-mates, way back when, one day, a tiny garden snake managed to get into our bathroom, of all places, and our screams rocked the hills, so loud the police were at our door within ten minutes. They'd laughed when they saw the perpetrator, picked it up, and threw it outside.

"Maybe she got over her fears," says David with a lift of his shoulders.

Luna shoots me a satisfied smirk. "I have. This morning, I actually did a scene with a boa constrictor—"

I let out a caustic laugh. "That's what you're calling my husband now?"

Before David can respond, Julia alerts us that it's time to eat. I'm not sure I'll be able to keep anything down because Luna's presence is nauseating, but I'll try. We meander to the table in the kitchen, sit. I pour another glass of wine. "Haven't you had enough?" David hisses.

Nope. Although I should be on high alert, I haven't had enough to deal with him.

Julia clears her throat. "Sorry, I need another minute with the boeuf bourguignon. Silly me, I must have set the burner on high," she says, meeting my eyes, "or somebody was out to sabotage my first real meal."

"Are you accusing Erica?" asks David. "I wouldn't put it past her."

I tap my fingers on the table. Now I know how he's going to play Julia—ride on in like her savior, make her hate me even more than she already does. He's going to protect her from me.

"No, I'm not accusing anybody of anything," says Julia. "It was just a joke." She bats her long eyelashes. "New kitchen. Getting to know how things work. I'm sorry if I've troubled you."

Ooh, I'm liking how this story is unfolding.

"You're no trouble at all." He shoots me a glance. "But Erica is."

Julia turns, returning to the table with our salads. One by one, she sets them down in front of us, brushing and leaning against David ever so slightly. "The main course will be ready soon."

And now I know how Julia is going to play him.

As we eat our salads, we watch as she adds more red wine to the sauce, bringing it to a low simmer. "Et voilà. It's perfect now." She locks her eyes on me as she ladles the bourguignon into deep bowls. Then she turns around, pulling something out of the oven. "I even made a baguette. Surprise."

Yes, a surprise, when I'd told her no carbs.

"Merci, Julia," says David. "So far everything is delicious. I didn't think a salad could taste so good."

Luna nods. "Absolutely incredible."

"Ce n'est pas rien," she says with a pop of her lips and David's brow scrunches with confusion.

"She said it was nothing," I explain and then turn toward Julia. I'm trying to communicate to her with my eyes, but I'm not sure if it's translating or if I look insane. "He doesn't speak French, only knows a couple of basic words. Could you please speak English? We *are* in America."

"Yes, Erica," she says softly, looking at me like I'm nuts.

Julia clears our salad plates, setting the bowls in the sink and then places our meal in front of us, the baguette in the middle of the table. "If you need more, eet's on the stove. Dessert ees in the refrigerator."

"What did you make?" I ask, noting her over-the-top French accent.

"Flan, topped with les fraises. I mean strawberries."

David digs in right away, his eyes scanning her cute little figure as he chews. "Absolutely delicious."

He's not talking about the meal.

David eyes her ass as she turns back to the stove. I'm running low on energy and out of time. I need Julia for my plan to work.

"David, eyes on your plate, not the chef. We're not running a cooking show here," I hiss with a smirk. I turn to face Julia, the tightest of smiles on my face. Her eyelids flutter with disgust. Mine, too. "You've done your job. We can manage the rest. The maids will clean up tomorrow. You're dismissed."

"What about breakfast?" she asks.

David clears his throat. "We're leaving early, around seven a.m. for Luna's costume adjustment."

"That's not all she needs adjusted," I mumble.

David shoots me a glare and continues, "Can you cut up some fruit and put it in the fridge?"

"I can do zat."

As Julia turns to slice mangos and pineapples, I watch her

intently. The way she chops as if it is second nature—fast and methodical. The blade flashes under the lights with every stroke. Luna stands up, blocking my view. "I'm exhausted. Think I'll turn in for the night."

"I'll show you to your room," I say, a thought coming to mind. "Oh, and I have a present for you—to celebrate your last scene."

Luna's eyes flicker. "A present?"

"Yes, something to remind you of the good old days. I do miss you, dear friend. The way we used to banter."

Luna grins, tilts her head to the side. "I do, too."

I return her smile, not because I'm happy, but because I'm an excellent actress and I know exactly how to play Luna.

THIRTEEN

JULIA

The following day, I don't wake up until two in the afternoon, a wicked smile on my face. Hours without Erica breathing down my neck. Hours of freedom. After pulling on my wetsuit, I grab the inflatable board from the garage and carry the heavy beast to the beach, filling it with air from the convenient electric pump, and then drag the board into the water. I lay down and paddle out, past the breaking point, the actual paddle under my body. Finally, I assume a standing position. Each stroke burns my arms. Feels good. Until exhaustion hits.

As I sit, the gentle sway of the Pacific Ocean beneath me, memories of past adventures with my parents flood my mind. I vividly recall the day we first encountered dolphins—or were they porpoises? My dad had a way of explaining the difference that made me laugh. "See," he'd said, pointing to a sleek creature leaping gracefully from the waves, "that's a dolphin. Look at its curved dorsal fin, like a smile. But over there"—he'd gestured to another group of marine mammals—"those are porpoises. They have more triangular fins and shorter snouts."

I can't help but smile at the memory of my dad, his eyes twinkling with excitement as he'd pointed out the subtle distinctions between the two. He even went so far as to give one particularly friendly porpoise a name. "That's Huckleberry Finn, but he likes his nickname, Finn," he'd declared with a grin, and the porpoise leaped as if to confirm his newfound identity.

I scan the horizon, hoping for a glimpse of Finn or any of his kin. Suddenly, a pod of dolphins emerges from the depths, their sleek bodies slicing through the water with effortless grace. I watch in awe as they playfully leap and frolic.

In this moment, surrounded by the vast expanse of the ocean and the playful antics of its inhabitants, I feel a sense of peace wash over me. My dad may not be here to share this moment with me right now, but the memories we'd created together feel like they'd happened only yesterday. I'm feeling a melancholy happiness—until I paddle back to Hummingbird House.

With dread, I put the gear away, and then shower, getting ready for my evening with Erica.

I'm in the process of prepping—chopping garlic, parsley, and shallots—when Erica meanders into the kitchen. Her kitchen. What a joke.

"It smells so good already," she says, taking a seat on one of the stools at the Italian marble center island.

I lift a brow. "I haven't even started cooking yet."

"It's the herbs. And the garlic. I love garlic." She grins. "What are you using to flambé?"

"Pastis. It's an anise-flavored liquor." I pause. "For drinking, it's usually served with water and ice. Some people say it's an acquired taste, although most people in France, at least those that drink, have acquired it. Would you like to try some?"

She pops her lips. "No, thanks. I'll stick to my rosé."

Her response surprises me. Maybe she isn't a Lushika.

Erica continues, "We'll eat here in the kitchen tonight. OK?"

"OK," I respond. "Along with the shrimp, what would you like? I bought rice, potatoes, the makings for an arugula salad with pomegranate..."

She raises a hand. "Stop. I already had my cheat day with you at Tra da Noi. You had me at salad." She pats her belly. "No more carbs for me until after the awards." She laughs. "I need to fit into my dress. I'd show it to you, but I have a feeling it's not a very good idea right now. A bit dangerous with fire, don't you think?"

I nod and continue chopping, thankful that nice Erica has come out to play. Again, she looks normal—her face scrubbed clean, her outfit a loose, white yoga ensemble, casual. I'm feeling overdressed in my l'Agence pants and blouse.

"Music?" she asks. "What's a good song to flambé to?"

I have no clue. I've never really thought about it. In a Michelin kitchen we only listened to classical music, whatever was piping in the dining room. I'm pretty sure by the excited look in her eyes she wants something with a little more oomph. God, I hope she doesn't hop off her stool and start dancing.

"My taste in music might be different to yours," I finally manage to say.

"What do you like?"

Anything my father listened to. But I'm not telling her that. I'll just be vague. "Old rock from the sixties and seventies. A bit of reggae. Some ska. Some modern groups." I meet her gaze. "Basically, I like anything but heavy metal, except for one song by Metallica called 'The Unforgiven'."

Her nose scrunches. "OK. I'm not into the oldies or metal." She taps her lips in thought, a glint dancing in her eyes. With a dramatic flair, she waves her hands in the air, as if conjuring up invisible flames. "If we're going to flambé, we need a song about fire. Fire doesn't follow the rules, it blazes its own path—the ultimate anarchist of the elements." Erica meets my eyes. "Are you forgetting where you are? You're in Malibu."

I haven't forgotten. No, I remember my past, specifically when the brush fires threatened to burn down my family home, the fire hopping over the canyons with its devastation and destroying over four hundred acres of trees. 2016. The Corral Fire, they'd called it on the news.

I tap my fingers on the countertop, thinking, struggling. "How about Sinead O'Connor's 'Troy'? I love the meaning behind—"

She cuts me off. "No. Too dark and old. I get burning down Troy, but I'd like something fun. Modern. On the pulse of the times."

She's doing my head in. I blurt out the name of the only recent group I know: "Imagine Dragons?"

"Yes!" she squeals a little too loudly. "Tyler listens to that group all the time. Perfect! Alexa! Play Imagine Dragons! 'Radioactive'!" Her lips twist into a devious grin and the music becomes so loud I can feel it thumping in my chest, in my bones.

OK. I kind of like this Erica. Although I really need to get dinner started.

She throws her head back and sways her body to the music. "We'll be the one killing dragons. And I'm not imagining anything. I dream about it..."

I stop chopping and turn to face her. I'm not sure I heard her correctly. "What?"

"Nothing—just getting into the music."

I whip around to turn the burner of the stove on, adding a dash of olive oil into the pan, followed by the garlic. "If there's anything I know how to do right, it's flambé." I smile, lift a brow. "Get ready."

"Can't wait." She rubs her hands together and jumps off her stool, walking toward me. "And I'm helping with the meal."

I add the herbs, shallots, and then the shrimp. After pouring a shot or two of Pastis, Erica strikes a long kitchen match and then dips the lit tip into the pan. The flame ignites with a whoosh, sending sparks of fire dancing before our eyes, the aromas of garlic and anise filling the kitchen.

"Ta-da!" she exclaims, a triumphant smile spreading across her face.

Her eyes flicker wickedly as the flames rise higher, bursting. A giggle escapes her throat. She rubs her hands together, leaning forward. OK, firestarter, calm down. I take a lid, snuffing out the flames before they destroy the kitchen.

"What are you doing?" she pants and then places her hands on her knees.

"Controlling the situation."

"Oh, Julia, don't be so boring. Fire and me? We understand each other."

Sure. Whatever you say.

A half hour later, satiated from our meal, along with a couple of laughs (Erica would love to flambé her fake friends), she still insists on watching a movie together when I was hoping to crawl into bed. "Have you seen *Swerve*?" she asks, crossing her fingers together. "That's the role I'm up for an Oscar for."

"I haven't," I respond. "It hasn't come out in France yet."

"Ugh, there was a translation issue." She throws her hands in the air. "Wine? And then to the home theater?"

"When in Rome?" I say, keeping my internal sigh to myself. Honestly, I'd rather curl up with Beurreboule, but she's being too nice and I don't want to be rude.

"But not the Miraval," she says. "That's for me. You take whatever else you'd like."

"I'll grab the glasses."

"Grab my bottle. It's chilling in the fridge. And follow me."

· · ·

As I step into a sanctuary of cinematic opulence, my jaw unhinges. This isn't just a home theater—it's exquisite. The first thing that catches my eye is the colossal TV screen, a mammoth display that spans an entire wall. Its dimensions are almost absurd, stretching wider and taller than any screen I've ever encountered. I'm sure we're in for a visual feast.

"Take a seat," she says. "This is our screening room. And also David's office." She lowers her voice and her head. "When he's here, which isn't often."

By the way he'd acted with Luna, by the way he'd eyeballed me, I'm pretty sure he's cheating on Erica. I don't know what to say so I don't say anything. Not my business.

Surrounding the gargantuan screen are plush, oversized leather recliners, each one a throne. Gilded accents adorn the walls, catching the ambient glow of hidden LED lighting that bathes the room in a soft, ethereal glow. A collection of rare vintage movie posters lines one wall, an homage to the golden age of cinema.

I settle into my chosen seat and the thump of excited anticipation washes over me. The room hums with a quiet energy, as if it knows the magic about to unfold. Erica reaches for the remote and my body tingles with anticipation. This is pretty cool.

With a press of a button, the lights dim to a cinematic twilight, and the screen springs to life. "It's Blu-ray—high definition." And in the opening scene I can see her every pore. "It's about a murder–suicide. I think you'll like it," she continues. "Very intense."

My eyes fix on the screen as the movie *Swerve* plays out before us. Beside me, Erica is watching me intently, her gaze like a weight upon my shoulders. I can feel her eyes boring into me, studying my every reaction to the film.

I'd seen her intense look when I handed her the lit match.

Now, she's even more fierce, like a tiger getting ready to pounce on its prey.

As one messed-up scene unfolds after the other, a flood of emotions well up inside me and I am trying to still my heart. I am trying so hard to keep my composure, when inside my head, my brain is screaming, so loud and unrelenting. But, despite my inner turmoil, I sit transfixed in shocked silence, like rubber-necking a car crash.

When the movie reaches its climax, a chill shimmies down my spine. I turn toward Erica, my gaze piercing and unwavering. She meets my eyes, her expression faltering for just a moment before she quickly masks it with a forced smile.

"What did you think of the movie, Julia?" she asks, her voice light and casual, though I can detect a hint of tension beneath the surface.

I bite down on my bottom lip, a lump forming in my throat. I pause for a moment, choosing my words carefully. "It was certainly... intriguing," I reply, my voice steady. "Powerful."

Erica nods, her eyes never leaving mine. "Yes, it was," she says, her tone neutral. She shakes her head from side to side. "Very tragic. Based on a true story."

I feel her watching me, waiting for some kind of reaction. But I refuse to give her the satisfaction. I won't let her see how deeply the movie has affected me, how it has stirred up a dangerous cocktail of emotions.

As the credits roll, I rise from my seat, my movements deliberate and controlled. "Thank you for the movie, Erica," I say, my voice cool and detached. "You were wonderful in it. I think I'll turn in for the night."

Erica's eyes flicker with something unreadable, but she simply nods, her smile tight and forced. "Of course, Julia. Sleep well. Wait. Before you go..." she says, leaning forward and rubbing her hands together. "Do you think I'll win the Oscar?"

"Of course," I reply. "Good night, Erica. I'll see you tomorrow. What would you like for lunch?"

"Oh, I didn't tell you? I have appointments. Antoine is taking me. I'll just see you tomorrow night." She lifts her chin when I don't respond. "I loved the salad you made. Maybe just change it up?"

"OK," I say, my spine stiffening.

"Don't forget. I need the recipes for the caterer tomorrow morning..."

I nod and turn on my heel, leaving the room without another word, making my way to my quarters. I stomp down the path, a fierce determination burning within me. I'm not thinking about snakes or spiders. I'm not thinking about the menu for her party. I'm thinking about her and how awful she is. Erica Drake will soon realize that she has made a grave mistake by bringing me into her life. Because I have a true reason for being here—and it isn't a pipe dream. She likes playing with fire. She wants *flambé*? That's exactly what she's going to get because I'm going to burn her entire world down to the ground.

ACT TWO
LE PLAT PRINCIPAL

(The main course: fuel for the soul.)

That I, with wings as swift
As meditation or the thoughts of love
May sweep to my revenge.

—William Shakespeare, *Hamlet*

FADE IN:

EXT. MALIBU BLUFF—DUSK

Three women rappel down a steep bluff, the
sounds of heavy panting. Feet slam into the
sand. Waves crash onto the shore.

WOMAN 1 (V.O.)

Are you sure it's safe? He can't
hear us?

                    WOMAN 2 (V.O.)

He can't. And we're going to do what we
need to do.

                    WOMAN 3 (V.O.)

And our plan has changed, thanks to you.

The wind hisses.

FADE OUT

FOURTEEN

JULIA

I'm getting out of the shower, in the process of getting ready for the day, and, once again, that creepy sensation slithers up my spine. I can't shake the feeling I'm being watched. Which gives me an idea. I'm going to watch Erica. I pull out my laptop and sign up for Amazon Prime, ordering six "spy" cameras: one that looks like a USB charger, the other a smoke detector. These are for the kitchen. The other cameras are tiny—two for the home theater/David's office, one for the dining room, and one for upstairs—if I can somehow make my way up there unnoticed. They all have sound and they will all be delivered to the house tomorrow.

Second floor off-limits, my ass.

To be safe, I also order a zester, a peeler, a garlic sleeve (best way to peel garlic), and a handheld fruit press.

I spend the next couple of hours coming up with recipes for Lushika's party. I'm really hoping she doesn't win the Oscar for best actress. If she does, I really hope she'll make a fool of herself during the acceptance speech—trip, fall down, or slur her words. David's office has a wireless printer, so with a press of a button I send the printouts off. Whoosh.

I look at the clock. It's half past nine.

I'm heading into the main house to gather the recipes so I can leave them in the kitchen for Erica to go over, but much to my surprise—she sits behind David's desk. Which is weird because it's almost as if she's looking for something on his computer.

When she notices my presence, her head snaps up. "Good morning, Julia, darling," she drawls. "Did you need something?"

"Oui," I say, waving a hand toward the printer. "I've done what you asked me to do for your party. I hope you approve."

Erica grabs the printouts, her eyes scanning the pages. "These recipes are divine! I'm glad you incorporated the flambéed shrimp." Her lips purse. She clucks her tongue. "But I was so hoping for that soup—the one I ate at Fouquet."

The one I want to drown her in.

"The potimarron velouté with the Parmesan crisp?"

"That's the one."

My jaw clenches. "Unfortunately, it's impossible to find that squash here."

She tilts her head to the side. "Surely there's a replacement. Think of it as a challenge. I think I read somewhere that cooking is about the art of adjustment."

She's quoting one of my idols—Jacques Pépin. How much does she know about me? Thanks to the cameras, I'm going to find out.

"Yes, Erica, I can replace that ingredient with butternut."

"Perfect." Her eyes light up. "Print that one out, too. And then drop everything off at Mel B's. They'll need to get everything in advance." She scribbles an address down and hands it over.

I force a smile. "I've ordered a couple of things from Amazon. The packages will be here tomorrow."

Her nose scrunches. "Why?"

"I needed a few more tools. For the kitchen."

"I'll reimburse you. Just give me the receipt." She nods and then straightens her posture, clucking her tongue. "Where is the one from yesterday? I didn't see it in the drawer."

Because I didn't put it in. "I must have forgotten."

"Please, don't be forgetful. And I really hope you went to Gelson's in Calabasas."

"I did, Erica," I snap. "Is there anything else?"

Her lips pucker. "Is something wrong?"

Everything is wrong. Especially you.

"No," I say. "I'm just looking forward to getting into the ocean."

She shivers. "It's only mid-March. Isn't the water awfully cold?"

"Not when you're wearing a wetsuit."

She nods. "Just drop off the recipes at Mel B's."

"Can't I just email them?"

"I really prefer that you deliver them by hand. She might have questions," she says, and I sigh. She grins. "Have fun today!"

I will. Because I'm going to be thinking about my recipe to destroy you.

When I arrive at Mel B's Catering, Mel isn't there, but there's a stressed-out girl around my age. She looks up from chopping vegetables. "Julia?"

I immediately recognize her, the sassier version of her sister, Solene. Much like me, Solene chose cooking over becoming a social media influencer, the reason I got on with her when we attended Le Cordon Bleu. Her sister? She's all about the posts and, well, posing with duck lips instead of confit du canard. "Chloe?"

She nods and exclaims with glee, "Oh. Mon. Dieu. I met Erica the other day. I texted her my number to give to you because I got a new phone. And, well, I lost all of my contacts. You know how it is? Oui?"

Not at the moment. I'm wondering why Erica didn't tell me. Maybe she doesn't want me to have a life. "She didn't give me your number."

Chloe grins. "Well, you're here now. Give me your phone."

I do as I'm told.

After plugging in her number, Chloe fans her face with her hand. "You didn't tell me you were working for the Drakes. I'd kill to get a part in one of his films." She huffs. "I have gotten a few bit parts—but they are always stereotypical—sexy French maid, gamine, little Lolita. C'est complement fou!" She throws her hands up in the air with an exasperated sigh and then she grins. "Desolée. I'm just talking about me. Are you settling in?"

Oh boy. There's too much to get into.

"Are you free for dinner sometime? Maybe we can meet at Taverna Tony's next week?"

She nods her head enthusiastically. "Parfait."

I hand her the file of recipes. "These are the recipes for the Drakes' party. You have my number. I have yours." I lift up an eyebrow. "Right now, I have a date."

Her eyebrows lift. "You've only been here five minutes and you've already met somebody? Who is taking you out? What dating app are you using? The only people I'm connecting with want to meet up for a *plan cul…*"

I laugh. Plan cul, literally translated, means *planned ass*, or rather a hook up/one-night stand.

"I didn't say I was meeting a man. I have a date with Mother Nature," I say with a grin and her head tilts to the side with confusion. "The ocean."

I also have plans to meet a man. He, too, worked for the Drakes and I'm heading straight to his surf shack at Zuma Beach. I remember what she'd told me about Tyler's lessons. I remember everything.

. . .

The moment I step out of the car, I recognize him—his total surfer look—long gnarly blond hair, tanned skin. I pick up my pace and make my approach. "Are you Oliver Shore? Ocean Ollie, the wave rider?"

He turns and grins. "The very one. You know who I am?"

Thanks to Google, I spout off competitions he's won, fan-girling him. "Nazaré. QuickSilver JAWS Big Wave. Pipe Masters—"

He places his hand over his heart. "You know surf?"

"I do. I grew up around here, but moved to France when I was fifteen." Merde. I didn't mean to slip my age. To recover, I say, "I mean, when I was eight. And, anyway, we have Biarritz. I've been going there every summer."

"France, huh?"

"Yep."

"You don't sound French."

"Eez dis butter?"

He almost falls down he laughs so hard. "What can I do you for?"

I want information on one Erica Drake. "I haven't been out on the water for a while, need to get my sea legs back in action. I'd like to paddle out, around Point Dume. Are you free?"

"No, it's two hundred," he says with a laugh. "But I'll give you a discount. I liked all the compliments. What's your name?"

"Julia. Julia Fouquet."

After an hour of polite conversation, stroke by stroke, we've made our way around Point Dume, spotting a couple of playful slick seals frolicking along the way. Breathless, I stop and sit on my board, my eyes focusing. Ollie points into the distance. "Why are you glaring at the Drake house?"

I gulp. My eyes dart from side to side. "Looking for dolphins."

Ollie chortles. "I mean, they probably have a saltwater pool, but, although smart, I don't think dolphins can climb steep bluffs. And they would definitely stay away from that man." He shoots me a sideways glance and points toward the house and sighs. "David Drake is darkness. He nearly destroyed me and my life."

I swallow. Now I'm getting somewhere. "How?"

"You sure you want to hear my story?"

I nod. More than anything. I wrap my arms tighter around my legs and then meet his eyes. I feel like I'm about to lose it. He must notice my shaky legs, but he doesn't say a word. I try to will my tremors down, the beating of my heart, and I finally say, "I do."

He lies down on his board. "Get ready, little lady. Hold onto your hat because it's supremely fucked up." He pauses and his eyes meet mine for a brief second. "I was in the prime of my career, but like most stereotypical surfers I liked pot. No, I didn't like pot. I loved it." He chuckles. "Things got out of hand and I started dealing, but only to my friends." He looks toward me. "Do you smoke?"

"I don't."

"Cigarettes?"

"Nope."

"Are you sure you're from France?" He sniggers and then shakes his head. He points toward the Drake house, and then props himself up on his elbows. "One day, David Drake approached me when I was doing a side deal behind my van at Zuma. He asked for some weed. I told him I didn't know what he was talking about. Unfortunately, I had a lit joint in my hand. He took it, took a puff, blew it out, and said, 'Your secret is safe with me.' Then he asked if I had any connections. And he'd pay big time. 'Stronger stuff?' he asked, and I looked at him blankly."

Ollie goes quiet for a moment, shaking his head.

"And? What did he want?"

"Coke, and a lot of it, for a party he called the Snowball," says Ollie with a shrug. "I told him I'd see what I could do. We exchanged numbers and then I asked him how much he wanted. 'One kilo,' he said." Ollie's voice raises in pitch. "'Dude, that's a tall order,' I told him. 'Do you know the cost per gram?' 'I do,' he said. He gave me thirty thousand in cash right then and there, the rest paid when the product was delivered. My dealer was pumped when I told him. I called David when I had the product. But he didn't show up, the cops did. They searched my house and, well, I was arrested for intent for distribution—not only for the cocaine, but also a rather large stash of pot. A felony. I pleaded guilty. Judge sentenced me to four years, a twenty-thousand-dollar fine and community service work. I served two years. By the time I got out, David's movie, *Caught in the Rip Curl*, based on a 'true story'"—Ollie pulls his fingers into air quotes—"hit the screens. The film solidified his career and was nominated for an Academy Award—it didn't win. And I knew he'd set me up."

Jesus. I want to tell him everything. But, although Ollie is being completely honest with me, a random stranger, I don't know if I can trust him. Instead, I glare at the house. "How did you bounce back from all that?"

"Ah, well, I've been clean ever since. Met Theo, he's an entertainment attorney. Opened my surf camp and training center at Zuma Beach. And, through Theo, got a book deal—telling the real story of my rise and fall, *Crashing into the Waves*." He smiles wistfully. "It hit the *NY Times* bestseller list before it was published. And I'm still getting royalties. I also stop by the Malibu Oasis, give troubled teens and adults lessons they can learn from me."

This is refreshing. Somebody being honest, telling me about their scars, and, might I dare say, proud of them. I wish I was that brave.

"Malibu Oasis?"

"A rehab center." He eyes me. "So, I've told you my story, are you ready to tell me yours?"

I can't. "Not much to tell."

"Julia, I see it in your eyes—a fire. And I wasn't born yesterday; it has something to do with the Drakes."

I go silent and stand up on my board, turning my back on him. I don't care if loose lips sink ships. I won't be working for them much longer anyway.

"Fine." I dig my paddle into the water, splashing him. "I work for them."

"Doing what?"

"I'm their personal chef," I mumble.

"Do you think you could poison his dishes?" he says with a laugh.

My thoughts leap to the belladonnas, planted right by the herb garden that Erica says isn't an herb garden.

"Funny," I finally reply.

"I'm not kidding," he snorts. "OK, pretty lady, I've got a lesson in an hour. Ready to paddle back?" I nod. Ollie shakes his head, water flying everywhere. "I have a couple copies of my book in my van. I'll sign one and give it to you, how's that sound?"

Oh, I want to read it. I need more ammunition. "I can pay you for the book—"

"Don't worry about it. Told ya, *New York Times* bestseller," he guffaws and then dips his paddle into the water, splashing me. "Plus, I'm not giving you that much of a discount. It's a bonus."

"Perfect," I say with a tight smile. "Sounds like a solid plan."

My plan: I'm going to figure out a way to take Erica down and reading is on my agenda tonight.

FIFTEEN

ERICA

My day at the spa was absolutely divine—the seaweed scrub has made me feel like a new woman. Now back home after hours of being pampered, I'm so relaxed and I'm taking advantage of some well-deserved me time. I'm sprawled out on a lounger by the pool, reading a psychological thriller, *The Lucky Widow*, and loving every word written in it, mostly because the protagonist's abusive husband dies. One can dream. I'm about to dive into the final chapter when Julia stomps onto the terrace, carrying one of the inflatable boards. She's wearing a wetsuit, unzipped to the waist, the sleeves off and hanging at her sides like extra limbs. Her little red surf bikini is cute, although I can only see the top. With her long hair all salted and scrunchy she does look like a little mermaid. I'm hoping she'll become more like a siren though, luring an unsuspecting man to his demise, not with her sweet songs, but her salty meals.

"How was it out there today?"

"Perfect, Erica," she growls and then turns to face me, shooting me a death glare. "Absolutely perfect. I mean, this *is* paradise. The sun is shining, birds are chirping... and, hey, every slice of paradise has its secret ingredients, but sometimes that ingredient isn't so sweet. It's bitter."

This personality shift of hers is interesting. I swing my legs over the lounger, placing my book down, and sit up straight. "Did something happen?"

"No, nothing happened." She straightens her posture. "Sorry for snapping at you like that. I'm just a little winded and overtired. I'm not quite adjusted to the time change yet. I haven't been sleeping well and I probably pushed myself too hard today." She drags in a deep breath, exhales slowly. "What would you like for dinner? And at what time?"

Damn it. She's played the take-away and she's quite good at it, too. Nice recovery. I could threaten to fire her for her lack of respect but decide to play it cool. She doesn't like me, let alone trust me. She probably wants me to fire her. I'm going to play nice, throw her off-balance. I shrug. "I don't know, a nice salad? I want to get to bed early. You should, too, catch up on sleep. Let's say seven thirty?"

"Anything for dessert?"

"No, merci," I say. "Will you be eating with me tonight?"

"I was planning on reading. I'll serve you and then head to my quarters," she replies, her tone terse. She raises her brows, shoots me a closed-mouth smile. "Unless that's a problem?"

Julia? She's lying about something. I can tell by the way her eyes dart to the side and won't meet mine.

"This isn't a prison," I say. "You can do as you please."

"For the salad—I'm thinking arugula, blood orange wedges, pomegranate, and goat cheese seared with a panko crust. Served with a citrus dressing." She meets my gaze, hers slightly intense. "Is that OK with you?"

Oh, I love blood oranges—the deep orange and crimson flesh reminds of the embers of a glowing fire, the taste rich and tangy.

"Sounds delicious."

"OK, Erica," she says, her lips pursed. Before walking off, she places a hand on her hip. "You didn't mention that you met my friend's sister."

Because the fewer people Julia knows, the better. "Oh, that pretty server? She's French, too..."

"That's her. Chloe."

"I'd forgotten about her. Sorry."

"Sure, no problem."

I watch her walk away, my eyebrows raised. My phone buzzes with a text. It's not from Moonbeam but David and my stomach lurches.

DRAGON:

I'll be home around six or seven tomorrow night. Tell that pretty chef of ours to get cooking.

I smile to myself. With this new attitude of hers, not caring if she pleases me or not, Julia is definitely going to bring on the heat.

At seven thirty sharp, I enter the kitchen. Julia turns and smiles. It's so fake. I hope she'll be able to play David better—that is, unless she's completely disgusted by him. Her eyes are a bit brighter now and she looks pretty, wearing one of the casual dresses I'd purchased for her—an emerald-green maxi dress that ties at the waist. She looks really good in that color and the cut is flattering to her figure.

"Good, you're on time," she says curtly. "Merci."

"I'm always on time," I reply, sitting at the round table in the kitchen. It seats six, useful for less formal meals and lunches. I actually prefer eating here than in the dining room. "You're looking rather cheerful. Feeling better?"

"Amazing what a good power nap can do."

"Yes, I agree," I say. "Fifteen minutes of wonder."

"I slept for an hour." She sets the salad on the table and then heads to the fridge, returning with the bottle of Miraval. She pours me a glass and sets the bottle down. "Anything else, Erica?"

"I'm good. Thank you." I look at her features, the frown pulling down her lips, the glare in her eyes. She definitely hates my guts. "Is there something you're not telling me? Earlier at the pool it seemed like you had something on your mind."

Her eyes dart to the side and she fidgets with the necklace I'd given her. I brace myself, my entire body buzzing and humming in anticipation. Do it, Julia. Tell me off. Do something. Anything. I lean forward, waiting. Hoping.

"No, like I said, I was just overtired," she finally says and the electricity racing through my body fizzles, especially after she drones on about nothing, making excuses for her snappish behavior. "If I don't get at least six hours of undisturbed sleep, I'm a walking nightmare. Again, sorry." My gaze follows hers as she glances at the clock on the wall. "I'm feeling a little woozy. So, if there's nothing else..."

She'll come clean. Eventually. And then we can get this party started.

I tap my chin. "There is one thing," I say, and she twitches. "Just a quick question. Do you like it here?"

Her lips curve into the tightest of smiles. I'm pretty sure she's holding back a laugh. "If I ignore the threat of snakes, who wouldn't love working and living in paradise?"

There it is—the cryptic dig.

"Good to know," I say. "Get some rest tonight."

She turns on her heel, walking quickly. "Merci."

As she scurries out of the kitchen, I remind her, "Don't forget..."

"I know. I know. David's coming home tomorrow. And he likes the meat from Gelson's in Calabasas."

She stomps out of the kitchen, down the hallway, and out the front door, each step echoing.

Before I shower, I lie down on the bed, turning on the news. The words *breaking story* flash across the screen, followed by

DAVID DRAKE'S SUNSET STRIPPER FILM ENDS IN TRAGEDY

An M&Ms commercial fades onto the screen. The headline has me praying something has happened to David. It would make life so much easier.

David had driven to Vegas in the Maserati, probably to lure one of the showgirls he's been promising a part to onto his lap. Seventeen years ago, I used to be that girl. Blame me for some very, very bad choices. And now I'm living with my mistakes. Literally. I used to be here for his amusement, now I'm just here for his abusement. It's a word now. And we both thrive on the drama.

Anyway, maybe he crashed his car—now that would be poetic justice. I cackle to myself and get comfortable on the bed, rubbing my hands together. The male newscaster, Brian something or other, blasts onto the screen, standing outside the Paris Hotel on the Vegas strip. An ambulance pulls away. "We have sad and disturbing news to share with viewers tonight..." He pauses, exhales a deep breath.

I ball my hands together and lean forward.

"Famed burlesque showgirl Luna Starlight, known to her family as Nellie Jones, was found dead earlier this morning, after falling out of an oversized champagne glass to her death."

I let out a gasp and clasp a hand over my mouth.

"The lead actress in David Drake's latest film *The Sunset Stripper*, Luna, born in Fort Worth, Texas, was only thirty-six years old at the time of her death. With me is David Drake. Mr. Drake, care to comment?"

The camera pans to David. He swallows, his Adam's apple bobbing up and down.

"I am devastated by the tragic loss of Luna Starlight. We all are. Luna's extraordinary talent brought immense depth to the film." He lowers his head, shaking it with remorse. "Luna was not only a gifted performer but a cherished colleague. My heart goes out to her family, friends, and the entire cast and crew who shared in her brilliance, the light she shone on all our lives."

A clip of Luna dancing in the tiniest of gold costumes with a wildly ornate headdress and a feather fan emerges onto the screen. I gulp.

"Can you tell us what happened?"

David rubs his forehead. "She wanted to rehearse her last couple of scenes. We didn't know she'd gone on set alone." He swallows again and chokes back a sob. "She's a perfectionist. She wanted everything to be perfect."

"Will filming continue?"

I already know David's answer before he replies. Of course it will.

"As they say in the biz, the show must go on. It's what Luna would have wanted." He clears his throat. "I'll be rewriting the end of the script. There's an open casting call tomorrow afternoon at my studio in Burbank from two–five p.m. For white females, five foot six, under one hundred and twenty pounds, and between the ages of twenty-five and thirty-five, who want to honor Luna. Just show up. More details will be posted on Drake Entertainment's site."

I pull up the last picture I have of Luna and me together on my phone. It was taken over ten years ago at my marriage to David. She'd surprised the crowd with a striptease, taking off her gown to reveal her costume, and launched into an impromptu performance, using me as a prop. She'd pulled up a chair and had me sit, while she shimmied around, fanning my face with one of her many feathered fans, to Shirley Bassey's "Big Spender".

She'd always been after my life, David's money. I did warn her about him; she just didn't listen. Look where sleeping with my husband got her.

SIXTEEN

JULIA

"Julia! Julia!" Erica's voice booms over the intercom. "Your packages have arrived. I'm still in bed. You go fetch them. The delivery people left them outside the gate." She mumbles, "Damnit. I need my beauty sleep."

Click. Mean Erica is back in action. Click. She doesn't know Julia is in action, too.

After reading Ollie's book, I'd spent all night thinking of ways to destroy her. I can't believe she's profiting by making movies about destroying people's lives. She's, simply put, not a good person.

- A: Blackmail, hence the cameras
- B: Seduce David, taking him away from her, thus destroying her marriage and acting career
- C: A combination of the above
- D: Be so obnoxious she fires me and I sue her for breach of contract

Yay for me! A couple of ingredients for my recipe of destruction have arrived.

I race out of the guesthouse, down the path, and sprint down the driveway, my heart racing. Back in my living quarters, I rip open the packages, balling them up so Beurreboule can play. By eleven, I've set up the cameras in the kitchen, the dining room, and David's office. I can't go upstairs because Erica is up there. But I know she has appointments throughout the week. I leave the packages of actual cooking tools like the handheld fruit press on the center island, along with a note.

Erica,

Went to Gelson's. Sliced fruit in the refrigerator if you're hungry. Bon appétit!

J

I want to write *p.s. your wine is chilling in the fridge. Have at it, Lushika.* But think better of this passive and very aggressive act.

Before I leave for the grocery store, I set up my EyeSpy account and test the cameras linked to my phone. And, Houston, we have lift-off. I jump into the Mercedes. And I'm going to take my damn sweet time. I'm not going to Gelson's but to Whole Foods. Much closer. And, with the way I cook, the way the flavors meld together, they won't know the difference. I really don't care about being reimbursed. All I care about is getting the truth and maybe a little payback along the way.

While driving and before shopping, I ring Chloe (thanks, hands-free Bluetooth) to see if she can meet me at the Starbucks in Malibu Country Mart. It's a beautiful day out (thanks, California) not a cloud in the sky—around sixty-five perfect degrees.

Just another day in paradise.

I click on Phil Collins's song, thinking about my parents. They used to slow dance to this, sometimes with me smushed in the middle. I park the car and for a moment I let the memories wash over me. My mom's perfume—Coco Chanel. The stubble of my dad's beard. Their love for each other. Their love for me.

Mom and Dad were free-spirited—not hippies, but connected to everything around them. Our house was filled with pottery my mother and me made when she wasn't baking. The earth, she'd say, we're taking the clay and transforming it into something new. My dad, formerly in finance, hated the money business. When he wasn't crushing numbers, he'd crush the waves with little ol' me. The water element. As for fire, they called me their little spark. And, air, well, it was everywhere, and they taught me to breathe in and appreciate every little moment.

With a sigh, I turn off the radio, heading into Starbucks.

After ordering, I wait for Chloe with two iced green teas at one of the outside tables. She walks toward me, a bounce in her step. She kisses each of my cheeks, the French way, and takes a seat, leaning forward. "Did you hear the news? I can't believe it."

"Why aren't you speaking French?"

"Because we're in America, not France." She grins. "Plus, I'm working on my accent. Anyway, Luna Starlight! I can't believe it."

"I don't know what you're talking about. I just met her the other night..."

"She died. On set in one of David Drake's films. The one he's filming now in Vegas." Chloe's eyes light up. "He's so good-looking. I'd kill to get a part in one of his films."

I gulp.

She blinks, her eyes going wide. "You've seen the tabloids—the speculation that Erica and David are over. There was even a video of him pushing her into the car and slamming the door in her face."

I am not one to keep up with the tabloids, and I know better than to reveal anything I've learned about their relationship. Good-looking? Sure, he wears that disguise well. "Chloe, what's your point?"

"This is my chance. He's having an open casting call this afternoon so he can finish the movie." She raises a brow, arching it high. "Could you put in a good word for me?"

My throat catches. This news has my heart pounding, thumping so hard and fast I feel dizzy. "No."

Her jaw drops and her top lip curls into an offended snarl. "Why? Because you want to be the only one with a connection to the Drakes? You have your in?"

What a joke. I want to be the person with the out. "No, it's because I work for them. I don't want to push the wrong buttons, have them thinking I'm using them to get ahead..."

No, I'm after something else.

"Julia, come on. This is LA. People do it all the time—especially for friends." She snorts. "Merde, I thought I was your friend."

Friend? I'd met Chloe a handful of times, but I'm seeing the real her right now. Funny how the light changes and you can truly see a person.

"If I can somehow work it into a conversation, I'll see what I can do." I swallow. "But I'd seriously reconsider this audition."

"It could be my big break."

I can't tell Chloe what I know about Erica, how horrible she is. I'm also a little disappointed with the ask. Chloe's proving she's just another Hollywood hanger-on, only out to get what she wants.

She kisses me on the cheek. "Merci, Julia. You're the best. I've got to go practice some burlesque dance moves." She nods to her cup. "Thanks for the tea. Wish me luck."

"Break a leg," I say with a tight smile.

. . .

Back at Hummingbird hell, I find a package waiting for me on my bed. I open it, finding a bandana with a smiley baguette and croissant print. The exact kind my mother wore. I lift the fabric to my nose, inhale. It even smells of her signature perfume— Coco Chanel. Who left it here? How did they know about my mother?

With resolve, I dry my hair and then I tie the bandana like a headband, with a little knot of a bow on the top. Erica, whatever game you're playing—it's on.

SEVENTEEN

ERICA

Julia's been slamming things around in the kitchen while David and I have drinks on the terrace. It's almost as if Julia is being noisy on purpose, baiting me to come in and yell at her. No, I'm saving my tirade for later. David and I have barely spoken a word, save for the usual trivial bullshit. Oh, yes! The weather is glorious today—not a surprise in southern California. Perfect. And we are perfectly incompatible. We've become experts at pretending that we tolerate one another, mostly for the cameras.

A loud crash comes from the kitchen, followed by Julia screaming, "Freaking putain!"

David stands up. "I should go see what's wrong."

"Don't. She's always like this. Chefs are very emotional, pouring their passion into their dishes. You'd only be distracting her," I say, taking a long pause as David makes a move to walk toward the house. "I saw the news about Nellie."

My tone is flat and cold. So is the look in my eyes.

David slumps back down into his seat. Sighs dramatically. "Yeah, it was quite the shock. Unfathomable."

"It certainly was."

I know I'm about to play with fire. But I like the flames.

What's that expression? If you can't handle the heat, get out of the kitchen? "Did you have anything to do with her death?"

I'm method-acting now, looking into what my character wants and needs, feeling every emotion. I'm not Erica Drake right now. I'm somebody else—the character I've created to get me through this farce of a marriage.

David slams his glass down on the coffee table and it shatters—not the coffee table, it's wood, but his glass, the fragments sparkling in the moonlight. Apparently, I've touched upon a very sore subject. He stands up, presses his fists into his thighs, heading over to the storage closet. "For fuck's sake, Erica, the police questioned me for hours yesterday. Now you?"

"Well, I have my reasons..."

"Look, I don't know why she did what she did, why she took that risk." He returns with a dustpan and sweeps up the glass, setting it to the side. "They think she was drugged or did drugs."

He's fidgeting with his watch, nervous. I'm going in for the kill. "What did the police question you about? Your affair with her? I know you were sleeping with her..."

"Damn it, Erica, stop with your crazy, drunk insinuations. Enough! I'm really broken up by this."

Of course he is.

I lean forward, meeting his intense gaze. David hates me more than Julia does. "Fine. When's her funeral? She was one of my closest friends."

"You don't have any close friends." He blurts out a caustic laugh. "You're lucky anybody speaks to you."

I'm not backing down. "I want to know. When is her funeral?"

"They're flying her home to Texas. Her funeral is set for Sunday," he says. "Sadly, we'll both have to miss it because we have more important things to do."

He smiles wickedly and raises a brow, a threat for me to stay in line.

I lower my head, keeping my scream internal. A tear manages to slide down my cheek. I wipe it away with my free hand. Motivation. Stay in character. "The Oscars. You're right," I say, my voice steady. "But we have to do something."

"I'll send a truckload of flowers to the church," he says glumly. "I'll even write a speech for somebody to read." He latches onto my hand and hangs his head. "I don't want to talk about Luna anymore. When's dinner? I'm starving."

I keep a straight face, willing my anger to go away. Instead of screaming, *you fucking bastard*, I scream, "Julia! Julia!"

She steps onto the terrace. "Yes, Erica?"

"When's dinner going to be served?"

She pauses for a moment, her eyes meeting mine. Fear or worry, something, flashes across her face. It's not the anger I'd seen earlier. Perhaps, now that David is back, she's finally catching on and will play her part. She holds up a finger. "I just need a couple more minutes. Did you want to eat in the dining room or the kitchen?"

"Right here is fine," David replies. "It's a beautiful evening."

She nods and meets his gaze, puffs out her bottom lip. "I'm sorry to hear about your friend, Luna. A tragedy."

"It was. But life is life and accidents happen. Sad to lose somebody so talented when they're so young." David lowers his gaze and sighs. "I'll eat my way through the pain. What are we having for dinner tonight?"

"Coq au vin."

"Perfection," he says.

Her smile is tight. She points to her head. "By the way, merci for zee gift, Erica. I love eet. So cute."

I gulp back a sip of wine. "I would never buy something as ridiculous as that."

"Then who sent it to me?" she asks.

"I don't know, darling. Maybe you have an admirer." My

gaze shoots to David and then back to Julia. "And I'd appreciate it if you took it off. Because I hate it."

David shoots me a disgusted glare and then his gaze meets Julia's. "Julia, I think your bandana is cute. Ignore Erica. Are you ever going to make us more croissants? And baguettes?"

"Why would she do that?" I hiss. "We're both carb free until *after* the awards."

"Understood," Julia replies and turns to leave.

No, she doesn't understand anything. Not yet. But she will.

I nod toward the shattered glass. "Julia? Since you're headed into the kitchen, can you please throw this out?"

Her mouth twists to the side, yet she doesn't ask what happened, just nods and grabs the dustpan. David heads over to the bar and refills a new glass of Scotch. When he returns to the table, we sit in silence, glaring at one another.

As Julia serves us, at one point, she meets his gaze and winks. I feel sick to my stomach. She doesn't know the rules just yet. But all I can do is sit back and watch how this plays out. This scene unfolding in front of my eyes, however, definitely needs another take or a thousand. Julia is playing hardball. Good. David cuts another obvious dig at me. Eventually, we'll see where her loyalties lie. Right now, they're not with either of us, but that will change.

"We'll take our desserts in the kitchen," I say.

"I'll set the table for you."

"After you've done so, you're dismissed."

Before Julia gracefully exits the terrace, I watch her with an eagle eye and mutter, "Honestly, the nerve of some people. Can't even serve a meal without attracting unwanted attention."

My comment is loud enough for her to hear. She goes rigid in the doorway.

"You're the one who invited her into our home," says David. "And, honestly, I'm happy about that. Very happy."

"I can't believe her dream is to open up a restaurant of her own one day," I scoff, watching Julia's spine straighten.

David looks up. "She told you that?"

"Yes, the other day when I took her to lunch." I roll my eyes. "I mean, she even told me she liked the same music you liked—classic rock and modern groups like Imagine Dragons. I'm pretty sure she's planning to use you, us, as a steppingstone to get what she wants."

"Isn't that why you used me?" says David, spitting out a harsh laugh. "Don't we all do things to get ahead?"

I chug back the last of my wine and then smile. "Oh, honey, I married you because you're the love of my life—"

"What a crock."

I curve my lips into a tight grin, raise my chin and my hands. "Then just divorce me."

If I leave him, he'll make sure I end up right back where I started, living in a trailer park. And that's not going to happen. Till death do us part.

"Shall we discuss terms?" he growls. "California is a fifty percent state. In addition to my fortune, did you want to cut Tyler in half?"

I gulp. What a terrifying image. He'd probably slice him open with one of Julia's knives and blame it on me so he could make a film about it.

EIGHTEEN

JULIA

As I look over my shoulder, observing Erica's intense gaze, a nagging worry creeps into my thoughts. What is she trying to do? What is he trying to do? I know I'm here for more than just cooking.

I'm standing in the hallway, my back pressed against the wall, listening to the most messed-up conversation I've heard in my entire life. It's like she's throwing me right into a shark's mouth. Here, chomp, chomp, here's some fish chum and her name is Julia. And David, by the way he looks at me, wants to eat me alive. I need to learn the rules of the game they are both obviously playing, and quickly. Breathless, I race back to the guesthouse and grab my phone, pulling up the feed from the hidden camera I'd placed in the kitchen. I watch as David gobbles down the dessert... and Erica slams down glass after glass of wine.

Her tolerance must be incredible. If I didn't hate her so much I'd be worried for her health. Plus, her eyes are always clear, no signs of jaundice. Her skin is blemish-free, too.

I should be packing my bags, but I need to expose them for what they do to people. The films based on true stories? Nope, they are based on lies. That is motivation enough for me. I mean, it's not like either one of them has tried stabbing me with one of my knives. Yet. What the hell was that conversation all about? Cutting Tyler in half?

Shit. I've now put that idea into my head and I haven't even met the kid. I rub my eyes and focus in on the screen, turning up the sound—earbuds on. If either of them are spying on me it just looks like I'm watching a scary movie with Beurreboule on my lap.

David licks his lips. "I'm thinking about working on a new concept after I finish up *The Sunset Stripper*."

Erica shivers, visibly. "You mean after you finished off Luna. Any parts in your new film suitable for me?"

David bangs his fist on the table.

I jump. So does Beurreboule because she's on my lap. Poor little puff ball nearly goes flying off the bed. My mind spins. Erica has just insinuated that David killed Luna. Which has the cogs in my mind ticking. Who else has he killed?

"Are you out of your fucking mind? I've had it with you. Do I have to remind you that if it weren't for me, you'd still be a nothing? Trailer trash. But you wasted that." He spits out his words. "Now you're just a useless, unlikeable drunk. Old. Not good enough to be cast in anything. You'd be lucky to get a part in a porno film. Maybe I'll give Julia a part in my next film. She's, what? Twenty-two? Twenty-three?"

Oh, hell no, I whisper to myself, cringing.

Erica's mouth quivers. She stomps her foot and staggers toward him. And then she slaps him. "Leave her out of this."

My throat constricts. I don't know what shocks me more—this messed-up conversation or the fact that Erica has just defended me. I really don't know what the hell is going on. I'm locking my door tonight.

"Screw you," he screams, rubbing his cheek. "I've had it with your meltdowns."

"Meltdown? I'm perfectly fine," she says, straightening her posture. "You know we both have our parts to play until the awards. After that, we're going to reevaluate our relationship."

"You can count on that," he hisses.

In the dim glow of the monitor, I'm witnessing moments of tension escalate, the way her voice rises and falls in pitch, his tense posture. This isn't a movie. This is as real as it gets. Unable to turn away, I grapple with conflicting emotions. He takes a step toward her, his face rigid with anger, his fists balled. I'm worried he's going to do something to her, harm her in some way. I'm facing a critical decision, a moral dilemma—whether to remain a passive observer or to intervene and protect Erica.

I jump up from the bed. I need to do something to help her, maybe say I forgot my knives in the kitchen. But what if he hurts me?

Should I call the police? And how would I explain what I know?

Before I do anything, I glance at the monitor. David storms out of the kitchen. And Erica sits alone, tears streaming down her face. For a brief second, I swear, her eyes meet the cameras and I can feel her pain, burning through me like a fire. She gets up and slowly leaves the dining room.

And I can't do anything.

My eyes sweep the room, landing on the bouquet of lavender that appeared while I was out. Erica wouldn't have been able to place it here when she'd been upstairs all day doing whatever she does—probably drinking. I would have seen her come down when I was cooking. And when I was in the pool, David was there. The bandana that matched my mother's favorite one, even smelled like her. David had the chance to stash it here.

If I've hidden cameras, he's probably placed some, too, the director that he is.

FaceTime buzzes. Marie. I'm not sure I want to pick up, but

I can't avoid her. Even if I'm being spied on, David doesn't speak French and surely he wouldn't understand all the slang. I push the button and answer.

"Coucou, Marie!" I say as lightly as possible.

"Thank God, I got you..."

"Parle en Française, Maman. Et vite, come d'hab."

If David is listening, I know he can't hear her, but he'll hear me.

Marie shakes her head, eyeing me with suspicion and then launches into rapid-fire French. "Bernard and I saw that movie *Swerve*. It finally came out in France. That actress, the one you're working for..."

I cut her off. "Je sais. Je l'ai vu."

Her jaw drops. "You saw it?"

I smile, eyes wide, and nod.

"Why in the world are you smiling like that? You look crazy."

I may be going crazy, putting up with these people. Still, the thoughts of bringing them—no, him—down outweigh any former sensibilities I might have had. That ship sailed when I'd watched *Swerve*, careening right over the canyon. I curve my lips into a tighter smile.

"Parce que tu me manques, Maman."

"I miss you, too. Pack your bags and get out of there right now. Don't spend one more second at that house. She's not a good person. They are not good people."

"Je sais, Maman, mais je ne peux pas."

"You can't. Why? And why do you keep calling me maman? You're scaring me. Are you in danger?"

Probably. But I'm ready to face all of my fears. Still, I have to lie to Marie, which hurts me more than I could have imagined. But if I even whispered a word about what I'm planning to do she'd try to talk me out of it. One thing about me, I'm stubborn and once I get an idea into my head there's no stopping me. So, I continue to lie. "Non, tout est parfait."

My eyes meet hers, my brows lifted. She knows my obstinate look, the kind where she knows she won't be able to convince me of doing anything else. Surf that wild fifteen-to-twenty-foot wave? I might kill myself. Stay under water for far too long? My lungs could burst. At least I'm being honest with myself. I'm not leaving the Drake house until one or both of them are destroyed.

She shakes her head from side to side, lips scrunched. "I really hope you know what you're doing. And you know I'm not happy about it."

The line clicks to a close. I know exactly what I'm doing.

NINETEEN

JULIA

I'm ready to face the day and I'm about to hop in the shower when I see a big black spider scurrying around on the floor of the bathroom. A freaking enormous and very hairy tarantula. With my throat constricting, I back out of the room slowly, tripping over Beurreboule. She hides under the bed as I slam onto the floor, my legs giving out from under me. The tarantula is moving toward me and the scream coming from my vocal cords reaches new decibels.

David races into the guesthouse and I feel like I'm about to have a heart attack. A tarantula? Now him? "I was doing my morning run around the property. Heard you screaming. Thought somebody was being murdered. Are you OK?"

How convenient. My eyes lock onto the window in the bathroom and it's cracked open. And I didn't open it. After witnessing what I saw and heard last night, I am more than fearful of him. I'd take a tarantula over David any day. But he can't know that. He places a hand on my shoulder. I point. "T-t-tarantula."

He nods and heads to the kitchen, grabbing a glass bowl and a plate. I'm smart enough to know what Erica is using me for.

Everything is making sense now. I saw the way she was trying to communicate to me subtly with her eyes. She wants David to fall in love with me so she can escape his hold. I get her game now. I'm supposed to act like a woman in distress—hate her, dote on him.

But why on earth would she put me in her position? Aside from being a little bitchy, I haven't done anything at all to her. To her, I'm worthless. Another victim for David. And that's completely messed up.

I watch him as he lets the tarantula loose in the garden and then turns to face me. "Crisis averted."

Not really. He's still here, his eyes scanning my body like a laser. It doesn't help that I'm braless in a tight tank top and wearing shorty pajama boy shorts.

"What if it comes back in?"

"It won't."

He saunters over to me and extends his hand, lifting me up off the floor. Then, he pulls me close into his chest. My heart is beating faster than the wings of a frantic hummingbird. His lips brush across my cheek nearly meeting mine and he whispers in my ear, "You don't have to be fearful of anything."

I can only nod.

"Are you OK?"

I just want him to leave, to let me out of his hold, especially after his hand slides down to my waist. But terror has rendered me into a limp rag doll. I whimper, "I'm fine. Merci."

He finally releases me and takes a step backward, lifting up my chin. "Julia, I have to leave now. Big day."

I gurgle out my response. "Uh-huh."

Once he's gone, my legs give out from under me. I may be in the deep end of the pool, but I do know how to swim, to tread water. With my heart still racing, I crawl under the bed to get Beurreboule. When I snuggle her into my chest, she's quivering, too.

. . .

An hour after the David and tarantula fiasco, Erica's voice booms over the intercom. "Julia! Get into the kitchen! Now!" There's a short pause. "Now! I said!" she screams. "Kitchen!!! Are you deaf? I said, now!"

I look at my phone. It's eight in the morning. This can't be happening. Just when I was starting to feel sorry for her, she's acting like a psychopath.

"I'm coming," I reply, after pressing down on the button. "Give me a minute. I just got out of the shower."

"I said, now!"

And so with a loud sigh I put on a pair of gym shoes, dress in Erica approved clothes, and stumble to the main house, my hair still wet. She crosses her twig-like arms over her chest. "I'd really appreciate it if you would stop looking at David the way you do."

I'm going to tiptoe around this accusation as best I can. She's really tipping the scales of manic behavior. And the way I look at him? It's the way he looks at me. Disgusting.

"I'm just trying to do my job, be friendly."

Her face flushes with anger, and she sharply retorts, "You're lucky that you're even here, Julia. Don't think I won't reconsider your position. People would kill to work for me."

Maybe they have. I eye my knives, unrolled on the kitchen counter. Tempting.

Her threat hangs in the air as tension and her heavy breath fills the room. I maintain my composure, standing firm. There's no use arguing with her right now, or, really, ever. She'd just twist everything around on me.

She turns her back on me and grabs a bottle of juice from the refrigerator. "Stop batting your long eyelashes at him."

I suppress an eye roll and blink, replying diplomatically,

hoping to shift the focus from blame to a resolution. "Of course, Erica."

She faces me. "What lash formula do you use?"

"I don't even wear mascara."

"Oh?" She nods, perplexed. "By the way, two things—Madison will be coming home soon. She's on her special diets."

How many personality shifts can one person take? I'm also surprised she's drinking a green juice, not the same consistency or color of her rosé.

"I know. I've already purchased ingredients. And you've approved this week's menu."

She snaps back her shoulders, shakes her head, and sneers. Something stirs inside me. I am so ready to quit. Right now. This very moment. Tell Erica I think she's a neurotic bitch. Go absolutely ballistic on her. And then I remember the reasons why I'm staying. I tell myself to stay strong, not easy considering who I'm dealing with. "I do need to pick up a few things from the store."

"Can you drop me off at Urgent Care on your way?" Her gaze drifts to the ceiling. "Antoine is stuck in traffic and can't get here in time. He's picking up Maddy at the airport."

I must have the patience of a saint because she's definitely testing mine to new limits. Now, instead of feeling angry with her, I feel sorry for her. I hesitantly approach her, wondering if David hurt her. "Is everything OK?"

Erica chuckles. "Oh, darling, I appreciate your concern, but don't fret. I have a Botox appointment. It's practically a ritual here. No harm, just a little maintenance." She flips her hair over her shoulder, evading the subject. "You know how it is."

I don't. Forget about the bizarre fact they give emergency Botox shots at Urgent Care, I don't understand anything.

"I can take you," I say with a sigh.

"I just need a half hour to get ready. Antoine can pick me up." Her eyes widen, flashing a look of warning, like the one she'd given me the other night. She exits the kitchen, rubbing her wrist. "I'll be back in two shakes."

I swallow, wanting to ask her what the hell is going on, but I stand quiet, thinking. While I wait for her return, I look at my phone. Chloe has been texting me non-stop. She's also left twenty voice mails. *Call me. It's important.* If it's so important—why isn't she telling me what it is? I try calling her and—it goes straight to voicemail so I leave a message.

On the ride to Urgent Care, Erica's on the phone with somebody from the Academy and then her agent. She doesn't say a word to me, just pretends like nothing is wrong. I drop her off and head to Whole Foods to pick up more flour and tons of butter. I am making more bread... and croissants.

Groceries in hand, or rather in one of the burlap faux-Chanel bags, I return around eleven, surprised to see a young brunette with shiny long hair, clutching a beet in her hand, its earthy texture pulsating between her fingers, the juices running off her fingers and onto the floor. "It's like a heart," she whispers to herself, her gaze fixated on the beet cradled in her palm.

I'm transfixed. The girl continues, embodying the character of Lady Macbeth's iconic soliloquy, her words laced with a haunting intensity. "Out, damned spot! Out, I say!" she exclaims, the beet's crimson juices staining her hands. She rubs her fingers across her face.

It's time to make my presence known. I cough. "Excuse me, I take it that you're Madison. What are you doing to my produce?"

Madison whips around, dropping half of the beet on the floor with a healthy splat, her cheeks streaked red. She eyes me up and down. "The bigger question is who are you?"

"I'm Julia—the private chef at Hummingbird House."

I know she's eighteen, so closer to age to me than Erica is, and she has a healthy, sporty look about her—lean and strong. Pretty. I'd looked up her mother, actress Valerie Morgan. She has her mother's large, beautiful brown eyes, perky nose, and full lips.

Her eyebrows pinch together. "You work here?"

"I do. Your mother, Erica, hired me. I live in the guesthouse."

"A: She's not my mother. And B: I'm thinking you're batshit crazy for wanting to work here." She holds back a laugh. "I mean, have you met David?"

I frown, thinking about this morning's almost kiss, the way he'd leaned into me, the way he'd made me feel violated. "Your dad? Of course I have."

"Adoptive dad," she says forcefully, twirling her index finger in circles on the right side of her head in the crazy motion and then pointing at me. "At least he's not around all that much, but when he is, if you enjoy dealing with him, I'm thinking you're nuts."

She has made a very good point. I'm beginning to think I'm nuts, too.

"Maybe, but I'm not the one squeezing beets with my bare hands and destroying this pristine kitchen."

She laughs. "Busted."

With a bemused smile, I approach her. She's still looking at the splattered beet with an intensity that mirrors Lady Macbeth's fervor. I'm wondering who she'd been thinking about. David? Erica?

"Back to my question. What were you doing to my beets?" I ask, a blend of amusement and genuine interest in my voice.

Madison looks up with a mischievous twinkle in her eyes. "I'm extracting the essence of ambition, just like Lady Macbeth would. This beet, it's like a heart filled with desires and struggles of power."

I chuckle, appreciating Madison's imaginative take on

Shakespeare. I think he would, too, especially with Madison's red-stained cheeks.

"Where are you from?" she asks. "I detect the slightest of accents."

Merde. I slipped into my American accent. I decide it doesn't matter because it's too late now and I won't be working here at the Hummingbird House of Horrors for very long.

"I grew up around here, and then I lived in Paris."

"Cool." She nods. "I love Paris. I only spent two days there, a stopover after my friends and me climbed in Montserrat, just outside Barcelona. We ended our little spring break jaunt in London. Saw Shakespeare in the Park. Loved *Macbeth*."

Picked up on that.

"Well, it seems Lady Macbeth has found a unique companion in our humble beet. Just be sure not to stain the whole kitchen in the process—or my head will be on the platter."

Madison grimaces. "Yeah, Erica is going to kill me when she sees the mess I made."

We burst into laughter just as Erica walks in.

"I really hope I'm not the butt of any jokes," she says, stepping forward. "Madison, my darling, what on earth is all over your hands and your face? You look like a murder victim."

"Just a little beet juice. I was channeling Lady Macbeth."

"I don't understand," says Erica, scrunching her nose. "But you're home. Wonderful."

I wonder why Erica isn't screaming at Madison for the juice dripping off the countertop and onto the floor.

"No thanks to you, Second Wife, and your lack of driving skills. But at least Antoine picked me up." Madison grins. "Darling Erica, I may need some things for school."

Erica clucks her tongue. "You know where the petty cash drawer is."

Madison flashes a wicked smile and saunters over to the

drawer. I watch her as she taps in the combination and grabs a small stack of hundreds. Erica is such a liar. She'd told me to never, ever share the combination with Madison or Tyler. I stand there, blinking, wondering what else she's lied to me about. Probably everything.

"How was Europe, you spoiled brat?" asks Erica.

"Better than being here, Second Wife."

"Would you please stop calling me that?"

They stare at one another for a long minute, the clock on the kitchen wall ticking like a metronome, punctuating the tempo of uncomfortable silence. I'm wondering what their relationship is like. Do they just banter and tease one another or do they dislike one another? Perhaps a little bit of both.

"OK, Stepmommy dearest." Madison snickers and to my surprise Erica does, too. "And you got the better deal. First wife, my mom, isn't around—"

"What a blessing! I get to take care of you." Erica fans her face and then fixes her gaze on me. "I spoke with Tyler. He'd like spaghetti Bolognese for dinner tomorrow night. With mushrooms. So"—she raises her hands in the air—"a change in this week's meal plans. And I'd like something light, another delicious salad."

"Obviously," I say, my tone edging on irritation, and Madison eyes me curiously. "What time will Tyler be coming home?"

"Second Wife, aka Stepmommy dearest, and I are picking him up tomorrow around three. He's at Malibu Oasis, right? That's the plan?"

Erica nods. "That's the plan."

Ollie had told me about Malibu Oasis. It's a luxury drug and alcohol rehabilitation center, the one he did community service at. Why does Erica lie so much? And can I catch her in this one?

"Malibu Oasis?" I cross my arms over my chest. "That's a strange name for a basketball camp."

Madison spits out her water. "She told you that? No, Tyler's been in rehab for a month. Got busted for a DUI—the influence was pot." She grins at me. "At least his sick car is being put to good use. I'm assuming you get to use it."

I scratch the back of my neck, glaring at Erica.

She meets my eyes, hers cold and stony. "What? Tyler's business is none of your business. You're not part of the family."

Thank God, I think. I feel like I'm living in a never-ending episode of the *Twilight Zone*.

Madison hops on the counter and leans toward the window facing the ocean. "Is everything set up?"

Erica shrugs. "You'll have to see for yourself."

Madison glances at me over her shoulder. "Do you climb, Julia?"

Yes, from the age of twelve, I used to climb with my parents in Solstice Canyon, all over California. When I wasn't surfing, I was climbing with them, having picnics in fields of wildflowers, laughing in the sun. But she doesn't need to know this.

So, like Erica, I lie. "No, I have a fear of heights. I surf."

Madison shrugs. "I have a fear of water. Maybe together we can get over our fears."

"I'd like that. And I'd like to know what you'd like for dinner."

"Oh, I'm easy," says Madison. "I eat anything."

"I thought you were paleo," I say.

She waves a hand toward Erica. "She's the one who is afraid of the big bad carbs. Keeping her weight down for the camera. Not me."

And Erica's lies just keep coming and coming like a typhoon.

"True. It's just us girls tonight," says Erica with a grin. "Will you be eating with us, Julia?"

"I... uh, I..." I don't know how to get out of this. And I do like Madison. She could be my ally. Or she could be another one of Erica's ploys.

"Please do," says Madison. "I can tell you about my time in Paris over dinner. Then we can watch another movie. I get to pick. What are your thoughts on dinner?"

I look at her magenta-red-stained hands, turning a purplish color. "Something with crushed beets."

"Borscht! Yes!" Madison squeals. "I'm a huge soup fan. Can I help you make it?"

I laugh and this time it's real, not the fake ones I've been spitting out for Erica. "I think you've already started the process." I wink. "Great technique, by the way."

Silvia and Karla race into the kitchen, embracing Madison and spinning her around, their smiles warm and welcoming. Madison, apparently, is fluent in Spanish. Me? I can only pick up on a few words that are similar in French—artist, café, tour, musique.

I politely excuse myself from the kitchen, leaving for the store. Among other ingredients for the borscht, I need more beets.

To irritate Erica, this evening to go along with the soup Madison has helped me prepare, I make another baguette. And Erica eats half of it. "This is delicious."

She's messing with my brain.

After dinner, we head into the home theater, naturally Erica bringing her bottle of wine, and Madison chooses the film. It's *Valerie*, the film her mother died in—committing suicide by taking pills and drowning in the pool. My jaw clenches. "Why do you want to watch this?"

As the lights in the theater dim, and the opening scene bursts onto the giant screen, Madison's eyes lose their former brightness. "Next year, I'm majoring in film at NYU and I like studying every little nuance. The camera doesn't lie. It captures all the moments." She swallows. Hard. "For me to be a great and honest filmmaker, I think it's important to face my past. Tap into the pain, you know?"

I nod, thinking *what you're doing is self-torture. Believe me, I know.*

TWENTY

ERICA

Today, I have a little surprise for Julia when she returns from the store—probably Ralph's or Whole Foods, just to spite me. Funny, I really don't care where she shops or if she does it daily. I listen for the front door to open. "Julia!" I call out. "Is that you?"

She sighs loudly. "Oui, Erica."

"Can you come into the living room, please? There's somebody I'd like you to meet."

"I'll be there in a minute," she says. "I have to put away the groceries."

"OK, darling, take your time."

I can feel her eyes roll, hear the swear words she's probably muttering under her breath. A couple of minutes later, Julia meanders into the room. The man I'm sitting with turns around and Julia's face pales ever so slightly, her eyes darting to the side. She's wearing one of the outfits I'd purchased for her, and looks all flustered and cute in it.

"I'd like to introduce you to Liam Harrington, Tyler's new teacher." I shrug. "As I told you, Tyler is being homeschooled for the rest of the year, mostly because he was expelled."

Liam's jaw drops as he stands up and he blinks with confusion. He's tall and lanky, with sandy brown hair. He has what they say is a nice face, open and honest. Well-scrubbed, well put together. Kind hazel eyes with golden specks. A nicely shaped mouth. If I was ten years younger, he'd be exactly the type of man I'd be attracted to.

He steps toward Julia, arm outstretched. She takes his hand and then quickly releases it, wiping her palms on her linen slacks. I lean forward with anticipation. "It's nice to meet you, Julia," says Liam, his head tilted to the side. "And, please, don't take this the wrong way, but I feel like I've met you before."

She's fidgeting, squirming. Won't meet his eyes. "I get zat a lot. I must 'ave one of those faces," she finally says, looking down at the floor.

Oh, boy, she's laying on her ridiculous, over-the-top French accent again. It's priceless.

"You're French?" he asks.

"Oui, I am."

"She's a chef," I say. "My private chef."

"Hmmm." He scratches his chin and shakes his head. He blinks. "I swear I've met you before. I used to know a girl. Her mother was French, owner of a bakery in Calabasas—lost contact with her, though. Years ago."

Julia swallows, her eyes darting to the window. She doesn't respond.

"I was going to invite Liam to stay for lunch." His gaze snaps to me. So does Julia's. My eyes meet his. "That is, unless you have plans? I mean, it will be a perk of working at the Drake house. Is that against the rules?"

"I don't think so," he says, looking at his watch.

Julia bites down on her bottom lip, her eyes wide.

"Lunch for four!" I exclaim. "Julia, what are you making?"

She shoots a scowl in my direction and forces a smile. "What would you like?"

"Something light," I say. "Maybe a ceviche? Madison loves it." I look toward Liam. "Do you like ceviche?"

"I do," he says. "A lot. My parents used to take me to this French restaurant in Santa Monica. I can't remember the name for the life of me."

Julia stands with her spine straight, clenching her teeth.

"L'Ondine," I say. "Julia's parents owned it."

"Yes, that was it." He grins. "I wonder what happened to them."

"My family moved to Paris," says Julia, her voice low.

"Uh-huh," says Liam. "Small world."

Lunch is a bust. Julia refuses to eat with us, just serves us and leaves, excusing herself. I'm thinking of sending Liam to check on her, but don't want to push Julia to the brink of insanity or, good Lord, to quit. I know she still thinks about Liam, keeping that old panda bear with all his letters tucked in them. Yes, I'm a snoop and I'd found them when Julia was at the store. I'd also found the photo of her parents.

Right after Liam leaves, such a polite and good-looking man, David calls, such a bastard.

"Erica."

"What?"

"I'm in the car on my way to pick up Tyler. And then I'll be heading back to Vegas."

This makes absolutely zero sense. He's up to something. I can feel it in my bones. He only shows love for Tyler when it looks good in the press.

"I don't get why you feel the need to pick him up."

"I forgot something at the house," he says flatly. "The brat home?"

I don't know if he's referring to me. "Madison?"

David and Madison have never really gotten along; they tolerate one another. I'm glad she's finally getting along with me, considering she knows full well that I was the other woman.

It took years to break down the barriers. But, in the end, she doesn't blame me for Valerie's death; she blames David. I'm surprised he'd adopted her when she's not even his; probably wanted the accolades instead of the bad press if he'd thrown her out on the street.

"Who else would I be talking about?" I hear the ding of his call waiting. "Gotta take this. See you soon."

An hour later, I'm watching the security monitor when the Phantom drives up. The Dragon, David, steps out, followed by Tyler. They walk toward the front entry, David's arm slung over Tyler's shoulder. They're laughing about something.

Acting all buddy-buddy with his son is not in David's arsenal of normal behavior. David was livid with Tyler's "arrest." He's the one who sent him to rehab, notably the one he'd sent me to as well. Malibu Oasis. Apparently, I was in the throes of another meltdown, bound to happen after filming *Swerve*. I actually adored my time in rehab—an escape from David and more like a spa. Maybe I'll have another meltdown. I open the front door, letting them in.

"Geez, Mom, stalk much?" says Tyler. "How'd you know we just pulled up?"

"Mom's—and wives—have a special kind of intuition," I say, catching David's eye. "About everything."

Tyler laughs. David glares. I curve my lips into a smile.

"It's good to be home," says Tyler, eyeing his Mercedes. "But what's my SUV doing in the drive? Has the suspension been lifted?"

"Nope," I say. "Julia's using it."

His nose scrunches. "Julia?"

"Our new chef," says David. His eyes glimmer. "You're going to love her."

And, just as if she's been cued, Julia rounds the corner.

She's wearing her wetsuit and red bikini ensemble, the top showing, carrying a surfboard. David licks his lips. Tyler's eyes go wide. Julia enters the garage and comes out board free. She waves and shoots us her pretty little grin and Tyler blushes.

"She can have my car," Tyler mumbles and David shoots him a look.

Madison races around the corner, wearing a climbing harness. She races up to us. "Tyler! You're home! The bluff is all set up! It's so rad. I'll go again if you want to—"

Tyler is about to respond with an enthusiastic yes, but David cuts him off.

"Madison, I paid for it. Tyler and I will have a go. A little father-and-son bonding time. And then I'll take off." He looks at his watch and slaps Tyler's back. "What do ya say, son?"

"Sounds good, Dad," says Tyler, clearly irked. He shakes his head, his eyes darting to the side. "Where'd Julia go?"

Madison blinks with irritation. David does what he always does; he ignores her, doesn't even ask her about her European adventure.

"It's her break." Madison slugs Tyler's arm. "Don't worry, you doofus, you'll see her tonight. She's making your favorites— spaghetti Bolognese with mushrooms and cookies. Just like you requested."

Tyler's top lip curls up and his shoulders lift. "I didn't make any requests. I didn't even know we had a chef."

"That was me. I know your favorites," I say.

"Mine, too," says David, frowning. "Too bad I'll have to miss it."

Such a shame.

I can't wait for David to leave so I can find out what he's up to. Flying back to pick up Tyler is the worst of excuses. He barely spends any time with his son and when he does they usually argue. "I'm going to take a little beachside power nap." I kiss Tyler's cheek. "I'm glad you're home. Have fun with your father. We'll catch up tonight over dinner."

Tyler grins. "What time is dinner?"

"Seven," I say as David shoots Tyler a look.

What? Does he think his son is competition for Julia's affection? Probably. I know how David's twisted mind works. Age, for him, is just a number.

There's a reason why Madison never invites friends over to the estate: David. He's hit on her girlfriends, serves them alcohol, tries to seduce them. One girl fell for his charm—a real *American Beauty* scandal that David quickly covered up by paying the girl's parents off.

"I have to respond to a couple of emails and then change into appropriate clothes," says David, eyeing his outfit—dark jeans worn with a tight white T-shirt. Why, hello, Simon Cowell. "Tyler, grab the gear and meet me at the top of the bluff in twenty."

Tyler nods.

"I'll head down to the beach with you, Erica," says Madison, holding up her phone. "Capture the moment."

"I'll be there in ten," I say. "I need to slather some sunscreen on."

Instead of napping, I watch the bluff with an eagle eye, Madison next to me, filming with her phone. They're both on the edge of the precipice and so is my heart. We're cringing with fear as we watch David rappel down the left side of the cliff, Tyler the right. And then relief. Five minutes later, they both climb up the bluff, gripping rocks, dirt and debris crumbling down to the beach as they search for crevices and foot-holes. Madison and I head back up the path, waiting. Tyler makes it back up first.

"Well, bonding with Dad for ten minutes was fun." He rolls

his eyes. "He's acting really strange. Kept asking me questions about Julia. Like what I thought about her."

"No shit, Ty," says Madison. "He's probably obsessed with her."

Tyler grins. "I might be, too. She cooks. She surfs. She's, like, my dream girl."

"You'd be jailbait." Madison slugs Tyler's arm. "She's seven years older than you."

"I'd go to jail for her."

"Dumbass, she'd be the one breaking the law, not you."

He grins. "A boy can dream."

It's at this moment David hoists himself onto solid ground, his brow covered in sweat. He looks at his watch. "That was exactly what I needed. I'm going to grab a quick shower and then take off." He kisses my cheek and hisses in my ear, "Be a good girl when I'm gone."

"Oh, darling, you know I'm always good." I blow him a kiss and he cringes. "I think Julia made you some snacks. They're in the refrigerator. I'm sure your climb worked up an appetite."

"Erica, I'm showering and then leaving."

Tyler grins. "Good. More for me."

As they walk away, Madison and I stand frozen for a moment. "Why don't we take a swim?" I suggest.

She nods. "Good idea."

We make our way back to the pool. After a quick dip, Madison heads over to Julia's, and I lay on one of the loungers, closing my eyes. Waiting. Fifteen minutes later, my phone beeps with an alert for the front door. He's gone.

I fly off the lounger and race to David's office. I search through his files, the ones in the filing cabinet and the ones on his computer, checking his latest notes for his scripts.

TWENTY-ONE

JULIA

I've been flipping out over Liam's surprise visit and David being back at the house. I'm not sure what Erica wants from me anymore and I'm sick and tired of her mind games, her odd glances of warning. After showering and dressing, I pull Liam's old letters out of the back of my panda, thumbing through them. They are always organized by date. Lo and behold, they are not in order.

Obviously, Erica or David had found them. And they'd seen the picture of my parents. I feel so violated. Like a criminal. And I haven't done anything wrong.

I put everything back in its place and I'm in the process of feeding Beurreboule when a knock comes at my door. If it's David, I'll scream bloody murder. I turn, a scowl on my face, and then smile; it's Madison. I wave her in.

"Sorry to bother you," she says. "I just wanted to tell you what a wicked surfer you are. You really slice those waves."

"Thanks," I say. "Can you close the door?"

"Why? It's, like, gorgeous out."

I point toward my orange, brown, and white ball of fluff and Madison squeals, "Oh my God, your cat is the cutest thing I think I've ever seen in my whole life! Can I pet her? What's her name? Does David the dick know she's here?"

I laugh. "One question at a time. Yes, you can pet Beurreboule, that's her name." I can't help but snort. "Does he know you call him David the dick?"

"I don't call him that to his face, mostly behind his back." She chuckles and scoops up Beurreboule, cuddling her. "I always wanted a cat or a dog. But he wouldn't allow it. He hates animals. Like beyond hates. Thinks they're dirty and diseased. Come to think of it, David the dick might be an animal."

"I take it you don't like him," I say, knowing I'm about to enter a topic that might upset her.

"Like him? I hate his fucking guts." She looks like she wants to say something else, but doesn't. Instead, she changes the subject. "Can I help you in the kitchen again tonight? I really enjoyed making the borscht and the bread the other day." She shrugs. "Erica barely knows how to boil water and I'd like to learn how to cook. One day, I'll be on my own."

I blink. Finally, I'm getting honest answers. I have another opening, one I have to be delicate with. "What's your relationship with her like anyway?"

Erica has profited greatly from her mother's death. Not only that, although David isn't Madison's biological father, Erica was the other woman.

"If I didn't have Erica and Tyler, I'd have nothing." Madison holds Beurreboule closer to her chest. "They are my family. David is not." She clears her throat. "And I do not want to talk about him. Kitchen? I can help?"

I nod. "Too bad I've already scrubbed the portobello mushrooms—I would have made you do it. You'll be on the chocolate chip cookies instead."

She salutes me. "Yes, chef."

"I do have another question for you," I say, before we leave. "Why did you really put that movie on the other night?"

Madison legs give out from under her and she sinks onto my bed.

"To remember her," she says, swallowing. "Just like in the movie, I was the little girl who found her in the pool. I was eight years old. He'd changed my name to Madeleine in the film." She shakes her head and then meets my eyes. "I like studying every scene in the film because I'm trying to find the lies." Madison's eyes lock on mine. She sets Beurreboule down and leans forward, almost with anticipation. "You look like you want to say something."

I clear my throat. "I just don't know how you could put yourself through that. And, honestly, I don't understand why you don't hate Erica."

Madison scoffs. "Don't you get it? Erica, like me, like my mom, is one of his victims." She puffs out her lip and swallows. "I did hate her for a long time. But after her last movie, something in our relationship shifted."

"What movie?" I ask, already knowing the answer.

"*Swerve*. Have you seen it?"

"I have," I say flatly, my eyes shooting toward the window and locking on the waves crashing onto the shore. Crash. My mind is swerving to the past. Crash. I need to keep it together.

"Anyway, Erica had a major breakdown after filming *Swerve*," Madison continues with a gulp. "Stayed at Malibu Oasis for a month. When she returned, we finally had the longest heart-to-heart—about my mom, about that film. About David."

My interest is piqued. "What about him?"

"We think he's pure evil. And so are his films."

No kidding.

"Why doesn't she leave him?"

"You'll have to ask her."

"What about you? I mean, you're eighteen, a legal adult. You don't have to stick around."

"I'm not sticking around. After graduating from Malibu High, I'm going to NYU in the fall and getting as far away from this shit show as possible." She gives Beurreboule one final pat and stands up. "I'm over talking about David the dick. I'd like to focus on something else. Let's hit it. I'll be your sous-chef."

We meander down the path, heading to the main house. I preheat the oven, and shuffle around opening cabinets, handing Madison a bar of seventy percent chocolate, flour, brown sugar, and we set to making chocolate-chip cookies—with my special ingredient, a dose or two, maybe three, of cocoa powder. Thanks to a mallet, once the chocolate bar is crushed to smithereens and everything is blended together, Madison dips her finger into the raw dough, tastes it.

"Oh my God! So good. Like I don't even want to cook this." She winks and then laughs. "Did I tell you I may be on a raw diet?"

I hand her a parchment-covered baking tray. "We're baking them."

"Fine," she says, placing spoon-sized dollops onto the tray. "What's next?"

"Making the sauce for the spaghetti." I turn and walk to the refrigerator, grabbing the mushrooms and some fresh herbs. I place them down on the chopping block and untie my roll bag of knives. One of them is missing.

Frantic, I search the kitchen, checking every drawer. Knives just don't get up and walk away. Somebody must have taken it. David? Erica? Why?

"What are you looking for?" Madison asks. "You're all jittery and weird."

"One of my knives is missing!"

"Maybe you left it at your place?" she offers.

I blink. It's quite possible. I did slice a kiwi this morning for breakfast. But I'm always so careful with my knives, cleaning and drying them after each use. And then putting them back in my roll bag. Then again, my mind has been a little scattered lately.

"Right. Right. Keep an eye on the stove. Take the first batch of cookies out in ten minutes. I'll be right back."

I'm about to sprint to my place when my gaze leaps to the bluff. Tyler, engrossed in his own world, is repeatedly stabbing the air in front of him, possibly imagining an invisible foe, maybe his father. And I've found where my missing knife has disappeared to.

"Hey, Tyler, what's going on?" I inquire gently, keeping a watchful eye on his hand and his feet, which are dangerously close to the edge of the cliff.

Tyler, with a bright smile, points to an imaginary opponent in the air. "I'm fighting dragons!" he exclaims and then stumbles. "Drake means dragon. Did you know that? I'm a dragon! Imagine Dragons! Love them." He blinks. "Wait, no, I'm not a real dragon. I don't have scales."

Panic washes over me. His eyes are crazed, dilated. He's definitely on something.

"Can I have my knife, please?"

He squares his shoulders. "I have to save us from the other dragons."

Tyler continues stabbing the air.

I honestly don't know what to do. "Tyler, follow me! Dragon slayers must get hungry."

He nods and wobbles, following me to the terrace. "Madison!" I bellow. "Take the cookies out of the oven. And come outside now."

Thirty seconds later, Madison rushes to my side. "What's going on?"

"You have to distract him. He thinks he's fighting dragons," I whisper. "I'll get the knife."

"Tyler! Julia and I made cookies! Chocolate chip, your favorite! Just for you."

I eye Madison.

"What?" she says. "He's crushing on you big time."

The knife drops from his grip.

"Tyler?" Madison asks. "Did you eat something before the dragons came?"

"They didn't come, they swarmed. Can't you see them? There's one right over Julia's head." He blows air into his cheeks. "Phew, it just swooped. Didn't get you." He grins and steps forward, his hand running over my hair. "You're so beautiful. Like a princess. And your hair is so soft. Like silk. I'm glad I saved you."

I take a breath. "What did you eat?"

He dances. "The mushroom snack you left for me and dad in the kitchen after our climb."

What in the world is going on? Madison glares at me. "I didn't leave a snack, Madison. I swear."

"What's in your cookie recipe?"

"Chocolate chips! You ate some of the batter!"

"I'm putting him to bed now. I'll make something up, say he has a stomach bug or something. Shit. This is bad." Madison meets my gaze. "Maybe he had something in his room, though it was searched. Like thoroughly."

As Madison escorts Tyler back to the house, I follow them, immediately throwing everything away, every ingredient in the garbage can—the cookies, the mushrooms, the meat, the noodles. Everything. I open the refrigerator; there is no snack, but there is a Post-it note on the floor.

Bon Appétit! xox, J

I pick it up. This is my handwriting. This whole situation, this place, is toxic.

As I race back to my living quarters, the belladonnas catch my eye. When I pull up the footage from the kitchen on my phone, the first clip is of Erica, grabbing her bottle of wine from the refrigerator. Then, she walks straight toward the camera with some odd device. It beeps. She shoots a satisfied grin and throws a kitchen towel over the lens.

Shit. She knows. But, with her look, maybe she thinks David is spying on her. That's what I'm hoping. I hear rattles and clanks. I can't see anything. A couple of moments later, she whips the towel off the lens, throwing it onto the floor with a smirk. She hisses, "I know you're spying on me, David. Guess what? You're busted."

Weird and kind of scary.

I shudder and fast-forward to the next clip. David pulls out a tray from the refrigerator—mushrooms with a soft cheese, on endive. Tyler enters the kitchen a minute later and David says, "Julia made these just for you."

Tyler smiles and grabs one. After he chews, he grins. "Delicious."

David looks at his watch. "I better take a quick shower and hit the road."

"I thought you were hungry. You don't want one?"

"I don't eat cheese," says David. "A bit lactose intolerant."

I'm stumped. Why would David drug his kid? Does he want him back in rehab? What does he want from me? I'm not leaving just yet. No, I'm coming after David, just not in the way he thinks.

TWENTY-TWO

ERICA

I switch the television off, livid. They're bringing up the past, calling me a liability on the news. I'm a drunk. I'm a high-maintenance bitch. I'm mentally imbalanced, the reason I'm able to switch personalities so easily, the reason I play women on the edge of madness. I'd tried tracking down the so-called "sources," to no avail. Because David *is* the source.

Being nominated for an Oscar has been my saving grace. Before Julia's arrival, I'd attended all the press junkets, the film festivals, hopped on from one talk show to the next. I've attended the luncheons, the industry mixers, the panel discussions. Sometimes the media loves me.

One interviewer asked me about my meltdown after filming *Swerve.* Of course, I'd already had my answer planned. "I'm a method actress—and that role, the character of Christine, took its toll on me. I suppose I took everything a bit too far. But I'm on the mend now and looking forward to my next part, hopefully a romantic comedy. Maybe *Love at First Latte 2.*"

This statement, of course, had everybody in stitches.

My cell buzzes. I look at caller ID: my agent, Lexi Gold. "Hey, hot stuff," she says. "There's a rehearsal tomorrow if—"

"Send a stand-in."

"Erica, you should really go."

"Goldie, this isn't my first time at the rodeo."

She sighs. "It's a preemptive measure. You have to show you're willing to play along."

I know exactly where this conversation is headed. I shake my head, sure that David has poisoned her mind against me, too. Time to test her loyalty.

"I read *The Lucky Widow*. Loved it. Connect with the story and the protagonist on so many levels..."

"That's great, but," she sighs, "it's a no-go."

"They don't even want me to audition for Emma's character?"

"Nope. I've been trying to convince them you'd be perfect. They don't want to awaken the dragon. And, honestly, I don't want to, either."

She's talking about David. He's claimed me as his own, his possession, and nobody in the industry will work with me because they're scared of the inevitable repercussions. He holds all the power and I feel powerless. I don't know why he doesn't just leave me. I suppose he's waiting for the perfect moment to make his move...and so am I.

"And if I win best actress next Sunday?"

"I think that could change everything," she says. "Go to the rehearsal."

"I can't," I say, not telling her the reason why.

I'm preparing for the biggest role of my life and the stakes have never been higher. All the characters have been cast, their fates intertwined with mine. There's just a major rewrite needed for the script I'd planned in my head, and I have to dissect each line, each scene, making sure the drama unfolds without David knowing what I've been up to.

"Fine," says Goldie, sucking in a breath. "I'll see you on Sunday."

"That's a given."

I end the call, seething. Here's the thing. I'm not afraid of David. He should be scared of me. What's that expression? Hell hath never seen fury like a woman scorned.

Julia—my thoughts race to her. I need her for the change in this new draft.

Madison races into my room, gulping. She paces in front of my bed. "Tyler, he's on something. I think David's trying to set up Julia for something."

I shake my head. "No, it's me he's after, trying to set me up like he did with Ollie Shore."

She slumps onto my bed. "Why would he do that to Tyler? I mean, he could have fallen off the bluff! He could have died!"

I know he could have, and the thought has my mind spinning.

I gulp. "Because maybe he doesn't want to get rid of just me. Maybe he wants to get rid of all of us."

I'm not saying anything we haven't discussed before. David only cares about one thing—himself.

"And Julia?"

"Oh, he wants to keep her."

"This is getting dangerous," she says, her eyes blazing with fear.

"Believe me, I know." I clasp her hands, trembling, not in fear, but anger like mine. "But he won't do anything until after the awards. And we still have time to prepare and come up with a new plan."

"How can you be so sure he won't do anything until then?"

"Because not only is he a sociopath, he's an extreme narcissist. He's expecting to win the Oscar with me by his side." My head pounds with uncertainty. I blink. "I wasn't counting on Julia's complete aversion to David. I thought hating me would be enough to drive her toward him. But she seems to hate him more. Has she opened up to you? At all?"

Madison sucks on her bottom lip and pinches her thumb and index finger, holding them an inch apart. "Almost."

I lower my gaze and shake my head in disappointment. "Keep trying."

Madison squeezes my hand. "I have to tell Tyler what's going on…"

"I agree," I say. "But let's wait until the effects have worn off." I grimace. "How long is that likely to take?"

"I don't know. A couple of hours?" Madison rubs her eyes and blinks. "He's sleeping it off right now. So, what do we do?"

"We need *her*," I say and Madison nods.

The two of us head down to the kitchen and Julia turns, her eyes flickering with dread.

"Erica, I'm sorry to be the bearer of bad news, but I have to get to the store for a change in menu," she says. "Something is wrong with the beef—it was bad or something."

I raise a brow. I know she's lying. She knows Tyler had been tripping the light fantastic.

"Yeah, Tyler ate some," says Madison. "He's really sick. Think he might have eaten raw hamburger."

"He's not a dog," I say, meeting Julia's gaze. "Did you get the meat at Gelson's in Calabasas?"

"Yes," she says, fidgeting.

"No, you didn't. I saw the containers with Whole Foods labels in the refrigerator. And you haven't given me the receipts for the petty cash." I stick out my chin. "Hand them over."

"Fine. I'll put them in the envelope later." She shakes her head with frustration. "Right now, I've got to get to the store."

I surreptitiously nudge Madison in the ribs with my elbow.

"I'll go with you," says Madison. "I need to pick up some things. Feminine things."

"Make sure Julia goes to Gelson's. The one in Calabasas. Not Whole Foods," I instruct. "Take Las Flores Canyon, it's quicker."

Julia's jaw clenches. "I am not taking Las Flores."

"Why? Is there a problem?" I ask, and she nods yes.

My heart races with anticipation. It's about damn time. She'll tell me what she wants. I'll tell her what I want. And we can all move on and get to the ending of the script: bringing David down.

"There was a mudslide on the road. It's blocked," she says, her eyes locking onto mine. "I saw it on the news. But I can take Malibu Canyon—and the better news for me is that there are no hairpin turns."

She shoots me a satisfied grin and I sigh. *Damn it, Julia, you're as stubborn as a mule.* Like the pet name she's come up with for me, the one I've heard her muttering behind my back: Lushika. Good one. I've now come up with one for her: Mulia. It's like she's made it her personal mission to test my limits at every turn.

"OK," I say. "Do what you need to do. I'm going to go check in on Tyler."

I leave the kitchen, noticing the surprised look Julia shoots Madison.

We all have our breaking points. Although Julia doesn't trust me, may hate me, she and Maddy have established a bond. As they leave, their footsteps echoing down the corridor, I cross my fingers, hoping Julia will finally come clean upon her return. It's a matter of life and death. On the latter topic, hopefully not mine.

TWENTY-THREE

JULIA

Madison and I are in the Mercedes, heading to Gelson's. In Calabasas. Although we're taking Malibu Canyon instead of Las Flores, I'm blinking with fear, my hands white-knuckling the steering wheel. Madison rolls her window down and gets comfortable in her seat, one knee on the dashboard.

"Music?" she asks, and I grunt out my agreement. "I'll link in my playlist."

She puts on No Doubt's "Different People" and I can't stop from blinking, my throat from catching. No Doubt was my mother's favorite band—and this was one of her favorite songs. She used to dance around the kitchen, her smile so big and bright, bopping around like a teenager, grabbing my hands and making me dance, too. The song is from the album *Tragic Kingdom*. No doubt, I've entered one.

"Is something wrong?" Maddy asks, lowering the volume.

"You like No Doubt?"

"No, duh. Gwen Stefani rocks. She's the coolest thing since... what's the baking expression?"

"Sliced bread."

"That's it," she says. "I have a question for you. You seemed really flipped out about driving on Las Flores. Did something happen?"

My grip on the steering wheel tightens. "Madison, I have to concentrate on driving. It's been a while. And I'm getting used to the roads here, OK? Las Flores has too many hairpin turns."

"OK," she says, eyeing me with suspicion.

Finally, we make it to Gelson's. We park and Madison and I barely step foot in the store when Barbara McGossip-Keegan rushes straight up to us, hitting my leg with her shopping cart. My nightmare of being recognized comes true and there is a witness—Madison.

McGossip—class president (people voted for her so she'd leave them alone), teacher's pet (the biggest kiss-ass on the planet), and a shark (nobody messed with her). She's rounder than I remember, but just as vivacious, annoyingly so, and bubbly. Her eyes light up with recognition.

"JoJo! JoJo! Oh my God! I thought that was you. My gosh, it's been what, seven, eight years?"

I stare at her blankly, pulling on my thickest, cartoonish French accent. "I'm so sorry. Desolée. I zink you 'ave me confused wif somebody else."

Barbara remains adamant. She tilts her head back and cackles. "No way! You're JoJo! Don't try to pull that on me! I'd recognize you anywhere."

Madison nudges my side and mouths, "What the hell?"

Maintaining my ridiculous accent, I try to defuse this bomb of a situation politely. "I assure you, I am not JoJo. My name eez Julia. Julia Fouquet."

"Good one! Julia! Haha! Do you keep in touch with Liam Harrington? He was quite the catch! I was always jealous of you."

"I don't know anybody named Liam. Excuse me. I 'ave to *faire mes courses*. I am chef."

My gaze shoots from Barbara to Madison, her brows raising.

She knows Liam is Tyler's tutor. Her chin lifts as if to say... got you.

Barbara insists, "You can't fool me, JoJo! What have you been up to?"

I'm about to lose it, growing beyond frustrated, and, once again, I attempt to redirect the conversation. "I zink zer has been a mistake. 'Ave a great day!" I wheel the cart around, praying for her not to make a scene, then nudge Madison to move along, feeling Barbara McGossip's eyes on my back.

Madison leans in and whispers, "OK, Julia, if that's your name, spill the beans. Who is JoJo, and why did you sound like a freak, laying the French accent on so thick you sounded like Pepé Le Pew? I've noticed you use it with Erica and David the dick, too."

Realizing my cover might have a chink, I chuckle nervously. "JoJo is apparently someone I'm not. Just a case of mistaken identity. And as for the accent, well, let's just say I was messing with that woman. Haven't you ever done something like that?"

"No." Madison raises an eyebrow. "You're a terrible actress, Jules. What's really going on?"

I sigh, realizing my slip. "It's complicated, Madison. I need you to trust me, OK? There are things I haven't shared, but it's for a good reason. Can we talk about it later?"

She nods, a mixture of concern and curiosity in her eyes. "OK. Whatever you say." She throws her hands in the air. "But that was a truly bizarre encounter."

We continue shopping, an unspoken mystery lingering between us, Madison shooting me sly glances. Finally, the torture ends, and we load up the bags in the car. Thankfully, we'd skirted Barbara and I didn't run into anybody else from my past. My neck hurts—rigid from being on the lookout. My head pounds, throbbing with uncertainty.

Something is off. Madison said she'd needed to pick up some things, but save for a box of ginger green tea, she didn't throw anything else into the shopping cart. I let out a grunt. "I thought you needed tampons or something?"

She laughs. "No, I just wanted to get away from Erica."

Understandable.

When we get back to the house, I slam the shopping sack onto the counter. "We went to Gelson's, Erica. Happy?"

Her eyes meet mine with one of those vague looks of warning.

"I don't know what I am." She brushes one finger over her lips, shakes her head, and mouths, "We need to talk. But not here." Her voice raises in pitch. "Madison, shall we show Julia the ropes before dinner?"

She nods. "I have to change, grab the gear. Meet at the bluff."

"I have to change, too," says Erica, eyeing me. "What shoe size are you, Julia?"

Where is this conversation headed? "Thirty-eight in Europe. Seven and a half here. Why?"

She nods. "Same size as me. Go put on something sporty, like what you wore the first day. And a long-sleeved T-shirt, if you have one."

I stand numbly, shaking my head. "Look, Erica, I'm not up for sunset yoga on the beach..."

"Hmm," she mumbles as if deep in thought. "That's not a bad idea. I haven't done that in such a long time." She turns and strides away, looking over her shoulder. "Just meet us at the top of the bluff. Ten minutes. And then we'll talk. Maybe do some yoga, too."

By the time I make it to the bluff, Madison is already there, unloading equipment from a large bag. She's on her hands and knees and she shoots me a grin when I make my approach. "You can take the path down to the beach. Erica and I will meet you there."

"You're climbing?"

"We are."

I jut out my chin. "Then I am, too."

Madison eyes me curiously. "I thought you've never been climbing, that you had a fear of heights."

"I lied."

"So did I. I'm a wicked surfer." Madison stands up and laughs, handing me a harness and a helmet. "When was the last time you climbed?"

"Eight years ago," I respond with a frown. "With my dad. I learned the ropes when I was twelve at an indoor wall." My throat catches. "Then, after I'd progressed, we used to go to Point Dume..."

Her eyes meet mine. She raises an inquisitive brow, but doesn't press on for more information.

"OK. So we have three anchor points, two bolts per setup, so two people can rappel down the bluff at the same time. For extra security, right now I'm installing a sling on one of the systems..."

I cut her off. "Prusik? Belay device? Got it."

"Yeah. Since you haven't done it for a while, I'll go over the safety instructions and all that. Erica will rappel down first..."

I jolt. "Erica climbs? I thought it gave her hives."

"No, she's really experienced. She's the one who taught Tyler, David, and me." Madison blurts out a laugh. "It was her idea to install the bolts into the bluff... and the anchors."

I stand, numb. Just fabulous. We're all liars. And I've been keeping the biggest secret of all. But something about the way Erica and Madison are behaving tells me they know the truth. I clench my fists into tiny balls when Erica rounds the corner.

"I'll go down first," says Erica. "I'll be on the ground for a fireman's belay. You'll go second. And then Maddy will join us."

Before I can respond, Maddy throws the rope over the side of the bluff. "We're all set. The first system is good to go. No need to hook up the second. Anchors are solid. Every knot is precise, every line taut."

Erica nods, securing the harness around her waist and legs, the belay loop at the front ready with a carabiner and ATC to receive the rope. For a moment, I forget my anger. I'm actually looking forward to doing this. With each check, each tug on the gear, a sense of anticipation builds up inside me. She clips the chinstrap on her helmet in place, clipped quickdraws and carabiners hanging off the harness jingling softly like chimes in the breeze as she stands poised on the edge of the bluff.

With a final glance at the azure sky above, Erica shakes out her hands and then drops to her knees. After positioning herself on her stomach, she leans back, her feet planted on the rocks. She winks. "See you on the beach."

I watch her rappel down the sheer face of the bluff, descending in controlled bounds, five feet at a time, the rope, a slender lifeline, feeding smoothly. Halfway down, like a dancer in mid-air, she pauses momentarily before springing off the rock, legs pushing against the stone to propel her downward. The rhythm of her descent is mesmerizing—bound, pause, bound, pause. I watch in awe.

Finally, her feet plunk into the sand. She yanks the rope three times. Madison smiles. "Your turn. Ready?"

"You bet I am."

"Remember, one hand keeps a firm grip on the belay device at all times, the other hand on the rope. Watch for loose debris. And if you need to stop, lean back and let the device do its work. Have fun." She grins. "Trust the gear. Trust yourself."

Oh, I trust the gear. I trust myself. I just don't trust Erica.

"How high up are we, anyway?"

"I think thirty-five meters, so around one hundred and fifteen feet." She shrugs. "Erica had bolts installed everywhere for the climb back up. Don't worry. It's not a hard climb—probably in between 5.7 and 5.9 and clear."

"Got it."

We do a final check on the gear before I descend. Madison gives me a reassuring nod as I ready myself at the edge of the bluff. And then I lean backward, using the rope to guide me, taking one step down, positioning my feet on the slight incline before the first drop. The adrenaline pumping through my veins, the thrill, the everything. The bluff, now bathed in glorious orange and pink hues from the setting sun, isn't imposing but magical. Ethereal. Before I know it, my feet plunk into the sand. Like Erica, I tug the rope three times, and soon Madison makes her descent.

"Julia," says Erica. "We can talk now."

My cellphone buzzes. I look quickly at it. Chloe. It buzzes again. Chloe. Another text. Chloe. I ignore it and meet Erica's eyes. "Sorry about that. Bad timing. Now tell me what what's going on."

"I will. No cameras here, except for mine," says Erica. "And, on that, the gardens should be safe."

"David planted cameras?" I ask.

"Only in the kitchen. And, since he's been back, he probably put one in the guesthouse to spy on you."

This explains Erica's odd behavior, how she'd smirked into the camera. It also explains why I've had that shaky feeling that somebody has been watching me.

"Look, would you just tell me what the hell is going on?"

"I'm getting to that, Julia." Erica smiles wickedly. "Or should I say, Josephine?"

My jaw goes slack. I'd done everything in my power to make sure nobody knew who I was and for very good reasons. My brain feels like it's about to short circuit as it flashes to the past.

Eight years ago, fate dealt me a cruel hand when a car crash snatched both of my parents away, leaving me orphaned. When I moved to Paris with my trustees, my mother's best friend Marie and her husband, Bernard, I wanted a clean break. I didn't want anybody to know who I was. I didn't want my past to follow me around. I didn't want pity. I wanted a new life. I wanted a new name. A new everything. Along with my name change, my adoption records were sealed. I have dual citizenship.

I thought working for Hollywood's golden couple would bring me one step closer to my dreams, but here comes the sickest twist. Her movie *Swerve* was about my parents. They made my mother, Christine, out to be a floozy French chef having an affair with a big Hollywood producer so she could put down the baking mitts and get into acting. During their torrid affair, she'd fallen pregnant and my father, Stephen Brooks, portrayed as a jealous and obsessive husband, drove their car off a cliff on the switchback roads of Las Flores Canyon, the car exploding in a drunk driving murder/suicide wake.

The only true facts portrayed in the film were that my parents died, and they were the owners of That French Café in Calabasas. The rest is fabricated bullshit. My mother wasn't pregnant—her autopsy report proves that. My mother wasn't having an affair with a producer. My parents were desperately in love. Knowing how my parents died is one thing; seeing how they died in Technicolor is another story altogether.

"It wasn't our fault," my mother's dying words echo in my mind. "There was another car on the road. I saw that actress." At the time, what she'd said didn't make any sense. But, when I watched that film, the pieces, her words, clicked right into place. *That actress* was responsible for my pain and suffering. She was there. She knows what happened.

My shoulders tense and I let out a bloodcurdling scream. "You've known who I was the whole time! And you've been messing with my mind! What the hell is wrong with you?"

TWENTY-FOUR

ERICA

I knew Julia would react this way. I would, too. I'd flip out. I'd
scream. I'd swear. Honestly, I would have killed me. I place a
hand on her shoulder. "OK, once you settle down, I'll tell you
everything."

She sinks into the sand on her knees. Her bottom lip trembles. "You better tell me everything," she chokes. "And I want
the truth."

Oh, she'll get the truth—at least my version of it. I've been
waiting for this moment.

I let out a low wheeze and whimper, "I don't want you to
hate me, even more than you probably already do. When I hired
you—and yes, I sought you out—I thought, she's the key to get
me out of this marriage to an absolute monster." I sit on the sand
next to her and Madison follows suit.

Julia glares at me. "Go on."

"I knew you hated my guts. I saw it in your eyes after you
watched *Swerve*—probably stuck around so you could take
some kind of revenge against me. Am I right?"

"Maybe," she says, not meeting my gaze. She whips her
head to the side, her jaw clenched. "Right now, I want to know

why? Why would you do this to me? Put me in this messed-up position?"

"First, I have to tell you about David. I was from the trailer parks in Fresno when I came to LA with glitter in my eyes, a starlet dreaming big dreams—"

"I know," she says with frustration. "I saw your interview on YouTube, the one with Tabitha Sinclair. Get to the point."

"Every story has a beginning, a middle, and an end. I'm starting at the beginning."

Julia leans back on her elbows, motions with her hand for me to carry on.

"I did bit parts, here and there, some extra work, and I even had a lead part in a film—a crappy film, *Love at First Latte*, the one you saw on the plane. And then one day David called my agent to have me come in and audition for the lead role in *Women on the Edge*. I got that part, and he promised me the moon and the stars."

"I really don't care," she huffs.

"You will. We had an on-again, off-again affair. At the time, he was married to Madison's mother, and didn't believe I was pregnant. He didn't speak to me for three years, avoided my calls. But after he'd met Tyler, he told me that I was the love of his life, and that he was finally going to leave her. He promised. He set me up in a little apartment. I was young and so, so stupid, I believed everything he told me..."

"Idiot," says Madison.

"I know I'm an idiot—don't rub salt into my wounds. He did take care of Tyler and me, making sure we had everything we needed. We saw each other two or three times a week. He told me, 'Hang on. It's only a matter of time.'" I focus on the horizon. A tear slides down my cheek. "He told me he was leaving her. And, finally, that day came."

"Erica played my mother—the psychotic breakdown, the suicide," says Madison. "The movie we watched."

"What about my parents?" Julia hisses. "My mother saw you that morning. She told me."

"I know. I saw her, too. Our eyes met in the headlights as David swerved the car into the other lane."

"It wasn't a murder–suicide..."

I shake my head. "I'm not sure. After reading the script and playing the role of your mother, Christine, I think he was chasing her down, maybe stalking her. I'd met her before at the bakery. I'd seen her interact with him." I rub my eyes, blink. "Anyway, that morning, he insisted on taking Las Flores. It was pouring and there were mudslides and he refused to turn around..."

"You weren't at the wheel?"

"No." I swallow. "After he swerved into the other lane, I saw their car lose control, I begged David to pull over. But he kept driving. I was three months pregnant at the time and when he slammed down on the brakes, the seat belt dug into my belly." I squeeze my eyes shut. "I lost my baby that morning. Your mother wasn't pregnant. I was. Yep, based on a true story."

She swallows. Hard. "And me? How did you find me?"

I meet her gaze, her eyes flickering with distrust, but not hate. "I was at the hospital, too. I saw you, saw the Fouquets. We'd eaten at l'Ondine so many times, I recognized them. Yes, I searched you out. Let's put it this way, the tears I cried in the movie were real. And shortly after filming, I did develop a drinking problem—stayed at Malibu Oasis for a month, trying to figure out a way to get away from him."

Julia launches herself off the sand, kicking it. She stomps toward me and pokes my clavicle with her finger. "You have had so many opportunities to tell me that you knew who I was, to tell me what you know. And you didn't."

"I was hoping you'd tell me."

"So, you've been torturing me? I mean, come on, putting the lavender in my room, the tarantula, sending me that bandana."

My jaw drops. "What bandana?"

"The one my mother used to wear. The one I wore the other night."

I lower my head, shaking it. "I didn't send it. David was obsessed with your mother. And I'm wagering that the bandana is actually hers."

The wind picks up around us. She shivers. "What is your goddamn plan? And how do I fit into it?"

My hair whips into my eyes. "People in Los Angeles are always after something. I was testing your character."

"I'm not a character. I'm a person," she hisses. "Tell me about this big plan of yours."

"When I saw the screenshots Jasmine sent me of you, so young, so beautiful, just like your mother, I knew David wouldn't be able to resist you. He's had his affairs, of course, but I needed him to be obsessed, like he was with her. I hoped you would hate me, fall in love with David to spite me, or pretend to when he promised you your dream of opening a restaurant." I grimace. "I was going to fake my own death, right on Las Flores —drunk-driving—and leave for Costa Rica." I look at the sunset. "I've been saving my pennies for a rainy day."

"Tyler and I were going to run away," says Madison. "Meet up with Erica there."

"You and Tyler both know about this?" she asks, blinking rapidly.

"Of course. We tell each other everything."

A long silence follows. We listen to the waves crashing on the shore. Julia paces on the beach, kicking up sand.

"First of all, I'd never let that man near me. I hate him. Profiting from my parents' death! Making up all those lies about them!" She leans back and screams into the wind, then straightens herself up and stomps toward me. Her body trembles with anger. "Second, this plan of yours is absolutely ridiculous. I'm wondering why I'm here. Why I've stayed."

"I'm wondering why, too," I reply, and her jaw goes slack.

She throws her head back and howls. "Because I want the truth about what happened to my parents. I want to clear their names!"

"And maybe a little revenge?" asks Madison, arching a brow.

Julia's shoulders cave forward. "At first, yes. But, right now, I want him to suffer... to know pain."

"Me too," says Madison with a heavy sigh. "That's why I've been studying the film he wrote about my mother. I think he may have played a role in her death, too."

A vein pulses in her neck. She clenches her teeth, shaking her head. Clearly, she's thinking everything over. Her eyes narrow. "I don't know how a woman who is constantly drunk can come up with a plan."

Madison tilts her head back in laughter. "She's a really good actress."

"I've seen her drinking. A lot."

"Have you tasted her wine? The Miraval? It's water with a little strawberry syrup."

She slams her hands on her sides. "Are you serious?"

"I do have a real glass now and then," I say with a shrug. "Now that you know what's going on, the choice is yours, Josephine. Stay or leave."

I'm hoping she stays. I need her.

"This is all so insane, but I'm in. I've stuck it out this far. That man needs to be destroyed before he damages anybody else." Her voice raises in pitch. "Because it's a lot of damage, leaving scars on your heart. Scars that will never heal. You can cover them up, but you know they are there." Her gaze shoots from Madison to me. "I still don't trust one bone in your skinny body, but I hate him more. What do you need me to do?"

"Play along, pretend you adore him, until we figure out our next move," I say. "Keep in mind, we still have to call you Julia."

"But I'm a terrible actress."

I let out a soft laugh. "No, you're much better than you think you are. Just tease him a little bit like you have been—before turning around and gagging. And don't reveal to anyone that your name is Josephine. You are Julia. Only Julia."

"Oh, and make sure you wear both contact lenses," says Madison with a snigger. "You kind of look like David Bowie right now—one eye slate blue, the other green. Heterochromia—that's what they call it."

"Damn it, I feel like an idiot." Julia slaps her hand to her forehead and blinks. "As long as we're getting everything out in the open, and my pathetic cover has been blown, you should know that I've been trying to trap both of you," she says, her voice just above a whisper.

"How?" I ask, feigning interest.

"I may have planted cameras in the kitchen and the dining room."

I wasn't born yesterday. I know and I'm glad she's fessed up.

"Keep them there," I say with a forceful nod. "And give me the codes. I'd like to keep an eye on him, too." I look toward the sky. "It's about to get dark. Shall we head back?"

Madison groans. "Rappelling is the fun part. Now we have our work cut out for us. Unless we take the path..."

"I don't want to take the path. I'm a method actress," I say with force. "David thinks he's a method director, but I don't think he has one creative bone in his body."

"I'm in," says Madison.

I look toward Julia. "Are you?"

She doesn't say anything for a moment, just stands there shaking her head and kicking rocks. She clenches her teeth. "Yes, to climbing. But, as to the plan, before I make any decisions, I have one question. And it's for Madison."

Maddy meets Julia's gaze, both of their eyes blazing with

determination. A fire. These young girls are putting the intense into intensity. "What?"

"If David isn't your biological father, who is?"

Madison licks her lips nervously and a tear slides down her cheek. "I don't know. I tried doing one of those DNA tests... found nothing. And my mom died before I could ask her." Her posture crumbles. "I was only two when they married, just happy to have a dad."

"Do you think your dad could be David?"

"Gawd," says Maddy. "I hope not. He's evil incarnate."

Julia places her hands on Maddy's shoulders. "I'm in. Just to be clear. I'm doing this for you. We're both looking for the same thing, right? The truth?"

"Damn straight," says Maddy. "I'm glad you're here."

"I'm not," says Julia. "Not exactly..."

Maddy wraps her arms around Julia. "I get it."

Good. It's hard to keep a satisfied grin from spreading across my face. I knew I'd eventually get Julia where I wanted her. It just took a lot longer than I'd thought.

ACT THREE
LE FROMAGE

(Stay at the table and, perhaps, order another bottle of wine.)

False face must hide
what the false heart doth know.

—William Shakespeare, *Macbeth*

FADE IN:

INT. MALIBU KITCHEN—DUSK

Hands sharpen a knife, the sound of scraping metal.

                    MAN (V.O.)

What's for dinner?

                    WOMAN (V.O.)

Something unexpected. I think you'll
like it.

                     MAN (V.O.)

I can't wait.

                    WOMAN (V.O.)

Neither can I.

The knife slams into a tomato. The tomato
splatters.

FADE OUT

TWENTY-FIVE

JULIA

Act like everything is normal. Pretend like I adore David. Great advice, Erica.

I'm only staying for Madison. We get each other. Erica does *not* get anything. Even when it appears that she's being honest, telling the truth, I know I'm not getting the whole story. To me, withholding information is just as bad as lying.

So, I'm protecting myself—and Madison. She's basically gone through the same things as I have.

My brain swims in between trust and distrust. I'm back to thinking that Madison could be one of Erica's ploys. But why? And for what purpose? She knows I'm dead set against seducing David.

I have two extra cameras. I'm placing one in my room, not to spy on myself, but to catch David in the act of doing something shady. The question is where? My eyes dart to each and every corner, finally landing on the middle window, a place to capture the entire space, save for the bathroom and the corner with the reading chair.

Erica's non-existent plan I'm now a part of percolates in my brain as I stomp down the path toward the main house. My thoughts meander to the dark side: a belladonna salad, prepared for David with a note. *Bon appétit, x J* I shake the thought off when Tyler shuffles into the kitchen, his head hanging low. "I'm sorry for yesterday."

"Not your fault," I say, my eyes darting toward the camera. Not the one I'd placed, but in the direction of the one I'm sure David hid.

"Sometimes I get a little messed up. I'm a work in progress." Tyler mouths, "I know."

"I'm just glad you're feeling better," I reply, sounding like a chipper French robot.

He shoots me a goofy grin. "I am. What's for breakfast, chef?"

Obviously, Maddy or Erica updated him on everything. We're all to act normal. As if we don't know a thing. As if we're not aware of David's hidden cameras. As if we're happy to live in paradise. As if we don't know he's a twisted sociopath.

"Whatever you want," I reply, and he blushes.

"Scrambled eggs and toast?" His voice cracks. "Maybe some bacon?"

"Coming right up." I'm in the midst of grabbing a pan when my cell rings. I hold up a finger. "In a minute. I may need to take this."

Tyler nods, sitting back on his stool. "Cool."

The moment I click on the call, Chloe bursts into tears, her breath ragged. "Thank God, I finally got you."

"You did. What's going on?"

"I didn't get the part in *The Sunset Stripper*," she gulps and then continues, "but David Drake is working on a new script he thinks I'd be perfect for and he had me read for it." She chokes back a sob and sputters, "I can't tell you what happened over the phone. I'm... um... still coming to grips with it myself. Can you meet me somewhere? It's important."

I feel the color draining from my face. The pan drops from my hand and onto the floor.

"Meet me in the parking lot, the one at the beach at Point Dume Cove in fifteen minutes," I say, my voice shaking, and Chloe sniffles her agreement. I turn to Tyler, my back rigid. "There's fruit in the refrigerator—"

"I overheard your friend. She's kind of loud and super upset," says Tyler with concern. "Don't worry about me. Go. I can fend for myself."

I grab my keys—or, rather, his keys off the hook. "Tell your mom I'll be back soon."

Tyler mumbles, "I will. If she is my mother."

I stop midstep. "What?"

He waves a dismissive hand and then rubs his eyes. "Nothing. Ignore me."

I look at his face—the shape of his lips, the freckles spattering his nose. It's just occurred to me that Tyler doesn't really look like either of them. He's lankier than David, but that could be attributed to Erica's side of the family. "Why would you say that?"

He shakes his head, his lips pinched into a frown. "I think I'm adopted. Like, how could I come from those people? They're both whacked." He snorts. "Might be paranoid, but..."

"But what?"

"I don't know. It's nothing. But there are so many lies in the house, I just kind of want the truth." He shrugs. "Madison is the only one who knows."

I swallow. "Why are you sharing this with me?"

He rubs his eyes with the tips of his fingers. "Maddy told me that I could trust you. She told me everything about you, how you're looking for the truth, too."

His gaze slides onto mine. He's expecting an answer. "I do."

Tyler lowers his gaze. "I, uh, actually sent in one of those

DNA tests. It's like a gut feeling. I mean, there are literally no baby pictures of me. Not one. Something is off."

Understatement of the century.

Off-season there's plenty of parking at the Westward Beach lot, just a couple of other cars, probably people taking advantage of the beautiful morning to hike the 1.8-kilometer trail. Situated atop buried volcanic rock with stunning ocean views, I'm taking advantage of the privacy. Chloe is waiting for me when I pull up, pacing in front of her yellow VW bug. The moment I hop out of the SUV, she races up to me, huffing and puffing and crying. She wipes off her tears and her nose with the sleeve of her hoodie. "Finally! You're here."

I give her a hug and then nod to the trailhead. "Let's walk. And you can tell me what's going on."

As we meander to the path, she rattles on in breathless French. "I met him. David Drake. I went to the open call for that stripper movie. Stood outside the front gates of the studio for hours until a man with a buzz cut pointed at me and said, 'You! You're up.'" She kicks a rock and lowers her head. "I was so excited. But, instead of going inside the studio, the man led me to an office."

"David Drake's, I assume."

"Uh-huh. The moment I walked in, he stood up, introducing himself, and his eyes scanned my body. And then I introduced myself, handing over my comp with my résumé on the back. He looked at it briefly and set it down on his desk. Then, he asked me if I was French. 'Oui, I am,' I said."

We stop on the path and she takes a deep breath, meeting my eyes. "Don't worry, I didn't tell him I knew you. But here's where everything fell to pieces. He said I was wrong for *The Sunset Stripper* role, but he may have a part for me in a film he's in the process of writing. He asked me if I'd like to read for it and I said yes, of course." Her jaw tightens. "The character he had me audition for... after she seduces the main lead and she falls in love with him, she kills his wife—" Chloe bursts into tears, her shoulders heaving up and down. "He asked me to do a little improv, to take my clothes off and seduce him. He-he-he—"

She doesn't need to tell me what happened.

"Chloe," I say, trying my best to keep my voice steady. I can feel the blood rushing out of my face. "Did you report him to the police?"

"No." Chloe's head drops with shame, her shoulders shaking. "And he didn't exactly rape me. I let him—"

I wrap my arms around her, pulling her in for a hug. "He used his power to get what he wants. Same thing."

"You've got to get out of that house. He doesn't want me. I think he wants you." She chokes on her sobs. "I think the film is about you. It's called *The Private Chef*."

When I return to Hummingbird House, I'm shaken to the core. Madison, Tyler, and Erica wait for me on the beach. "What's going on?" Erica asks.

I let out a disgusted grunted. "David is in the process of writing a new script.."

"*The Evil Wife?*"

"No, *The Private Chef*." I explain what Chloe shared with me.

Erica's face blanches. "That poor girl. Did she report him to the police?"

I shake my head no. "She's scared of what it would do to her career."

Erica's jaw goes slack. "We have to get our hands on his script or his notes." She shakes her head with dismay. "There's just one problem. He'll be home in a couple of hours. Let me think on this. Until then—"

"Yeah, Mom," says Tyler. "Act like everything is normal."

"I'll argue with him," says Madison.

"I'll pretend I'm drunk," says Erica.

All eyes shoot to me. I squeeze my eyes shut. I'm supposed to flirt with him, make him think I want him. "I don't know if I can do this."

"You can," says Erica. "You have to. Just put your mind in another place, like an out of body experience. Focus on the outcome, the final scene."

I bite down on my bottom lip. My life has turned into a horror film.

My hands move with practiced precision as my knife slices over the scales of a cod, flakes of silver floating into the sink, but my mind is elsewhere. Erica's plan is insane, which might make me insane, too. Not paying attention to what I'm doing, I nick my hand, slicing my palm. Regardless of the cut, the droplets of blood raining down onto the floor like thick raspberry jam, I need to keep calm and cook on. I wrap a kitchen towel tightly around the wound and then head back to the guesthouse.

After slathering the cut with petroleum jelly and then wrapping up my hand again with some gauze, I'm in the process of shaking out Beurreboule's dry food into her bowl. She usually skids right up to me, knocking over her water dish. I call for her. Nothing. Not one little meow. I look under the bed. I look in drawers, in the closet. This can't be happening. She's missing.

Frantic, I race around the property, panicked, screaming, "Petit chat!"

And then I see David holding her, stroking her under the chin by the pool. "Oh my God! You found her!"

"She's yours?"

"Oui," I say. "I don't know how she got out."

"You must have left the door open." He hands her over to me. "You should be more careful. Coyotes. Snakes. It's a wild world in SoCal."

He doesn't need to remind me. I'm looking at a savage animal. And I did not leave the door open.

I will my heart to stop racing. "Merci for finding her."

His eyes lock onto the gauze wrapped around my hand, to the blood splatters on my cream linen pants. "Did you cut yourself?"

"I did. Eet's a hazard of the trade. Burns, too."

"Do you want me to dress your wound?" he asks. "I'm pretty good at it. Tyler's always been accident prone."

Does he have a bandage big enough for my life? Enough words to tell me that everything will be OK? No, he doesn't. Because he's the one who created the scar. I'm supposed to seduce this man, make him think he stands a chance with me. But I almost blow it when I get all twitchy and nervous. I have to follow Erica's advice, find my motivation, put myself in another space, detach myself from the current situation. Become someone else.

I tilt my head to the side. "Zat would be very nice of you."

He winks. "I'll go grab the first aid kit."

With my smile dropping from my face, I scramble back to the guesthouse, placing Beurreboule on my bed. I pull up the video feed on my phone, pretending to check emails. I never got the chance to place the cameras upstairs—so I placed one in mine. A cough comes from the doorway.

David is leaning against the frame, holding a first aid kit.

I want to scream.

TWENTY-SIX

ERICA

I'm having a glass of "wine" on the veranda while David drinks a Scotch. Julia walks by, her left hand bandaged like a mummy. A lump forms in my throat. I'm wondering if this was David's doing. He knows all about cuts—but mostly when he screams out the word when filming.

"Julia, what on earth happened to your hand?" I ask, slurring dramatically.

"Just a slip of my knife," she says, *slip* sounding like *sleep*. "Nothing to worry about. David helped me with the wound. I'm fine now."

Hmmm. Maybe she could accidentally slip her knife into David's neck. There's an idea, one that has me grinning internally.

"I'm less worried about your hand than the blood on the kitchen floor. Clean it up," I snap. "And I really hope our meal isn't infected with your germs. What if you have a disease?"

"I am not diseased," she says, her eyes wide. "And I can wear gloves..."

"I'm thinking we should order in," I say.

David clears his throat. "Oh, Erica, stop being so mean to

Julia. Damn, you really are insufferable. Like a viper." He grins at Julia. "What's for dinner tonight, chef?"

For a brief moment, she goes silent until I clear my throat. She snaps to attention.

"First course is a vichyssoise—a leek and potato soup. Then, seared fillets of cod served with a salad and roasted rosemary potatoes—"

There are many ways to fillet a fish—especially when Julia bats her eyelashes at David and then glares at me. She's got this. So do I.

"I told you no carbs! No starches! Damn it, why don't you listen!"

"Zey are for Madison and Tyler," she says, lowering her head, her mouth in a pout.

"Erica, would you calm the hell down? Have another glass of wine," says David. "Dessert?"

"Mousse au chocolate."

"Sounds delicious," says David, licking his lips. He sniggers and glares at me. "Your idea to hire a chef. We are not ordering in."

Julia looks at her watch. "Alors, I better finish up the meal. Dinner will be served in an hour."

As Julia heads toward the kitchen, David's gaze glides onto her ass. He blinks with every step she takes. I slam back my fake glass of wine, needing a real one. I'm not stressed about Sunday's awards ceremony. I'm stressed about David and our plan to get rid of him. I close my eyes, manifesting the outcome in my head and he's not in prison.

An hour later, Julia announces that it's time for dinner, using the intercom. The four of us—Madison, Tyler, David, and me—convene in the dining room. Tyler's wearing his earbuds, listening to music. Madison scrolls on her phone. I pour myself another glass of wine.

David slams his hand on the table, the plates and bowls

trembling like they do during an earthquake. "How many times do I have to tell you kids—no phones, no gadgets at dinner?"

"It's not like we talk anyway." Madison looks up and then continues scrolling on her phone. She grumbles, "And I'm not a kid anymore. I'm a legal adult."

David stands up and stomps over to Madison, ripping the phone from her hands. "My house. My rules," he hisses and then he shoots Tyler a death glare. "I mean it. Both of you will get your devices back after dinner."

"Fine," says Tyler, taking out his earbuds, handing them over.

David takes his seat, locking eyes with Tyler. "Heard you weren't feeling that well the other day. Anything you want to tell me?"

I know Tyler wants to say, *you drugged your own kid, I could have fallen off the bluff or worse, and we're going to find out why*, but Ty knows better.

Tyler shrugs. "Just had one of those twenty-four-hour bugs. Something I ate. No biggie."

David's eyes narrow. "Something Julia made?"

"I was still hungry after the climb, and I found some granola bars in my room." Tyler grimaces. "They must have gone bad. After I ate them—man—explosive diarrhea, like it just came pouring out of me—"

"Ew, disgusting, dumbass." Madison makes over-the-top gagging noises. "Like, we're about to eat dinner."

Good one, Ty. He'd come up with his little lie yesterday and, judging by David's expression, it's worked, throwing his dad off. David clenches his teeth, shaking his head from side to side. "Madison, don't call Tyler names."

She snorts. "But it's the truth. He is a dumbass."

Tyler slugs her arm and David mumbles something indiscernible under his breath, most likely *I can't wait to rid myself of all of you.* The frown pinching his lips turns upside down when Julia carries a tray into the room.

"The first course is a classic recipe, a vichyssoise, but, although created by a French chef, Louis Diat, eet ees not exactement French as eet was invented at the Ritz Carlton in New York." She places a bowl in front of David, leaning slightly into him and brushing her hand lightly across his arm. "It's déli-cieux." She brings her fingers to her lips, blowing a French chef's kiss with a tiny smack of her lips. "This puréed leek and pomme de terre soup is also made with cheeken broth, onions, cream, garnished with chopped chives and served chilled."

Over David's shoulder, Julia shoots a sly wink in my direction, serves the rest of us, says "bon appétit," and saunters out of the dining room, David's eyes following her every step.

"I think I'm in love," says Tyler, picking up his spoon.

David scoffs, "You don't know anything about love."

Under my breath, I mumble, "Neither do you."

"Why doesn't she eat with us?" asks Tyler.

"Because she works here, dumbass," says Madison.

The rest of the meal goes the same way—a stilted conversation, me drinking my wine, David practically drooling every time Julia serves us dishes or clears the plates away. It's also obvious that Tyler is crushing on her big time, the blush creeping across his cheeks proof of that. Before dessert comes, I excuse myself from the table, explaining I need to take a long bath, that I'm so very tired and so very stressed out. I grab my bottle of wine, preparing to leave.

"Don't drown," says David, a wicked look in his eyes.

Madison fidgets uncomfortably in her seat. She shakes her head from side to side and then blinks. "Yeah, like my mother," she mumbles. "If you drown, Daddy dearest might make a movie about it."

We are entering dangerous territory here. I'm hoping David didn't hear her. If he did, he's ignoring the comment.

"Oh, I'm just having one more," I say, shooting Madison a look of warning. "It relaxes me."

"This meal is relaxing me. I'm stuffed, but I've saved room for dessert," he replies with a low groan. "Sadly, I'll be missing out tomorrow."

I stop in my tracks, looking over my shoulder. "Where are you going now? The awards are this Sunday. There are preparations that need to be done."

"I'm prepared for everything," he huffs. "I'm leaving early in the morning, back Saturday afternoon."

Good to know.

"Are you going to the rehearsal?" he asks.

"No," I snap. "Been there, done that. I have my hair and makeup team coming by for another trial run."

"You're looking kind of haggard," he says with a laugh. "Tell them to work their magic."

I wish I could ask them to make David disappear. I grip the bottle of wine and turn on my heel, heading upstairs to the bathroom. After locking the door, I pull out a makeup wipe, cleaning the haggardness off my face—the smudged mascara, the blotchily applied foundation. I'm making sure David sees what I want him to see. As I run the water, I text Julia.

ED:

He's leaving early. Bluff. I'll text when he's gone.

JF:

OK. Plan?

ED:

Thinking now.

JF:

How did I do tonight? Overkill?

ED:

U were perfect.

Since I'm filling the tub, I add some bubbles, and slide right into it, thinking. With him out of our hair, we have an opportunity to find what he's working on without the fear of being caught. I know he backs all his files up to the cloud and to the computer in his office. He's paranoid he could lose something, or a file could become corrupted. He did this with the films *Valerie* and *Swerve*, possibly every film he's ever written. I know because I've seen him do it. "Sometimes I like going back to my original notes or a previous version," he said. "You can never be too careful."

I know we have to be careful, too.

Half an hour later, David knocks forcefully on the door. "Erica, not that you care, but I'm sleeping in the guest room. Leaving around six."

"OK, darling," I reply, my words garbled. "Sleep well."

I listen to him rummaging through his things, listen to him leave the room. Once he's gone, I get out of the bath, dry off, and pull on my nightgown. In case he should come into the bathroom in the morning, I pour out the contents of the Miraval bottle, leaving the empty bottle on the floor. How could I be planning anything when I can't even think straight? No, not me, I'm always bombed. After brushing my teeth, I crawl into bed, pulling up Snapchat.

SUNBEAM:

Paddle out tomorrow. Beach.

MOONBEAM:

Safe?

SUNBEAM:

Yes. Have new plan.

MOONBEAM:

Julia?

SUNBEAM:

Not exactly.

MOONBEAM:

Time?

SUNBEAM:

7 am

MOONBEAM:

C u then.

I watch the messages disappear and curl up in bed, my gaze focused on the ceiling. I will not be getting a good night's rest. No, that won't happen until David's out of the picture. David blurs the lines between reality and fiction; I'm going to make sure his life becomes very real for him—so real, it'll be unreal.

TWENTY-SEVEN

JULIA

The sun is peeking up over the horizon. I've been up since six, waiting for Erica's text. Finally, it chimes in.

ED:

He's gone. Now.

I kiss Beurreboule on her little head and double-check the door. It's closed. To be safe, I lock it.

As I race down the path toward the bluff, I clench my hands, my nerves on fire. I'm not as good an actress as Erica is. Although David seems to like it when I play stupid. Or like I need to be saved—the time he saved me from the spider, the hero when he saved the cat. And he also likes it when I snap or glare at his wife.

Madison and Erica round the bend. Erica looks as wrecked and sleep deprived as I feel. My mind spins. My ears ring. I hiss, "I don't think I can do this. Last night was torture..."

"My marriage to David is torture."

I scream, "Jesus, Erica! This is all so messed up. I can't take it anymore!"

"Julia, why are you flipping out?" Madison asks, placing a hand on my shoulder.

Why? Does she need reasons? Why isn't she flipping out?

"Because I think he knows who I am," I say. "The bandana. I'm worried. He also catnapped Beurreboule."

"He doesn't know who you are," says Erica flatly.

"But what if he does?" I eye Madison, curiously. "Shouldn't you be in school?"

"I'm taking a sick day," she responds. "We need to get our hands on whatever he's writing. And all the other scripts, don't you think?"

"I don't know what I'm thinking anymore," I mumble.

"Let's head down to the beach," says Erica. "I've called in reinforcements."

"What?" Madison and I shriek at the same time.

"You'll see," she says, looking over her shoulder. "Come on."

We head down the path, Erica unlocks the gate, and we meander onto the sand. That's when I see him: Ollie Shore. Erica waves, ushering him to the beach. I clear my throat. "What's he doing here?"

Erica shrugs. "He's here because he hates David as much as we do."

As Ollie paddles toward us, I turn to Erica. "Explain."

She makes her way to a chair and sits. "When I had my stint at rehab, Ollie came by once a week and we got to talking— about everything, about all my suspicions. I told him about my plans for divorcing David, but how he'd fight for custody of Tyler and probably cut Madison off after she turned eighteen." She clears her throat. "He told me his story and we decided to come up with a plan."

"A plan that clearly involved me," I growl.

She lifts her shoulder into a shrug.

"You mentioned suspicions? What are they?"

"He's not just a method director, using people as inspiration for his scripts." She flinches. "I think he's a serial killer."

Madison hangs her head. "I do, too."

A cold shiver of fear, of anger, runs down my spine. For a moment, I can't open my mouth to speak. I can't even breathe. It's almost as if the ground has dropped away beneath my feet and I'm free-falling into an abyss. Everything around me blurs.

Never in my wildest nightmares could I imagine what she's implying. I get that he profits from movies "based on true stories." I get that the man is creepy and amoral, but a serial killer?

My dad was obsessed with true crime. I know all about Ted Bundy, the serial killer who kidnapped, raped, and murdered dozens of women and girls in the seventies. He was charming, good-looking, and charismatic. I want to vomit.

Once I regain my focus and the world around me stops spinning, I stomp my foot and walk toward Erica with purpose. "You think he's a serial killer? And you've been using me as bait? I thought you just wanted to get away from him. What the hell, Erica?"

"I'm sure he killed your parents."

"And I'm sure he killed my mother," says Madison.

A thought sucker-punches my brain, bashing it in. "You brought me into this. What's to stop him from killing me?"

"He doesn't want to kill you—at least, not yet," Erica says.

Madison clasps my hand. "Don't you get it? He wants to kill us. And then make a movie about you—you'd be the new star, replacing Erica."

"I don't want to be a fucking star. And I definitely don't want him," I scream, whipping my hand from her grip. I storm off toward the path, calling over my shoulder, "This is so messed up. I don't want any part of this. I'm leaving."

"Don't you want to find out what he did to your parents?" Madison screams. "I don't know about you, but I'm not stopping until I get the truth about what really happened to my mother and he's behind bars."

There must be something wrong with my wiring. Why am I not trusting my gut? *Get out of here. Get away from these people. Follow your dream. Honor the memory of your parents.* Why has vengeance gripped me in its hold?

Yet, Madison's words stop me in my tracks. I turn just as Ollie pulls his board onto the sand. I sigh, placing my hands on my hips. David has taken everything away from me. I pick up a rock, throw it, and then watch it skim across the water. "I do. I want him to pay. For everything."

"Good," says Erica as I make my way back to them.

I'm staring blankly at the horizon, the chorus to OneRepublic's "Run" playing in my head on repeat. My mom played their music all the time while baking. Although she'd never gotten a chance to hear this particular song, she would have loved it. And she would have told me to run while the going was good. My gaze snaps to my sneakers when Ollie races up to us and then to his face. Ollie is staring at Erica like a lovesick teenager. "Are you two an item?"

Ollie shrugs. "Not yet. But we want to be."

"We were going to run away to Costa Rica together, after I'd staged my death," says Erica. "He's my moonbeam, my guiding light."

"She's my sunbeam, she makes my life bright."

"Oh God, stop being so corny, I'm going to gag," says Madison, scowling. "Neither of you are running away. We're all going to bring him down together, right?" Her head whips in my direction, her gaze fierce. "Are you in or are you out?"

Erica titters out a laugh. "You just quoted Heidi Klum."

"Not the time for jokes!" I huff.

I don't say anything for a moment, just stare at the horizon, my thoughts vacillating like the tides. A pod of dolphins swims by, a couple jumping and gliding over the waves. Freedom. I need freedom from my past. I need to clear my parents' names. My words come out in an angry whoosh. "As long as you really don't think I'm in danger."

"I'll see to that," says Ollie, nodding his head. "Power in numbers."

My eyes meet Erica's. "What now?"

"Get a hold of the scripts, obviously," says Erica. "I'm not too savvy with computers. You and Madison come up with something. Ollie and I will be lookouts in case he comes back."

Insanity isn't what I've signed up for, but I want to see this through.

Madison and I head back to the house and into the home theater that doubles as David's office. She pulls out a rhinestone-encrusted USB stick from the pocket of her shorts. "It holds two terabytes. I use it for the film projects I've been working on."

We sit behind David's desk and she opens a browser, pulling up a recipe for tom kha gai soup.

"Maddy, I don't see how that's going to help us…" I begin.

"In case he comes back." She shoots me a grin. "By the way, I'm really computer savvy," she says, minimizing the window. She shoves the USB drive into the computer, taps keys, and searches. "What did your friend say the new script he's working on is called."

"*The Private Chef.*"

"Nothing. I'll try TPC." She grins. "Bingo. We've got it— and we also have WOE, V, SW, CITR—all his films." She opens up the folder, copies them onto the stick.

The timer reads thirty minutes, then ten, then five. My heart races and launches into my throat when a cough comes from the doorway. He's ba-ack, just like Jack Nicholson's character in *The Shining*. My panicked gaze shoots to Madison's. She mouths, "Thirty seconds."

Great. I have to distract him. My legs tremble as I get up from my seat. I round the desk, blocking the back of the iMac. "What are you doing here?" I ask, my forced smile quivering. "We zought you left…"

"I live here," he says with a scowl. "And I forgot something. A benefit of flying private is that my plane will wait for me." His lips pinch together tighter. "The bigger question is: What are you doing on my computer?"

"Mine died and we were looking for recipes," says Madison. "For soup. Oh yeah, I need a computer. The Mac went all wheel of death on me. And it won't start up."

"Julia, you don't have a computer?"

I shake my head no. "I don't. I have an iPad. But I'd left it in the guesthouse."

"And you couldn't make the two hundred meter trek to get it?"

Madison and I exchange a look. "That's my fault. Erica said it was OK to use yours. Because you weren't here. What's the big deal? Afraid we'll find your porn stash?"

I stifle a laugh.

"Madison, you're crossing a line. I don't watch porn and you shouldn't speak to me like that." He tilts his head to the side, meets my wide-eyed gaze. "Soup? What kind?"

"Tom kha gai," I say, pointing to the screen. "It's Thai. I am French. I don't know many Thai recipes. And Madison has requested it for lunch."

His gaze locks onto Madison. "And why aren't you at school?"

"Really bad women problems. Like the red tide has rolled in. Big time. I'm bleeding through my clothes. And I have the worst cramps."

He growls with disgust. "Too much information, Maddy."

She shrugs. "It's just nature. Human nature. I can't help it that I'm a girl."

"Yes, eet's horrible," I say with a wide-eyed nod. "You're so lucky you're a man."

He grimaces. "Wouldn't change a thing. Are you two almost finished here?"

"We just need to print zee recipe out." Madison sends the page to the printer. Thankfully it's not too long. I grab the page from Madison's hand. "Merci, c'est fait! I can get to the store..."

"I'd go with you, but—" begins Madison. She scrambles out of the room, yelping, "I need to get to the bathroom. Now. I feel another wave rolling in—"

David's eyes shoot down to the seat she'd been sitting in. He lets out a sigh of relief as I make my way to leave. He sits down in his chair and I feel like I'm about to have a heart attack. "Did you need something, Julia?"

Why, yes, I do. I need to destroy you. I feel the heat rise in my face, though it probably looks as if I'm blushing.

"Yes." I wave the paper over my head. "Ingredients for the soup," I say with a quivering smile and head to the doorway. Before leaving the room, I look over my shoulder. "Have a nice time in Vegas, David. One day I'd like to go. I've never been."

"One day I'd like to take you there." He clears his throat when I tilt my head to the side with a confused pout. "I mean, we'd all have fun. And you and Madison seem to be getting along." He stands up, striding over, and then places a hand on my shoulder. "I'm sorry for the way Erica has been treating you."

I shrug, his touch rendering me immobile. *Please take your hand off me.* "Eet's OK. I'm here to work, make you all happy with my cooking. I'm not here to make friends."

His gaze meets mine. "I'd like to be your friend."

Keep your friends close and your enemies closer.

"I'd like dat, too." I blink and turn to leave. "See you tomorrow."

I hear him say, "Can't wait."

I turn on my heel, walking slowly and then I pick up my pace, racing to the guesthouse with the recipe in hand. My breathing picks up, too. I fight the urge to throw up. But there are three things that are absolutely certain right now: he's after me, he doesn't know who I am, and I'm really playing with fire.

Back in my space, I flop down on the reading chair, the only place a hidden camera can't find me. I'm shaking with fear and relief. Before I'd left the home theater, I'd glanced at the back of the computer. No rhinestone drive.

Erica texts me the moment Antoine pulls the Phantom out of the driveway.

ED:

Watched the footage from your link. Did we get what we need? Meet you at the bluff?

JF:

The beach? And, yes, I think so. Madison has it.

ED:

🙂

With shaky legs, I walk the path down to the beach. Ollie's sitting on his board in the distance. He stands and paddles away when Erica shoots him the thumbs up.

"Well, that didn't go as planned," Erica says.

"You think?" I hiss.

"Oh my God! I was shitting bricks," says Madison.

Erica shudders and then places her hands on her skinny hips. "But you got his files? Yes?"

"I did. We have a slight problem. There are over a hundred," says Madison, her lips twisting. "And they're all encrypted."

My heart drops.

"So, what do we do?" I ask.

"I'm on it. Found a bunch of de-encryptors—is that a word? —on Fiverr. I'm figuring we hire a bunch of them." She pauses. "But there's another problem."

"What?" Erica and I say at the same time.

"If I use my credit card, he'll know. Because my card is linked to his card. I mean, he may think I've hired somebody to write papers or something, so it's a risk and he'd probably demand to see the bill, even if I lied and said it was for a film I'm working on. And Erica can't use hers for the same reason. Also, if he sees Erica using Fiverr, it would be a huge red flag."

Their gazes shoot to me, eyebrows raised, eyes blinking with expectation.

"Fine. I have a credit card," I say. "Let's get on this."

Erica grins. "And I have a drawer full of petty cash. I'll reimburse you."

"Oh, apparently, I need a computer and tons of tampons," says Madison with a laugh. "But he'll pay for those. I'll head to the Apple Store in Santa Monica and then CVS."

"I better go get the ingredients for tom kha gai." I shake my head. "Good call to use that as a distraction. I hope you like it."

"I love it," says Madison with a grin. "It's the reason I pulled it up."

After going to the store, not Gelson's, I'm preparing the soup when Tyler and Liam walk into the kitchen. Liam sniffs. "Oh, my goodness, that smells so good."

He comes up behind me, peeking over my shoulder. "You smell good, too." He pauses and then whispers in my ear, "JoJo."

I turn to face him, my eyes wide with shock. I shake my head and mouth, "Don't say another word." I smile with clenched teeth, mouthing, "Or else," and raise my voice. "We'll have lunch on the beach. Talk a little. What do you think?" My eyes are saying what my lips aren't: agree or I'll go ballistic. He lifts a curious brow and his mouth twists. He's about to speak, but I cut him off.

"What do you think, Tyler?" I ask loudly.

"About what?"

"Having lunch on the beach with Julia," says Liam, enunciating every syllable in my name.

I kick his shin lightly, shooting him the stink eye. Paranoid about cameras? Why, yes, yes, I am.

"Hell yeah. And the waves are righteous today." Tyler grins and then blushes. "I get a half-hour break. Julia, do you want to hit the water with me?"

"Not today," I say. "But I'll take a rain check. Maybe tomorrow?"

His bottom lip puffs out with disappointment. "OK. I'm going to grab a board."

Along with a container of soup and bowls, I grab bottles of water, and Liam and I make our way down to the beach. Once we're on the path, I stop walking and turn to face him. "How'd you know?"

"The little tattoo on your shoulder. The yin. Did you forget I had the yang?" He looks up toward the sky. "Why are you pretending you're somebody named Julia?"

"I'll explain once we're on the beach," I say, unlocking the gate.

Liam follows me to the small table and chairs, and we sit. As I unpack lunch, after settling my shaky hands down, I tell him everything, how I didn't want people to know who I was. Well, I tell him almost everything. I don't tell him that Erica, Madison, and I are trying to figure out a way to bring David down or that David may be a serial killer. I also don't tell him that Erica knows exactly who I am.

"So, that's why you're speaking with a weird French accent?"

"Yep."

He shakes his head, frowning. "Look, JoJo..."

I send a scowl in his direction and then turn my head. "Don't call me that. Not anymore. You can't. And you have to promise you won't tell anybody about me. Not a soul."

"I promise." He sighs. "But Julia's going to take some time to process."

"Call me J."

His eyes focus on the horizon. He's deliberating. I clear my throat.

"OK, J." With one hand, he raps his knuckles on the table. "I get why you changed your name. And I sort of get why you changed your appearance." He fights back a grin. "And you look incredible, by the way." His grin slowly drops into a frown. "What I don't get is why you cut me out of your life and then pretended you didn't know me. It really hurt me. And it still hurts."

"I'm sorry, Liam. Hurting you is the last thing I ever wanted to do. But I told you my reasons. And that's all I can do right now."

He squeezes his eyes shut and shakes his head. After a moment of silence, he looks up. "Do you miss your parents?"

"Of course," I say. "Every. Single. Day. But I really don't want to talk about them or what happened to them right now."

His eyes meet mine, his lashes fluttering. "Did you miss me?"

My lips pinch into a melancholy frown. "Like you can't imagine. I still have Riku, the panda. He's here with all your letters stuffed inside."

His expression brightens for a moment or two. "Really?"

"Really."

"So, what do we do now?"

I look at the spread set out before us as Tyler makes his approach. I shrug. "For now, we eat."

As much as I'd like to get my relationship with Liam back on track, maybe have some fun, the timing is so off it's unfathomable. My eyes latch onto Tyler's. If David had harmed Tyler because he'd thought somehow Tyler would be competition for my affection, ridiculous as that notion is, I can't imagine what he'd do to Liam. No, I can't bring Liam into the dumpster of a situation I've put myself in. The mess needs to be cleaned up first, starting with David.

TWENTY-EIGHT

ERICA

I'm in the master bedroom watching Julia and Liam reconnect on my phone, wondering how much she's told him. We'd agreed she'd just confess to being his long-lost Josephine Brooks... and to make him promise not to tell a soul. So far, he hasn't jumped out of his seat screaming bloody murder, which calms my fears. A flash of disappointment crosses his face. She's either letting him down easily or telling him they need to take things slow.

I know she still cares for him.

I'd forgotten to tell Julia that the cameras I'd installed turn with a little control on my phone, that I can position them so they face the water, the bluff, or the beach. I'll tell her later. Right now, I'm wishing they had sound.

I leave the master bedroom, knocking on Madison's door. She calls out, "Give me a minute."

I never barge in. I wait for her to open the door. She tilts her head to the side. "I've been trying to decrypt the files myself. I can only get as far as the info page, with the actual titles, not the acronyms. It's so frustrating."

"Take a break," I say. "Hungry? The soup is on the stove. I thought we could go for a climb, then eat."

"You are a mind reader, Stepmommy dearest." she says. "I'm taking the middle."

After gearing up, helmets included, we rappel down the bluff, the sun on our faces, and then we climb back up, covered in sweat. Every muscle in my body aches, but it's a good kind of pain—the kind that makes me feel whole. The two of us amble to the kitchen, rubbing our hands with anticipation. Julia has placed the soup in the Thermomix, keeping it warm, two bowls set to its side along with garnishes like chives, limes, and sliced spring onions. The smells of all the ingredients—ginger and citronella and coconut—waft up to our nostrils. We help ourselves and sit at the kitchen table.

"That was fun," says Madison. "And I'm totally starving now."

"Me too."

While we eat, I turn on the news.

BREAKING NEWS: BODY FOUND ON THE MISHE MOKWA TRAIL IDENTIFIED: JASMINE ANDERSON, PERSONAL ASSISTANT TO ERICA AND DAVID DRAKE

Madison spits out a mouthful of soup. "One of the titles he was working on is called *The Personal Assistant*! It's the only one that wasn't encrypted!"

We sit in stunned silence as the report plays out before our eyes.

"Good afternoon, viewers. Beyond the glitzy lights of Hollywood lies a trail in the Santa Monica Mountains: the Mishe Mokwa to Backbone Trail. Although moderately experienced hikers often amble down the trails for its stunning views, the hike can be deadly in windy or slippery conditions, due to its steep and narrow paths along the ragged cliffs.

"It was here under one of these rock formations that the

body of Jasmine Anderson was found a couple of hours ago by two brave hikers, who earlier this morning took an undesignated route."

A picture of Jasmine and David fades onto the screen.

I think David hired her because she's a younger version of me—blond hair, glimmering blue eyes. He'd insisted, of course, that nothing was going on between them. But there is more than a business relationship going on in this photo—what with her head tilted back in laughter, leaning into him, his arm wrapped around her waist.

"According to the initial coroner's report, the cause of death was blunt force trauma to the head, presumed to be from a fall."

The reporter pauses. Madison shoots me a panicked look, her eyes as big as saucers.

"Joining me now is David Drake, coming to us via satellite from Las Vegas."

The screen splits, half with the reporter, half with David's smug face.

"Mr. Drake, do you have anything to say?"

"Jasmine quit working for us a couple of weeks ago—just left, no notice. I'm pretty sure she couldn't take Erica's high maintenance demands anymore. And that was that." He sighs. "She was a really great assistant. The best..."

While he drones on, I leap up from my chair, knocking it over. Madison places a hand on my back. I gulp, my eyes meeting hers. "We don't have much time. We need to act quickly. Play the offensive."

Madison eyes me curiously, tears streaming down her cheeks. "I, uh, really liked her. We hiked that route all the time. All of us. Aren't you upset?"

"Of course I am," I whisper. "I've learned to control my emotions. And right now, they are telling me to protect us from him."

"We have to go to the police!"

"With what? We have no evidence. They'll never believe us."

"We have his notes for *The Private Assistant*—the only file that wasn't encrypted!"

"No, Maddy. All we have is his logline. A driven private assistant plots to kill the wife of a Hollywood producer for a twisted desire, only to find herself tangled in a deadly game where the hunter becomes the hunted."

She blinks. "You saw it?"

I swallow, my eyes darting to the side. "Not exactly. He shared his idea with me the other night, told me I was too old for the part." I place my hands on her shoulders. "Look how he just played this. I'm going to come off looking like the scorned wife."

Madison gasps and wheezes. "I don't think you care about what really happened to my mother. You say you care, but you don't."

I wrap her in a tight hug. "But I do, Madison. Right now, we need to loop in Julia before we do anything."

"Fine," she says, wiping her cheeks. "But I think your plan sucks."

"It doesn't. We can't catch him with things he's done in the past. We need to catch him in the present."

I pull out my phone, sending a text to Julia.

ED:

Taking you to dinner with Madison. I'll stop by. Put on a show. Argue with me. And then sigh when Madison begs you to go and says she doesn't want to eat alone with me.

JF:

What about Tyler?

ED:

Make him fries and chicken nuggets. He'll be fine. He's sixteen. We'll tell him it's a girls' night.

Julia's acting skills are improving. After having our fake argument in the kitchen, we straggle out to the car, Julia pretending to be put out, me following her, telling her to drive safely. On the ride to Nobu, we don't say a word. I sit in the passenger seat, filing my nails, Madison in the back, scrolling on her phone. At the restaurant, we're immediately seated at a table outside, whispers of "that's Erica Drake" following my every step.

Most of the time it's good to be me. A bonus of being a celebrity—I never have to wait for anything. Ever.

Once seated, Julia says, "I don't think we should talk in public."

"I do," I reply. "Just keep that scowl on your face, pretending you can't stand to be with me."

She clamps her mouth into a tight grin. "What if I'm not pretending?"

I roll my eyes and then Madison plasters on a smile, updating Julia about Jasmine. It's like they're two young girls connecting or commiserating. When Madison finishes, Julia's eyes flash with fear and then she pulls herself together. She places her napkin on her lap. "What now?"

"Have any of the other files been decrypted yet?" I ask.

Julia pulls out her phone, shakes her head as she scrolls. "Nope. Not yet."

"Can you push for a rush? I'll pay for it."

"I'll try. Let me email."

The server comes to take our order. I hold up a finger. "We need a couple more minutes."

People keep stealing glances at me. A few patrons nod in my direction, whispering. Thankfully, nobody has the nerve to make an approach.

"Any luck, Julia?" asks Madison, her voice raspy.

"Yep. We'll have most of the files early tomorrow morning." She frowns. "All but one—*The Private Chef*. There's a problem with it. It won't open. Might be corrupted or something. The guy is trying to figure it out but needs a couple more days. He'll try to get it back to me by Sunday."

"We're going to have to read a lot in a very short time. I'll loop in Ollie," I mumble.

The waiting game begins. We order our sushi and, as I stab at my dragon roll with a chopstick, I'm thinking there are many ways to scale a fish.

I hold back my laugh. Make that a dragon.

TWENTY-NINE

JULIA

The following morning, I'm sitting at the little dining room table with my ocean view, coffee in hand, iPad before me. I didn't sleep well last night, the weight of our plans pressing down on me like a lead blanket. Fear grips me as I contemplate the consequences of our actions. What if David finds out what we're up to? What if he does something to us before he can be stopped? We can't afford to wait any longer. We need to find out what David's plans are before he strikes, stripping him of his power and influence. Better? Sending him to jail.

I glance at the clock, realizing time is ticking away—although only 7:30 a.m. Even Beurreboule is still sleeping, curled up at the end of the bed. I open the emails on my iPad, praying. Quickly, my eyes scan for Shazam124. Bingo! My contacts at Fiverr have come through—we have files in!

Hi Julia, I still need more time for the TPC file. It's a mess. Hope to get it to you soon.

Shazam

I rub my eyes, disappointment setting in. After setting my coffee down, I bite down on my bottom lip, looking for the original notes for *Swerve*. Dare I? Erica didn't say I'd have to wait for her to read them. Can I? I'm not sure I'll be able to handle it. But I have to.

Music. I need something calming. Madison had played Mr. Probz "Waves" in the car the other day. I really connected to the lyrics and loved the melody. I link my phone to the sound system, pulling up Spotify. As the song comes on, I take a steadying breath and click the file of his original notes open, my heart racing. And I read, surprised to find the first note crossed out.

~~A Hollywood producer, infatuated with a French pastry chef, begins to stalk her and her husband, obsessively tracking their movements and routines. As his obsession grows, the woman denies his advances. If he can't have her no one will. He meticulously engineers a fatal "accident" by tampering with her car, ensuring her and her husband's demise along a treacherous canyon road with hairpin turns.~~

My heart pounds inside my chest.

As I read the words, each short sentence carries a horrifying realization. Regardless of whether I thought he'd been involved with their death, him causing it is beyond all comprehension. My heart is beating so furiously I feel like I'm about to have a coronary. This is it. The truth staring back at me in stark black ink. A confession, disguised as a screenplay note. David—he murdered my parents. I feel like I'm drowning, being pulled under, and the room spins, the text swirling on the screen.

I place my hands on the table to steady myself. I don't want to scream; David may come running to "save" me again and I wouldn't be able to act my way out of the hatred I feel for him. I am sick to my stomach. With trembling hands, I'm about to forward the files to Madison, but my finger hovers over the send button, and I read the next note.

A French pastry chef has an affair with a Hollywood producer so she can put down her baking mitts and get into acting. What she gets is a bun in the oven. After she becomes pregnant, she tells her obsessive husband she's going to leave him, but he ensures both of their demises along a treacherous canyon road with hairpin turns during a mud slide. A murder–suicide.

That's the script he wrote. These are the lies he wrote, bound by twisted threads in a sinister plot. Based on a true story, my ass. I've never been more determined to bring him down.

I force myself to push through the current of anger rocking my system. I've come too far to turn back now. I hit send, the action feeling both liberating and terrifying all at once. Fear gnaws at my gut, but beneath it lies a flicker of resolve. We may be playing a dangerous game, but we're doing it for the greater good. Or at least, that's what I keep telling myself.

With a heavy sigh, I steel myself for the challenges ahead. Whatever happens next, we'll face it together, come what may. Since we think David may be spying on us, we're only communicating by text. I'm not expecting Erica to be up, but she'd mentioned wanting to climb with Madison early in the morning to see the sunrise.

JF:

Got the notes for his files in. All of them except TPC.

Three dots.

ED:

Good. Need to get everything printed. Divide & conquer.

JF:

Plan?

I watch the screen on my phone, waiting for her answer.

ED:

Will tell David you're taking the kids to doc.
Taking me on last minute errands. Argue with
me in car.

JF:

Why?

ED:

Bugged? Don't know.

JF:

OK

ED:

Garage. Car. 1/2 hour

I nod and set the phone down, heading to the shower. My blood is running so hot, I keep the water cold. As I get ready, my movements are mechanical, like I'm not really grounded in the moment. Flashes of grief, anger, and betrayal flash in my mind, despite my efforts to stay composed. And then I feel numb, dressing as if I'm on autopilot. I feed Beurreboule, giving her fresh water, and leave, grabbing my big sunglasses and then locking the door.

I stomp down the path. Erica, Tyler, and Madison are already waiting for me in the driveway in front of the garage. I don't say "good morning," or "how are you feeling?" I just stomp to the car and jump into the driver's seat.

"Let's go," I say. "I have to get to the store! I haven't got all day!"

Yes, I've snapped.

Once everybody is buckled in, I start the engine and I

scream at Erica. I've been waiting to scream, to yell, and now I have a chance to. "Driving you around! Taking your kids to the doctor! Zees is not my job!"

"It is today," she replies with a hiss. "I'm paying you a fortune. You're lucky you work for me."

"Lucky? Ha! If you weren't paying me so much, I'd quit!"

"Then do it," says Erica.

"But I have not poisoned you yet," I say, and Erica mouths, "Don't give him any ideas."

Oh, I've thought about it. He probably has, too.

On the ride, Madison and Tyler sit in the back seat, trying to hold back their sniggers. This situation is not funny. I glare at them in the rearview mirror, but, thanks to my enormous, black-tinted sunglasses, they can't see my eyes. Finally, we pull up into the parking lot of the UPS store, conveniently located spitting distance from Urgent Care in case David is tracking us. Before exiting the car, Erica throws on a big floppy hat and sunglasses, and we get out. I slam the door and Erica startles. Once we're away from the car—which may or may not be bugged—Erica asks, "What's the matter, Julia?"

My head snaps in her direction. "Like you don't know."

Her lips purse. "I don't."

"I read the original notes for *Swerve*," I hiss, wondering how much she knows.

She nods with thought. "Like I told you, he was obsessed with your mother."

"You didn't tell me he killed them—purposefully messed with their car," I respond, my voice so low it sounds like I'm growling. And I am. I'm growling on the inside.

"I told you I had my suspicions. That's why we're doing this." She cocks her head toward Madison and Tyler. "This isn't just about you, Julia. She needs answers, too. We all do."

Madison, Erica, Tyler, and I stomp into the store, full of

intent. Like a gang. Behind the counter, a guy's jaw drops and his eyes widen.

"We need these files printed out," says Erica, handing over the USB stick. "Right now."

Hurricane Erica is a force to be reckoned with. This I know first-hand.

"How many files? How many pages?" the guy stammers.

"A lot," says Madison. "Around ten or eleven thousand."

The guy holds up his hands. "Sorry, no can do. We have other clients. It'll take at least three or four days."

Erica holds up a wad of cash. "Five thousand dollars says you'll have our prints done in two hours or we'll be taking our business elsewhere."

"Yes, ma'am," he says, reaching for the cash.

"Don't call me ma'am," Erica retorts with a guffaw. "I'm not a grandma yet. And there's an extra thousand if you have every printer in this place running, churning out the pages. We'll be back in an hour. You don't get the bonus or this cash until the job is completed, got it?"

"Got it. And wait. Aren't you—"

"Absolutely diabolical," I say, cutting him off, and Erica glowers at me.

We exit the UPS store, where Ollie waits outside, worry creasing his forehead. "How long will it take?" he asks.

"An hour," says Madison. "Maybe more."

"So, what do we do until then?"

Erica's eyes flash to the nail salon. "I'm treating us girls to a little pampering—manicures, pedicures, and neck massages. You boys, check out the surf shop. Get a wheatgrass shot at Vitamin Barn." She hands Tyler a wad of cash. "We'll reconvene at Starbucks. Sound good?"

Madison shoots me a look. I think she's as confused as I am.

The last thing I'm thinking about is being pampered. Erica really is a piece of work. How can she remain so calm?

An hour later, we're all sitting at a table in Starbucks, printouts in hand. Nobody, thank God, recognizes Erica. Fellow coffee and tea lovers sit at tables, laptops out, probably working on scripts, some alone, some in groups. For the next hour, we sit reading, flipping pages, letting out occasional gasps of disbelief and pained groans.

After reading his notes on the original script pertaining to my parents, my heart aches and I can't stop the tears from falling, no matter that we're in a public place. The man deserves to be locked up in prison for the rest of his twisted life. He stalked my mother. She didn't want him. So, he followed her, found her schedule, and purposefully drove them off the road. If he couldn't have her, nobody would.

Madison's bottom lip trembles. She looks up, tears in her eyes. Her voice comes out as a whisper. "After Valerie discovers her husband is having a passionate affair with another woman, she's found dead in a swimming pool and her death is ruled out as a tragic suicide..." Her throat hitches. "That's the final script. B-b-but the other note continues. Valerie's husband, wanting to leave her, orchestrates her demise, plunging her into a watery grave." She bites down on her bottom lip. Her voice raises in pitch. "I really don't think we should be reading, let alone talking about anything here. We're at fucking Starbucks and the world is crumbling beneath my feet. I feel like I'm going to burst."

The hiss of steaming milk, the grind of the espresso machines, and the clamor of nearby chatter doesn't drown out the tension at our table. A couple of people shoot us curious glances, eyebrows raised. I get it. They're working. But this isn't the library.

"We have to go to the police," I finally say.

Madison, Tyler, and Ollie nod their heads with a firm agreement.

"Yes, now, this very instant," whimpers Madison.

"Not yet," says Erica, shaking her head. "We have to wait until Monday."

Jesus, this woman is placing our lives in danger because she's up for an Oscar? Not cool. I'm beginning to question her true motives. From what I've learned and what I've seen, she really is an excellent actress. My mind spins. Why would she play us? She keeps telling us that it's her life on the line—not ours. Something is so off.

"Your career is more important?" I hiss.

"No, it's the timing. We'll have him exactly where we need him. Begging for forgiveness. Held accountable for everything. Isn't that what you want?"

"Right now, I want him rotting in prison," I say with force, my voice low. "This? Your plan? It's a recipe for disaster."

"No," she says. "It's a recipe for his destruction."

"They must be brainstorming a thriller," a patron at a neighboring table says to her friend. I shoot her a death glare and she goes back to typing.

As the woman's words hang in the air, I feel a shiver crawl down my spine. I never wanted my life to end up like this. I never wanted to be in danger. I just wanted to build my dream to honor my parents. Now, that dream has been tainted. My gaze drifts to the window. Right now, I'd like to make a run for it, never look back.

"Which is why we need the last script," Erica finally says. "We have to wait or we—meaning me—won't be taken seriously. David's seen to that. He's destroyed my reputation."

I blink back my anger, my frustration. "We wait for him to kill me? I'm bait? Not in my plan."

"Oh, Julia," she says with a placating tone. "I'm fairly

certain he doesn't want to kill you. He wants to kill me. Just like he did to Madison's mother. Your parents. The question we should all be asking ourselves is, how is he going to do it? So, we need his notes for that script. You'd be saving my life..."

Tyler's head hangs low. "What about me? Why'd he drug me? Did he want to k-k-kill me, too?"

Erica reaches across the table and grips Tyler's hand. "It's a possibility."

"Why? I'm his son..."

"He thinks I just used you to trap him into marrying me."

My eyes pop open wide. Even if it's true, this is something she shouldn't be sharing with her kid. Sometimes I think her brain needs to be rewired, like big time—every neuron reconnected.

Before she answers, Ollie snaps, "Jesus Christ, Erica, don't say anything else. You'll give the kid a complex for the rest of his life."

Tyler's face crumbles. "I already have a complex—it's the reason I turned to pot. Made life a lot more bearable. And, honestly, tripping was..."

Ollie sighs. "Tyler, man, don't talk that way. You and me, we're going to Malibu Oasis together after this. We'll both speak with Dr Reynolds. I do not want to see you relapse because of that man."

"I'll come, too." Madison grips my hand, pulsing her grip. "We're all in this together," she reminds me.

When I meet Madison's eyes, they are no longer filled with tears but determination. I know she's feeling the same pain I am.

Erica's phone chimes. She stands up, her chair scraping the floor. "I'll be right back."

Stunned, we watch her walk out to a black Porsche with tinted windows. The passenger window rolls down and Erica reaches into her purse, handing somebody a package. I can't see because she's blocking my view. The car drives off and Erica walks back in, taking her seat.

Ollie scowls. "What the hell was that all about?"

Erica sighs. "Jasmine. Her parents wanted the necklace she'd always worn and a couple of other personal effects. Sent a delivery man to pick it up."

"How did he know we were here?" I ask.

"I texted while we were getting our nails done."

Madison's head lowers. "I can't take much more of this."

Erica shrugs and looks at her watch. "It's almost noon. We need to get back to the house. The caterers and my makeup team will be arriving soon, not to mention David."

Madison and I exchange a look.

My mind is trying to arrange the pieces of the puzzle, but nothing is fitting into place. Right now, I'm thinking Erica may be the missing piece. Maybe she and David are working together? I have to figure everything out, snuff out the fire that's been lit inside my heart before I explode.

THIRTY

ERICA

On the ride back to Hummingbird House, Julia is silent, save for letting out irritated grunts. I understand her desire to loop in the police with what we have, but it's a very bad idea, especially with my reputation. How many times do I have to tell her that they'll never believe me? We need something concrete.

I need something to happen.

Of course, I'd been planning on leaving David by staging my own death—and Julia had been dead right. Such an ignorant notion—especially when dealing with a would-be serial killer. I guess when things get so bad and you don't know what to do, you hold on to whatever hope you can catch. Tomorrow night, I'll be catching the stars.

My respect for Julia has sky-rocketed to the moon, the stars, and back again. Like me, she's a fighter and won't give up until she gets what she wants. If I told her this, though, she'd prob-ably burst out laughing. Regardless, she is more like me than she realizes, and we have established a bond—well, as close to one as I can have with anybody.

I'm not a fool.

I think Julia, Madison, Tyler, and Ollie are angrier with

David than they are scared of him. If that wasn't the case, Julia would definitely pack up her bags and leave and I wouldn't hold it against her. I think we all see the big picture, the details: if we don't band together and stop him, nobody will.

Then again, I know they are all doubting me.

A thought has me shivering. What if the guy at the UPS store alerts David to our ambush today? Would he? My thoughts drift to poor Jasmine. I'm honestly not that broken up over her death—-she'd just been after David, probably wanted to be the third Mrs. Drake. If she were still alive, she could have him.

A buzz from the guard gate chimes, nearly making me jump out of my skin. I stumble over to the intercom, wondering if it's the police coming by to question me about Jasmine or Nellie's deaths. "Yes?"

"Mrs. Drake, Elodie and Calvin are here."

"Thanks, Kyle, send them in."

I rub my eyes and head downstairs. Now I have to play dress-up. Oh, I'm so not in the mood for this. Regardless, I open the front door, pasting on a smile.

"Elodie! Calvin! Thank you so much for coming over!"

"We can't wait to get started," says Calvin. "You are going to rock the red carpet. Can we see the dress?"

"Uh-huh," I say. "It's to die for."

Hopefully, I won't be dying in it.

Two hours later, after being poked and prodded, my scalp tingling with pain, my hair pulled this way and that from the many up-dos Calvin has tried, we finally agree on the look: I'm wearing my hair down—sleek like a blond seal.

As for my makeup, I scrub it off, telling Elodie to give me a more natural look. Gwyneth Paltrow, Jennifer Lawrence, and Julianne Moore all looked radiant with their understated looks.

I want people to see the real me, not the gloss or the lies of perfection.

Elodie tsks. "Are you sure? I mean, the lights might drown out your features—"

"Oh, I'm sure," I say. "Plus, you haven't seen the dress."

"I can't wait."

Calvin fans his face with his hand again. "Neither can I."

I grin. "Give me two seconds and I'll change in the bathroom."

I head into the closet to grab the dress, unzip the protective bag. The dress has been slit right down the middle, sequins tumbling to the floor. And there's a note attached to the silk with a safety pin: *Bon Appétit!—J*

Yes, the note is in her handwriting. She always leaves little notes, usually on plates in the refrigerator. I'd told David how excited I was to be wearing an original Dior. Paranoid of sabotage, I'd purchased the dress I'm now holding at Nordstrom's Rack for two hundred bucks and had Silvia sew in a Dior label. I'd hidden the *real* dress where nobody would ever find it—in Madison's room in her vault.

I step out of the closet with a sheepish grin.

"Is something wrong?" asks Calvin.

"No," I say. "Silly me. I forgot I was storing the dress in my daughter's room. My closet, as you can imagine, is about to burst." I hold up a finger. "I'll be right back."

Half an hour later, I'm all dolled up in the stunning silver, art deco beaded and sequined number with scalloped details and a plunging neckline, when David walks into our suite. I turn to face him, tilting my head to the side. "How do I look?"

He swallows and then blinks. "I must say, I'm amazed."

I'll bet he is. "Are you ready for tomorrow's big event?"

"I'm ready for everything," he says with a scowl.

"I need a good night's rest. Can you pack up what you need and hunker down in one of the guest rooms? But not the suite. Calvin and Elodie are spending the night. We have an early start tomorrow."

David stands quiet, shaking his head and glaring at me. If anything, he should be in a good mood. I am. I mean, come on, we've both been nominated for Oscars.

Calvin clears his throat. "Once I'm finished with Erica, I can assist you, Mr. Drake."

David grumbles and heads to his closet. "Erica's the one who needs help. Not me. Just give her a bucket of wine and a straw."

I lower my eyes and tuck my chin into my clavicle, holding back the laugh I want to blurt out. I know David is insinuating that I'm not right in the head, that I'm a drunk. He knows I wouldn't dare bring such a topic up with Calvin and Elodie in the room. It's like a Mexican standoff. He raises a smug brow; I shoot him a tight grin. I think he enjoys dancing this ridiculous dance of ours. We've both been doing it for so long we know all the steps.

I wag a come-hither finger. "David, can I have a quick word with you while you pack?"

He rolls his eyes and I follow him into the closet, closing the door. Our closet is four hundred square feet, his and hers sides. I grab the destroyed dress, my lips pinched. "Look what Julia did to my dress! She cut it! Right down the middle!"

His eyes go wide. "Is that the one you're wearing tomorrow?"

"No," I say.

"And you're sure Julia did it?" He sneers. "Or is this another of your cries for attention?"

I blurt out a laugh. I'm an actress. He knows full well that I'm an attention seeker. Maybe he's projecting his own insecurities onto me. His parents basically ignored him when he was growing up, the reason he lashes out sometimes. He likes the spotlight on him. Maybe it's too bright because I see every single one of his flaws.

"I think *you* cut the dress. And tried to pin it... literally... on her. There was a note attached." I hand him the Post-it and he crumples it into a little ball, shooting it like a basketball into the waste bin in the corner.

"I didn't mess with your dress, Erica," he scoffs. "And if you think Julia is out to sabotage you and cuts up your clothes when you're not looking, then you confront her and you fire her."

"Maybe I will," I say. This is a plot twist I didn't see coming. I thought he'd become obsessed with her. Maybe he's outgrown his boyhood obsession of getting the unobtainable girl.

"Good," he replies, throwing his things in an overnight bag.

A few minutes later, David stomps out of the room with his tux slung over his shoulder. The door slams behind him as I settle back into my chair. Calvin and Elodie share a look.

"Oh, he's just nervous for tomorrow," I say, waving a dismissive hand.

"I can imagine," says Elodie, clucking her tongue. "The pressure is on. You seem to be cool, calm, and collected, though. I'm wondering how you do it. It's like you have ice in your veins, while the rest of us are melting. Whatever your secret is, I could use some of it right now. If Calvin and I don't get your look right, we could be blacklisted."

Calvin nods in agreement. "What she said."

"Oh, you'll get my look right."

"Perfect canvas, those cheekbones of yours," says Elodie with a sigh. "You're going to be drop-dead gorgeous, as usual."

"Hopefully, I won't drop dead," I say with a self-deprecating laugh. "I'm old, you know, for Hollywood."

"Bullshit," says Calvin. "Forty is the new twenty. And you, my darling, don't have anything to worry about."

I am worried, but not for the lame reasons I'd puffed out. Julia really needs to get her hands on that script. The clock is ticking.

THIRTY-ONE

JULIA

As I mull over Erica's twisted plans, I'm in the process of prepping for tomorrow's party when David comes up behind me, once again standing way too close. I clench my teeth together, turn and plaster on a smile. "You are back," I say, my tone low.

He grins. "I am. Did you miss me?"

I don't know how to reply so I force a smile and lower my head. "Did you need something?"

I can feel his eyes raking over my body. "Depends on what you're offering."

What I'm offering? I'm currently envisioning taking the paring knife I'm slicing herbs with to his neck. At least the fresh aromas of dill and basil overpower the stench of evil. Dread pounds in my heart. I do have a good excuse to get rid of him.

"Desolé," I say with a little pout. "No meals today. We are preparing for tomorrow night's party. It *weel* be absolutely delicious. I assure you."

He raises a brow and licks his lips. "I'm sure it will be."

Ugh. Could he be any more disgusting? My back tenses

under his penetrating gaze. "Erica's upstairs with her hair and makeup team."

"I know. Just saw her." He then mumbles, "She needs a team. But you don't. You're naturally beautiful." And then he clears his throat. "And Tyler? Where is he?"

He wants to know where the son he'd drugged is, and tried placing the blame on me? This man is a real piece of work. I've never been more motivated to bring him down, no matter that I'm putting my life in danger. I don't know what that says about me. I just know that David isn't as smart and powerful as he thinks he is. I may have googled the subject last night and one way, one how, serial killers all get busted because they make a grave mistake. Ted Bundy? John Wayne Gacy? Jeffery Dahmer? David Berkowitz? The only person that got away with their crimes was the Black Dahlia murder; Elizabeth Short's killer has never been identified, though the case continues to inspire theories, including the possibility that the killer was involved in other crimes.

Unlike David, he or she got away with it.

David's mistake? His notes. His original scripts. Now, unbeknownst (I hope) to David, I'm the bait. Nom, nom, nom. I want to chew him up and spit him out, watching as he's arrested and sentenced to life in prison. Sometimes the prey has to outsmart the predator. Survival of the smartest.

Breathe. Find your motivation, like Erica has said. You're in it to win it. Bring this sick and twisted ass-wipe of an excuse for a human being down. Breathe. Smile for the cameras. Breathe. Keep calm and cook on. Breathe. Trust in yourself. I continue to chop the basil, hoping David will just grab a snack and leave.

Wishful thinking. He stands there, watching me chop.

"Julia, I asked you if you've seen Tyler."

"I have not seen him." I shrug. "You know how zee teen-agers are."

"I do," he says with a laugh. "I used to sleep in for hours. And then walk around like a zombie."

I blink, the song by the Cranberries—"Zombie"—about to play in my mind. My fear is fighting my determination. And I can't let fear win.

"I better get back to prepping," I say, hoping he'll pick up on the hint to leave. "The caterers will be here any minute."

"Seriously?" he says, and I turn, sighing with exasperation. "No lunch?"

He puffs out his lips into a pathetic pout and I want to punch his mouth. How could Erica have fallen for such a tool? She's smart and scrappy. She must have seen the warning signs. I mean, they are practically flashing over his head—I'm a crazed sociopath. He doesn't even like animals! Come on, who doesn't like animals? Maybe because he thinks they're competition. At least Erica can see him clearly now and so can I.

"I can make you a sandwich, eef you like."

"Make two," he instructs, leaning against the center island's counter. "Tyler and I will need energy for our climb."

"D'accord," I say, worry coursing through my veins. What if he tries to harm Tyler again? I have to warn Erica.

As I gather the fresh baguettes, some ham, cheese, and lettuce, I feel David's eyes following my every move. Internally, I groan while I wrap up his meal in tinfoil, place it in one of the faux-Chanel shopping bags with chips and drinks. I turn to face him. "'Ere you go. Special order."

He kisses my cheek when he takes the bag. "Thank you for looking out for me, Julia."

After he leaves, I race to the bathroom, dry heaving, wiping my cheek. Then, I text Erica.

JF:

He's back.

ED:

I know.

JF:

Wants to take Tyler on a climb.

ED:

I'll warn him.

The caterer and her crew arrive. I buzz them in. All of a sudden, the house is a whirlwind of activity while, thanks to David, I feel like I'm in the eye of a tornado. I know he's probably watching me. Should I smile for the camera?

I really don't think Mel B has the greatest first impression of me. I'm laying on my French accent so thick it sounds weird even to my ears. My eyes take in Mel. She's in her fifties, short, has bright red dyed hair—an odd color, almost purple. You definitely wouldn't confuse her with the Spice Girl. No wonder Erica had laughed so hard.

"So," says Mel, looking up from chopping sage with disbelief. She lowers her funky purple glasses to the bridge of her nose. "*You* went to Le Cordon Bleu?"

"Oui, I did," I respond.

Her face lights up. "I did, too. In Pasadena?"

"No, in Paris." I pronounce Paris the French way. *Par-ee.*

Her lips pinch together into a tight line. She raises her chin. "That's right. You're French. Well, la-dee-da. Aren't you fancy?"

Not exactly. I'm a hot mess. And Erica's nasty attitude has definitely rubbed off on me. Time to backpedal. I smile. "Zey are both excellent schools. I mean, it is Le Cordon Bleu. Did you 'ave any problems or questions with zee recipes?"

"Nope. I think everything is set."

"I've just finished the soup. Did you want to try it?"

Mel smiles, holds up a finger. She picks up a spoon, lifts it to her mouth, swallows. "Oh my! This soup is out of this world!

Ginger! I love the ginger." She dabs her lips with a white linen napkin and leans forward. "I'd steal you away from Erica and hire you, but I don't think I could afford you. What's she paying you, anyway?"

She didn't just go there. My brows pinch together.

"Sorry," says Mel, tucking her chin into her neck. "Rude question. I was just curious."

"Do you have any other questions regarding the recipes or tomorrow's event?" I say flatly.

"No, I think we're all set."

"Bon. I'll see you tomorrow morning."

Erica's demeanor is definitely rubbing off on me. Maybe I have two personalities, too. That would explain why I'm still here, putting my life at risk and treating a nice woman with disdain. Instead of heading straight for the guesthouse, I find myself wandering into Erica's hummingbird garden, searching for any semblance of inner peace, I suppose. I sit on one of the cement benches, pop my earbuds in, and decide to play roulette with one of my dad's playlists—putting it on shuffle. Whatever song comes up will tell me what to do. I press play and close my eyes.

Note by beautiful note, Bob Marley and the Wailers's "Three Little Birds" floats into my ears and my eyes widen with surprise. Just at that moment, two hummingbirds zip by, one, once again, hovering in front of me, darting from side to side. The other electric green bird joins their partner and it's almost as if they're dancing for me, telling me not to be scared, not to worry.

Everything is going to be OK.

Entranced, I sit staring off into the distance until the song comes to an end and the birds dart off into the sky. My parents are together for eternity and, someway, somehow, they are keeping an eye on me. I need to believe this.

With a sigh, I take the path to the guesthouse, passing by

Tyler and Madison, carrying boards—Madison's painted with bright smiley faces, Tyler's like a shark. Madison grins. "Join us, Julia! You can give me some tips."

Tyler blushes when I say, "Maybe." My gaze locks onto his. "Thought you were going climbing with your dad."

He snorts. "Mom warned me. I bolted and hid in Maddy's room before he could ask."

Smart kid.

He grips his board. "By the way, I should have my DNA results next week."

Madison snorts. "Hopefully, you're truly not the Devil's spawn."

Tyler punches her in the arm with his free hand.

"Ouch. That freaking hurt."

"What?" Tyler laughs. "The Devil made me do it."

"Are you going to slice the waves with us?" asks Madison, squinting. "Please? Pretty please. With sugar on top. I know you want to. Plus, you can become a member of our pre-sunset ritual..."

She doesn't have to beg. It's exactly what I need to do, and I have a couple of hours to kill. "I'll meet you in a few. Just have to change and grab a board."

After feeding Beurreboule, I'm about to dash to the garage to pick up a board when FaceTime chimes. Marie. I can't bear to face her right now. She knows my every expression. She'll know something is desperately wrong. She'll know I'm lying through my teeth when I tell her that everything is OK. I send her a quick message.

JF:

> Can't talk. Preparing for big Oscars party. Will call later in the week, when things settle down. Tu me manques. Bisous. Xox

I press send, staring at my message. *Tu me manques.* I do

miss her so much and I feel guilty for lying. If she knew what was going on, she and Bernard would fly to California and grab me by the hair, dragging me back to Paris kicking and screaming.

With a gulp, I grab a board and head down to the beach, surprised to see Tyler and Madison, straddling their boards, just talking. I wave, zip up my wetsuit, and throw my board into the water, paddling out on my stomach past the breaking point to join them, plunging under the waves. We're about thirty meters, maybe forty, from the shore.

"Anything I should be aware of?" I ask, not sure if I want the answer.

"Kind of." Madison clears her throat. "He slit Erica's dress wide open and left a note signed 'Bon appétit—J'."

"He blamed me?"

"Yeah, but don't worry about it. Erica thinks he did it to give her a reason to fire you..."

"Her dress for the awards is ruined?"

Madison stifles a laugh. "No, it was a plant. We're keeping her real dress in the vault in my room. I have a massive safe with a steel door to protect all my camera equipment. You know, film school—that shit is expensive. And, no, David didn't buy it for me, Erica did."

I swing my body onto my board, straddling it like Tyler and Madison. As we bob up and down, my mind bobs, too. In the distance, on the bluff, the dark figure that is David looms. We all watch as he clips the rope to the anchor, rappels down.

"He's not wearing a helmet," says Tyler, watching his every movement, a glare in his eyes. "What an idiot. God, I hate him."

"We all do," says Madison. "The tie that binds us together."

I go silent, ocean water lapping over my thighs. I've never hated anybody with so much intensity. I don't even think I've ever hated anybody—not like this. Although the water is a chill

14.7° Celsius, the anger sparking every nerve in my body keeps me warm.

"Any luck with that last script?" Madison asks.

"Nope," I sigh. "And I know we really need it."

Once David lands on the beach, he shields his eyes from the sun, staring in our direction. He shakes his head, mouths something. Then he turns and climbs back up the bluff, clipping into anchors, hands and feet searching for the holds and pockets on the face of the bluff. His foot slips and debris falls down to the beach.

My eyes go wide, a wicked thought taking hold of my brain. "Am I the only one envisioning him falling and cracking his head open like an egg?"

"Nope. I was thinking the same thing. The rocks at the bottom? Brutal." Madison blurts out a laugh. "He's probably trying to impress you with his machismo strength, prove he's young and strong."

"Ugh, I kind of want to throw up right now."

"Wouldn't matter. Vomit doesn't attract sharks. Blood does." Her eyes go wide. "Maybe you could cut him with one of your knives and then Tyler and I will throw him into the water. The sharks will swarm—"

"You have a wild imagination," I say, spitting out a laugh at Maddy's suggestion.

"That's why I want to be a filmmaker—a real one, not an impostor."

Our gazes shift to the bluff, watching David watching us. We can't see his expression, but I'm sure he's pissed. He turns and leaves, stomping off. A shiver runs down my spine. "I feel like we're sitting ducks."

"No, we're sharks," says Tyler, beating out a rhythm on the front of his board. "I got it. Imagine Dragons. 'Sharks'."

"Sing," Madison demands, meeting my gaze. "We're all in this together."

She's right. We sing out the lyrics at the top of our lungs while beating our boards. It's almost tribal. An initiation of some sort. A release.

Tyler looks over his shoulder. "There's a nice swell coming in. Let's see who catches the quality wave first." He cackles. "Last one in is a rotten egg. On one, two, three, get into position and paddle like your lives depend on it."

Oh, I am.

THIRTY-TWO

ERICA

It's seven in the morning and I've already showered. Now, I'm just waiting for Calvin and Elodie to help me get ready for the big event. Honestly, they don't need to do much; I have fantastic bone structure and a flawless, porcelain complexion, at least that's what everybody tells me. Well, everybody except David.

Thankfully, last night was a non-event, David avoiding me, me avoiding him. The usual. Today, we have to pretend we like one another, maybe even love one another—and that's going to be hard for both of us. But I've been doing it for so long, lying comes naturally. As for David, sometimes I think he likes being kept on his toes. Maybe I'll step on one of his as we walk down the red carpet for the pre-event. Whoops! Sorry, honey, didn't mean to stab you in my high stilettos with knife-like heels. Imagining his pained expression has me grinning. Winning the Oscar? That infuses my soul with so much happiness I can barely contain myself.

I've manifested this day since I was eleven, clutching onto my first journal filled with dreams—namely escaping the trailer park. Back then, fluorescent light flickered in our cramped and dirty living space, the smell of alcohol and cigarette smoke overpowering everything. The lash of one of my mother's many boyfriend's belts. The sting on my cheek when my mother accused me of seducing her boyfriends, when they were lying on top of me, drooling in my hair. Instead of running away, I ran into my dreams, even though the odds were stacked against me.

Hmmm. *Against All Odds.* I loved that movie.

I am the girl who fought tooth and nail for a new life.

One day I'd be a bright fire, a star, lifting the Oscar in my hands. Instead of tears of pain coursing down my cheeks there would be tears of pure joy. I'm going to prove myself. With my eyes shut tight, I rehearse my acceptance speech in my head, knowing that if you dream it fiercely enough, if you believe in yourself with every fiber of your being and your soul, your dreams can come true.

Today, it's my time to shine, to prove all those naysayers wrong—not under crappy fluorescent lights, but on the red carpet and on the stage, the flashes from the cameras of photographers and the searchlights seeking me out. I'm going to absorb every last moment.

Walking into my closet, I step up onto my tippy-toes to grab my special box. David thinks the pristine package holds expensive shoes—Louboutin's—and it kind of does, but my feet are way too big to fit into them. Sitting on the closet floor, I pull out the pair of special editions—Versace Barbie®, a blond wearing a ribbon-corseted, silk chiffon champagne-colored dress with a sexy slit, showing off her legs, and Louboutin "Anemone" Barbie®, with auburn hair, wearing a chartreuse-colored silk gown with a purple bow train and lavender heels. I'd purchased the latter because the doll came with three additional pairs of shoes and the cutest miniature signature red shoe bags, complete with their own boxes. I don't need the Tailored Tuxedo Ken doll—he's not in this scene. I throw him to the side.

Today, Versace Barbie (representing me) will wear the strappy gold Louboutin's. I slide the doll out of her box, followed by the shoes and the doll (representing a reporter) from the other box. Such a Cinderella moment, getting ready for the ball. Growing up, I'd only had one Barbie—but it was a knock-off made of cheap plastic and her arms broke off.

With the characters ready, I need one more accessory to set the scene—a red scarf. I stand up, heading to one of my sets of drawers, quickly finding what I need, laying it on the floor. Then, I grab both dolls, one in each hand. I sashay down the red carpet and the reporter stops me.

I lower my voice. "Erica Drake, you look absolutely stunning! What are you wearing tonight?"

"Right now, I'm wearing Versace, but I'll be wearing Dior," I say, high-pitched, making a mental note to search out the Dior doll.

"How does it feel, winning the Oscar?"

I titter out a laugh. "Wonderful! Wonderful! All of my dreams have come true!"

I'm still sitting cross-legged on the floor, gripping the dolls, when my cell buzzes with a text. Damn interruptions. Just when I'm finding my Zen. Annoyed, I look down at my phone.

JF:

Did you want me to bring you breakfast?

In fact, what she's proposing is a good idea. I tap in my response.

ED:

Yes! Enough for all of us. You, me, Madison, Elodie, and Calvin.

JF:

Got it.

ED:

Leave something for David with a note. Bon appétit!—J

JF:

OK?

                                                    ED:

Maybe wish him luck too. He'll need it.

There's a knock on my door and my heart rate accelerates. I do not want to deal with David this morning. It's bad enough that we have to share the car to the Dolby Theatre. One hour of torture, maybe more if there is traffic.

"Erica?" comes Madison's voice. "You awake?"

"I am. Give me a minute," I say. Quickly, I put the dolls and shoes back in their original packaging, pack them in the box, and place it back on the shelf. "Come in."

The door rattles, shakes. I'd forgotten I'd locked it. One can never be too safe. "Hold on," I say. I twist the lock and Madison walks in with my dress. She grins and walks over to my closet, hanging the magnificent showstopper on a hook. "You are going to knock them dead today."

I wish I could knock David dead. Bang bang. He shot me down...and I got right back up.

"Darling, could you run downstairs and help Julia? She's bringing breakfast up here to my room and she'll probably need some help carrying everything."

She turns on her heel. "OK."

Should she run into David, I need one of my props. I don't have to explain this to Maddy; she knows all about my act. "Bring me my wine, too."

"Got it."

Soon, my bedroom is a whirlwind of activity—with me the center of attention. Madison flops down on my bed with Julia, watching as Calvin and Elodie preen and pamper and prod me. As Calvin brushes out my hair, pulling it, an idea comes to mind—one to mess with David's head. With Calvin and Elodie, we can't say exactly what's on our minds, have to talk without talking, if that makes sense. I clear my throat. "Julia, how would you feel about inviting Liam to the party tonight? Maybe he could come over early and watch the awards with you?"

"Good idea. I'd like reinforcements. I'll text him now." A moment or two later, she grins. "He thanks you for the invite."

I tap my chin and nod.

"Perhaps Chloe, too?" I ask. "Any friend of yours is a friend of mine. And, as they say, the more the merrier..."

"Do you think she'll come?" Madison asks.

"I think so. Other industry people will be here and she's all about making connections. I'm texting her right now."

We wait a few moments, Julia staring at her phone. Finally, she meets my eyes and says, "She's in. But she'll probably want to steer clear of David, especially after what happened. Maybe she can hang out with Tyler?" She meets my gaze and I glare at her. "I'm just thinking out loud."

Understood. Tyler can run interference, but Julia shouldn't have said what she said in front of Calvin and Elodie. I have to correct her error before they pick it up. "Yes, David told me she was not only a horrific actress, but a terrible dancer and she ran crying from the audition when she didn't get the part in *The Sunset Stripper*."

Julia's eyes meet mine. She shakes her head. She knows I'm lying. Whatever. The girl should be used to it by now.

"That's so sad. I'm glad I play behind the scenes. No dents to my ego," says Elodie with a groan. "Unless you don't like my magic, Erica."

"I love your magic."

"There's just one problem," says Julia, and my heart lurches.

"What?"

"She doesn't have anything to wear."

"Not a problem. She seems to be the same size as me." I wave a dismissive hand. "Head into my closet and pick out a couple of options for her." I pause. "Which dress are you wearing tonight?"

"I'm not sure."

"Wear the blue one," I instruct. "And maybe go braless."

She cringes.

"Trust me," I say.

Calvin agrees, "Yes, you pretty young thing, you have the perfect figure and perky breasts. You can so get away with it."

Madison clears her throat. "Erica, what about Moonbeam?"

My gaze snaps from Julia's dropped jaw to Maddy. Ollie would never, ever walk into this house—unless he had a gun aimed at David's head. Instead of responding to her question, I say, "Good idea. I think you meant moonlight, though, the song used in *Swerve*. We need music." I tap my chin. "Alexa, play "Dancing in the Moonlight" by King Harvest."

"One of my parents' favorite songs," says Julia, her head dropping. She swallows. Hard. My heart goes out to her, but I can't stand up to squeeze her hand because Elodie is currently slathering a hyaluronic acid cream over my face. It's good for the complexion, tightens up the skin.

The intercom buzzes. "I can't move," I say.

"I'll get it," says Madison, scrambling over to press the button. "Yes?"

"Mrs. Drake, Mel B's Catering is here."

"Send them in, please. Thanks, Kyle." Maddy turns to Julia, whose bottom lip quivers. She clasps her hand, pulsing it. "I'll help you out. OK?"

Julia mumbles her agreement and then says, "Good luck, Erica."

"You've got this," says Madison with a fierce nod.

I blow them kisses. I better have this.

. . .

By 1 p.m., I'm in the back seat of the Phantom, waiting for David. He slides into the seat next to me, wearing an Armani tux with a silver tie that matches my dress. He's also donned dark shades, but from the side I see his eyelashes blink with approval.

"You look beautiful, Erica," he says.

"So do you," I lie.

"Do you think we can get back to the beginning?"

"Of what?"

"Us."

"If both of us win," I say, and he nods.

I lean back and close my eyes, rehearsing my acceptance speech.

THIRTY-THREE

JULIA

The caterers have arrived, and the house explodes with activity —people running around everywhere, setting up decorations— silver balloons and stars to match Erica's dress and, apparently, David's tie. The house pulses with excitement. Madison follows me into the kitchen and I head straight for the butternut soup. I still need to incorporate the final touches, adding in cream and making the Parmesan crisps.

"What do you want me to do?" asks Madison as the catering crew scrambles around us.

"Grate the Parmesan."

"By hand?"

"No, with the Cuisinart grating attachment," I say, pulling out the machine, followed by the Parmesan, placing everything in front of her. "We'll need enough for seventy."

As Madison sets to work, I take out a small pot, spoon a couple of ladles, followed by a dash or two of cream. Time for a final taste test. Once simmering, I pour it into one of the little glass bowls we'll be serving them in, add the garnish. I place the bowl in front of Madison.

"Taste this," I instruct.

She salutes me. "Yes, chef."

Madison sips from the bowl and immediately starts coughing and wheezing, her eyes watering. "It's so spicy! Flu-ugh-water, water. Need water now!"

Mel B's gaze shoots in my direction as I throw a dish towel over where I think David's hidden a camera and then grab a bottle of Perrier from the refrigerator. "It's not spicy. It was perfect yesterday."

Normally, I'd have cast suspicion on Mel, but I know there's only one person out to sabotage me, the same one who'd tampered with my boeuf bourguignon and catnapped Beurre-boule. I hand Madison her water and then pull out my phone. As Madison chugs straight from the bottle, I click on the kitchen footage on my EyeSpy account, getting an error message.

SORRY. YOU'VE EXCEEDED YOUR DAILY LIMIT OF VIEWS. PLEASE TRY AGAIN TOMORROW.

My entire body trembles with anger. Erica. I shouldn't have given her the log-in information. I mean, is she constantly spying on all of us? I wouldn't put it past her. I'm not sure if I like her or if I hate her—it's a thin line.

I clear my throat, my words coming out louder than they ever have. I don't even bother using my fake French accent. "This is an important party. Everything we prepared yesterday needs to be tasted now. This very instant."

"What the hell?" whispers Madison. "Why would he do that?"

"I don't know. Maybe he wants Erica to fire me in front of all the guests, so I'll hate her even more. Maybe he wants me to cause a scene? Make her look bad?" I whisper back. "I need you to get to the store and pick up fifteen more butternut squashes. And anything else we might need."

Thankfully, the soup was the only dish David had messed

with—the one thing he knew Erica had specifically requested. When Madison returns from the store, I spend the hour preparing a new batch, roasting the squash first, Mel by my side.

Before we leave to head into the home theater to join Tyler, Silvia, and Karla, I instruct Mel: "Taste everything before it's served. If any complications arise, come find me."

She swallows, her eyes wide.

Madison and I make it just in time to see Erica and David's red-carpet entrance. Hot and sweaty, we sink into our seats. Erica looks absolutely stunning as she struts down the runway, the cameras flashing.

"She looks incredible!" gasps Silvia, and Karla agrees. "So natural!"

Karla sniggers. "She better win."

"She will," says Maddy. "And I know you just want whatever is in the suitcases she brings back."

"Can you blame us? It's our bonus!"

"Well," says a reporter from E News, "you definitely have my vote for best dressed. Good luck tonight. Who are you wearing?"

Erica winks. "Dior, darling."

David stands by her side, blinking with irritation. Probably because Erica is getting all the attention and he's just her side-piece, one she barely glances at unless it's to shoot him a fake smile.

The front gate buzzes, alerting us to Chloe's arrival. Since Erica and David's categories aren't until much later, I have time to shower and get ready. I meet Chloe out front. She hops out of her yellow VW bug, eyes the house. "I can't believe you live in such an amazing place," she says and then swallows. "And I can't believe I'm here."

Me neither. Yet she's here for a reason.

"I do. And don't worry. He won't come near you." I pull her

into a hug and we exchange les bisous. "Ready to see your dress choices?"

"I kind of can't wait," she replies.

"Erica told me to tell you that you can keep all of them—or at least the ones you want."

"How many are there?"

"A lot." I lead her down the path to the guesthouse.

She's up to something. I know it.

As we get ready for the party, I put on one of my dad's playlists, laughing when Blue Öyster Cult's "Don't Fear the Reaper" comes on. I'm not scared of David. He should be scared of me. Ignoring Erica's advice, I am wearing a bra under my blue silk dress. Braless? No, my ladies will be strapped in. I am not shark bait. I am the shark.

It's almost showtime. The guard alerts us to Liam's arrival. I race to the front door to greet him. He's looking stylish in a slim-cut suit. "You clean up well," I say with a grin.

He clears his throat. "So do you. You look beautiful, J."

"We're watching the event on the big screen in the home theater," I say, and Liam nods. "Follow me."

We enter the room.

Tyler's gaze drifts back and forth from me to Chloe, finally landing on Chloe. He grins and blushes. Apparently, he has a new crush and will certainly enjoy his duties for the night. We all settle in the theater, glasses of champagne in hand, waiting in anticipation.

It's time...

Li Wei, last year's winner for her portrayal of Mei Lin in *Eternal Promise*, steps onto the stage to present the nominees for best actress. I squeeze my eyes shut, holding my breath, my heart beating with anticipation, until I hear, "And this year's

Oscar for best actress goes to..." A long pause. "Erica Drake for her role as Christine Brooks in *Swerve!*"

A tear slides down my cheek. She's profited—big time—by exploiting my parents' deaths in the most heinous of ways. They both have. And my emotions are raw, as if my heart has been lanced with a knife.

Liam squeezes my hand as Erica takes the stage. Li Wei kisses Erica's cheek and then smiles as Erica holds up her Oscar high above her head. The camera view snaps to David, who nods with a smug grin.

"I want to punch his mouth," says Tyler flatly.

Silvia and Karla share surprised glances.

The applause dies down to a low roar when Erica clears her throat. "I guess the second time is the charm," she says. "This is all so overwhelming. I am honored and thrilled and I'd like to share this triumph with all the amazing women in this category. This. This Oscar is for all of us." She pauses, lifting up the statue. "I guess Oscar can make the rounds. And, of course, we'll also need to share Oscar with the cast and crew. We all came together as a team and there is no I in team. Thank you. Thank you, of course, to the Academy. Thank you for recognizing all of us." She pauses, looking into the crowd as the applause settles down. The camera flashes to David. "I'd like to thank the love of my life and my inspiration, the one dream I've had." Her mouth curves into a wide smile and David straightens his posture. And then she says with a wink, "Of course, I'm talking about acting."

The crowd rips into wild laughter. And the expression on David's face is priceless. The way his lips turn down, the humiliation in his eyes. I'm reveling in it.

On the big screen it's almost like she's looking directly at me when she says, "David, my husband, took extreme creative liberties when he wrote the screenplay for *Swerve*. I'd like to say it was based on a true story, but I know it's a lie. Christine and

Stephen Brooks were deeply in love with one another. I know this because I met both of them a few times at That French Café in Calabasas." She takes a dramatic pause. "I dedicate this award to Josephine Brooks, the beautiful daughter they left behind. Every tear I cried on screen was real, thinking about how a child should never have to experience losing their parents so young." She raises the Oscar again. "Josephine Brooks, wherever you are, this is for you."

I hang my head low, my heart beating furiously. Liam squeezes my hand again, pulsing his grip.

As Erica gracefully exits the stage, the camera pans to David. He blinks and then smiles, nodding his head while clapping slowly. The room falls quiet when the winner for best original screenplay is announced. It's not David. And he doesn't win best picture either. He purses his lips, shrugging cockily.

I stand up. "The guests will be arriving soon," I say, gulping. "I'm going to check in with the caterers."

I leave the home theater, head to the powder room and lock the door. Finally alone, I let out the tears I've been holding in, sinking to the floor and sobbing.

Erica and David arrive at Hummingbird House a little after nine. Antoine carries two large suitcases into the foyer and Silvia and Karla's eyes light up. With over fifty guests in attendance, the applause and shouts of congratulations for Erica are deafening. "Where's Oscar?" Madison demands.

"He'll be here in a couple of weeks. They like keeping everything a secret until the winners are announced." Erica grins. "They're engraving my name."

David scowls, pushing by Erica, heading to the bar.

"What a sore loser," somebody whispers.

Silvia and Karla start serving, helping the caterers. Chloe,

Tyler, Madison, Liam, and I huddle in the corner as Erica makes her rounds. All our eyes are locked onto David.

His jaw drops when he sees Chloe. David slams his drink down and storms over to us. "Who is this?"

I shrug. "Chloe. She eez my guest. I was friends with Chloe's sister, Solene, in Paris. We connected a week ago," I say. "Why? Do you know her?"

"You're sounding a lot less French," he hisses.

"I've been working on my American accent," I say. "Erica's been helping me."

He clenches his jaw. "Guests need to be cleared."

"She was," I say. "By Erica."

Erica saunters up to us. "Is that a problem? Julia does have a life outside this home."

He glares at Erica and then stomps back to the bar. Madison raises her brow. "Let's grab something to eat before it's all gone," she says. "Come on."

She escorts Chloe, Tyler, and Liam to the far side of the room. Liam mouths, "I'll be right back."

Erica stands before me, silent for a moment.

"I think he's reaching his breaking point," she finally whispers, our eyes following David's every move. It's almost as if he's putting on a performance, pretending to be happy—slapping the backs of men, air-kissing women's cheeks.

David's eyes scan me, my dress. He licks his lips.

I'm in the process of shuddering, willing my disgust down, when Erica lets out a groan. "Julia, you're about to meet my friends. Just roll with the punches." She turns, nodding to each of them. "Miriam, Cindy, so glad you made it!"

"Congratulations on the win. Didn't see that one coming," titters Miriam.

"Neither did I." Erica coughs out a fake laugh. "But life is full of surprises, isn't it, Julia?"

I plaster on a smile. "Eet eez."

Cindy's gaze rakes over my body. "You must be Erica's French chef."

"Oui, c'est moi."

Miriam laughs. "Why'd you hire a chef if she isn't even cooking?"

"Maybe she's heating things up elsewhere," says Miriam, her gaze landing on David.

"Because she's prepared everything in advance," Erica says, lifting up her chin. "Have you tried the soup? It's phenomenal." She waves to a server and the woman comes sashaying over with the tray. "David and I had this at Fouquet, in Paris. It's one of the reasons I sought Julia out."

Cindy eyes me up and down, and snickers, "I'm thinking David sought this one out."

Now I know why Erica doesn't like her friends, both of them nasty hyenas.

The women each take a small glass bowl, served with little spoons. "And what is it?" asks Cindy.

"It's delicious," says Erica.

I straighten my posture. "Usually, I prepare this velouté with potimarron, a chestnut-flavored squash, but zees time, I use butternut because—impossible to find here." I shrug. "Still good. Taste it. See if you can pinpoint my special ingredient."

Miriam licks her lips, dives her spoon right into the bowl. Her eyes open wide. She licks her lips. "Ginger!" she exclaims. "Oh my lord, this is phenomenal. I'm stealing you away from Erica. How much is she paying you?"

Definitely not enough. And what's up with people asking me that question?

David has been circling around us, within earshot of the conversation. A muscle twitches underneath his left eye. Once again, he storms off toward the bar, shaking his head. Oh, sorry, saboteur, did you think I wouldn't taste every dish before serving? You did. Shame on you.

A few hours later, I'm talking with Liam, laughing—flirting a little bit, pulling invisible lint off his jacket. And he's flirting back with me. I feel David's eyes boring into my back. And then I feel his hand grip my upper arm. "Two guests, Julia? You invited Chloe and your boyfriend to our event..."

Liam clears his throat. "Mr. Drake, I'm not J's boyfriend, I'm Tyler's tutor. I'm here every day of the week. Mrs. Drake invited me."

David's eyes narrow into a glare. He gives Liam the once-over. "I didn't recognize you."

Liam's eyes go wide. "I think this is the first time we've met."

David scowls at me and turns on his heel, heading to the bar for what I think is his fifth drink. To my surprise, Chloe saunters up to him, whispers something in his ear. She gingerly touches his arm, winks, and then grabs his tie. Sophie Ellis-Bextor's "Murder on the Dance Floor" is piping through every speaker in the house and Chloe is dancing, circling around David and he laughs. It occurs to me, right in this moment, how I don't really know her or what her agenda is.

Erica raises a brow, shakes her head, and then cuts off the music. Silvia hands her a microphone. The crowd turns to face her. "I'd like to thank everybody for coming here tonight to celebrate my win. Apparently, the second time is the charm," she slurs, her gaze locking onto Chloe, her chin lifted. "Or maybe it's the third. I dunno. At any rate, I'm glad we're all able to have fun tonight and that I finally won"—she hiccups—"best actress before I reach my expiration date. I'm turning thirty-nine this year so apparently that date is coming soon." She raises her glass. "To Hollywood! Let's pop open the champagne!"

Aside from polite applause, people don't know what to do, mostly shooting each other confused looks. David takes the microphone from her hand, scowling at her as she teeters on her heels. "Winning the Oscar has clearly gone to Erica's head. But champagne is always a good idea."

A few chuckles. Whispers of "she's wasted." But I know she isn't. This is an act. And this is awkward.

"Erica was sober two seconds ago, speaking clearly." Liam eyes me curiously. "J, something feels really off tonight and I'm feeling like a pawn in a really messed-up game of chess. Like I'm supposed to witness a meltdown." He blinks. "Did Erica hire me to tutor Tyler because she knew who I was? That I knew you?"

He's calling it out just like it is. My face, the way I blink, the way I can't meet his eyes, is my tell.

"Damn it, Josephine, answer me."

I hiss, "Do not call me that. Not here. You don't know—"

"I'll scream your name out right now if you don't tell me what's going on. I mean, seriously, you're working for the people who made a film about your parents' death, profiting from it." He lifts his chin with defiance, his eyes dark and fierce. They're intense. "Don't test me."

"Don't threaten me. You don't know what you're doing." I grab his wrist, my body tensing. "We're going outside. To the beach."

For a moment, Liam stares at me blankly, most likely deliberating if he's going to create a scene. "Jesus, J, tell me what's going on."

"I will. I'm trying to," I say, my eyes meeting Erica's. She scratches her cheek—a sign she wants to talk to me. She clasps her phone, nodding toward it. Blinks. "Liam, give me a couple of minutes. I need to use the ladies' room. Meet me on the terrace."

He squints and shakes his head. "Fine."

I make my way to the powder room, digging my phone out of my purse. The screen jumps alive when I wake it.

ED:

I don't trust Chloe. Be careful. Liam. David is jealous.

I will the headache pounding like a hammer in my brain to go away, but it is slamming my head like a drum. Before meeting Liam on the terrace, I peek into the great room. Lo and behold, Chloe and David are whispering in a corner. His hand glides surreptitiously down her side.

My heart sinks as I walk out onto the terrace. Liam stands quietly, wringing his hands, staring at the stars sparkling in the sky. I wince when he turns to face me. This party is a nightmare. My life is a nightmare. Worse, I've probably put Liam in danger. And, well, Erica likes to flambé anything that stands in her way. I can't shake the image of her lighting the match.

Liam shakes his head and my throat goes completely dry.

THIRTY-FOUR

ERICA

It's after two in the morning when the last guests finally leave—of course, Miriam and Cindy and their equally horrific spouses. I'm exhausted, and yawn dramatically as they fake kiss and congratulate me again. The horrible duo of hyenas will be talking about me behind my back tomorrow. I can already hear their cackles and their words.

Can you believe she went au-natural with her makeup?

She thought she could pull that look off.

Her dress was beautiful, but it would have looked better on somebody younger.

I can't believe she actually won. Must have paid somebody off.

David stands to my side, laughing with the husbands over something, hopefully not me, but I wouldn't put it past him. Golf plans are made. Yada-yada-yada. Go away. I'm looking forward to reliving this night—the win, my win—over and over again in my dreams. Yes, I'll be replaying every stunning moment in my head.

Silvia and Karla step up to me as the front door closes. They eye the suitcases filled with swag. I laugh. "Have at it," I say. "But remember to keep some things for Julia and Madison."

They nod, wide grins stretched across their faces. "And Mr. Drake?"

A reminder of his failure, he probably won't want to look at them.

"I don't even know why they give me stuff when they know I can afford it," he says with a low chortle. "They're up for grabs, too. Maybe put some things aside for Tyler."

"I love working here!" they squeal. "Congratulations! Again!"

"My win is your win." I wink and David shoots a nasty look in my direction. "Just make sure everything is shut down tonight and that the caterers clear all their stuff out."

"Will do."

The catering crew scrambles to clean up the bulk of the mess and I stumble upstairs to the bedroom, a satisfied smile on my face. Before undressing, I grab my phone, pulling up Snapchat.

MOONBEAM:

Could you hear me screaming? I knew you'd win.

I smile and type in my response.

SUNBEAM:

Thanks. What a night!

MOONBEAM:

He must be pissed. Any danger? I'll come running with a sword…

SUNBEAM:

Oh, he's angry. But it's nothing I can't handle.

I watch the texts disappear, my words spoken too soon.

David storms up behind me and he grabs my arm. "You

ungrateful little bitch. You didn't even thank me in your speech."

"But I did," I scoff. "I looked you right in the eyes."

He slaps me so hard I see stars. The sharp sting on my cheek blooms into a fiery pain. For a moment, my vision blurs, the room spinning. Once the world comes back into focus, I taste the metallic tang of blood on my lip, where his watch caught me. His face, contorted with rage, hovers in front of me. I feel the angry heat of his breath on my skin.

He jabs my clavicle with a forceful finger. "And then you made a joke."

I know what I'm about to do will push him over the edge. I laugh.

"The crowd loved it," I say, spitting out my words.

His eyes swirl with a crazed anger I've never seen. "Don't forget, Erica. I made you," he hisses. "And I can destroy you, too."

I narrow my eyes into a glare. Without me, he'd still be writing crappy films. I'm the one who gives him the big ideas. I'm the one who reads the first drafts for all of his scripts. I'm the one who suggests the changes to make them more powerful —more human. Once I gather my wits, I say, "David, don't you dare forget. We made each other."

He pushes me onto the bed.

His hands fly to his temples, an attempt to restrain himself from lashing out again. "I don't want to hurt you, Erica. Damn it," he says, his voice strained with pained remorse. "Why do you get off pushing me the way you do?"

Like I'd been asking for it? It's such a twisted narrative, one we've gone through so many times, as if I mentally abuse him. Ridiculous.

I prop myself up on my elbows. "I believe you're the one who pushed me."

As I rub my neck, trying to swallow, he stomps toward the

door, turns. "You're firing your French chef tomorrow. She's on the beach with Tyler's tutor. We're paying her a fortune... and she hasn't even been cooking," he screams, and points at me with a solid finger, and then he mumbles, "I really don't know why you brought her into your twisted world."

"My twisted world?"

Is he kidding me? He's the twisted one. He is so jealous. This could be good for my plan. Or it could be bad. I may need to rewrite this script. Again. I'm always thinking.

"Yes, Erica," he says, pacing, "but no matter how much you enrage me, I love you. And I'm proud of you." He sits on the edge of the bed and kisses me on the cheek. "Look, I'm spent. I'm going to sleep in the guest room again... unless you want me to stay..."

"I don't." No, I want him as far away from me as possible. I've already pressed David's limits beyond his breaking point. I need to stay safe. Should he do something to me tonight—he'd have a hell of a lot of explaining to do. He won't take the risk—not now, not with the media crawling down our backs. I've got him where I want him—he's about to snap and I'm counting on him making a huge mistake. One thing I learned a long time ago is to kill 'em with kindness. Instead of retaliating, I slump onto the bed, my hands cradling my head. "I have a pounding headache."

Thanks to you.

"Good night, gorgeous. I'm sorry for the way I reacted," he says softly, almost like a little dog who was slapped on the nose with a newspaper. "Congratulations on your win."

"Thanks, my love," I say, and he blinks. "Before you leave, can you unzip me?"

He nods and I stand up, my back to him. He's probably thinking about wrapping his hands around my skinny neck, but that would be very, very unwise of him, especially with Madison and Tyler down the hall. Plus, the caterers are still here, and they'd hear me scream bloody murder. I do have lungs.

His hands run down my back, to the zipper. I can smell his Creed Aventus cologne, all woody and musky with notes of blackcurrant, pineapple, and birch. I used to love the scent. I used to love him. Now they both make me sick to my stomach.

The zipper slides down my back. He kisses my neck and, as if reading the thoughts swirling around in my mind, he says, "No matter what happens between us, I'll always love you," and then he exits the room with a sigh.

My eyelids flutter. I wonder if that's what he'd put on my epitaph.

The moment he leaves, I close and lock the door. After hanging up my dress, I text Julia.

ED:

Send Liam home. D jealous.

Talk plans in morning.

JF:

Already morning.

I pull up the cameras on my phone, adjusting the movement. Julia and Liam are just lying down on loungers, looking up at the starry sky, talking. She gets up, yawns, stretches her arms. He links an arm into hers and they start for the path. Before they cut out of view, Liam tries angling in for a kiss. Julia places one hand on his chest and I can make out the words, "Not yet."

She's putting off a chance for love to help me. Taking one for the team. And I know David was just pacifying me. I'm sure he's expecting another one of my so-called meltdowns. Once the excitement from my win dies down, he'll unleash the dragon and my plans for a better life could end up being flambéed. I have to warn Julia.

ED:

D wants me to fire you.

I head into my closet, pulling out the Ken doll from the box, thinking about lighting him on fire. Then, I think better of the idea, mostly because a lot of my dresses are highly flammable not to mention the smell of burnt plastic. Horrible. Instead, I tie a cord from one of my dresses around his neck and hang the doll from the bar of my closet. I swing it back and forth and then head into the bathroom to grab a pair of nail scissors from the vanity.

Snip.

Oh, how the mighty have fallen.

THIRTY-FIVE

JULIA

Mental stress is like a ninja sneaking up on you, and I can barely move a muscle in the morning. Of course, I didn't sleep well, not with my mind spinning, but adrenaline eventually gave way to exhaustion.

Last night, I didn't tell Liam everything, but he knows enough; namely that I've put myself in danger. He'd tried his best to convince me to leave with him right then, and he'd quit working for this deranged family, too, but I stood my ground.

"Liam, the only deranged person in this equation is David," I said. "And I'm not leaving until he's ruined and exposed."

"You're no better than he is then." He shook his head. "Revenge won't get you what you want—"

"How do you know what I want?" I spat. "You don't even know me. Not anymore."

"It's obvious. And I know you better than you think I do. You want your old life back. You want your parents back." He sighed. "And that's not going to happen. They're dead."

Talk about getting straight to the point.

"I know they're dead, Liam." I glared at him. "I know I can't change the past, but I can change the future. I want to live out their dreams for them, the ones they couldn't because David took them away."

He went silent for a moment. "What dream?"

"Opening a chain of That French Café." I paused. "I want to honor their memory."

"I could get on board with that." He pursed his lips, tucked his hands behind his neck. "But you're not telling me everything."

Because, no matter how much I wanted to, I couldn't.

"Just answer one question."

"Depends on what it is."

"How does Erica fit into this dream of yours?"

Good question. A whisper of doubt and hesitation crept into my mind. I'd already shared too much with Liam. But I could be honest with him. "We share a common goal."

"I'm putting my number in." Liam grabbed the cellphone I'd been clutching from my hand, but before he could open Contacts the phone buzzed. "She just texted you."

"And?"

"She's warning you. Apparently, David wants her to fire you. I honestly don't get it."

"What's there to get? He probably saw the way I looked at you."

"And how do you look at me?"

I sighed. "Liam, you're a smart guy. Figure it out."

He gripped my hands.

"Do you think there's still a chance for us? Maybe we could pick up where we left off?" He tilted his head to the side. "I mean, I'd like there to be. You're the one that got away, the only girl—woman—I've ever thought about."

As he spoke, my mind raced from the present to the past—both with problems and conflicts I've yet to overcome. I still care for Liam, always have, and my heart tugs at the memories—like when he took me to his senior prom, me, a sophomore, wearing a blue dress and the most beautiful orchid corsage on my wrist. When we slow-danced and it was as if our hearts beat as one.

"There's a chance," I said, head down. "But not yet—it's too much, too soon."

My words delivered a shooting pain into my heart, like somebody was holding a knife and twisting it. I can only imagine how they impacted Liam. His face crumbled from hope into disappointment. "I'll walk you back up the path. It's dark out."

We didn't say a word until we reached my front door. "I'll see you tomorrow, J. Promise me that you'll call if you're in any danger. And I'll come running."

This morning, Liam's words ring in my brain.

Running? After last night, I've been thinking about it. Everything is catching up with me and I'm tired. No, I'm absolutely spent. Life used to be a lot less complicated, and I still have unfinished business to attend to before I leap into anything. Which sucks. Still, I make my way into the kitchen, which looks like a tornado swept through it. Empty bottles of champagne litter the countertops, half-eaten hors d'oeuvres are strewn across the floor, and the sink is overflowing with dirty dishes. The caterers did a half-assed job of cleaning up. With a sigh, I roll up my sleeves and start tidying the mess—one crumpled napkin at a time. It's going to be a long morning of cleaning, but at least I have time to think and prepare something simple for brunch.

It's around 9 a.m. when I hear footsteps. I'm hoping to see anybody else—Erica, Tyler, Madison, Silvia or Karla. But there he is, all sweaty, a towel draped around his neck: David. I swallow back the dread in my throat. Say something. Say anything but *I know you killed my parents, made a movie about their death, profited from it, and I'm going to make you pay.*

"Good workout?" I ask, shifting my weight from side to side.

He nods and takes a step closer.

He must have gotten loaded last night because, along with his sweat, I smell the rancid and pungent scent of alcohol coming off his skin. Keeping from gagging, I scramble over to the refrigerator to grab the homemade raspberry jam I made last week—thanks to the Thermomix. I stare at the jar, thinking it looks like blood, its dark crimson hue, the texture. And then my eyes flash onto David. He has the blood of my parents on his hands. I shudder and then paste on a smile, although it's getting difficult—enormously so—to pull this act off.

"What can I get you, Mr. Drake?" I ask, eyeing my kitchen knives, unrolled on the counter and gleaming in the sun. But, unlike David, I'm not a murderer. I wouldn't kill a fly.

"It's David. And you can get me a new wife," he mumbles. "One who appreciates me."

His lips part as if he wants to say something more, but he clamps them shut. Good.

I turn back to the fruit I'd been cutting, focusing on the sweet aromas. In my head, I think of flavors: sweet, salty, bitter. And I am so bitter right now. "How about a nice glass of fresh squeezed *jus d'orange?*"

"That'll work. Put some champagne in it while you're at it."

I force out a fake laugh. "Rough night?"

"You don't even know." He hangs his head. "What time is your boyfriend coming over?"

I snort and place the oranges into the fruit presser. "Boyfriend? I don't have a boyfriend."

"Liam."

"Liam is not my boyfriend. He's Tyler's tutor. And he usually gets here around ten."

"What time does he leave?"

I pour the juice into a glass and grab a bottle of champagne from the fridge, popping it open.

"Cinq heure. Sometimes a little after." I hand him his drink with a forced smile. I'm hoping he doesn't notice my shaky hands. He doesn't. Because he's not staring at my hands. I clear my throat. "I take it after all the excitement Erica is sleeping in."

"She is." He grins. "Your English—the accent—has really improved. I'd almost think you were American."

You think?

"It's all coming back to me." I look at my wrist. There isn't a watch on it. I'll just pretend it's there and hide my arm behind my back. "What would you like for dinner tonight? And for brunch? I'm leaving for the store in a couple of minutes."

I need an excuse to get away from him.

"I won't be here for brunch. Need to take care of something at the studio. For dinner, something simple with loads of carbs. I missed out the other night. How about spaghetti Bolognese? And brownies for dessert. It's not only Tyler's favorite, it's mine, too." He lifts his chin. "Plus, we can have all the carbs we want now."

"Parfait."

He chugs back his mimosa and sets the glass down. He winks and steps forward to kiss me on the cheek. He angles in, twisting his body so his lips lightly brush against mine. He whispers, "I'll see you tonight, ma belle."

Internally, I'm freaking out, but I'm getting used to forcing smiles. I lower my head, pretending I'm blushing and reply, "Can't wait."

He leaves and I let out the breath I've been holding in. I don't know how much more of this I can take without losing my mind. I clench my fists and close my eyes. When I open them, two hummingbirds hover just outside the kitchen window.

Keep calm. Cook on. Until the shit hits the fan.

THIRTY-SIX

ERICA

It's one in the afternoon. Liam and Tyler are on the veranda, studying. Tyler is smiling and laughing. Liam is a good teacher —because Tyler is completely engaged. Their voices float up to me—they're discussing Shakespeare. Julia knows how to pick them, whereas I do not.

Julia's face drops when I finally wander into the kitchen. Her jaw tenses. I know she wants to talk. I shake my head and mouth, "Not here." And then I say loudly, barking out an order, "I have the worst headache. Please, do your job and make me a cure."

"Mimosa?" she asks, eyes wide.

"Oh, Julia, I need something stronger."

Until we know what he's up to, we're playing out our roles. Sometimes Julia overacts, but it comes off as authentic—as if she's sweet and innocent, only trying to please. Brava for that.

"How about a screwdriver? Zat is zee name, oui?" She smiles. "Congratulations on your win! I'm so very, very proud of you."

I hear footsteps. David? It wouldn't surprise me.

"Would you just make me my damn drink?"

Silvia and Karla are about to come into the kitchen. And they sneak right out. I feel terrible that they have to clean up after the party, but I can't let them off the hook. Not when we're trying to catch the big fish. I laugh to myself. Moby Dick.

I slam my hand on the table. "Now."

Julia's chin tucks into her neck. "D'accord, Erica."

"And stop sounding like a stupid French robot," I mumble.

Julia makes the screwdriver and sets it down in front of me. "Oh," I say. "I'm not drinking it here. I'm thinking some fresh air will do me good. It's a beautiful day. I'd like to go down to the beach. I need help walking down the path." I rub my forehead dramatically and meet her eyes. "I'm not feeling so well."

She stomps her foot. "Is zat in my job description? Because I don't zink eet is."

Even though I want to laugh at her ridiculous accent, I meet her eyes, my gaze steady. "It is now. Pick up my drink. And follow me. I need to lie down."

On the way, we pass Tyler and Liam. I give them a slight wave. Liam looks concerned. And he should be because he doesn't know what's really going on. Yet, the less he knows the better. "Do you need help, Mrs. Drake?" he calls out.

Tyler stands up, a worried look on his face. "Mom, are you OK?"

"I'm fine, sweetie," I say, lifting up my chin. "I have Julia. Get back to your Shakespeare."

Finally, after I pretend stumble down the path, we can speak without the threat of hidden cameras.

"That was some performance, Erica," says Julia, eyeing me with concern.

"There's a reason I won best actress." She hands me the drink and I set it down. "I don't want it. Do you?"

She nods. "Kind of."

"It's yours."

She takes a gigantic sip of the drink and then gasps. "And

you are one hundred percent sure he doesn't have cameras down here?"

"I am." I blink and then I smile. "I may have hired a crew to sweep the place when they were installing the anchors and pilons."

Julia's voice quivers. "Erica! This is getting really serious."

I nod. "Just hold out a little longer until you get his latest script."

"I don't know," she says.

"If we know what he's planning, we can bring him down." I meet her eyes, my gaze steady. "I saw his reaction to you in the kitchen. I have a feeling he's going to do something tonight. It's a gut instinct. And we need to be prepared for anything."

"And what's that?"

"He thinks you hate me. And he wants you." I shake my head. God, it hurts. "He's killed before, you know..."

Julia's eyes bug out. "And? Should I warn Liam?"

"No. The less Liam knows the better. And what I'm going to do to you will hurt you more than it hurts me." I focus my gaze on the bluff. "We know how his twisted mind works. He wants me to fire you, so just be prepared. I may slap you really hard."

Her hand automatically shoots to her cheek. "How hard?"

"Really hard."

"And then what?"

"You threaten to sue me and then you take off in Tyler's Mercedes," I say, and then I stare off into the distance, mumbling under my breath. "Maybe I'll take off, too. Montenegro looks spectacular this time of year. The climate and landscape are similar to California..."

"What?"

"Nothing," I say, rubbing my eyes with my fingertips. "I'm tired. Exhausted. A vacation from stress is what this woman needs..."

Her nose scrunches. "I guess I'll start packing."

"And help yourself to a handful of petty cash."

"I need a vacation, too," she says. "I'm thinking about taking all of it."

She'd better not. I need it.

Dinner, as usual, is awkward. Stilted conversations. David eyeing Julia lasciviously. Me one-upping David with my win. Him glaring at me. Finally, the moment I've been waiting for. Julia comes in to serve dessert. Brownies. Tyler's eyes go wide. "You are my most favorite person in the world, Julia. I love you." He blushes. "Well, I love your cooking."

"She's a really great cook." David grins and pats his belly. "No arguments here. Is there vanilla ice cream, Julia?"

"Bien sûr," she says, her eyes meeting mine. "I'm so happy for the Thermomix. I'll go grab some."

Tyler picks up his fork. "I can't wait. I'm digging in."

Thirty seconds later, Tyler chokes and gags. He falls off his chair and onto the floor, writhing and gripping his throat. "Are there peanuts in this?"

"EpiPen!" I scream. "Second drawer in the kitchen!"

Madison races out of the room as Tyler's breath grows more labored, wheezes mingled with desperate gasps of air.

David screams, "Didn't you tell Julia about Tyler's allergies?"

"I did," I hiss. "She knows everything."

Madison comes back into the room, quickly releasing the EpiPen from its case and ripping off the safety cap. She presses the pen against his thigh, stabbing it firmly. Our eyes meet. Tyler's breathing calms down to an almost normal level.

Julia races into the room, dropping the ice cream on the floor. I get up from the ground, walk up to her, and slap her hard across the face. So hard my hand hurts. "You are fired!

Pack up your things! You and your creepy cat can leave the premises immediately."

Her hand flies to her cheek, her eyes wide with confusion. "What did I do?"

Come on, Julia, don't fail me now.

"There were peanuts in the brownies. And I told you about Tyler's food allergies. You could have killed my son! My son!"

"I did not put peanuts in the brownies," she hisses. "And you just physically assaulted me." She lifts her chin and I meet her eyes with a fixed, intense glare. "I'm fired. Fine. But I'm taking the Mercedes."

Good, chef. Now you're cooking.

I take a step toward her. David tries to intervene, holding me back. "Calm down," he says.

"She is not taking the car," I hiss.

"Oui, I am." Julia sends a death glare in my direction and then stomps her foot. "I'm being let go for something I didn't do. You hit me. I will sue you. Read the contract I signed." Julia looks at her watch. "It's after nine. And nobody walks in LA."

David walks over to Julia, placing a hand on her shoulder. "Take the car. We'll figure everything out later." He shoots me a look. "My wife is obviously having another one of her meltdowns—"

"I am not having a meltdown. She could have killed our son!" I scream and then I screech at Julia, "Just get out of my face, you little slut! I saw you on the beach with Tyler's tutor." My eyes latch on to David's. "You make sure she's gone before I get back. We have to take Tyler to the emergency room. Madison will drive us."

"Uh, yeah, I will," Madison replies, her eyes wide.

I'd forgotten to prepare Maddy for this scene. My bad. I bite down on my bottom lip so hard I draw blood. Meanwhile, David is pretending he cares for Tyler, bending over him, one hand on his chest.

"What's going on?" Madison mouths.

I raise a brow.

On her way out, Julia's shoulders tremble. But she manages to lift them up and turn. "Va l'enfer, salope."

Go to hell, bitch. Good one, Julia.

THIRTY-SEVEN

JULIA

I wasn't expecting Erica to slap me so hard. My jaw rattles. My heart races. Thankfully, I'm already packed, save for Beurreboule, and I know I need to act quickly. It's hard to think straight, to move, not when my body is trembling. I stack my suitcases on top of one another, so I can wheel them down the path together. Beurreboule sits in her kitty carry-all, slung over my back, my purse slung over my shoulder.

After loading my suitcases in the back of the SUV, kitty in the back seat, I think I'm in the free and clear. I sit, shaking in the seat for one minute too long. A tap comes at the window. I roll it down, my heart rate picking up to dangerous levels. If anything, David will just think I'm upset about what transpired. I mean, he can't kill me now. Can he? I cannot meet him in the eyes, so I keep my head down, trying to swallow.

It's not hard to act upset when you're truly reeling from the shock of everything. David has done something to Tyler again. I know it. Erica knows it. Madison knows it. And so does Tyler. This man's mind is so twisted.

"I-I-I'm so sorry," I stutter, trying to shift the blame on me as best I can. "I must have forgotten about Tyler's allergies."

"Julia," says David, his tone low and placating. "I'm sorry for everything that's happened tonight. Erica, well, she's more than a handful, especially when she's drunk. Are you OK?"

Words do not form. I'm not OK. I'm flipping out.

"You packed pretty quickly," he continues.

I shift in my seat, hoping he doesn't know I'd been prepared. "I don't have many things."

He lifts up a brow. "Where are you going? To your boyfriend's? Liam?"

"I told you this before. He is NOT my boyfriend," I snap, and then change my tone. "I think I'll just stay at a hotel."

"Good to know." His gaze shoots from me to the car. "One of the tires on the car seems a little low. Before you take off, let me check it out."

"M-merci," I stutter as he stoops down.

I sit in the driver's seat, waiting, shaking, thinking: Oh my God! He could be messing with the car, doing something to it so I crash just like my parents. The Devil, indeed, does wear Prada and he has a killer smile. It's like he wears a Halloween costume —good-looking on the outside, evil inside. I've never met an uglier person. I can't believe my life may be on the line. I'll drive slow—so painfully slow when I want to speed out of here just like the film *Fast and Furious*, a movie I'd watched with my parents. I want to be fast. And I am furious. Then again, Paul Walker, the actor in that film, died in a crash, the car, a Porsche, bursting into flames.

I'm so out of my element.

Think. Think. Think.

If something happens, I could easily do what I'd learned as a child in emergency fire situations.

Stop: Do not run. Drop: To the ground. Roll: Snuff out the fire.

Why didn't they teach us how to jump out of a moving car? He could be tampering with the brake system. I don't have time to google the method. David's head pops up again, scaring the crap out of me. "It was nothing. A trick of the eye. You're good to go." He slaps the hood and I startle. "Madison and Erica have already taken Tyler to Urgent Care. Gate's open, I'll close it when you leave."

"Merci," I reply. "I hope he's OK."

"Me too." He shakes his head. "Drive safely."

Oh, I will.

I shift the car into drive, and peel right out of the driveway, slowing down as soon as I reach the gates. Good news: the brakes work. I'm trembling so badly I know I shouldn't be driving, but I press my foot down on the accelerator, David's figure looming like a malevolent shadow in the rearview mirror. Finally, after driving through the security gates, I pull over before turning onto PCH. Erica has sent me a text.

ED:

Tyler OK. You OK?

JF:

No.

ED:

Sorry I hit you so hard. Get script?

JF:

No.

We've all gotten so good at sending cryptic messages. I don't need a translator to figure out what's going on. We're all relying on gut instincts. Once my breathing calms down, I dial Chloe's number. Something about the way she'd played up to David at the party isn't sitting right. I need to find out what she knows about him. More importantly, she may have a copy of the script. She did audition for it. She picks up on the first ring. "Ch-chloe?"

"Julia? What's wrong?"

"Everything!" I sob. "Erica fired me. I don't know where to go. Can I come over?"

"Bien sûr," she says, giving me her address. "Got it?"

Not that she can see me, I nod and plug it into the GPS. She lives about ten minutes from here in Western Malibu, just off PCH on one of the canyon roads. Thankfully, nowhere near Las Flores.

"I didn't hear you," says Chloe after a few beats.

"Yes. Got it. Merci. I'll be there in a few."

I'm still trembling, but I manage the drive even with visions of David flickering in my brain. When I arrive at Chloe's house, I leave my bags in my trunk, bringing in my purse and Beurreboule's kitty carry-all. I'm stumbling up to the front porch as Chloe opens the door. She grabs Beurreboule's case, and the cat meows. "We'll put your kitty in my room, OK?"

I nod, standing numbly.

She heads down the hall, opens a door, returning a minute later, ushering me to sit down on the couch. "Wine?" she asks, and I shrug.

Chloe saunters into the kitchen, fumbles around.

"My roommates are both flight attendants, so they are not here. Always traveling. They share the bigger room, the veranda." With her free hand, she points down the hall. "I have the small room. It's very tiny, but comfortable." She grins. "If you need a place to crash for a couple of days, you're sitting on your bed. I have spare blankets."

Her home is large, probably over a thousand square feet, and well decorated with a beach vibe, including a whitewashed design element pointing out the beaches. It's cute—California bungalow style, set on a garden, and, in the distance, there's an ocean view.

She sits down on the couch next to me, setting the wine and glasses down on the coffee table, followed by her phone. I can't be sure, but I think I see the initials DD flash on her screen. She flips her phone over. Fiddles around with a necklace—one that looks exactly like Erica's. "What's going on? Why are you so upset? You're shaking."

I already told her why I was upset. But I didn't tell her everything. Perhaps I'm being paranoid. Maybe I'm just on full alert. Might as well get on with my hunch. "How well do you know David Drake?"

Her eyes darken and she sinks into the couch, her head lowered. "I told you what happened. He, he—"

I rub my forehead. "I saw you talking to him at the party. I don't think you told me everything."

She puffs out her bottom lip and her eyes glaze over. "I know he's having marital problems. Maybe I'll be the next Mrs. Drake."

I want to scream *Are you that stupid?* He's not only married, he could be dangerous. A freaking serial killer! Get with the program, girl! Then again, she's impressionable and he's clearly pulled a number on her, probably pays her portion of the rent, promised her everything—exactly like he did with Erica when she was her age. This is unfathomable. She'd basically accused him of rape. "So, you lied to me?"

"I didn't lie. I just didn't tell you the whole truth. I didn't want you to think less of me." She lowers her head. "I shouldn't have made up that story about him. I was the one who went after him, suggested the seduction at the audition. Nothing happened—"

Nothing?

"The film he's working on. The one about me," I say flatly. "Do you have his notes? The script?"

She shakes her head no. "Only what I told you."

If she's been seeing him, possibly falling in love with him, something isn't adding up. "Why did you tell me about it?"

"I wanted to see your reaction," she says. "Because I'd be playing a character based on you."

"What if I end up dead, Chloe? Would you still want to play the part?"

Her gaze snaps onto mine. "What are you talking about?"

"His personal assistant, Jasmine, was just found dead in the desert. It's all over the news."

Her brow scrunches. "What's going on?"

"You're going to have to trust me." I clamp my lips together. I'm not going to tell her who I am or what my plans are. "He's a method director..."

Her mouth forms a large o and doesn't close for a moment or two. She grabs her phone off the coffee table and points to a trunk. "If you need somewhere to stay tonight, blankets are in there. Feel free to help yourself to anything in the fridge. I can't deal with what you're implying. I'm going to bed." She shakes her head. "And I'd like for you to leave in the morning."

Right before she's about to stomp down the hall, a forceful knock comes. "Julia, it's David Drake."

No kidding. I can see him through the glass. He can see me, too. The big bad wolf. He's come to huff and puff and blow the house down.

"Chloe!" I say, and she stops midstep. "How does he know I'm here?"

She tugs at her bottom lip. "I don't know."

Panic rises in my body. I swallow and squeeze my eyes shut before Chloe opens the door. "Mr. Drake, this is a surprise. W-w-what are you doing here?" she asks.

On his way to greet his lover.

"I'm here to talk to Julia." Chloe swallows hard when he shoots her a pointed look. "And I know this is your home, but I need to speak with her alone. It's important. Could you please give us some privacy?"

She nods and shuffles down the hall, slamming her bedroom door closed. David leans against the frame of the door. "Julia, I didn't get to say what I wanted to say to you before you left. I couldn't. I think she's hidden cameras everywhere."

Uh, that would be me. And Erica had told me David is the spymaster. "Cameras? But you're the director—"

"Not in my house."

I can only blink.

"Look, I want to apologize for Erica's behavior." He grimaces. "I can't believe she hit you. She's a bit off-kilter and I'm so sorry she fired you. I told her that mistakes happen, that you probably didn't know about Tyler's extreme allergy."

I swallow and nod. "Is Tyler OK?"

"He's fine. Poor kid. They're keeping him for a couple of hours to monitor him," he says. "Mind if I come inside for a moment? It's awfully windy tonight. I think the Santa Ana winds are picking up."

So is my heart rate. I gulp, stepping to the side. "How do you know Chloe?"

More importantly, how did he know I was here? I do not ask this question.

"I talked to her at the party the other night." He chuckles and then rolls his eyes. "She'd begged me for a role in one of my films. Like they all do."

"You don't *know* her?"

He shrugs. "Not really. Why? Does it matter?"

I blink. It does matter. Somebody is lying. For some reason, my gut is telling me that it's not David.

David walks into the living room, handing me my roll bag. "You left this at the house. Thought you'd like it back. I know how chefs like their knives."

"Merci," I say, my throat hitching. I can't believe in my haste to leave I'd forgotten my knives. Big mistake. "That's really kind of you."

His eyes scan the room, landing on a full bottle of red wine. "Got anything to drink? I'm parched."

My heart thuds against my ribcage. "Honestly, I'm in the mood for a glass, especially after the evening I've had. We just opened a red. Or water?"

Keep it together.

"You're preaching to the choir. A red would be great." He grins and then chuckles. "Unless you have a bottle of Miraval?"

I sneer. I know he's trying to make a joke about Erica; it's not funny.

With a shaky hand, I point toward the couch and the bottle. "I'll be back in a second. Just need to use les toilettes."

"I'll be right here," he responds.

With my heart racing, I set my knives down on the counter in the kitchen and then head into the bathroom, splashing cold water on my face. I face my reflection and tell myself to find my motivation: clear your parents' names and take him down along the way. When I return to the living room, David is fumbling around the bookcase, his hands shooting to his pockets. I gulp, wondering if he's planting a camera or something else. He grins. "Sorry. Just admiring all the travel books."

"Chloe's roommates are flight attendants. They're not here." Merde. Why did I say that? He could kill both of us. Think quickly. "But they'll be back any minute."

The floorboards creak and David raises an inquisitive brow.

"My cat," I say. "Chloe probably let her out of her carry case."

He scowls and then lets out a beleaguered sigh. "Have a seat. There's something important I need to discuss with you."

"One second." I hold up a finger and pour the wine, handing him a glass, surprised wine isn't sloshing over the side and onto the couch.

"Julia, I didn't really come here to return your knives. I'm here for another reason. I'm sorry for the way I've behaved toward you. I'd like to apologize to you for that, too." He squeezes his eyes shut. "You just remind me so much of some-body I used to know."

I swallow, setting my glass down. I can't hold on to it. He's talking about my mother.

"She was so beautiful. You are so beautiful, Julia, but you know that, right?" He angles his body toward mine and grabs my shoulders. "I'm here to warn you. Erica is out to get you," he says. "She's dangerous. She's not right in the head. She's setting you up for something. Me too." He squeezes his eyes closed. "I've been trying to get her the help she needs, but she refuses. I honestly don't know what to do."

This man is a real piece of work. He's the one who needs help—the kind they lock you up for. I can't help but choke out a laugh. "What about your new script?"

He blinks. "What new script?"

"Are you kidding? The one you're writing about me. *The Private Chef?* Ring a bell?"

His eyes go wide. "I have absolutely no idea what you're talking about. I'm not working on a new script. I actually wanted to take a break, maybe travel."

"Chloe auditioned for y-y-ou," I stutter. "For a p-part. Playing me."

He sits back into the couch, his head dropping. For a moment, he doesn't say anything. When he does, my heart nearly jumps out of my ribcage. "This has Erica's stamp all over it. I'm going to try and find out what she's up to." He rubs his temples. "Although it jumpstarted my career, I should never have made that film." He rubs his eyes. "And then she came after me."

"What film?" I ask, my throat hitching. Maybe he'll tell me what he did. "*Swerve?*"

"No, my first film—a low-budget horror film about a teenage girl from a trailer park. She'd set her trailer on fire—with her mother and one of her mother's boyfriends inside it..."

Fire. Flames. Her bizarre reaction when I'd flambéed the shrimp.

David continues, "She was a minor. Only fourteen. They kept her name out of the papers. I didn't know the story was about her until she'd had her first meltdown—four years ago." He clamps his lips together. "You always want to see the best in people, you know?"

I blink, not sure if I want to ask my next question. "What about Valerie?"

"Madison's mother? She was the love of my life." He squeezes his eyes shut and then opens them, meeting my stunned gaze. "Look, Julia, I'm not perfect. I have faults. A lot of them. When Val found out about Tyler and my affair with Erica, it destroyed her..."

Anger courses through my veins. "You made a movie about her death!"

He reels backward. "Look, Julia. I used to think art imitated life. Like somehow all the darkness could be exposed onto a canvas, through a melody, or the greatest medium of them all— film. But art isn't imitation—it's a reflection, a mirror of every- thing we're trying to hide. Through pain, through real-life struggles, the struggles I like to tap into, that make everything real. Only then can we evaluate raw, unfiltered human emotion.

"So yeah, I like to take in all the darkness and mold it into something—something real. Because in the end my films are a desperate attempt to make sense of the chaos inside all of us." He sighs. "Erica was the one who taught me that. I used to think I loved her, but I don't know how I feel about her anymore. I guess it's something I have to figure out."

Nothing he's saying is making sense. I need to think, which is impossible to do when he's staring me down. I mean, he could just be a really excellent liar. Sociopaths usually are. He drugged Tyler. He put peanuts in the brownies. He sabotaged my soup. Erica told me she'd seen him do it, using the link from the cameras I'd given her.

David places a hand on my thigh. "Julia, I think we have a connection. I think you feel it, too..."

"You've got to be kidding me!" My eyes narrow into slits. The nerve. What's wrong with him? Such a narcissist. A sociopath. A freak. I stand up and point to the door. "I think you should leave. Right now."

He clenches his jaw and sets his wineglass down. Then he walks to the front door and leaves, looking over his shoulder. "Be careful, Julia. Consider yourself warned. Erica is out to get you."

I do not reply, just stand there, my eyes wide. A gust of wind slams the door behind him.

Chloe races out of her room, tears streaming down her cheeks. "I heard everything. What the hell is going on?" she spits out. "Me? Throwing myself at him. Begging for a part? N'importe quoi. And there is a script for *The Private Chef*. I-I read for him."

I hold up my hands in the stop position. "Chloe, keep your voice down. We'll talk when he leaves."

The headlights from his car shine into the living room, flashing on the walls. A sense of relief washes over me for a moment, followed by panic. I pull up the video surveillance on my phone. There is nothing. Every single clip has been deleted from my account.

I race into the kitchen, unrolling my knife bag. There's one missing.

THIRTY-EIGHT

JULIA

The truth about everything is falling through my hands like grains of sand, leaving me right where I started—with nothing tangible. I'm about to text Erica when I see an email alert from the guy I'd hired from Fiverr:

Will have the file to you later tonight or early tomorrow morning. Cleaning it up. Lots of strange characters breaking up the document, like pages and pages of alien-text garble. Sometimes happens with corrupted documents.

I place my phone down and growl, pacing. Then I scream, "Merde!"

Chloe nearly jumps out of her skin. "What?"

I frown. "I'm texting Erica."

"Good idea," she replies, nodding her head.

It doesn't take an idiot to realize that she's way more involved than I thought. And nothing is making sense. My eyes meet hers. She looks away. "How well do you know Erica anyway?"

She gulps. "Not well at all. I just met her that one time at the luncheon. And then again at the party."

She's lying. Everybody is lying. Including me. Funny, because I'm only searching out the truth. And my truth is already out.

Chloe slumps onto the couch. "I-I, uh…"

"I'll talk to you in a minute. OK?"

"OK."

I tap in my message.

JF:

> David came by Chloe's. Told me to be scared of you.

> We need to alert police now.

ED:

Not yet. Need final script/notes. They will think we are crazy.

JF:

> I think we have enough ammo.

ED:

We don't. Hang tight.

I really don't understand her reasoning at all. Why does she keep putting this off? Also, she didn't ask me how David knew where I was staying. When he was checking out the tires on the SUV did he put some kind of tracking device on it? Maybe Chloe did text him, but that doesn't make sense either.

Chloe taps me on the shoulder. I turn to face her. "He's such a liar," she says.

And so is she. I don't know where the truth lives anymore; probably buried under the sand, waiting for somebody to find it. What's real? What's fiction? Who can I trust? For some reason, my thoughts swim to Ollie. I know he hates David Drake as much as I do and he'll know what to do. Plus, he's been helping us and he's been more than honest. Every nerve in my body sparks.

Chloe stands in front of me, blinking. I turn my back on her and dial. "Ollie, it's Julia..."

"This better be important. I'm watching the last episode of *Ripley* on Netflix..."

"It's important. Erica fired me. I'm staying with Chloe. David Drake was just here, and I thought you might know what to do."

"Address?" he asks, and I give it to him. "I'll be there in five, maybe ten. We don't have much time." He mumbles, "Fuck, not this again."

Ten minutes later, there's a loud knock at the door. I leap out of my seat. Ollie's first words are, "This is all too uncanny. He's setting you up. Like he did me." His voice raises in pitch, so high it hurts my ears. "We need to act quickly. We're searching the place. Where was he sitting? Or was he standing?"

I point to the couch with a shaky finger. "He sat there."

Ollie hurdles over Chloe's dirty laundry and rips the cushions off the sofa, throwing them to the side. He sweeps a gadget over the bookcases. "Nothing. No hidden cameras. I'm checking out the car." He holds up a finger. "Back in a minute."

Chloe slumps onto the couch. "I can't believe what's going on. She didn't say—"

What the hell? "She?"

"I meant he. Erica is obviously nuts, like he said."

"He told me he barely knows you."

She frowns. "And that's a lie. I told you what happened."

Ollie clomps back into the house, holding up a bag. "This was in your car, stuffed under the passenger seat. Peanut oil. Mushrooms. A scarf. A necklace..." He looks at his watch.

"That motherfucker is up to it again. The cops will probably be here in a few." He races out the door. "I'll get rid of this. Back in ten. Maybe longer."

My heart rate accelerates. I'm no longer thinking about clearing my parents' names, not when I may have to clear mine. Numb with panic, I stand watching as Ollie jumps into his red Corvette and peels out of the driveway and onto the road, gravel spraying.

I should have left the Drake house on the first day. But I didn't. No, like an idiot, I thought I could deal with all of the craziness, save up my centimes, and fight for my dream of opening a chain of That French Café. I must be insane. I'd had the opportunity to leave so many times. But instead of my dream, I'd started focusing on revenge. Look where that got me.

Chloe taps me on the shoulder, breaking me out of my thoughts. "Julia," she says, "I know we're friends, but I'm thinking maybe you should leave."

I snap my head toward her, my eyes shooting daggers. "If I do, you'll be the one with the connection to the Drakes. You told me that's what you wanted. Because I'll tell the police what you told me—how David forced himself on you. Let's see how that plays out."

"I l-lied about that." Her bottom lip quivers. "But I did audition for *The Private Chef*—"

"For who?"

"For him." She grimaces and takes a step back. "I-I just don't know what to do. This is all so messed up..." Her mouth twists to the side. "Actually, you can stay. I'm scared. But just for tonight."

She knows exactly what to do—play her part. The same way she's been playing me. I don't know what Chloe's role is, but I'll find out later. Right now, just like she does, I'm thinking about one person. And that person is me.

"Chloe, how good of an actress are you?"

"If you're asking if I can cry on a dime, I'd ask you what eye do you want me to cry from, the right or the left, and how far do you want the tear to fall?"

"Jesus, you're quoting Leonardo DiCaprio—"

"What can I say? If that guy can do it, so can I. I studied. A lot. Method acting." Chloe swallows. "What do you want me to do?"

Until Ollie returns, I honestly don't have a plan. All I know is that David is definitely setting me up and I don't have proof. I shrug, turn back into the house, Chloe following. "It's all about improvisation, got it? Just follow my lead."

She closes the front door and stumbles over to the couch, sinking into it. "Got it."

Chloe lowers her head, breathes in and out. Then she shakes out her hands and blinks. Her mouth twists from a smile into a frown. She repeats all of the above two more times. I leave to check in on Beurreboule and she's curled up on Chloe's bed, a bowl of water on the floor set beside a dish of her food. When I return to the living room, Chloe still looks like she's having some kind of bizarre seizure. This time, her head is tilted back and she's opening and closing her mouth and croaking and grunting. For a moment, I'm entranced until the sounds emitting from her throat get louder. This is too much.

"What in the world are you doing?"

Her gaze snaps onto mine. A fat tear slides down her cheek. "Finding my motivation. I'm getting warmed up."

I'd love to tell her about my motivation: getting to the truth. Save for Ollie, Madison and Tyler, everybody is fake as shit.

A couple of minutes later, flashing blue-and-white lights strobe in the driveway. I peek out the window. A patrol car pulls up. Two men get out of the vehicle, one of them inspecting the Mercedes. A forceful knock almost shakes the house down.

"Los Angeles Sheriff's Department. I see the lights on. Open the door," he demands, and I do as I'm told.

Chloe sinks onto the couch.

"Can I help you?" I ask, my voice quivering. He's a tough-looking man with eyes so dark they're almost black, a scar running down his left cheek. I'd say he looked kind of familiar, but my head is done in and I don't know any cops. I've never even been pulled over. My eyes land on his name tag. "Deputy Sanchez?"

"Sorry to bother you, ma'am, but we got a call about a stolen car." He points toward the Mercedes, and I notice the dark ink of tattoos on his hands, one a cross. "Can you explain why that vehicle is parked in your driveway?"

I'm not expecting this accusation. My face pales. "I can. I worked for the Drakes. Erica Drake fired me tonight..."

He squints. "And you took her car?"

I honestly don't know how to explain anything. Tell him that her firing me was planned? That she was going to slap me and that we're trying to get more evidence on David. Nobody would believe that story because it's absolutely insane—like all of Erica's other plans. Seriously? The woman was going to stage her own death and then take off to Costa Rica. Worse. I'd fall in love with David and become Mrs. Drake number three. I think it's time to trust myself and my own decisions.

"Car stealing? Julia would not steal a car," says Chloe, coming to my side, squeezing my hand. "She's a very nice French girl."

I surreptitiously nudge her in the ribs, releasing her grip. She's dressed in shorty-shorts and looks like a little nymph.

I straighten my posture. "I didn't take the Mercedes. They gave it to me. A car was in my employment contract. Which is the reason I have the keys—" I walk over to my purse, pulling them out, dangling them. "See?"

Deputy Sanchez frowns. "Why did Mrs. Drake fire you?"

I snort. "Wrongful dismissal. She accused me of doing something I didn't do."

"I'm afraid to ask what," he mumbles, and then clears his throat, his eyes darting to the side. "Again, I'm so sorry to bother you, but I'd like to see your employment contract before I do anything."

"Like what? Arrest me?" My pulse races. I did not see this coming. It's like a fist flying and hitting you in the face before you can move out of the way. Another sneak attack. "I assure you I do not have a criminal record. I'm just a chef..."

My shoulders tense. I'm also an orphan with a gigantic chip on her shoulder, but I don't tell him that.

He holds up his palms. "I'm trying to make sense of the situation. The Mercedes is registered to the Drakes." He points. "It's in the driveway. One of them called reporting it stolen. You have the car." He rubs his eyes. "Let me see your contract. We'll take things from there, Ms. Fouquet."

I did not tell him my name. I gulp and wave a hand toward the living room. "Entrez-vous."

"Come again?"

"Exactly," says Chloe. She'd been so quiet I'd forgotten she was here. "It means come in. So sorry, sometimes we speak in French. Together. We bof French. Learning English. Eet is zometimes a problem. Two Frenchies. One house." She pumps her fist and then kisses my cheek. "We love Los Angeles. Go Lakers!"

I glare at her. Just then, Ollie's little red Corvette pulls into the driveway. He rolls the window down. "What's going on, girls? I saw the lights! Did something happen? Are you OK?" He holds up a DVD and a bag of freshly popped popcorn. "I have the movie, the snacks," he says, eyeing the officer, "but I'm thinking, rain check?"

The deputy's gaze locks on Ollie. "Aren't you Ollie Shore? The surfer?"

Ollie's shoulders snap back, straight and proud. "The one and only."

"Man, I'm a fan of yours."

"Awfully kind."

"You got a rough hit. That asshole, David Drake—" He clenches his teeth. "But you didn't hear that from me."

Hope blooms in my chest with the deputy's statement. Maybe this surprise interrogation won't be so bad. Maybe, just maybe, I'll share a little more about what's going on. I'm sick and tired of the Drakes controlling the narrative. I have a voice, too.

"Should I leave?" Ollie's eyes go comically wide. "I mean, I'd like to sit in with the girls. Unless it's a problem?"

The cop eyes Chloe and me almost lasciviously and it really creeps me out. "Nah, that's OK. You can stay."

The Santa Ana winds are picking up, leaves swirling in the driveway. There's a storm brewing. Ollie sits in a chair, twiddling his thumbs. Deputy Sanchez sits on the couch, eyes me. "Your employment contract?"

I nod, pulling my iPad out of my purse. "Give me a second, OK? I have to search for the email from Jasmine, the Drakes' personal assistant. She's the one who hired me."

"Jasmine Anderson?" he asks.

"Yes," I respond.

"They just found her body on one of the trails." He scratches his chin. "So, you knew her?"

"Nope, I never met her in person. We'd only communicated via Zoom and email." I clear my throat. "I was expecting to meet her when I arrived in California, but Erica told me she'd disappeared."

He pulls out a pen and pad of paper. "When did you say you arrived here?"

"Almost two weeks ago."

"From?"

"Paris."

He cocks his head to the side. "You speak English really well."

"Thanks," I say, wondering how much I should tell him. "I was born here. Well, not here, at UCLA Hospital. My family moved back to France when I was young."

"Good to know," he says, rubbing his chin. He writes something down. "Jasmine's family reported her missing two weeks ago. When was the last time you'd heard from her?"

Great. Now I'm knee-deep in what is most certainly a murder investigation.

"Around a month ago," I say. "She'd sent me the final contract, flight information, and everything else I needed to know. It's in the email, the one I'm about to share with you."

"Did you want a glass of water, deputy?" asks Chloe, her eyes clouding over.

"That would be great," he says, and Chloe scrambles into the kitchen.

As she does, he eyes her ass. Not very professional. But what can I do? Arrest him?

I pull out my iPad, opening the email with the contract. Deputy Sanchez's eyes skim each and every page, his finger flicking the screen. He mumbles, "That's some salary." Finally, he looks up. "I don't know why Mrs. Drake reported the car stolen, when it's clear in your contract that you'd have rights to the car. I think you'll have to settle this with her."

My heart thuds inside my chest. "Wait! Erica called, not David?"

He shrugs. "Or somebody pretending to be her. I don't know. I'll listen to the call to Dispatch again when I return to the station." He stands up. "I'm sorry for wasting your time. And I hope you sort things out."

Ollie clears his throat and Deputy Sanchez shoots a look at him.

"Something you want to add, Mr. Shore?"

"Not me." Ollie waves a hand in my direction. "Her. Tell him, Julia."

"David Drake stopped by here around half an hour ago," I say with a groan. "As you saw in my contract, I was the personal live-in chef for the family. He was returning my roll bag of knives. And one of them is missing."

Deputy Sanchez blinks. "Stay inside. Lock the door. Don't answer it or open it for anyone. I have a hunch. I remember what he did to Mr. Shore. I read your book," he continues, his attention on Ollie. "The guy set you up. I'm surprised you didn't use his real name..."

"Couldn't," says Ollie. "He would have sued the shorts off me."

Deputy Sanchez frowns and meets my eyes. "He may be out to get you." He slaps his hand over his mouth. "But you didn't hear that from me."

Regardless of what Erica said, I'm going to tell Deputy Sanchez what I know about the threat relating to me. She's leaving me to fend for myself and I have an opportunity to share what I know. Right now. Of course, I'm not going to mention my birth name, not yet—that would be fishy. Like I'm some kind of con-artist or something.

"He's working on a new script," I whisper. "I think it's about me, considering it's titled *The Private Chef*."

Deputy Sanchez's brows pinch together with concern. "Can I see it?"

I shake my head no slowly. "Sorry. I don't have it yet. See, I got into David's computer, found the file, but it was corrupted. Somebody is working on it now." I swallow, nervously. "I should have it later tonight or tomorrow morning."

"I don't understand. How did you hear about this script?"

I point to Chloe and her face pales. "She auditioned for it."

His eyes lock on Chloe. "And you don't have it?"

Her shoulders slump and she doesn't respond. "I'm taking that as a no." He exhales. "Look, I'm not supposed to give out my personal number, but should you receive the file, call me before you do anything," he instructs. "Got a pen and a piece of paper?"

Chloe scrambles to the kitchen, returning with a notepad. Deputy Sanchez scribbles down his cellphone number and email, handing it over to me. "We'll figure out what's going on, OK? Get a good night's rest. And stay safe."

Ollie stands up. "I'm staying here tonight—I'll keep an eye on the girls."

I swear the deputy mumbles, "Lucky man," but I can't be sure. Deputy Sanchez salutes him and then turns to me. "The moment you receive the file, call, OK?"

"Will do."

He leaves and the three of us flop onto the couch. At least Deputy Sanchez didn't think I was nuts. No, he'd been more concerned. For a moment, we all sit quietly, thinking. Tonight has done my head in and Chloe took that little act of hers too far. "Why were you pretending we were lovers?"

"Improv," she says. "Men love that."

I grimace. "No, they don't."

"Um, yes, we do." Ollie coughs out a laugh and then blows out a sigh of relief. "I hid the bag David left in my compost pile." He pauses. "The scarf? The necklace? They were both Jasmine's. I recognized them. She'd worn them when she visited Erica at Malibu Oasis."

"Should I have told Sanchez?"

"Nope," says Ollie. "On top of the stolen car, that would have looked really bad. Like, righteously bad. "

"But I didn't steal the car. And aren't we withholding evidence? Tampering?"

Ollie's hands slap over his cheeks and eyes. "Shit. I didn't think of that. Fuck. We'll figure it out later."

I'm sick and tired of waiting for the hammer to drop, because it's already bashing me on the head. I pull out my phone. "I have to text Erica on Snapchat. Warn her. David's playing a really dangerous game."

"Yeah, good idea," Ollie agrees.

JF:

Why did u call police, telling them I stole car?

ED:

I didn't.

JF:

Who did?

ED:

Who do you think? Obvious.

Three dots.

JF:

D said he wasn't working on a new script.

ED:

He's a liar.

JF:

He planted evidence in my car.

ED:

Police find it?

JF:

No. It's gone. Found it.

ED:

Now u know what you're dealing with.

I'll try to figure out next move.

JF:

OK

Ollie is here with Chloe and me.

ED:

Ollie?

JF:

Called him for help. Good thing, too.

ED:

Talk tomorrow. Getting late.

Chloe leans over, looking on as the messages disappear. She gulps and then turns her head, not meeting my eyes. Then, she wrings her hands. She is withholding information. "What are you not telling me?"

"What? Nothing. I'm just really tired." She swallows. "I can't believe what's happened tonight. David..."

"Told me he barely knows you," I say again.

"Obviously, that's a lie." She stands up. "Ollie, I'll show you to my room. I changed the sheets this morning. They are clean."

"Can't believe I'm involved in this situation again." Ollie yawns. "I'm spent." He winks at me. "See you in the morning. Sweet dreams."

More like a nightmare.

Chloe points. "You and I can share the couch. It's a pull-out. Could you move the coffee table?"

I can. I'm thankful she's letting me and Ollie stay. With people around, I feel safe. Sort of. "What about Beurreboule? She's under your bed."

"What's a burble?" asks Ollie, stopping midstep. "Should I be scared?"

"Non," says Chloe. "It's Julia's cat. She's in my room, so you'll have a bedmate tonight, too."

"I love cats." Ollie grins and then his lips curl into a frown. "But I don't like David Drake. Tonight, I'm having dreams about slaying dragons."

Soon, we all turn in. I'm lying, rigid, next to Chloe. She snores and mumbles in her sleep. With everything that's going on how did she fall asleep so quickly? I will not be resting tonight. Just when I thought I had everything figured out nothing makes sense, especially David. He'd almost seemed sincere tonight. Why would he warn me about Erica if he's the one trying to set me up? The cops left hours ago, but flashes of light still pulse and throb in my brain.

ACT FOUR
LE DESSERT

(A satisfying conclusion to any meal.)

*The sweetest honey is loathsome
in its own deliciousness.
And in the taste destroys the appetite.*

—William Shakespeare, Romeo and Juliet

FADE IN:

EXT. MALIBU BLUFF—DAY

Three women rappel down a steep bluff, the
sounds of heavy panting. Feet slam into the
sand one by one.

                    WOMAN 1 (V.O.)

Are you sure it's safe?

                        WOMAN 2 (V.O.)

    It's safe.

                        WOMAN 3 (V.O.)

    I can't wait for this all to be over.

Waves lap on the shore. The wind hisses.

FADE OUT

THIRTY-NINE

JULIA

I've been pacing for hours when I hear a loud ding. Finally. An email alert. I grab my iPad with anticipation. *Please. Please. Please.* I'd really like something tangible to go to the police with before David does something to anybody. I can't take much more of this waiting game; I just want to get on with my life and get as far away from this messed-up situation as possible. After rubbing the sleep out of my eyes, I click my email open and my prayer is answered.

Shazam124: Finally got the file cleaned up. Here ya go. Attached.

With shaky hands, I open notes for *The Private Chef*. My eyes skim the words and my stomach lurches. I have to read through the page again, my eyes locking onto every single messed-up word, a cold, sick feeling shimmying its way down my spine.

When a renowned French chef is hired by a Hollywood actress, sparks fly between her and the actress's famous husband, igniting a deadly recipe of passion and betrayal that leads to a fatal finale.

~~French chef seduces husband, the actress tries to kill both of them, fails, and ends up in prison.~~

~~The actress kills the French chef.~~

French chef purposefully tampers with meals endangering the actress's son.

The French chef learns this couple made a movie about her parents' death and she's out for revenge. French chef kills the actress either by poisoning her with belladonna or cutting a climbing rope when the actress is rock climbing. Then, she goes after the husband, cutting the brake line on his car, causing a fatal accident on Las Flores Canyon Road.

The French chef and the actress kill the husband, making it look like an accident.

The husband, a serial killer, kills the actress after she wins an Oscar, making it look like an accident, and then he kills the French chef because she denies his advances—and if he can't have her nobody will.

The blood rushes from my face. I accidentally bite down on my tongue, drawing blood. These notes are absolutely insane, worse than I could have imagined. I blink at the text. David knows exactly who I am and if I hadn't been scared for my life before I'm terrified now.

In a complete state of panic, I scramble for my phone to text Erica. She needs to be warned. When you read the words "he kills the French chef" and you know that person is you, they are pretty unbelievable. When you realize your life is actually in danger, you know you have to act. Unfortunately, I can't find my phone and I'm knocking and throwing things around—namely Chloe's dirty laundry, trying to find it. I moan loudly. "Damn it! Damn it!"

"What's going on?" Chloe mumbles, one eye open, from the pull-out couch.

I don't trust her. In fact, I don't even know why I'm staying with her when I had other options—like an Airbnb. Unbelievably, there are over sixty thousand French in Los Angeles and I happen to be connected to one who only cares about herself and becoming a famous movie star. An opportunist. I have so much more in common with her sister, Solene. My eye twitches. Maybe I just didn't want to be alone in case something happened, which it did. My mind wanders to Liam. I should have called him, but I'd be putting him in danger, too. Maybe I already have? I've got to calm down.

"I'm just looking for my phone. I can't find it," I say, blowing out an irritated sigh. I'm not telling her anything. She'd probably go straight to David. Even though he denied it, she's connected to him somehow. "Go back to sleep."

She mumbles something and pulls the covers over her head. I continue my manic search. After dumping out the contents of my purse onto the floor, rummaging through receipts, change, and random crap, I take a deep breath, and squeeze my eyes shut. *If I were a phone, where would I be? Not in the bathroom.* The answer comes to me in a flash. Finally, I find my phone, charging in the kitchen—right where I'd left it. I'm not thinking straight, but I know I have to text Erica.

JF:

Danger! Leave house! Go anywhere!

David plan! Kill you! Kill me!

Panicked, I stare at the screen, waiting for her to respond. There is nothing and my texts don't make sense. My breathing picks up. I have to talk to her. A matter of life and death, I don't care if I piss her off by calling so early. I tap in her contact. The phone rings and rings and rings. No response. I call again. No response. She's probably sleeping and put her phone on silent. I'm in full-on panic mode. What do I do? Merde. Call Deputy Sanchez!

Last night, I'd tacked his number on the refrigerator with a magnet. My hands shake as I punch in his number. If he doesn't pick up, I'll keep calling until he does. He answers on the fourth ring. "Who in the hell is calling me so early in the morning?"

"It's J-J-Julia Fouquet…"

He groans. "What do you want?"

I'm not sure if I'm going to make any sense. I grip my phone tightly, willing my heart rate to calm down.

"David Drake," I say, breathlessly. "I just received the notes for the script he's working on, the one pertaining to me. Everybody in his films dies or goes to prison. Luna? Jasmine? Valerie?" I choke back a sob. "My parents."

"Your parents?"

"My birth name was Josephine Brooks. He killed my parents so he'd have material for his script, *Swerve*." I gulp. With each word, I'm wasting time. I need to get to the point, no matter how crazy I sound. "Look, he's planning on killing Erica. And maybe me."

I'm shaking like a leaf. Ollie comes out of Chloe's bedroom, racing over to me when he sees my face. He places a hand on my shoulder, squeezing it. He stands to my side, listening to the conversation, eyes wide. He mouths, "Holy shit."

I point to my iPad and he nods, heading over to it. He slumps into a chair and his eyes dart back and forth, reading. He looks up and meets my gaze, shaking his head, jaw clenched.

"That's a very serious accusation," says Sanchez.

"I know it is." I'm pacing as I speak with him, panting. "I think he's going to do something to Erica today. Something with my missing knife. And you have to stop him before he does. Ollie and I will meet you at their house with all of the scripts, the notes. Then, you can arrest him..."

"Jesus Christ," he says. I hear somebody cough, the roar of an engine.

"Are you at the station?"

"I'm on patrol," he says gruffly. "Did you call Dispatch?"

"N-n-no, not yet."

"Don't. I'm on it," he snaps. "I'll meet you at their house."

"OK. You know where they live—"

The line goes dead. Stupid question. Of course, he knows the Drake house. Everybody does—even those tour buses looking at the *magnificent* lives of the Hollywood elite. Ollie looks up from my iPad, his face paling. Both of us leap into action, getting dressed. We race to the Mercedes and stop in our tracks. Somebody has slashed all four tires.

FORTY

ERICA

David didn't sleep in the master bedroom last night, but like clockwork, he storms into the bedroom pushing by me, raging and spitting out insults. I'm a lunatic! I should be locked up! I poison everything I touch! I didn't thank him! I'm an ingrate! Why did I involve Julia?

The grump. I'm assuming he didn't sleep well, probably stayed up all night replaying my acceptance speech in his head. I don't say anything, just let him have his little temper tantrum. He'll get over it; he always does.

Once he calms down, his next words are: "Erica, I still love you, but we really need to talk. Things can't go on like this. I can't go on like this."

No kidding. Somebody needs a major lesson in anger management. One moment he's hurling insults like grenades, the next second he's claiming he still loves me, pleading for us to reconcile. It's a dizzying roller-coaster ride, his emotions fluctuating wildly. I'm surprised I've been able to hang on for so long.

Finally, he stops, noticing me dressed in my athletic wear. Very cute, might I add. Lululemon—black with a pink stripe.

"Are you going climbing?" he asks.

"It's a beautiful morning."

His eyes shoot to the window and then he gives me a look of concern. It's anything but beautiful out there. According to the weather report, the Santa Ana winds will soon hit the coast. The air is dry and unusually warm for the end of March and the sky looks surreal with shades of orange and pink, tiny dust particles floating in the atmosphere and glimmering like iridescent confetti.

"I don't think it's a good idea—"

"I do," I reply, sitting down on the bed to pull on my shoes. "Madison and I do it all the time, usually around now. I wanted to get one in before the weather turns bad."

"Shouldn't Madison be in school?"

"She's in confinement. Had Covid when she returned from Europe—probably caught it on the flight home."

David clears his throat. "Damn it, Erica. She could have contaminated us. Do we have to alert everybody at the party?"

"You can be so paranoid sometimes," I say, rolling my eyes. "She tested negative a couple of days ago. Took her to Urgent Care on Saturday morning. She's fine." I make my way to exit the room. "Maddy and I are looking forward to this morning." I grin. "I'm taking the right side."

"You haven't been climbing in a while," he says. "That's the harder track down. You're going to kill yourself."

I look over my shoulder, batting my eyelashes. "I thought that was your dream."

"No, Erica. Whether you think so or not, I still care for you." He blinks. "I'm sorry I lose my temper. It's something I need to work on. We both need to get help—"

I'm pretty sure he's not referring to couples' therapy. Been there. Done that. Didn't do a thing to solve our problems, mostly because we both lied through our teeth. He probably wants to institutionalize me. Little does he know, my break-downs are an act.

"The only help I need right now is getting some exercise in. I'm preparing for my next role. The biggest one of my life." I slip on my climber's grin. "I'm a shoo-in. So Goldie says."

He rubs his chin. "You talked to Goldie?"

"Of course. She was here at the party." I lift a brow as I pull on my gloves. "Winning the award has helped build up my reputation in a big way."

"I'm happy for you. Really," he says with an appreciative grin. "And if you're climbing, I'm going with you. I could use a good workout." He holds up a finger. "Just give me a minute. I need to change."

"Whatever you say," I say with a smile. "Don't change too much."

I hate him just the way he is—all smug, pretending like nothing is wrong, thinking we can work things out.

Quick as lightning, he throws on a pair of sweats and a long-sleeved T-shirt with the Drake Entertainment logo printed on the front, a dragon on the back. I make my way down the hall and knock on Maddy's door. She opens it, flashes me a grin that fades the moment she sees David standing behind me. "He's going with us today," I say, tilting my head to the side.

"Good morning, Mads," says David. "I see you're ready to go. It'll be like the good old days..."

"I think I'm going to sit this one out. I'm exhausted." She holds her hands up and then brings them to her face, rubbing her eyes. "I did set everything up, though."

She turns and slams her door shut.

David sighs. "She's always pushing me away. I try..."

"Try harder," I hiss. "You'd know how wonderful she is if you took the time to get to know her better..."

"Enough with the guilt trips, Erica," he growls. "I think I do enough to provide for the family. Don't you?"

He wouldn't like my answer—that we're all just props—so I keep it to myself. Don't want to push him over the edge.

David shoots me a look of irritation and stomps down the hallway to the stairs, heading to the kitchen, me following. Before we head outside, he stops midstep, picking up a knife with a black handle. "Isn't this Julia's?"

"Probably," I say with a snigger. "You know I don't cook."

He points to the cutting board, to a bowl of chopped berries. "Then who did this?"

I shrug. "Probably Madison. Julia has been teaching her to cook. You'd know that if you were around more."

He sets the knife down and picks up a sheet of paper. "Ooh, Julia's recipe looks good. Death by chocolate. I'm dying from anticipation already."

I'm sure he is. When he's not looking, I tuck the knife into my fanny pack, fearful of what's to come. I don't trust him. And he sure as hell doesn't trust me. "I'm ready. Can we go?"

He nods and flicks the switch on the wall for the floodlights. "It's still a little dark out. Better to be safe than sorry."

"We need to grab the rest of the gear and suit up," I say, and we head through the mudroom off the kitchen to the garage.

His eyes meet mine as he grabs his harness. After he buckles himself in, he says, "I'm looking forward to this."

I throw him a helmet and he catches it, setting it down. He throws on a baseball cap—Drake Entertainment. "I don't need a helmet. I've done the descent three times on my own already. I'm a pro. Let's go."

We make our way down the path and the light is even more surreal on the bluffs, the cliff almost looking like a living being. Plants wave ominously, blurring as a strong breeze blows in, the fronds of the palm trees cracking like whips. A moment of doubt creeps into my mind. I take a step backward, licking my lips nervously. "I changed my mind. You're right, this was a bad idea. I don't think we should do this."

"I know how good a climber you are. You taught me." He grins. "I think working together, descending and climbing back up, could be good for our relationship, don't you?"

He eyes the anchor. "I'll clamp you in. And wait until you're halfway down before I start to rappel. The engineers were smart the way they designed everything—the anchors are solid. It's safe."

"I know," I say. "I'm the one who managed the entire project."

"Once we're on the ground, we can have a nice heart-to-heart on the beach, talk about our future." He grins again, the morning light, the sunrise mirrored in his eyes. "I'll probably pass you. I'll be waiting at the bottom."

I raise a brow and thread the rope into the ATV, my heart racing. After double-checking the gear, I lie down on my stomach. Soon, I'm rappelling down, my feet slamming onto the rocks, when David's form passes mine in a flash. I hear a loud crack.

David. He is waiting for me. At the bottom. But his head is smashed into a rock and his body is limp. Debris tumbles down the bluff. Frantic, I stumble toward David, falling down onto my knees, water lapping on my legs, my hands.

Kneeling, numb in shock, a haunting version of Blondie's "The Tide is High" plays in my mind as I watch the ocean water swirl and mix with the thick, dark blood pooling around his lifeless body, drops of crimson clinging to the sand. With each lapping wave, the water retreats, carrying his blood with it, and the sun rises higher, illuminating his face.

"Erica," he wheezes. "Do something."

Of course I should do something. He's still alive. I can see his chest rise and fall. I pull out the knife from the fanny pack and I plunge it into his neck, slicing it open. Oddly, it's a paring knife and I've unpaired us. Like a sudden earthquake, his body trembles and quakes, his eyes staring blankly at the sky, his mouth frozen in a scream.

Finally, I stand up, stepping over his still form. Once my limbs cooperate, I race up the path, my heart beating furiously, my clothes trailing pale red water.

I drop the knife on the ground, thinking some dragons just can't fly.

FORTY-ONE

JULIA

I'm on my way to Hummingbird House with Ollie in his little red Corvette. He's speeding like a bat out of hell and shaking so hard I'm surprised we don't get into a wreck. On the ride, he keeps mumbling, "If he harmed one hair on Erica's head, I'm going to kill him."

Chloe has stayed behind, using the excuse that she'd just get in the way. Which is true. Either that or she'd launch into some odd role she'd conjured up. All I really know is that she's overheard way too much and she could warn him. So, before we left, I'd snagged her phone. I'm not sure what our plan is, how we stop David. What if he has a gun? I wish I'd brought my knives. Then again, you don't bring a knife to a gun fight.

We finally reach the guard's outpost and I'm glad we've made it here alive. Kyle, on duty, eyes me curiously. "Just open the gates, Kyle!" I bark.

"Is there a problem?"

"Obviously," Ollie yells.

We pull up to the front of the house and I open the gates. I'm expecting to see Deputy Sanchez and maybe his partner, but there is no sign of him. I punch in the code for the door. "Erica!" I yell. "Where are you?"

Madison and Tyler race down the steps. "What's going on?"

"I-I received the notes for the last script," I pant. "Where's Erica? He's going to kill her..."

Madison gulps. "They went climbing this morning."

"Fuck," says Tyler.

We race out of the house to the bluff, tripping over our feet. When we reach the edge of the cliff, we peer over the side. David's body is splayed on the rocks. He's not moving and the tide is high, waves rolling in. The sky is the strangest color. Everything is strange. Erica is nowhere to be seen. We all stand with our mouths dropped open. A glimmer on the ground near my feet catches my attention. I point. "That's one of my k-knives," I stutter. "The missing one. The paring knife."

"Don't touch it," says Ollie. "Leave it there."

"We have to call the police," says Madison, blinking.

"I'll do it," says Tyler, pulling out his phone. He puts the call on speaker.

"Nine-one-one. Please state the nature of your emergency."

"This is Tyler Drake. Um, we just found my dad, David Drake, and we think he's dead."

"Think?"

"He's all bloody at the bottom of our bluff. And not moving."

"Paramedics and responding officers will be arriving short-ly." She pauses. "You said 'we'?"

"Yeah. Me, my sister, Madison, our chef, Julia, and Ollie Shore." Tyler clears his throat. "There's one more thing..."

"Yes? I'm listening."

"My mother, Erica, is missing. We can't find her. We don't know where she is."

"OK. Please stay on the line until the responding officers arrive."

"Uh-huh. I'll open the gates and the front door."

"Where are you?"

"We'll be outside. On the terrace."

The four of us stumble to the terrace, not one of us saying a word, my heart feeling like it's going to explode out of my chest. The air is so dry and I'm parched, but I don't want to move. I sink into a chair and stare at the pool.

"Anybody thirsty?" asks Madison, as if reading my mind.

"Uh-huh," we mumble.

"I'll go grab us some waters from the fridge," she says numbly.

Like a zombie, she ambles into the house. She returns a minute later, her eyes wide. She doesn't have water in her hands. She takes a breath, lets it out slowly. "The petty cash drawer was open—and all the cash is gone. She must have taken it. There's also some chopped-up devil's cherries on the counter... with one of your recipes, Julia."

"What the hell?"

We don't have much time to ponder anything because sirens blare at the front of the house and a man makes his approach a moment later, a group of men following. "I'm Deputy Sanchez..." he begins.

"There are two of you at LASD?" Ollie cuts in.

"No, I'm the only one at the Lost Hills Malibu outpost."

"That can't be true," I jump in. "We met him last night. David reported the car stolen, saying I did it. I called him this m-morning. He gave us his cell number..."

"Officers of the law do not give out personal information. And even if we did, you didn't call me." His brows pinch with confusion, as do mine and Ollie's. "Before I address that question, I need to know. Where's the body?"

"At the bottom of the bluff," says Madison, pointing. "You can rappel down or take the path."

"The path would be great," he says, and I hand him my set of keys.

He calls one of the other men over, gives him the keys, and instructs him, his voice a low whisper. Then, he returns his attention to us. "Did any of you touch the body?"

We all shake our heads no, shuddering.

He takes a seat, leaning forward. "Could somebody please tell me what's going on? Starting with how you found the body. And we'll move on from there."

One by one, we complete each other's sentences, filling real Deputy Sanchez in: namely that David Drake is a possible serial killer, using real-life murders that he'd committed for his scripts. His face blanches. "Jesus, I thought I'd heard it all."

Two hours later, we're still sitting outside at the iron table on the terrace. A forensics team is surveying the grounds, collecting evidence. The coroner has come to take David's body away. The real Deputy Sanchez clears his throat. "For now, we're ruling the cause of death as murder—something to do with a deteriorated belay loop and"—he clears his throat—"a fatal stab to the neck. I'll get to the knife in a moment. Do you know where he stored his harness?"

I can feel the blood rushing out of every pore in my body. Erica has set me up. I don't know where to look so I stare blankly at the ocean, my heart racing.

"In the garage," says Madison.

"By chance, are there chemicals in the garage or batteries?"

"I'm not sure," says Madison.

"OK," Deputy Sanchez says, unclipping his radio. "I'll have the team check it out."

We watch him as he instructs somebody on his radio. Then, he turns. "And what about the rest of the gear?"

"We keep everything in a couple of big blue suitcases with

wheels on them," replies Madison. "David kept his sporting goods separate from the rest of the family's."

"Why?"

"He didn't like rummaging through everything to find his stuff," she says, throwing her hands up in the air. "Plus, he was a germaphobe."

"I see." Deputy Sanchez scribbles something down on his notepad. "Why was he wearing a baseball cap, not a helmet?"

"He never wears a helmet," says Tyler. "He thinks they're stupid."

Sanchez mouths, *Idiot*.

"What about the knife? The one found on the ground? Pretty high-end," continues Sanchez, looking me squarely in the eyes.

"It was mine," I squeak. "When David, when Mr. Drake, returned my roll bag to me, one was missing."

"Convenient. Although the rope Mr. Drake used to rappel down wasn't cut, somebody sliced his neck..."

"I didn't do it," I say, straightening my spine. "I wasn't even here. I have two alibis. You'd better fingerprint it."

Deputy Sanchez glowers at me. "We are."

My posture slumps.

"And the recipe in the kitchen?"

I gulp. "It's mine. But I wasn't even here. And that's the truth."

"Look," he says, smirking. "I'm trying to uncover the truth."

"We all are!" screams Tyler.

"You've all made serious accusations this morning. You claimed David Drake may be a serial killer, using real-life murders for his scripts."

"It's not an accusation," says Ollie, and we all nod. "We have proof. He's a method director. He takes his inspiration from his real-life crimes. Crimes he committed—"

"There is no proof."

"Yes, there is!" says Madison, tapping the stack of papers. "It's right here. Everything you need. Written in his own words. His original scripts, his notes. It's like a confession."

"And how did you happen upon these?"

"Julia and I found them on his computer. The files were encrypted, so we had them decrypted," says Madison.

"I'll need to see the original files—on his computer." Deputy Sanchez coughs into his hand and then rubs his eyes. "Where's Mrs. Drake?"

All of us shrug and grunt out inaudible murmurs.

"You don't know?"

We shake our heads no.

"She's missing," says Ollie, tears forming in his eyes.

"People don't just disappear," Sanchez says, eyeing me again. "We'll find her. Until we do, none of you are to cross state lines or fly back to France. Understood?"

My heart stutters. This is when I know that there is definitely a method to Erica's madness.

FORTY-TWO

ERICA

Orange is definitely *not* the new black. I look much better in blue—the color of the athletic gear I'd changed into after leaving what I'd worn this morning in the guesthouse—with Julia's DNA all over it. Thanks to my 'climbing gloves,' even the knife won't have my prints because they're made of nitrile. A black Porsche Cayenne pulls into the driveway, and I hop into the passenger seat, throwing three large duffel bags in the back. I lean over, kissing the scar on the driver's cheek. "Go. Now."

"Erica, don't you worry your pretty blond head," says Enrique, as he shifts the car into drive. He pats my leg. "It's all good."

"Not my name, Deputy Sanchez," I respond with a laugh, slinking into my seat as we pass the guard gates.

"Karen, did you get the rest of the cash?"

"Not my name anymore either," I say, shooting him a mock glare. He knows I've always hated my birth name, especially after a widespread meme referenced the name for middle-class white women who exhibit obnoxious behaviors that stem from privilege. I didn't come from a privileged background.

"I like your new name," says Enrique, squeezing my hand. "Karla."

"I like my name, too," I say with a wink. "Yes, I got the cash. It's in the blue duffel bag. Two hundred thousand in addition to the money we've been saving up. You get my new passport?"

"I did," he says. "The chef called just as I was pulling into the driveway. Set her up?"

"The police will definitely place some heat on her," I say, hoping Julia can wiggle her way out of this one. I actually like her. And I don't like many people. I go silent for a moment, saying a silent goodbye to California, to this life.

Like Julia, when I'd arrived in Los Angeles, I shed my former identity, including my name, thanks to being adopted when I was sixteen. Karen Martinez—hardly a name for the bright lights of fame I'd envisioned. But the journey to my shining moment was more than tumultuous. At the age of fourteen, a devastating fire claimed the lives of my mother and her boyfriend, leaving me orphaned. Instead of finding comfort with a new family, I'd bounced around from foster home to foster home, a nomad in the system.

They labeled me as troubled. And I was. Big time. I searched for trouble, whether in the form of a bottle, a cigarette, or the flicker of a match, igniting the world around me. Each new foster family saw me as a liability. Confession time: I started the fire, killing my constantly drunk mother and her pedophile boyfriend, and I don't regret it.

Amid all the chaos, I met Enrique, a kindred spirit, if you will, a friend who knew exactly what I was going through, what I'd needed to numb my pain. I liked seeing people suffer more than me; he did, too.

At the age of sixteen, the Moore family took a big risk, adopting me. You'd think my life would have taken a turn for the better, maybe I'd find some stability; it didn't. The couple looked on me as a domestic slave—I did all the cleaning, all the cooking, all the ironing. I ran away when I was seventeen, living with Enrique in squalor. We started off grifting—coming up with false charities, selling fake merch as the real thing, exchanging fake gift cards for cash with sob stories—and I got pretty good at it, my acting skills growing day by day.

But, over time, the spark was missing. We both needed something more.

After David made the movie about the girl from the trailer park killing her parents, I set my sights on him. I got off on thinking about becoming a movie star. Enrique got off on taking everything away from the rich, leaving them powerless—both of us real-life Robin Hoods with killer instincts.

We decided on a long con... with a huge payday and I became the very unreliable narrator of my own life.

David always had a wandering eye, and I took advantage of that, seducing him at an audition. Our affair lasted for a year... until he broke it off with me. I'd tried getting him back, told him I was pregnant, but he didn't believe me—until the day I showed up at the studio with Tyler. Enrique had found him at a mall, hiding from his parents in between clothing racks. When opportunity knocks, you answer the door, and he bribed the kid with a kitten. The kid walked right out of the store with him, holding his hand. I didn't know what to do with a kid, but I'd figure it out. I also didn't know how old he was. Two? Three? It didn't matter. At the time Enrique had been "dating" a nurse at UCLA Hospital's maternity ward, one who happily accepted $15k to forge Tyler's birth certificate, listing me as the mother and putting us in the system.

I forget the nurse's name. So does Enrique.

At any rate, David melted when he saw Tyler, didn't even question his paternity. Why would I lie about something so serious? Plus, Tyler was the spitting image of David when he was younger, with stormy hazel eyes like his.

David put me up in a small apartment in Studio City, got

me an audition for *Love at First Latte*, ensuring I got the role. At the time, I was twenty-two and using my adoptive name: Erica Moore. Yes, the Moore family crawled out the woodwork. Yes, Enrique took care of them for me. Poor couple! Stabbed and mugged in an alley! During this time, David promised me he'd leave Madison's mother, Valerie. He didn't. And, well, Enrique took care of that little issue for me, too, getting rid of the evidence, namely the pills I'd put in the bottle of wine we'd "shared" before I held her under water until she'd taken her last breath. I'd come over to their house, introducing myself as the new neighbor. The plan was I'd feed Enrique cash until I fulfilled my dreams, winning an Oscar.

Dreams don't happen overnight. To make a long story short, I'm the one who convinced David to write the script for Valerie, tapping into his pain, the loss. Granted, I was nominated for my portrayal of Valerie, but I didn't win. And David doesn't know how Valerie really died—he thought she found out about his affair with me and committed suicide. David and I married when Tyler was five.

Unfortunately, David's eyes kept wandering—latching onto Christine, Julia's mother. He'd been beyond obsessed with that woman. I didn't lie to Julia. I was pregnant at the time. I told her everything... except for how I was the one who told David to take Las Flores to Gelson's. And I was the one who screamed and grabbed the wheel, swerving the car into the other lane. I was the one who'd cut their brake line. I was also the one who insisted on driving straight to the hospital, promising I'd tell the police what had happened. I didn't.

As for Jasmine, she was starting to pick up on everything, questioning my motives, especially during the filming of *Swerve*. So, I had Enrique take care of her—the blunt force trauma to the head on her hike: a rock. Good thing I kept her phone. Luna? She shouldn't have been having an affair with David and lying to me about it. The gift I gave her was an expensive bottle of tequila—her favorite—laced with a heavy sedative. I figured she'd drown in a tub, not fall from an oversized champagne glass. At least she died somewhat in style.

Aside from Enrique, David is the only person on the planet who knows my real name. And Enrique knows more than that— he knows everything about me. My true nature. Now that I've won the Oscar, I don't need another script, namely *The Private Chef*, to achieve my dream. More importantly, I don't need David. I've acted out the role of my life.

"Erica, you've been quiet," says Enrique.

"My name is Karla now. Get used to it."

He sighs. "Karla, how'd you set the chef up?"

"Changed in the guesthouse. And I planted some evidence. One of her knives with his blood on it."

"That's my girl." Enrique pats my leg again. "What about that Ollie Shore? I kind of like that dude."

I snort. "He'll get over me, especially when he realizes I played him."

We're on Las Flores Canyon Road, heading to a private airport in Westlake Village when Enrique pulls the Porsche over on one of the hairpin turns onto Gorge Road. The last time I was at this spot was when I'd caused the "accident" that killed Julia's flake of a mother.

"Why are we pulling over?"

"We're switching cars. Bumpy is meeting us. Should be here any minute." He laughs wickedly. "He loved playing the sidekick to my deputy. Wants to keep the costume and the cop light."

I hate Bumpy. He's terrifying with his compact form and messed-up skin. Why Enrique likes him is a mystery to me.

"We should just get to the airport," I say forcefully.

"No," he says. "We can't take any chances. Your security guard saw the Porsche."

I suck in my cheeks, blow out the air between my lips. "Right."

We get out of the car and my hair whips into my eyes. The Santa Ana winds have blown in with a vengeance, transformed from gentle breezes into raging gusts, howling like coyotes through the canyons and valleys. Dust and debris dance like wild spirals through the air, sometimes obscuring the moonlit sky. Trees bend and creak, branches thrashing. They can last from days to weeks, creating hazardous conditions, such as wild-fires and power outages.

The Santa Ana winds remind me of me—unstoppable. Bumpy's Honda peels over to the side of the road. Enrique takes a container, pours gas on the Porsche. Bumpy joins us, grabbing the bag of cash. Enrique eyes me. "Want to light the fire?"

I shoot him a wicked grin. He knows me so well. The pieces that make me who I am all snap together, click right into place. I hold up a finger, grabbing another one of the bags from the back seat and wink after throwing it onto the ground. "We can sell my jewelry. And I do need a wardrobe change."

Enrique hands me a box of matches. I shake the little sticks into my hand and then light ten, because why not? Life doesn't come with a dimmer switch.

A hiss. Flames burn hot and heavy around me. My eyes spark up. Alicia Key's "Girl on Fire" loops in my brain. Fire and me? We get along. It's part of my nature.

FORTY-THREE

JULIA

Stunned, Maddy, Tyler, Ollie and I watch the real Deputy Sanchez stand up. "I need to see the original files now."

"I'll take you to his computer," says Maddy. "But it won't do you any good. All the files are encrypted."

He scowls at her. "Just show me where it is."

She nods and we all get up, following Maddy to the home theater. Deputy Sanchez's eyes go wide, and he mumbles "holy shit" under his breath. Maddy sits in the chair, with Sanchez leaning over her shoulder. "The files are here." She taps a couple of keys and then shakes her head. "They were here."

Sanchez raises his eyebrows. "Setting somebody up for murder is a serious crime."

Maddy jumps out of her seat. "Wait! I have the originals on my USB drive." She bolts out of the room. "I'll be right back."

Tyler stares at nothing in particular, frowning. Ollie's eyes dart to every corner of the room. I stare at my feet, thinking. "Cameras!" I blurt out. "Cameras!"

Deputy Sanchez locks his gaze on me.

"I planted cameras in the kitchen. And here."

"Why?"

"Because I was trying to prove they had something to do with my parents' death."

"I don't see the connection."

"I'd get something on them and they'd confess."

"You're talking about blackmail..."

Shit. Could I be tried for that?

"I just wanted to get to the truth. Justice. Right? You believe in that!" I gulp. "I'm sure I have videos of David doing something—drugging Tyler, coming into my room, poisoning the brownies with peanuts, taking one of my knives..."

He squeezes his eyes shut, shaking his head. "Just show me the footage."

Erica was right—they think we're crazy. Or maybe they think we're guilty of something. With shaky hands, I log into EyeSpy, but my password doesn't work. I try again. Nothing. I swallow. Hard. "I think my password has been changed. I'll reset it."

Madison screeches back into the room with her bling-bling drive. She holds it in her hand, her arm lifted high. "I got it."

"Great," says Sanchez. "While you try getting into your account, I'll have a look at the files."

"Time stamps. On documents," he says, pushing the blinged-out drive into the iMac. He sits in the chair behind the desk. "Command I will tell me when they were created."

"I should have thought of that," says Madison, peering over his shoulder.

Five minutes later, I'm still on hold with customer service, listening to elevator music and watching Deputy Sanchez with an eagle eye.

One by one he goes through the files. "The dates for the actual scripts—they are correct, the years spanning over twenty years to the present. But the original notes? They've all been created within the past week, one created just a few days ago."

David's words ring in my ears.

I didn't write the script.

This has Erica written all over it.

"Did any of you write them?"

"No!" we all say forcefully. He rubs his forehead, meets my gaze. "Any luck with the videos?"

"Not yet. I'm still on hold," I say with a sigh just as a human voice blares into my ears. I hold up a finger, putting the call on speaker.

"Hi. This is Tanya from EyeSpy. How can I be of service today?"

I swallow. "Hi, Tanya. I can't get into my account."

"Account number?"

"Hold on a sec, please. I have to look it up," I say.

After going through the rigmarole of confirming my identity, email address, and so on, Tanya tells me, "You canceled your service last night."

"But I didn't. And I've been having problems with it."

"We emailed you to confirm."

"I never received an email," I explain, giving her the email I signed up with.

Tanya says, "Hold on. Give me two seconds, please." I hear her typing away. "You changed your email address."

I am about to go into a rage. A storm. But I keep calm. "No, I didn't. I think I've been hacked. I'd like my account restored immediately, using my original email, and a link to change my password."

"OK, Ms. Fouquet, I'll just need some more information to confirm your identity," she says. She fires out question after question and I give her the answers, including the last four digits of my social security number. "Good, I'm working on re-establishing your account right now." She clears her throat. "But it looks as if all the files are in the trash bin. Did you want me to delete them?"

"No," I say, "restore them." I draw in a breath. "Thank you,

Tanya."

"Everything should be up and running in about ten minutes. Please contact us again if you experience any other issues or problems."

Ten minutes later, finally, I'm back in. After hooking my phone up to the computer, Sanchez scrolls through the videos—and there are quite a few of Beurreboule. I now know what she does when I'm not around—she sleeps and cleans herself. A lot.

And then we see Erica. We see Erica messing up my soup, pouring hot chili sauce into the pot. We see her dribbling peanut oil over the brownies. We see her chopping up mushrooms, grinning, rolling them into cheese, and placing them on endive. We see her slapping David, slapping me.

I want to slap her, too. Harder than she'd slapped me.

And then we see her grinning, sitting behind David's desk, typing and smiling. Like a mad woman.

Maddy chokes back a sob. Tears stream down her cheeks. "I remember something. It just hit me."

I squeeze her shoulder. "What?"

"David was out of town the night my mother died." She swallows. "But there was somebody else there that night. A woman. They were swimming in the pool. The woman looked up and said, "Shouldn't you be in bed? We're playing adult games." I think I blocked it out of my memory because I was the one who found my mom floating on her back the next morning and that's the memory that stuck with me."

Nausea. I feel it roiling around in my gut.

Deputy Sanchez sighs. "Anything else I should know? Anybody else involved?"

There's only one person I can think of: Chloe.

We're in a police van about to leave Hummingbird House, my mind spinning. I don't want to go back to Chloe's, but I have to pick up Beurreboule before we check into a hotel—that's if I'm not going to prison.

We pull into Chloe's driveway. My heart stutters.

We get out of the van. I don't bother knocking or ringing the doorbell, just storm right in. Maddy races in front of me. She storms toward Chloe. "You lying little bitch. You never auditioned for *The Private Chef*. I think you made that shit up. She's going to be arrested. And so are you."

Chloe bursts into tears. "I thought it was a game, my in! I didn't know she was batshit crazy. She promised to help me with my career! She... she... Erica told me to play my part, to cry and... I'm so stupid!"

"She's not stupid—she's savvy like a fox," says Deputy Sanchez.

I swallow, thinking about what she'd told me when we flambéed. *I love playing with fire.*

"Her name is not Erica," I say. "David told me he'd made a film about her life, but he didn't realize it was her when he first read the story." He meets my eyes, his gaze intense. "The girl in the film, *Evil Ignited*, had set fire to a trailer with her mother and her mother's boyfriend in it. They weren't able to prove the girl did it. She'd been put into foster care..."

Deputy Sanchez eyes me. "Do you know her birth name?"

"I don't," I mumble. "Sorry."

Maddy screams, "I think I'm going to need therapy for the rest of my life."

Me too, Maddy, me too.

Chloe sinks to her knees. "What if she tries to come after me?"

"Right. Save yourself. Before psycho-mom kills us!" Maddy stamps her foot. "Damn it! I don't know what to do." She stops screaming, meets Deputy Sanchez's eyes. "Self-defense? That's a thing, right? Like she might be stabbed with a knife?" She looks over her shoulder, eyeing my roll bag. "Can I borrow one?"

Deputy Sanchez's expression falls into what I can only call disturbed. "Please, don't do that, and don't talk like that in front of me. I could arrest you."

Maddy faces him. "With her on the loose, I'd feel safer behind bars." She holds out her arms, wrists crossed. "Arrest me!"

Tyler scrambles to her side. "Arrest me, too."

He lets out a breath. "The only person I want to arrest right now is Erica Drake."

Funny, although I don't actually have the nerve to do it, I'm thinking about killing her, too.

FORTY-FOUR

JULIA

One week later

I've rented a three-bedroom Airbnb in Malibu, right on the beach. Tyler and Madison are staying with me and pitching in financially. Sadly, to receive their inheritance, it could take six months to a year with possible delays at the probate registry. Plus, the police still need to find Erica, the main beneficiary in David's will. Deputy Sanchez has told us that she'd filtered out a couple of million dollars from their joint account, but David's personal account is untouched, along with his investment account at a private bank. No matter—Madison received a trust of one million dollars when she turned eighteen this past January and Tyler has a hefty savings account. Thankfully, it's still off-season and we're able to book a place with a discounted rate.

We've decided group therapy might be a good idea, especially after Deputy Sanchez gave us the card of somebody he was recommended. Doctor Alexandra Cruz, a police psychologist, is coming to us today. A regular therapist wouldn't cut it— not with what we have to unpack.

The doorbell rings and Tyler escorts Doctor Cruz into the house. She's petite with dark brown shoulder length hair and eyes—has a serious look about her. We decide to sit outside, quickly changing our minds when we hear the clicks of cameras.

The paparazzi have been out in force, prowling the beach in front of the house. We can't leave, haven't even been able to unwind and surf—the reason we'd wanted this place.

Doctor Cruz sits down in a chair, smiles. "Before we start, you can call me Alex."

We all nod, sitting on the couch, me in the middle. Madison clutches my hand.

Alex claps her hands together. "Deputy Sanchez has updated me on everything that's been going on." She sucks in a breath. "You are all victims of extreme traumas. But the good news is that you're also survivors. I'm here to help you see that. Where would you like to start?"

Tyler and Madison lean forward sharing a look, shrug and then nudge me. "I'm not sure we know," I say, clearing my throat. "We're all coming to grips with everything. It's almost like none of this happened, like it doesn't seem real."

"I understand," she says. "Rather than focusing on the far past, I think we should start with Mr. Drake's death. Can you talk about those feelings?"

Tyler snorts. "I can't believe she killed him. I'm just glad I'm not related to either of them."

My head whips to Tyler. "You got your DNA results back?"

He shrugs and then hangs his head. "Yeah, I paid for the rush service. My parents are Jack and Linda Elliot from Three Forks, Montana. Apparently, I'm seventeen years old, not sixteen, my birthday is July eighteenth, not February four-teen, and I have a thirteen-year-old brother named Thomas." He coughs. "My real name is Robert. Little Bobby."

Madison chokes on her glass of water. As I tap her back, the room is silent for a moment.

Alex leans forward. "And how do you feel about learning the identity of your birth parents?"

Tyler slowly shakes his head, looking down at the floor. He sighs. "I don't know. I don't even remember them. I just remember not feeling truly connected to this family. Well, except for Madison. We connected."

"I understand," says Alex. She taps her pen. "Do you want to connect with them?"

"Yeah, one day, but not now." He gulps. "They sent me a message, but I haven't replied. I'm trying to figure out what to say, what to call them." He circles his fingers on his temples. "In a way it's a huge relief knowing that Erica isn't my biological mother. It gave me nightmares to think I might have the blood of a sociopathic serial killer running through my veins." He pauses. "As for David, he was OK—not the greatest fake dad in the world, but he didn't deserve to die."

"Right?" says Maddy, clearing her throat. "Erica poisoned our minds against him, making him out to be the bad guy—the sociopath." She blinks, her eyes focusing on the ceiling. "I mean, I was always angry with him for having an affair on my mom, but I never hated him. And I agree with Tyler. He didn't deserve to die. Not like that. But I will never, ever forgive Erica for anything she's done."

Madison crosses her arms over her chest.

Alex nods thoughtfully. "Part of the grieving process, and I'm here to help you through it, is finding some form of forgive-ness—or at least understanding..."

"You expect us to forgive and understand a sociopath?" spits Maddy. "Get real."

"No, I'm asking you to think about what made her the way she was, how she'd been a victim when she was very young, and how very sick she was." Alex lifts a brow. "Erica needed serious psychiatric help. I'm not saying she should be absolved for what she's done. I just want you to understand how profoundly damaged she was."

Madison crosses her arms over her chest, breathing heavily. "She was profoundly fucked up in the head."

"Exactly. She needed help, but unfortunately, it's too late to give it." Alex directs her attention to me. "Julia, you've been quiet. What are your thoughts on the subject?"

"I thought I hated David. I thought he'd killed my parents. But now that I know Erica was the one pulling the strings I don't hate him as much." I pick at my cuticles, nervously. "And I guess, as long as we're talking about her, I'm devastated about Erica. Because I did like her and I did relate to her. I'm just having a hard time—a really hard time—trying to understand what she did."

"So." Alex lifts a brow. "She had some redeeming qualities? Something that made her, let's say, less of a monster and more human?"

The three of us burst into tears, sobbing uncontrollably. Honestly, it feels good to cry and I don't think one of us has released the pain, mostly because we were angry and in shock. We need to let loose, let those tears cut right through us. We are crying for everything—letting the eruption of pain out.

Once we settle down, Alex hands us tissues, and tilts her head to the side. "What if I told you they found her?"

As I blow my nose, my eyes go wide with shock. "Where? Did she flee to another country? Costa Rica?"

"Nope, she didn't get that far," says Alex, raising a brow. "Deputy Sanchez wanted me to be the one to tell you. She's dead."

"What?" we gasp, our words overlapping.

My posture straightens to full attention. "Am I-I-I a suspect..."

Alex's lips turn into the subtlest of grins. "Nope, all of you have the tightest of alibis."

"I don't understand…"

"She died the same day as David. You were with Deputy Sanchez." Alex lifts her shoulders. "The cause of the death was a car explosion. And, well, not the best choice of words, but she'd been flambéed."

"Jesus," says Tyler as Madison and I choke on our tongues.

My cellphone rings and I stare at it. "I'd take that," says Alex, looking at her watch. "And then we'll talk some more."

After helping Madison and Tyler make funeral arrangements for David, we stand in front of his grave, hands linked. There are over three hundred people in attendance, not one dry eye. I can't say I'm completely broken up, and neither are Maddy or Ty. Acceptance is a melancholy feeling, a creeping sadness. With the help of Alex, we're working through the stages of grief. One of David's friends is having a party to celebrate his life, but, along with Ollie, we have other plans. Tabitha Sinclair is meeting us at the Airbnb—her call was the one that came in when we'd been with Alex.

From the cemetery, we hop into Madison's BMW, making our way back home. The cameras are already set up on the terrace and, after a little touch-up from the makeup team, we take our seats.

BREAKING NEWS: REMAINS OF ERICA DRAKE IDENTIFIED

"Good evening, viewers. I'm Tabitha Sinclair. Welcome to tonight's edition of Nightwatch 60. The nationwide manhunt for Academy Award winning actress Erica Drake has come to an end. One week ago, a Porsche Cayenne was set ablaze, with two bodies beside it, a third victim's DNA found inside the car. Thanks to dental records, we can say with one hundred percent certainty that the remains are those of Erica Drake. The other two victims are Enrique Santos and Javier "Bumpy" Mendoza, both men affiliated with the Eastside Vipers. The Los Angeles Sheriff's Department suspect foul play and an investigation is under way.

Aside from recently winning the Oscar for best actress for her portrayal of Christine Brooks in the movie *Swerve*, Erica Drake will most likely be remembered for being a murderess, tampering with the belay loop of film magnate husband David Drake, which resulted in him plummeting from the cliffs below their mansion; when he survived the fall, she stabbed him to death. In addition to this heinous crime, if she were alive, Mrs. Drake would also face other criminal charges including kidnapping, multiple murders, and embezzlement.

With me we have four victims of Mrs. Drake: Josephine Brooks, daughter of Christine and Stephen; Madison Drake, adoptive daughter of David Drake; Tyler Drake, kidnapping victim and assumed son of David and Erica Drake's, and famed surfer, Ollie Shore, whose story I'm sure we all remember.

Can you tell our viewers what happened?"

FORTY-FIVE

JULIA

Three weeks later

Sometimes when searching for the truth, the answers aren't quite the ones you've been looking or hoping for. Since Erica's death, I've become a celebrity—and I'd rather hide in the sands of the Mojave Desert, bury myself in oblivion under a Joshua tree. The truth doesn't always set you free—no, it binds you with the weight of reality. And revenge just leaves a bitter taste in your mouth.

I'd thought that exposing the Drakes would heal my heart, make my pain go away, but it will always be a part of me. In a way, I can understand Erica's deceit, manipulation, and sociopathic tendencies... though I still can't believe I fell for her act. Worse? She was the one responsible for killing my parents. I don't think I'll ever come to terms with her madness.

Ollie is torn up, too. Deputy Sanchez pulled up the Dispatch call from many years ago, the one Ollie thought David had made to set him up. It wasn't David; it was Erica. Apparently, Erica liked assisting David on the sidelines to write his scripts, convincing him that real art is human pain, so she brought on all the pain—and, while she was at it, wrote her role into the script as the 'cute' and devastated California surfer girl.

On the plus side, I have a new-found family with Tyler and Madison. While I re-establish my connection with Liam, we've rented a bungalow near Ollie's—a cute three-bedroom. Madison, through a little magic, has convinced the courts that she's a responsible adult and she has custody of Tyler, with me named as the guardian. Considering the circumstances, Malibu High is lifting his expulsion and he's super pumped to return to school —with his car, now with new tires, which means I have to get a new one. To tide me over, Madison "loaned" me David's Lexus SUV. They've put Hummingbird House on the market, priced $25 million below its actual value at $65 million. She and Tyler, the sole heirs, are hoping for a quick sale. Not only that, they are now the owners of Drake Entertainment. For the time being, they're placing the company in CEO Max Blackwood's capable hands.

Tonight, I'm making dinner for all of us. Liam and Ollie are coming over, and, because Ollie insisted, we've included Chloe. As Tyler sets the table, Madison plays sous-chef, helping me prepare. "What's on tonight's menu? And what can I do?"

After all the drama, I'm keeping things simple tonight. "We're making crêpes—savory for dinner, chicken and criminology mushrooms—haha," I say with a snort, but my joke goes stale. "Fine. Cremini mushrooms with a béchamel sauce, fresh herbs and a salad. Sweet crêpes for dessert. And little cheese puffed pastries called gougères for the apèro, cherry tomatoes, and olives."

"Hey, I want to learn how to make crêpes, too," says Tyler, racing into the kitchen, and Madison shoots him a look.

"What? One day, I'll impress the girls." He wiggles his brows. "A guy that can cook? It'll be on."

Madison laughs and punches him on the shoulder. "Dumbass, you're such a horndog."

"I'm seventeen," he says, nudging Madison with his hip. "And I'm a guy. Don't judge. Plus, I'm visiting the Elliots for a month this summer once school is out. So, there's that."

Madison frowns. "What if you don't come back?"

"First of all, they are complete strangers to me. I don't know jack about horses. I'm all about the surf." He gives her the crazy eye. "Plus, they didn't raise me. You did…"

She lifts a brow. "A good job, little Bobby."

"Do *not* call me that," he says with a grin.

Madison blurts out a laugh and then cringes. "I may have an idea for my first script. It's, um, based on a true story. I've already come up with a title."

"And?" I ask.

"*The Method Actress.*"

My mouth forms into the subtlest of grins and I wink. "Just stick to the original script—don't rewrite it."

"Clearly." She snorts. "And, not to change the subject—but I am: while we prepare tonight's feast, we need music." She pulls out her phone, linking it to the sound system. "This one's for all of us. Julia, you're twenty-three, I'm eighteen, and dumbass is seventeen. And, well…"

She presses play. Imagine Dragon's "Waves" booms in the kitchen.

I squeeze my eyes shut, listening to the lyrics. Everything has changed. Now, it's time to come up with a new recipe for my life, leaving the bitter taste of revenge behind me.

One by one, our guests arrive, Liam the first. He looks so handsome in a blue button-down shirt and khaki pants, his sandy brown hair slightly disheveled. I have to fight the urge to run my fingers through it. He smiles and now I'm fighting the urge to kiss him. We haven't gotten to that point yet, mostly holding hands, whispering sweet nothings.

"What can I do?" he asks, handing over a bottle of champagne.

"Pop it open. Meet me on the deck," I say. "I'll grab glasses."

"You got it."

I grab four glasses from the cabinet and head outside, the appetizers all set. Ollie and Chloe arrive together. Odd. I indicate for them to sit down at the table with my free hand and they do. "Well, all of us together again," says Ollie.

"Under much better circumstances."

For a moment, Chloe's eyes won't meet mine. Finally, she looks up. "I have something to tell you."

I blink. Now what? I set the glasses down, Liam steps out and pours the champagne, and I signal for her to carry on. "I have good news." She bats her eyelashes at Ollie. "I'm learning to surf. And I can't wait to go out with you..."

"For a role?"

"No, for fun."

Something isn't adding up. Ollie is holding her hand. "Are you two together? Like, together, together?"

Ollie's grin is sheepish. "We are."

"A fifteen-year age gap isn't that much," says Chloe.

I do the math in my head. Chloe is two years older than me. Twenty-five. Which makes Ollie forty. I'm not judging, but I didn't see this one coming. Chloe's head hangs. "Julia, I've learned a lot. I also want to apologize for being so selfish." She looks up. "I was a very bad friend, got swept up into everything. I'm sorry."

I'd gotten swept up in everything, too. "There is no need to apologize."

"At least something good came out of the Drake nightmare," says Ollie.

"Hey," screams Maddy. "There are two Drakes here! And we're finishing up your meal."

"Good thing you're not really Drakes," says Ollie. "Or I'd be questioning the ingredients. Death by chocolate?"

"That's not funny," says Tyler, storming out on the deck. "And this is a nut-free meal. Got it?" He cracks up, hunching over. "Nuts!"

"I guess it's not too soon for jokes," I say, and honestly it feels good to laugh.

"Nah, we all need some laughter, especially to move on." Liam puts his arm around my shoulder, pulling me into him. He smells so good, clean and fresh. I could breathe him in all night. "On moving on, have you texted that Paul guy yet from Solstice Group?"

I gulp and shake my head. I've been putting that one off. I know I need to find a new job, and soon—and definitely not as a private chef.

"I haven't."

"Are you planning on going back to Paris?"

"I'm not."

"Then text him now."

"Yeah," says Ollie. "The worst he can say is no. Do it."

With all eyes on me, I pull out my phone. "Fine."

JF:

> Hi, Paul. I don't know if you remember me. The girl with the cat. The chef. At the airport. Was wondering if your offer still stands?

"OK. Done," I say, placing my phone face down on the table. "He probably won't respond. I wouldn't. I'm all over the news..."

My phone buzzes.

PB:

It's PB. Hey, PB & J. A perfect combo. Peanut butter and jelly. Get it? Never mind. Have position open for an exec pastry chef. Would need to test you out.

JF:

Pastries are my specialty.

PB:

How does a one-month trial period sound?

Absolutely perfect.

ACT FIVE
LE DIGESTIF

(Ensuring everything goes down smoothly.)

Revenge shall have no bounds.

—William Shakespeare, *Hamlet*

FADE IN:

EXT. DOLBY THEATER—DAY

Security guards scan the area. Limousines
drive up, high heels emerging. Crew members
hustle.

MAN (V.O.)

This Oscar season has the entire
industry abuzz with one particular film
up for best original screenplay, best
director, and best picture. Today could

make awards history—usurping Matt Damon
and Ben Affleck, who at the ages of
twenty-seven and twenty-five, were the
youngest duo to win best original
screenplay for 1997's *Good Will Hunting*
and Damian Chazelle winning best
director at the age of thirty-two for
2016's *La La Land*.

Cameras flash. Various celebrities, male and
female, stride down the red carpet, pausing
and posing for photos.

FADE OUT

FORTY-SIX

JULIA

Five years later

It's been five long years and my nightmare with the Drakes is finally over. I worked for Paul for three years, mostly to create some buzz around my name—not that I really needed any— before I opened my first café. Paul knew of my plans, mostly because I'm honest and I'd told him.

"Hey, you're talented and we all need to start somewhere," he'd said with a laugh. "Just not with cereal killers. Kind of crumb-y."

I'd looked at him blankly and he'd recoiled.

"Too soon?"

"No," I said, cringing. "Really bad jokes."

Madison insisted on being my angel investor for my start-up, a chain of bakeries—especially since I'd looked after Tyler while he finished up high school as Madison spread her wings, attending NYU. Now, the two of them are running the renamed Drake Entertainment. Because what's in a name?

They picked out a good one: Phoenix Studios. Yes, we all rose from the ashes. Well, except for Erica. They still haven't found her killer. I'd given Deputy Sanchez the description of fake Deputy Sanchez, assumed to be responsible for Erica's demise, but nothing. Zero. Zip. Nada. Maybe he's already in prison?

On names, Hummingbird House sold within two weeks of being on the market—at its estimated value of $80 million—to Anthony Griffin, a porn magnate. Apparently, he'd fallen in love with the private cove.

From Dragons to Griffins to Phoenixes.

Today, we're putting the past behind us. And we are going to shine.

I'm not looking forward to walking the red carpet, preferring to stay out of the limelight, but I have Liam by my side for support. And I'm here to support Madison and Tyler. A reporter shoves a microphone in my face. "Who are you wearing, Julia?"

"A dress. And my name is Josephine," I say, and the reporter shakes her head, turning to Chloe, Ollie, Maddy and Ty.

I eavesdrop on the interview.

"We're here on the red carpet with Academy Award nominees for best screenplay and best picture, Madison Drake and brother Tyler, for their original screenplay, based on a true story, *The Method Actress*, as well as *New York Times* bestselling author of *Escaping the Dragon*, Ollie Shore, who plays himself in the film. And, up for best supporting actress, Chloe LeFevre, for her portrayal of chef Julia Fouquet, or rather, Josephine Brooks. It's an exciting night..."

Before Liam and I move on, I'm stopped dead in my tracks, another microphone shoved in my face. I'm kind of enjoying this moment. It's freedom. Liberating. Like the day Madison, Tyler, and I beat out tunes on our boards. I actually have everything I came back to California for.

"Ms. Brooks, tell us, tell the viewers, now that Erica Drake has been exposed, how are you feeling?"

"I'm just glad the truth, like cream, has finally risen to the surface."

"What are your plans?"

"I've been opening up a chain of cafés to honor my parents' dream—"

"Does the chain have a name?"

"That French Café," I say, turning on my heel. I turn, looking over my shoulder. "In addition to desserts, we'll also be known for our savory dishes." Liam grabs my hand. I wink. "Life is both savory and sweet."

Liam kisses my cheek. Hand in hand, we walk into the auditorium, cameras flashing. As we walk, I FaceTime with Marie and Bernard, showing them the glitz, the glamor.

"We'd better see the two of you at Christmas," she says.

"We were thinking of celebrating the holidays here." I grin, nudging Liam in the side.

"Marie, Bernard, I'd love your blessing to marry JoJo."

Marie sucks in a breath and smiles. "Liam, of course, if you make her shine this brightly, you have our blessing." Bernard grins. "Congratulations! Your parents would be so proud of you. We are." He clears his throat, tears glimmering in his eyes. "I think you've found your happy place, Josephine."

Yes, indeed, I have. I'm living life for myself and for my parents. Life can't get any better than this. We say our goodbyes, blowing air kisses, and I click out of FaceTime. We enter the auditorium, taking our seats, Liam gripping my hand.

The event passes by in a blur, my heart racing with anticipation. I'm holding my breath as the announcements are made.

"And the Oscar for best actress goes to Chloe LeFevre..."

"And the Oscar for best original screenplay goes to Tyler Elliot and Madison Drake."

"And the Oscar for best director goes to Madison Drake."

"And the Oscar for best picture goes to Tyler Elliot and Madison Drake for *The Method Actress*."

The applause is deafening.

Fleetwood Mac's "Landslide" plays inside my head. A fitting song for this new beginning. In their speeches, Chloe, Tyler, and Madison thank me for being an inspiration, for my strength, for my friendship. Tears stream down my cheeks. I lean into Liam and whisper, "Before Maddy and Ty's party, gosh, I'm so happy they won, there's something I need to do. And I'm driving."

He eyes me curiously. "What's that?"

"Pick up some flowers and drive up Las Flores Canyon to say a final goodbye."

I don't have to say another word.

He knows I'm finally moving on, coming to terms with everything—my parents' deaths and, while I'm at it, trying to forgive Erica. We're at the light, about to turn onto Las Flores when my phone chimes. My eyes go wide as I read a text from a blocked number on Snapchat. I find myself holding my breath, my eyes swimming over the words:

> Greetings from sunny Costa Rica (or some other obscure place where I'll never be found.) You played your part perfectly, darling. We both fulfilled our dreams, getting exactly what we wanted. I'm truly hoping you'll set the world on fire.

I'm in the process of hyperventilating when another text chimes in. The light turns green, but I don't turn the car. Liam pats my thigh. "What's wrong?"

Everything.

I don't answer him right away, my eyes locked onto the screen.

In case you're wondering, David always knew
how driven I was; he just didn't count on how
far I'd go to fulfill my dream. Don't worry. The
bones they found—presumed to be mine? I
took them from a studio set. With love, sparks,
and a killer smile (glad I kept a couple of teeth
from my dental implants a few years ago) xox

"JoJo? What's the matter?"

"Nothing," I lie, not wanting to worry him. I let out a long breath. "Just another crazed message from a sociopath."

"Are they ever going to leave you alone?"

I clench my jaw. "I hope so."

In the blink of an eye, the messages disappear. My spine stiffens so tightly, so rigid, until I turn the car onto Las Flores with resolve. If there's anything I've learned from Erica it's that cooking, like acting, is about the art of adjustment. Although I've come to terms with my parents' deaths, I'll never forgive her. No, I'm going to concoct a new menu, rewrite the script— one that finishes with Erica Drake behind bars. I can practically taste the ingredients as I imagine each course, each scene.

Erica isn't the mastermind she thinks she is. As I steer the car along the hairpin turns of Las Flores, I'm replaying every detail in my mind, thinking back to the one day she slipped. And I know *exactly* where she is.

Thank you for reading *The Private Chef*. If you'd like to keep up to date with all my Storm Publishing releases, you can sign up here:

www.stormpublishing.co/samantha-verant

And if you'd like to hear about all my upcoming releases and bonus content, including the occasional French recipe, please feel free to sign up for my author newsletter.

www.eepurl.com/UH8cP

If you enjoyed this book and could spare a few moments to leave a review, that would be hugely appreciated. Even a short review can make all the difference in encouraging a reader to discover my books for the first time. Thank you so much! Merci beaucoup!

When I was sixteen, I attended the Chicago Academy for Performing and Visual Arts. Although I'd auditioned for voice, I ended up choosing acting as my major, taking voice lessons once a week. This book was somewhat inspired by my experience at the Academy, namely knowing how competitive the performance arts world is—one of the major reasons I prefer being behind the scenes and writing. The idea of somebody "killing for success"—a method actress or director taking things way too far—flickered in my mind, but it needed more normalcy, a character you could root for. Please note: I live in France, I'm a very determined home chef, and I adore cooking up twisted plots. For a brief stint, I also lived in Malibu, right off Las Flores Canyon Road. Voilà! The concept behind this book, just like a star, was born!

Thanks again for being part of this amazing journey. I love hearing from readers and I hope you'll get in touch!

All my best wishes,

Samantha Vérant

www.samanthaverant.com

The Private Chef Playlist:
www.youtube.com/watch?v=N-aK6JnyFmk&list=PLxnchx-t8uUwWEp69FAdi4-8i6oOzCXvI9

facebook.com/AuthorSamanthaVerant

instagram.com/samantha_verant

tiktok.com/@authorsamanthaverant

bookbub.com/profile/samantha-verant

ACKNOWLEDGMENTS

What an amazing cast! We brought this book to life!

A huge merci goes to my fabulous editor, Kate Smith (producer). Thank you to Oliver Rhodes, founder of Storm Publishing (studio executive); editorial director Alexandra Holmes, copyeditor Anne O'Brien, and proofreader Amanda Rutter (script doctors); page designer Naomi Knox and brilliant cover designer James Macey (set designers); the marketing team of Elke Desanghere and Anna McKerrow (publicists); and, finally, thank you to book narrator Caitlin Shannon (actress).

Thank you to my beta reader, thriller author Lyn Liao Butler for sharing her initial thoughts and ideas on the storyline with me. Thank you to scriptwriter Laurie Whittaker for fine-tuning the introductions of each of the book's sections so they were more script-like! Thank you to Patricia Marsh's eagle eye. And, as always, thank you to the Debut 2020 author group for their ongoing support and cheers.

To Deputy Serna from the Los Angeles Sheriff's Department, thank you for answering my questions about how law enforcement agencies work in California, particularly who would respond to the crime scene in Malibu. Thank you to Jason Martin from American Alpine Institute for guiding me through rock-climbing terminology and, well, answering the craziest questions you've probably heard in your life: how can a fictional character kill off someone when climbing? Can a bolt fall out?

Finally, thank you to the readers I've connected with and those I've yet to connect with—thank you for joining me on this wild publishing journey. Happy reading! Cheers!

www.ingramcontent.com/pod-product-compliance
Lightning Source LLC
Chambersburg PA
CBHW011029190726
48290CB00011B/2763